D0504251

PYNTER BENDER

JACOB ROSS

Pynter Bender

FOURTH ESTATE • *London*

First published in Great Britain in 2008 by
Fourth Estate
An imprint of HarperCollins*Publishers*
77–85 Fulham Palace Road
London W6 8JB
www.4thestate.co.uk

Visit our authors' blog: www.fifthestate.co.uk

A catalogue record for this book is
available from the British Library

ISBN 978-0-00-722297-1

Typeset by Newgen Imaging Systems (P) Ltd

Printed in Great Britain by Clays Ltd, St Ives plc

Mixed Sources
Product group from well-managed
forests and other controlled sources
www.fsc.org Cert no. SW-COC-1806
© 1996 Forest Stewardship Council

FSC is a non-profit international organisation established to promote the
responsible management of the world's forests. Products carrying the FSC
label are independently certified to assure consumers that they come
from forests that are managed to meet the social, economic and
ecological needs of present and future generations.

Find out more about HarperCollins and the environment at
www.harpercollins.co.uk/green

ACKNOWLEDGEMENTS

Deep-felt gratitude to:

David Godwin, my agent, and Nick Pearson, my editor/publisher, for offering something more valuable than support – a belief in the work.

Bernadine Evaristo, without whose wonderful gesture of solidarity and friendship this book would have taken much longer to arrive.

Manisha Amin, Jackie Clarke and Raksha Thakor, for the quality of their insights.

Yvonne Malcolm and Anthony Grainger, for timely reminders of weather and plant and season. And Pauline Cohen, for the virtue of forbearance.

For Esau and our father,
Janine, Jamal, Nichole and Akilah

For Grenada, and those who will come after....

Being lost is worth the journey home...

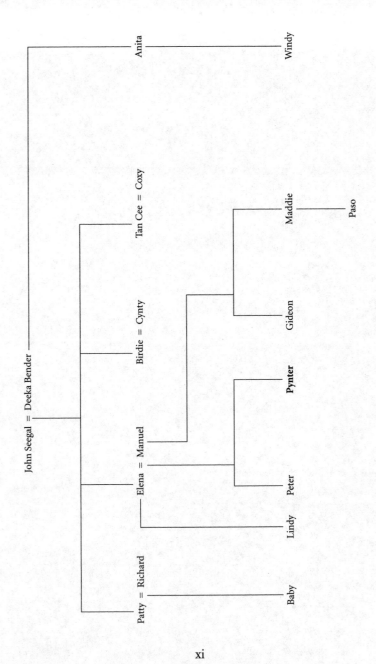

John Seegal = Deeka Bender

Anita — Windy

Patty = Richard

Elena = Manuel

Birdie = Cynty

Tan Cee = Coxy

Baby

Lindy

Peter

Pynter

Gideon

Maddie — Paso

BOOK ONE

Eyes

1

Saturday mornings, the women came down to the river. They were larger than their menfolk. They balanced basins as wide as ships on their heads and their voices carried across the foothills and washed the bright morning air.

As soon as their babble reached him, Pynter left home, let the slant of the hill carry him down towards the water to watch them wash and talk the day away. He chose a large boulder that overlooked the field of stones around which the water boiled and frothed before disappearing through the dark leaf tunnel of the bamboos overhead. He just sat there, feeding his eyes on the glitter and the green and on the throbbing reds and yellows of their washing spread out on the soap-bleached stones. The glare hurt his eyes. Aunt Tan Cee kept reminding him that he must rest those eyes of his, they were new and delicate, taking in the shapes of things, still making sense of the darkness and the light and all the mixing in between.

Each woman had her own little acre of stones on which she spread her washing. Up to their knees in water, they beat the clothing against the boulders and flashed their soapy corn husks over them. He'd grouped their names in his head according to the sound of them – Ursula, Petra, Barbara and Clara; Cynty, Lizzie, Tyzie, Shirley. And then there was Miss Elaine, her name all pretty and by itself, just like the way she was.

Pynter knew them by the stories they told each other and laughed over: the illnesses of their children, the appetites of their menfolk, the little things they wanted for themselves that their men would never give them. He heard them even when their voices dipped; they seemed to bring their heads together, especially when their talking turned to terrible things. Like why pretty Miss Madrone no longer came to the river with them. She carried an illness between her thighs, which her man had brought home to her from the tourist ship he worked on. He was due back in three months and only God knew what he would bring back to her this time. Pynter learned about the child that Sadi Marie's eleven-year-old daughter was carrying for Sadi Marie's man, while Sadi was accusing every young bull in Old Hope because she could not make herself believe the truth. And then their voices would go lower still and the women would speak of what a man called Gideon had done to his mother a coupla months before Peter and he were born. Gideon – he'd heard the name before, always said with lowered voices, always with a sideways glance as if he might be there among them listening. Once Deeka, his grandmother, had used that name in the yard and it had paused his mother's hands over the dishes she was washing, brought a deadness to her face.

Suddenly the women seemed to notice he was there and they fell silent. Miss Lizzie would not take her eyes off him. Her eyes were dark and shiny like the berries that grew on vines beside the road, berries Aunt Tan Cee said were poison.

His presence bothered Miss Lizzie. She said so all the time, and loud enough for him to hear. She said so with steady staring eyes, and lips that barely moved. She repeated it so often, the others no longer seemed to hear her: that he, dat 'Jumbie Boy', didn have no right just sittin on dat stone an' watchin people; that he, dat ugly likkle mako-boy, was like a shadow on her shoulder and she hated it.

He'd grown accustomed to her words the way he had the sandflies that bit into his skin and left little needle points of itching there. He'd put it down to what the women said about her. That her belly was poisoned. That something in there killed the babies she was carrying a coupla months before they born. That she blamed it on the weakness of the men who placed their seed in her, and she would have any woman's man if she thought his child would survive her insides. Which was why, Miss Dalene said, a pusson was prepared to put up with the natral badness of that woman.

This morning Miss Lizzie came to the river with an ugly mouthful of words for him. She saw him there and laid her basin down. She moved her lips as if she was about to speak and then, without a word, she turned her head down to her washing. He could sense the heat in her; it came out of her skin like smoke. And soon enough she began tossing words over her shoulders at him.

'What he doing here! What it want 'mongst big people, eh? Why dem don' go an' play with devil-chilren like theyself? Eh?'

It was a river morning, brimming with sunlight, the kind that made everything glitter and vibrate, and above the babble of the water he could hear the leaves of the bamboo shu-shuing like so many people making polite conversation. A shower of dragon-flies, little strips of foil, drew his gaze away from her, and when he looked round to her again she'd left her patch of stones and was moving towards him. His heart began to race because she'd never looked so mad before. Miss Elaine called out her name and Miss Lizzie swung her head around, her arm flashing out behind her as if to squash a fly.

She was breathing hard when she reached him, and all he could feel was her hate, like the sting of the sun on his naked skin. He turned his eyes down to where her feet were in the water, studying the busy weave of light around her ankles. The other women were saying nothing.

'Whapm, you born without a tongue too? Say something. Talk! You can't talk?' She turned towards the others. 'What kind o' people make funny chilren so? I hear he come from beast not yooman been. Dat so? Dat's what your modder get from sleepin wid de Devil, y'hear me?'

He unfolded his legs from under him, shifted his gaze towards her face, worked his mouth because something hard and choking had caught itself inside his throat and he could not get it out.

'Leave 'im, Lizzie. Is trouble you askin for,' Miss Elaine said.

Miss Elaine reminded him of his Aunt Patty – tall and brown and wavering like the bamboos. She had moonshine eyes too, large and shiny white. Miss Elaine had coiled the red dress she was wringing around her arms. It ran like a snake from her shoulder, the water was spilling onto her chest.

Miss Lizzie laughed. 'My arse! Trouble from who? Dat Bender tribe don' frighten me. Your ever see yooman been with eye like dat? Look at 'im, black like sin with whiteman eye!'

Before he realised it, he was running through the canes, the saw-edged leaves cutting at his face and arms and legs. And then he was running home across the field of stones that took him all the way down to that thick green copse of almond trees, Miss Lizzie's laughter trailing behind him like an accusation.

Aunt Tan Cee's hands woke him that night. Most times he chose to sleep on the long wooden bench in the place they called the kitchen which no one ever cooked in. He slept on his back with his eyes wide open, they said. His twin brother, Peter, told him they shone like polished marbles in the lamplight.

Tan Cee had unbuttoned his shirt without his knowing. She'd brought the lamp down close to his skin. With the other hand, she was passing a warm, damp cloth over his chest and arms and stomach. Pynter looked back at her through slitted eyes. She stroked her thumb across his brow and he felt a warmth seeping into his head.

'Tell me what happm,' she whispered.

All he could see were her arms and face framed by the blue headwrap she always wore. The rest of her had melted into the darkness beyond her shoulders.

'Don' wan' my eyes no more,' he said. 'Wish I never have dem.'

She eased herself backwards. The lamplight dipped and fluttered and the whole room seemed to teeter with the flames.

'Which you prefer, Sugarboy? If Santay come to take back your eyes, yuh'll agree to give dem back?' She lifted the cloth from his stomach and brought her face down close to his. She smelt of plant things – nutmeg oil, and the bay leaves she picked to make him tea. 'You still got your baby eyes, that's all. Ever see how baby eyes look? Just like yours – light like a whiteman eye. Time goin come when all dat daytime sun goin darken dem, like how fire darken wood. If whiteman used to born an' live here, you think he eye not goin to get dark too? Just give it time, Pynto.' Her fingers traced the welts across his arms and the small gashes on his face. 'You not goin tell me what happm down dere, not so?'

She came to her feet as if lifted by some invisible hand behind her. Now her face was a dark full moon above him. 'Well, Elaine done come an' tell me.' She'd pulled her lips back so that he could see her teeth. 'Come Saturday, you'n me goin down dere together.' And suddenly she was no longer there, just the scent of nutmeg oil and the throb of her thumb above his eyes.

The throb was still there when he climbed to the top of Glory Cedar Rise next morning to get nearer to the sun. To turn his face up towards it and outstare it. But the sun was a hot metallic eye that didn't blink, and so it left a burning ember behind each socket in his head and reduced the green of the world to a charred and shapeless darkness.

His eyes stared back at him from the glass of the cabinet in his mother's hallway, the enamel of the cups in there, the flake of mirror above her bedhead, the water in the buckets brought home from the standpipe by the road. From the liquid, broken light of running river water. They stared back at him, pale like a washed-out sky, from behind the red curtains of his lids; were still staring back at him on Saturday, when Tan Cee arrived, placed a hand between his shoulder blades and steered him down towards the river.

He could hear his naked feet pounding like a heartbeat against the earth and feel the sweat running down the drain of his back. He could smell the danger rising from his aunt as she pushed him along the winding path towards the women.

He was thrust by his aunt's hard hand among the swirl of voices: Miss Maisie's teasing, Miss Lizzie's laughter, bright and sharp like a blade against a stone. The chorus of chuckling and curses and the quietness that always surrounded Miss Elaine. Miss Elaine – tall and bright-eyed, under the bamboos as usual – another red dress coiled around her elbow as if she'd never left the river.

Tan Cee left him standing in the water and walked towards the bank. The sun was a hot sheet on his skin, and the swirling cold water numbed his feet. He wanted to call to her, but the tightness in her face stopped him – that and the little knife that appeared in her palm, curved like a fingernail. Miss Lizzie saw it too. Her eyes followed the arc of the tiny blade as his aunt's arms darted among the shrubbery, slipped through stems, gathering leaves.

The women turned their heads back down to their washing, their large round shoulders hunched against the day. In the midst of all of them, Miss Lizzie seemed alone, her unblinking eyes fixed on his auntie's face. Pynter turned towards the women and shivered. The silence among them was dense and tight and terrible.

Returning from the bank, his auntie walked through the water towards him. She dropped the herbs on a stone beside his feet, tossed a handful of water on them and bent down to crush them with the heel of her palm. The plants surrendered their odours, which prickled like needles in his nostrils. And when the herbs had been mixed into a green and oozing paste, Tan Cee reached out and dragged him towards her. He was aware of her hands at his armpits, of his feet leaving the water, his body being lifted onto a tall stone so that all of the river lay before him, and all of the eyes of the women.

She dragged his shirt from his shoulders, slipped his short trousers past his knees, and now he was naked, and he wasn't embarrassed or afraid.

Pynter stood there with her propping him up, still shivering in the heat, looking down at himself as if his body no longer belonged to him: his small penis dark and curved like a bean-pod; his stomach round and tight and smooth; his navel a tiny hill which his grandmother said had anchored him so stubbornly to his mother that when they'd severed it, it had almost killed her. And his feet, which his mother said had to have come from his father, Manuel Forsyth, because they were too long and narrow to be a Bender's.

The water fell in a sudden scalding shower down his shoulders. Its coldness knocked the breath out of him. It stopped his shivering. Tan Cee coated him in the sap of the plants and he felt his skin grow stiff and tight like paper, and then very, very slowly she rinsed the paste off him.

Now he saw that each of the bruises he'd suffered the week before had risen up again, and stood like purple worms against his dark skin, as if they had only retreated to wait for his auntie's hands to bring them back.

'Look at 'im,' she said. 'He got anyting y'all boy-chile don't have – dat is those of you who kin have! Hi skin don't bruise-an'-bleed like everybody own? He different? Yes, he different. Lemme tell y'all what make 'im different: he mine! Dat's what make 'im different. He mine.' Her voice had climbed above the bamboos. It was bright and hard like the blade she carried somewhere in her bosom. 'An' so help me God, if dis ever happm again, I kill de bitch who cause it.'

9

She swung her head away and turned to leave, with his clothes still tucked under her arm. He climbed down the stone to follow her.

'Where you goin?' Her rage washed over him like cold water. 'You not leavin here now. You leave here when you ready. Y'hear me!'

He watched the blue flash of her bright headscarf receding as she climbed the hill through the restless netting of the canes. He was left naked on the stone in the middle of the river before the eyes of the women.

Santay was the woman who had given him back his sight. Hers was the first face he'd ever seen, the first lips that had shaped words before his eyes, the first eyes he'd ever looked into with his own.

They hadn't prepared him for her coming. Santay was Tan Cee's friend – the woman who lived in a small wooden house above their valley, who spoke to the departed and knew every plant on earth that cured or killed. She knew poisons that could put a man to sleep for good or kill the fire in his loins. Tan Cee told him that. His aunt also told him that men never went to her, only the women. They carried their illnesses, their children and their tiredness to her. And there were those like Tan Cee who, every new moon, travelled to her place, lit a fire in her yard, danced and sang songs which she repeated to him from time to time.

He'd woken one morning and she was there – a woman with a man's voice. He knew it was a woman because there was more breath around each word, and of course her smell. Men smelled of sweat and earth and meat things. They never smelled of plant things. His body had tensed, his skin flaring with the awareness of her presence. A hand that belonged to no one he knew rested briefly on his shoulder. Then two thumbs pressed hard against his eyes.

'Leave 'im to me,' the voice said.

They left him in the room with her and it became a war in which her hands seemed to reach out from anywhere and hurt him. His body was crouched, his nerves all flared and snarling, and whenever he felt her move he struck out in a wide, violent arc. But she was too quick, seemed to be everywhere at the same time. He lashed out until his arms were aching, and then two strong hands were pinning his arms against his sides. He stood there screaming for Tan Cee.

She said her name was Santay. She called him by a name different from his own. Santay lowered him to the floor and told him that she was there to give him back his eyes and that he must stay with her. That meant leaving the yard with her with a bag strapped to his back, guided by her hands at the nape of his neck. It meant going up a long, steep hill that seemed to have no end.

Pynter felt himself rising out of the valley to lighter, chillier air. A low, deep-throated snoring replaced the rustling of the canes, the sound of the World, she told him, the wind mixed up with all the noises and movements that came from down below and bounced against the bowl of the sky above their heads.

If he was to have back his eyes he would have to lie on the floor at nights and listen to the cheeping, whistling, tik-tok-tinkling of the world outside which slipped into his ear and filled his head to overflowing. It meant learning her moods by the way her feet sounded on the floorboards. It meant being fed the flesh of fruits he'd never before tasted, especially when the pain in his eyes curled his fingers in, made talons of his nails that sunk into her arms as she prised the bandage loose and replaced it with a fresh one.

Once, her hand had paused against his face and he could hear her breathing. 'You'z a real pretty boy,' she said. 'You should see yourself one day.'

Those last few words had made it easier for him.

'Plants,' she said, 'carry in their sap, their bark, their roots, their leaves, the answer to every livin sickness in a yooman been.

Some know what should be in a person blood and what don' ought to be in dere. Some unnerstan de skin. Some have knowledge of de eye. Same way y'have heart doctor and eye doctor, y'have plant that carry the exact same unnerstandin. In fact, sometimes a pusson get to thinkin that God make tree and den tree make we.'

She fed him light the way she fed him fruits, slowly and in fragments. She took the bandages off at night and brought him out into the yard. She showed him where the stars were, the dark unsteady rise of trees, the dizzying slope of hills and the patterns they made against the paler sky. She made him watch a full moon rise until his head began to throb.

It was raining when she first took him outside during the day. Through the thick white haze, she stretched out her finger at shapes and places and said their names to him. Mardi Gras Mountain, tall and dark, pushing its head up through the mists way beyond his vision, at whose feet Old Hope River flowed. The cane fields of Old Hope, whose sighs and whisperings he knew so well. The houses were brown pimples against the green of the hillside, his own home hidden behind a tall curtain of glory cedar trees.

They were sitting on a stone above the valley. He was feeding himself on guavas – the glistening white-fleshed type which smelled of a much gentler perfume than the pink-fleshed ones. She pointed down at the canes and showed him gauldins skimming with outstretched wings above the green surf of the canes. He watched them wheel and settle on the topmost branches of the bamboos that fenced the river in, and he remembered something Tan Cee had told him when the skin still covered his eyes and he'd asked her what the world was like.

'De world is life; and life is de world,' she told him. 'S'like dis room, but it so big-an'-wide it ain't got no wall around it. An' it carry millions an' millions an' millions of other living things inside itself. De world is like dat – an' dat's just a little piece of it.'

'Miss Santay,' he said, softly, hopefully. 'I – I don't want to dead.'

His words swung Santay round to face him. The scarf on her head was a throbbing yellow. It framed a face so dark he could barely see her features. She looked down at him and his heart began to race.

'My granmodder ... Deeka, say I dead soon,' he explained, looking down on the rain-swept canes, the birds fluttering above them like a host of living lilies. 'When I reach ten, she say.'

'If that granmodder of yours have she way, everybody dead soon.'

Santay lowered herself onto her haunches and placed a hand on his shoulder. She felt different from every person who had ever touched him. In all the time he had been with her, he'd never heard her laugh. She moved so silently, as if she did not dare to disturb the air.

'Listen, sonny, I don' know what your people make you out to be. Talk reach me that you have to be one of de Old Ones come again – Zed What's-iz-name again ... ? On account of the way you born. And lookin at dem eyes o' yours, I not so sure they wrong. But ... ' She got up suddenly, went inside the house and returned with a sheet of plastic and threw it over him. She told him he would spend the day out there and watch the way night came.

When it was too dark to see the valley any more she called him in and made him change his clothes. He was shivering by then – shivering and hungry.

'Eat,' she said, placing a plate of fried fish and bread in his hands. She sat on the small table before him, her elbows almost touching his. 'Now tell me what happm, Osan.' It was the name that she had given him.

'Tell you ... ?'

''Bout dis fella you s'pose to be.'

He was surprised she did not know the story. Everybody knew it, even Miss Lizzie. The story was always there, even when no one was telling it, there in his grandmother's eyes whenever she turned her gaze on him. Perhaps she knew but she wanted to hear it from him.

He chewed the bread and stared at her uncertainly. He swallowed and closed his eyes.

'My auntie, Tan Cee, say the cane was always there – the cane and us. She say we come with the cane. A pusson got to count a lot of generation back till dem reach Sufferation Time, when we didn belong to weself, because de man who own de cane own de people too.'

He lifted his head in incomprehension. Santay nodded slightly.

'Had a fella name Zed Bender. He didn feel he belong to nobody, but in truth he belong to a man name Bull Bender. Bull Bender had a lotta dog. He teach dem to hunt people down. He teach dem to rip off de back of deir leg when he catch dem. If is a woman, he bring 'er back. But he never bring back a man.

'It happm one day Zed Bender decide to run 'way with a girl name Essa. She was pretty an' he like 'er bad, real bad. He like 'er so bad he wasn' 'fraid o' nothing o' nobody. He run 'way with her. Bull Bender catch 'im – catch 'im … ' He lifted his eyes past Santay, frowned, shook his head and pointed where he thought the purple mass of the Mardi Gras might be. 'Up dere. 'Cross dere it have a tree. S'big. It got root like wall. Part of it like a lil house. It got a lotta little bird in dere. Dey ain' got no feather on dem. It don' smell nice in dere eider. Missa Bull Bender catch dem dere after de dog tear off de back of Zed Bender leg.'

He placed the bit of bread he was holding on the table and looked at her. He was tired. Wasn't hungry any more. He wanted to sleep.

'Finish,' she told him quietly.

'He put hi back against one of dem wall root. He want to stand up. He make 'imself stand up cuz he want to watch Bull Bender in hi eye – like a man in front of a man. Bull Bender tell 'im to kneel down. He won' do it. He tell Bull Bender if he have to kill 'im, den he have to do it with 'im standin up. He tell 'im dat he put a curse on him an' all hi famly, an' de seed of all hi famly to come. He dead. Dead real vex. He tell Bull Bender that is come he goin come back. Don' know when, but he goin come back, and when he come back … '

Pynter looked away. 'I don' know, don' know what goin to happm when he come back. Nobody never tell me dat part.'

Santay brought the heel of her hand up against his eyes, so softly he barely felt it. 'You cryin,' she said.

He watched her move across the floor towards the back door in that quick, whispery way of hers. She stood there and sniffed the air. The rain outside had stopped and he could hear the rising-up of the night-time bush sounds. He heard her call his name.

'Come, look down dere.' She was pointing at the black hole that was Old Hope Valley. He saw showers of lights stippling the darkness below them. 'Firefly,' she said. 'Never seen so much in one night.'

While he watched and marvelled, she turned her gaze on him. 'Dat tree up dere, de one where dat young-fella get kill, your auntie tell you dat part too?'

He stared back at her, said nothing.

'Well,' she said, turning back to face the night, 'sound to me like dis Zed Bender fella had a real mind of hi own. You don' fink so? The way I figure it, if he decide to make someting happm, den is happm it goin to happm. It cross my mind dat if he really come again an' he decide he don' want to go back, nobody kin make 'im go until he damn-well ready. A pusson have to ask demself a coupla question though. Like why he come back now, an' whether he come back alone. Cuz dat lil Essa Bender lady he run 'way with the first time was sure to meet 'im up again – in the end, I mean. Love like dat can't dead. An' if she loss 'im once, she not goin to loss 'im twice. She goin want to follow 'im. An' if what them say 'bout you is true, your brodder should ha' been a girl.'

She switched her head back round to face him. 'So! Let's say dat girl come back with him – mebbe different passageway – and she somewhere on dis island, what you think goin happm if dey meet up?'

He looked at her, but she did not seem to expect an answer. She got up and tightened the knot of the cloth on her head.

'Well, I figure she come to take 'im back. I figure dat she not good for 'im. Come, catch some sleep. Tomorrow I take you home.'

2

HOME WAS THE yard his grandfather had blasted out of rocks. It was a hill above the road that no one had found a use for until John Seegal claimed it for himself. Ten years it took her husband, Deeka Bender said, ten solid years to break through the chalk and granite with dynamite, crowbars and sledgehammers.

The work was as simple as it was breathtaking. With every girl-child he gave Deeka, he carved out a place where one day they would build their house. He went further up the hill each time a girl-child came. As if he knew that they would never leave his place. Or perhaps it was his way of tying them to this rock above Old Hope Road. Or maybe it was just his way of making sure his words came true.

And what were those words? Deeka splayed her fingers wide and laughed: that no man alive would ever rule his women. He said it when Tan Cee, their first girl-child, was born; said it again when Elena arrived a couple of dry seasons after her; said those very same words a final time when Patty the Pretty was born.

For Birdie – the only boy – he made no place at all. He told Deeka something different. 'Man,' he said, 'have to make a way for himself.'

He wasn't thinking about Birdie when he laid a nest of stones in the middle of the yard to make a fireplace. Or when he perched the great metal cauldron he'd brought from the sugar factory on three boulders, under the ant-blighted grapefruit tree

17

which he'd planted with his hands. He put it there for the times they would need to feed a wedding or celebrate a birth, or when, just for the hell of it, one of the women decided to clear out the leaves, fill it with water and toss the children in.

It was the only thing he ever built, because all his life he had been paid to pull things down. Used to be the person the government called to blow up hills and buildings. Old bridges too; or when, during the rainy season, the face of one of those mountains on the western coast broke off and, on its way down to the sea, flattened every living thing in its wake, including people foolish enough to put their houses there. He was the one they sent for to clear the mess. Once he blew up the house of a man Deeka had worked for as a servant girl for the liberty he'd taken with her.

No wonder then, that in the eyes of lil children and a lot of foolish wimmen, her husband, John Seegal Bender, was the nearest thing to God, since with a little red box and a coupla pieces of wire, he could make thunder.

He'd built his house with storms in mind. A kind of ark on thirty legs, it half stood, half leaned against the high mud bank, which was, in turn, reinforced by the roots of a tres-beau mango tree. The posts were cut from campeche wood, chopped down at the end of the dry season, just before the new moon, since the blood-red core was hardest then.

He'd rebuilt the house in '51, the year before he 'walked'. Four years before Hurricane Janet pulled the island apart, lifted most of what people were living in and flung them at the Mardi Gras a thousand feet above them.

The house had grown since then, in various directions and according to its own fancy, to accommodate the swelling family. Elena added a couple of rooms to the west side with the money that, in Deeka's words, Manuel Forsyth's conscience had given her when Peter and Pynter were born. And because the house could not decide in which direction it wanted to lean, different parts leaned different ways.

They called it home because, although Patty and Tan Cee had their own places, John Seegal's was the one in which the family always gathered.

Deeka Bender ruled it with her presence, especially those evenings over dinner when she chose to talk about John Seegal. Theirs had been the greatest love story in the world, she boasted. And whether they wanted t'hear it or not, she was going to tell them. These days they watched her more than listened: for the way her own words changed her, and how the white mass of hair, let loose like an unruly halo round her head, threw back the fire-light. How the long brown face, the cheekbones and nose – high-ridged like the place from which she came – was alive once more. They watched and marvelled at the miracle of those fingers, thin and knotted like the branches of sea grapes, becoming supple and young again.

She was a north-woman, and when a pusson say north-woman they mean a woman with pride. And Deeka Bender was prouder still, becuz she carry the blood of de First People: Carib blood, thick-hair-long-like-lapite blood, high-steppin, tall-walkin blood. And in them days Deeka walked taller than every-body else, no matter how high they was above her.

'But what God leave for a pretty young girl to do in a lil ole place sittin on the edge of a precipice over de ocean? Eh? Especially when she don' want to live and dead like everybody else up dere with no accountin fo' the life she live. And life for a woman in those days could mean just movin out, knowin a lil bit o' de world, hearin different voices an' seein whether everybody cry or laugh the same way. It wasn' askin much, but it mean a lot.

'It so happm that one day news reach me that Missa John Defoe's wife want a servant girl,' Deeka said. 'Defoe was a big Béké man who own the coconut plantation an' most other plan-tation you find round there. Everybody work for Defoe because it don't have no work apart from the work that Béké fella have to give. And for poor people girl-chile with a lil bit of ambition it was a good position to start from. So 'twasn' a nice thing to come home six months after, bawling like hell wid me pride mash down an' bleedin becuz dat man grab hold of me in de back o' de kitchen, tell me he will kill me if I make a sound for hi white-'ooman-wife-from-Englan' to hear 'im. And den, well, he take advantage of my situation. Make it worse, nobody couldn do nothing 'bout it becuz, like I tell y'all, everybody work for Defoe, including my own father.

'Must ha' been a week after I decide to go back kind of meek and quiet to that man house. People find it kinda funny. My fadder who never go anywhere widout hi couteau – his special kind o' knife he use for openin lambie – even he was more surprise than everybody else. An' that was kinda funny becuz he leave dat knife right on de little table in de room where I used to sleep. Still, you should see de shock on hi face when I tell dem I goin back to John Defoe house.

'I went back to de kitchen same way, and start doin de cookin and de washin same way, and sure enough I see 'im throwin eyes at me.'

A soft throaty laugh escaped her.

'It don't have a woman who don' know how to stop a man. For good. Most woman don' know dey know. But I know. I know it from since I was a girl bathin under the same standpipe with my little brothers. You see, lil girls not de same as lil boys. Y'all tink you know dat, right?'

She'd turned her eyes on the men: Patty the Pretty's man-friend, Leroy, Tan Cee's husband, Coxy Levid – deep-eyed and always with a cigarette and a small smile on his lips, and Gordon and Sloco, who had come to have a couple of quiet words with Coxy.

'Well, y'all don't, becuz you don' know what I going to tell y'all in a minute. You see, lil girls don' see what lil boys got. Dey see what lil boys got to lose. Is something I learn from early.'

The visitors shifted on their seats.

'Y'all think that is that lil dumplin' y'all got that rule the world. So y'all use it like a gun, like a nail, like a stone, like something y'all got to shame woman with. Y'all hear say that God is a man and God have one, an' dat give y'all de right to rule woman de way God rule de world. Well, fellas, I got news for y'all. Me – Deeka Bender – I have a cure for God.'

Coxy placed a cigarette between his lips, struck a match and lit it. Held the burning stick up before his eyes while the flame chewed its way down to his fingers. The fire fluttered there a while, like an injured butterfly just above his nails, and then went out.

It was the way Deeka told these stories, the events the same, the messages different every time. It might be about daughters who disappeared in secret and returned home with children whose fathers they refused to name, in which case her eyes would keep returning to Elena. Or her tongue might rest and remain briefly on the sorts of women who married themselves in secret and who, for some sin known only to themselves, hadn't given any children to the world. This time the bony shoulders would be turned away from Tan Cee, for this daughter's tongue was quieter than hers, her temper very, very slow to wake. But when it did, it knew no respect or boundary.

The first time Patty brought Leroy to the yard she spoke about girl children who came home with their men, locked themselves up in their bedrooms with them for days, doing *what* she just could not imagine. She was beautiful then – beautiful and terrible – with the firelight sparkling those dark north-woman eyes, her voice so high and clear it seemed to come from a different person altogether.

'In fact, I always believe dat what Delilah cut from Samson wasn' no long hair from hi head. But y'see, de Bible not a rude book. Missa Moses find another way to say it, an' so dem call it hair. But I tellin y'all dat is not no dam hair dat she take 'way from dat Samson fella. Anyway, I spend eight months in jail for de damage I do Defoe and it would ha' been longer – p'raps me whole life – if I wasn' carryin proof o' de liberty he take with me. I was six months pregnant wid dat man chile when I walk out o' Edmund Hill Prison. I wasn' going back home. I know dat from de time the warders open de gate and left me standin outside in the hot sun. I walk down dat road with a lil cloth bag in me hand and a coupla wuds in me head dat a man lef' with me almost a year before I got in trouble. You see, de time I was workin fo' John Defoe, dis fella used to come buy dynamite becuz dat Béké man was de only one allow to sell it on de islan'. I used to watch 'im from de kitchen without 'im noticing. I s'pose 'twas because I never see a man like 'im before. Most times a fella come to Defoe he stay outside the gate. But this fella walk right in. He put hi hand on hi waist and look round him, like a surveyor. Big fella, strong fella – the kinda man God build to last.

'When he talk to Defoe he watch 'im straight in hi eye.

'He was there when I come out with de washing. He look at me like if he surprise. He look at me like if he jus' make up hi mind 'bout something. It cross me mind dat for me to get to the clothes line I had to pass under dem eyes of his. Not only that, but I was wearing one o' dem cotton dress without no sleeve, and for me to hang up dem clothes I had to stretch to reach de line. I didn like dat. I didn like no man making me feel so confuse without my permission. I was vex like hell. I look at 'im an' tell 'im, "What de hell you looking at?" He look back at me like he more vex than me and say, "Tell me what you don't want me to be looking at and mebbe I won't look." An' den he laugh.'

Deeka laughed out loud at the memory.

'I never hear man laugh so sweet. He start comin more regular for dynamite, till I got to thinkin that he mus' be plannin to blow up de whole islan' o' someting. Missa Defoe get wise to 'im and start refusin to sell 'im any more dynamite. An' den one day that Béké fella tell 'im straight, "Oi'm never going to sell you no more dynamite."

'"I'll come anyway," John Seegal tell 'im.

22

'"Then Oi'll have you arrested for trespassing, or shoot you moiy-self," Defoe say.

'"Make sure you succeed first time you try," my husband tell 'im back.

'Lord ha' mercy, them words frighten me. Them frighten me to know dat I become a woman dat a man prepare to kill for. He keep comin like he promise. Used to stand up on the lil hill across the road an' watch me. I never talk to 'im. But if I look up an' he not 'cross dere, I start to sorta miss 'im. It last a coupla months till he couldn take it no more. One day he stay 'cross the road an' call me. Was de kinda call dat make you know dat if you go, you was sayin yes to a question he didn ask you in the first place. Was like sayin, "I give in, I'z yours." I never go. I should ha' gone. I didn go. He call my name again an' tell me if I didn come to 'im right now, he never comin back.

'"I tired holdin on," he say. "You wearin me down," he say. "Dat lil Béké man 'cross dere make it clear he want you for himself. I could break his arse as easy as I look at 'im but you have to give me reason. I won't bother you no more. When you ready, you come to me." He stay right across the road and shout it. Then he leave. Was de last time he come.'

Deeka had been standing all the while. Now she sat on the steps, her elbows resting on her knees. She seemed to have forgotten they were there.

'Still, it don't take a half a man to have a woman come to him from jail carryin a child that not his, far less a child for a man who was threatening to shoot 'im. He cuss me, he even bring hi hand to me face. But was de beginnin of a kind of forgiveness, although he never accept the child. A woman know these things. Is what a man don't say. Is how he look at that baby when he think you not watchin. Is how he dress an' undress dat chile if he have to. Is how he look at it when it not well, that sorta thing. Must ha' strike 'im, every time he look at her, dat it ain't got no way dat lil red-skin girl could pass as hi own child. And in Ole

Hope here, a man who take in a woman dat carryin another man seed, he either born stupid or born wrong-side. Is all of dat must ha' got to 'im in the end. And of course my lil girl, Anita.'

This was the place they were waiting for her to arrive at. Perhaps this time she would go past it and tell them the bit that seemed to stop her right there every time. Over the years she'd been inching closer to it. A word here, a sentence there, softly mumbled sometimes, like slipping on pebbles at the edge of some precipice. She always recovered at the last minute. She became herself again, the weight of all her years settling back on her shoulders and bowing them very slightly. The light in her eyes receding.

3

THE TALK OF WOMEN taught Pynter Bender one thing: men walked.

The women spoke of it as if it were an illness – a fever that men were born with, for which there was no accounting and no cure. It could come upon them anytime, but more likely halfway through the harvesting of the canes in April – those months of work and hunger that Old Hope called the Stretch, when the children were thinnest.

A man stripped and cut the canes for ninety-four cents a day. A woman tied and packed and lifted bundles onto trucks for seventy-eight. And with the coming of the first rains, the tractors with the ploughs arrived. They walked behind them for a month, clearing the valley floor of stones and the diseased roots of last year's crop.

That was when their men started looking southwards at the triangles of blue between the hills. Over dinner, the man would not really hear his woman when she told him something trivial about their child: that it would have his lips or eyes and be as good-looking as him. He might nod or stare through her, wondering aloud if she'd heard that another stoker in the sugar factory south of Old Hope, or in one of the little mills further east, had lost an arm to the machinery. That some quick-thinking friend had the presence of mind to cut the arm off at the shoulder before the cogs could pull him in. Or that an overladen truck, carrying a couple of tons of cane, had rolled over and crushed the loaders – boys really, boys barely old enough to earn a wage.

It was not always the rumour of an accident that started the man off daydreaming. One ordinary day he would look up from pulling ratoons from the earth and suddenly see nothing but the canes, stretching all the way to the end of his days, beyond life itself. And he would imagine himself walking on streets with lights, or standing at the foot of some tall glass building with cigarettes and money in his pocket, a coat around his shoulders and a newspaper tucked under his armpit. His woman would sense the change in him because he was irritable with her all the time, raised his hands at her more often, couldn't stand to hear the baby crying.

Over the months, the savings, the borrowed money, would go towards the beige felt hat with the widish rim, a couple of thick Sea Island cotton shirts, two pairs of heavy flannel trousers, that started narrow at the heels and got looser all the way up to the waist. And of course a coat. Nothing was more confirming of his intentions than that coat. It would be the last thing that his friend – the only person he'd trusted with his plans – would hand over to him as they stand on the Carenage in San Andrews with their backs towards the island. And he would promise that friend, over a quick and secretive handshake, that he would make a way for him as soon as he got 'there'.

'There' was anywhere, anywhere but home. 'There' was wherever in the world someone wanted a pair of hands to do something they didn't want to do themselves. 'There' was anywhere a man could turn his back on cane. And it all started with that walk which, one quiet night, took him past the small dry-goods store with the single Red Spot sign, past the crumbling mansions that sat back from the road, their facades half-hidden by ancient hibiscus fences.

At Cross Gap, the last and only junction that marked Old Hope from the rest of the world, the man would begin to walk faster, the beige felt hat pulled down over his eyes, his last journey up Old Hope Road, his arms swinging loose, the walk of no return.

There were other Old Hope walks too, shorter walks, the night-time disappearances that lasted until morning. After dinner he would get up, wash his hands, hitch his trousers higher up his hips, and with barely a turn of the head he would say, 'I takin a walk.'

'Where you off to?' a woman's quiet query would come.

And just as softly his answer would reach her: 'Don' know, jus' followin my foot.' And the soft pad of his shoes would melt into the night.

Tan Cee's husband would never explain himself. Wednesday nights, Pynter would watch his auntie watching her husband sitting cross-legged on the stool a couple of feet away from her. He imagined her counting the cigarettes he pulled out of the packet, the gestures his left hand made to light the match, how close to the butt he smoked each one and the slowness with which he crushed it into the dirt between his feet. That long, still face of his was always lifted slightly, like a man whose head was buried in a dream. And as the night drew in, he took longer drags and made the match burn closer to his fingers.

Tan Cee's head was angled just like his, but slightly away from him, her eyes switched sideways so that only the whites showed in the firelight. He could hear the whisper of Coxy's clothing as he came to his feet, smell the Alcolado Glacial he'd rubbed along his neck and shoulders. It was only when his sandals hit the asphalt on the road below that his aunt got up and headed home.

Pynter had his eye on Coxy too. There was something about the soft-voiced smoking man that made his aunt a different person. However quietly Coxy called her name, she always seemed to hear him. She would lift her head, drop whatever she was doing and go straight away to him. It was as if she had an extra ear that was always listening out for him.

Sometimes Pynter would catch Coxy's eyes on him. It was a different look from Deeka's. It didn't seem to wish he wasn't there. It didn't switch from him and then to Peter and back to him again. It was quiet and direct; and if he looked back at him, Coxy would nod his head and smile.

He was going to get an answer to the question that Coxy always left behind every Wednesday night. It felt a natural thing to do because lately he had been following his eyes. He left the yard on mornings and made his way to places he'd spotted in the distance. The week before it had been the high green rise of a silk-cotton tree on the slopes of Déli Morne. The day after that a patch of purple down the furthest reaches of the river, or a bit of rock that stood bare and brown like a scar against the green face of that precipice they called Man Arthur's Fall. His eyes had even taken him down to that stinking place of tangled roots and mangroves into which they said his grandfather had disappeared. He'd stood there staring at the boiling mud, wondering what could ever make a person want to do a thing like that.

Now, he'd only just got back home from the sea. He'd sat on the pebbles that faced the ocean and looked out at the grey shape of the land that rested like a giant finger on the water, beyond which were darkness and the boom of water breaking over reef. He'd repeated in his head the last words Santay said to him the day she returned him to his yard: that to truly rid himself of Zed Bender's curse, he would have to cross that ocean.

Deeka was talking about John Seegal again when he arrived. He wondered if she'd ever been to see the swamp that her husband had left her for. He wondered if anyone in the yard had ever done so.

His mother came and placed his dinner in his lap. He wasn't hungry, but he fed himself all the same, keeping his eyes on Tan Cee and her husband. He glanced across at Deeka's face. She was talking too much to notice him, and for that he felt relieved.

Following Coxy in the dark was easier than Pynter expected. He had been behind him for so long his heels were aching and a film of sweat had broken out on his face. He was not afraid of the night. It was never the kind of deep black that Deeka spoke of in her stories, where you couldn't see your hands even if you held them up before your face.

The night was full of shapes, some laid back against the sky-line, some leaning hard against each other. The track curled itself around the roots of trees that rose as high as houses. It dipped into small ravines, turned back on itself so suddenly he some-times lost his sense of where he was.

He thought there would be no end to Coxy Levid's walking.

Past Cross Gap Junction, Coxy turned left and suddenly they were in the middle of a cocoa plantation that spread out before them like a warren of dark tunnels. Pynter had a sense of how far ahead of him Coxy was because of the glow of his cigarette and because he sometimes whistled a tune. Sometimes he stopped and pulled his shirt close because it was cold beneath these trees.

Tan Cee had told him of the snakes that lived beneath the car-pet of leaves which every cocoa tree spread around its trunk. Crebeaux, she told him, were creatures so black they glistened. They moved like tar but were quick enough to knot themselves around the foot of a careless child, a rabbit or a bird and make a soup of their bones before swallowing them whole.

He'd lost sight of Coxy, had emerged on the edge of a small hill and hung there, leaning against the bark of a mango tree, looking down at the houses scattered along the hillside facing him. Lamplight seeped through their wooden walls. Their gal-vanised roofs glowed dully in the dark.

He was about to turn and make his way down when he caught the smell of cigarettes. He brought his hands up to his face. A hand reached around his shoulders and he felt himself thrown backwards. He'd lost his balance but he wasn't falling. He felt his breath leave his body as the hand lifted him and slammed his back against the tree. Pynter opened his mouth and drew his breath; and there was Coxy Levid's face, level with his own.

'Why you falla me?' Coxy shook him hard. 'Yuh aunt send you after me?'

Pynter shook his head, made to speak, but his tongue had seized up like a stone inside his mouth.

'You lie fo' me, you never leave dis place.' Coxy made a circle with his head that took in the bushes and the darkness around. 'Y'unnerstan?'

A match exploded in his face again. Coxy's lips were peeled back, his teeth white and curved like seashells. The light-brown eyes glowed in the matchlight like a cat's.

'Why you falla me, boy!'

'I don' know, jus' … You squeezin me.'

'That woman send you after me?'

'No. I come – I come by meself. You, you squeezin me.'

'So if I break your fuckin neck right here fuh mindin big man bizness, nobody goin to know.' The fingers pressed harder against his forehead.

Pynter looked into Coxy's eyes. He searched his head for words. Found nothing.

'So what you fallain me for?'

'I – I not goin to tell nobody.'

'Tell nobody what? What you got in your mind to tell nobody, eh? A man cyahn' take a walk? You think anybody could walk behind me for me not to know? You feel say you is spirit? You feel say all dem shit dem talk 'bout you is true? You feel say you can't dead. You wan' me to prove it?'

Coxy shifted his hand sharply down beneath Pynter's chin. Now there was a terrible pressure at the back of his neck. His jaws were so tightly locked he could barely whimper.

'You so much as breathe my name to anybody, you so much as tink a lil thought about where you falla me tonight, you so much as dream 'bout tryin it again, I make you wish you never born.'

The hand released him suddenly and he fell backwards.

Pynter stayed leaning against the tree, his breathing coming fast and hard. He listened to Coxy's footsteps going down the path until he could hear the man no more. A little way off a dog barked. A few others across the hill replied, followed by a man's voice – low and deep like far-off thunder. A woman's laughter climbed the night air, so bright and musical it made him think of ribbons in the wind.

4

FROM THE SETTLEMENT of twenty dwellings or so east of Glory Cedar Rise a man sat hidden under one of the houses, dreamily looking down on Old Hope Valley.

The occupants did not know that he was there. He could have chosen any of the houses scattered about the hill, since they all offered the same view of the valley. After resting a couple of hours there, he'd picked up enough from the conversation that filtered through the floorboards to know that the woman's name was Eunice and the man's was Ezra, and that he worked in one of the quarries in the south.

He had dozed a little and then woken up. His feet still ached from the walk from Edmund Hill. The eight miles had taken him longer than he'd anticipated, but that was because for many years he had lost the habit of walking distances.

Having also lost the habit of sleeping a whole night through, he would sleep again for another couple of hours and then wake up to watch the morning come. By then, those above him would begin to stir. He would take the mud track down towards the river, or perhaps wait a couple of hours longer. The quarryman might find him there. He might move to say something, as any man would do to a stranger sitting beneath his house, but then the quarryman would stop and examine him more closely – the coarse old cotton shirt with faded numbers stencilled below the breast pocket, the heavy pair of leather boots, resoled and passed

32

on to him as a present. And of course his face. The quarry man's eyes would pause there and he would think better of whatever he was about to say and maybe go inside to tell his woman.

It was what always happened when, every few years, a man found him beneath his house waiting for the morning.

In the valley below, he'd counted the fires in the yards as they went out one by one with the deepening night, each bit of dancing yellow like a tiny signal of hope against all that darkness. He had watched the moon rise and smelled the morning, and had begun to wonder how they would receive him this time and what, if anything, had changed since he last saw them. And then the sky lit up a couple of hills ahead of him. It was in the general direction of where he wanted to go. He eased himself forward, thinking how strange it was that anyone would want to light a boucan this time of night, in fact so close to morning. He watched it burn till the flames died down, becoming no more than a glowing scar against the dark.

It was daylight and the valley filled with birdsong. He got to his feet. He moved with the litheness of a man accustomed to hard work. It would take him a couple of hours to get there, perhaps longer, because on his way up the other side of the valley he would pause to gather guavas, water lemons, perhaps carve a spinning top or two for the children. He always brought home something for the children.

He turned his face up to the morning, the almond-shaped eyes catching the soft, indifferent light. A gold tooth glimmered between his parted lips and his large head dipped down. He picked up a cotton sack, which he swung onto his left shoulder. The sudden flurry of air raised the scent of bread. His eyes were still fixed on the scar against the hillside when he started marching down the hill, the smell of yeast and hard-dough bread following him.

He emerged into a bright, harsh day from the cocoa plantation near Cross Gap Junction a couple of miles away. And it was from there that he started greeting people.

Tan Cee heard him first about a quarter of a mile out on the road. Somebody must have set him off laughing. Her head cocked up like a chicken's and suddenly she was squealing, 'Birdie! Birdie!', running down the hill towards the road with the tub of washing spilt all over the ground and Coxy's trousers trailing in the dirt behind her.

'That sister o' mine crazy,' Elena laughed, but she too was dancing on the steps.

Birdie brought Tan Cee back up the hill kicking and choking with laughter in between her pleas for him to put her down. He was holding her high above his head and tickling her at the same time.

They collapsed in the yard together and before he knew it they were all over him. Patty arrived running and simply dumped herself on them. Elena almost took a flying leap from the steps and trusted Birdie's body to take care of the rest. Tan Cee was somewhere between them. They pinched him, they bit him, they kicked him, they dug and squirmed their fingers in his ribs, which brought out thunder-rolls of laughter from him and set the whole yard laughing too. For Birdie's was the kind of laughter that was in itself a joke.

He rolled them off eventually and they sat in the dirt and stared at him, the giant they saw once in every few years. They reached out their hands and brushed the bits of grass and dust from his beard, wiped the sweat off his forehead with their hands. Tan Cee straightened the collar of the khaki shirt they'd just crushed while Patty and Elena rested their elbows on his shoulders. He got to his feet, bringing them all up together with him, like a tree might move with all its branches, and now that the children could see his full size they were open-mouthed.

If Birdie had been born after his father's passing, they would have said he was John Seegal born again, and he had the same effect on Deeka. She was sweeping up the fallen flowers of the grapefruit tree when she heard his laughter. The sound of him had frozen her. She hadn't moved from under the grapefruit tree, still held the broom in her hand in mid-swing.

She didn't say a thing when he got up, eased the three women aside and turned around to face her with a grin as wide as a beach.

Birdie lifted his mother off the ground and held her, broom and all, as one would do a child. The smile gone now, he looked down at her face and rumbled softly, 'Ma!'

Everything was in that single word, all the time and distance there had been between them. Deeka dropped the broom. She reached up and looped her arms around his neck.

'Put me down,' she ordered.

He held her for a while longer then carefully let her down among the stones, passing his hands through his hair, his beard, then his hair again.

'When you goin back?' she asked.

'I goin straight this time, Ma. No more jail for me.'

'Until you break in somebody house again and clean it out? I try to straighten you out from small, but this son o' mine born crooked. Come lemme feed you some proper food, you thief!'

His laughter filled the house till evening. He ate everything they placed before him, and when he finished he kicked the heavy boots off his feet, reached for the canvas bag that hadn't left his shoulder, even when his sisters were wrestling with him, and pulled out several loaves of bread.

It was what they had been waiting for: Birdie's prison bread. Pynter and his brother knew more about his bread than they did about their uncle himself. It was the taste of Birdie's bread they talked about when they were really missing him. It was a way of talking about his strength too, for the secret to his making the best bread on the island – and a pusson won' be surprised if it was de best bread in de world, Elena told them – lay in the power of those hands. She'd said those last words the way a preacher in church would say them. Only she didn't get an amen at the end but a loud 'Uh-huh!' from Tan Cee.

Those hands – they kneaded dough so tight a pusson could hang it on a branch and swing on it and it won't stretch loose an' make dem fall an' bust their tail. That was bread – that was de fadder an' modder of all bread. In fact, bread was Birdie salvation. God might forgive him his thiefin ways on account of his talent for baking. And not just bread. Dumplings too. Cornmeal dumplings, plain-flour dumplings, cassava dumplings: dumplings for oil-down and crab stew; for pea soup and fish broth. Or jus' dumplings stan'-up by itself.

You bit into one of Birdie's dumplings and it protested. It stewpsed. It sucked its teeth like an irritable woman. It went 'chi-iks!' Like it was answering you back or something. Like it asking you what the arse you playin, biting it so hard.

In fact, a woman could get de measure of a man by the dumplin' that he make. By de size of it, the toughness and de strength of it, an' whether it could answer back when you sink your teeth in it. And if a pusson want proof dat Birdie was a real man, dem only had to eat his dumplin'. Just one. In fact, you didn even have to go to all that lovely trouble. All you have to do is ask his woman, Cynty. Cuz soon as Birdie reach from jail, he does go an' cook she food!

Woman-talk. Sweet-talk. Bender-talk that sent them up in quakes of laughter and left the children smiling back suspiciously at them.

Birdie spoke of prison as if it were another country – one with walls too tall to escape over. And why a person goin want to do that anyway? They could break a leg, and if they got away, where they goin to hide on a little island that the sea fence in better than any barbed wire? And that was only if they got that far, because there were dogs – he knew the name of every one of them. Real dogs. Not no bag-a-bone pot-hound like people got in their yard at home, but Rockwylers and Allstations. Them is serious dog! Them could follow a man shadow in the night. No joke! All they need was a little sniff of the bench that fella sit down on a coupla years ago. And they good as got him.

He told them of troubles they knew nothing about, and of men who'd spent their entire lives behind those old stone walls, who, when let out, were so confused and terrified of all that light and air around them they ran straight back inside. Some spent all their days trying to figure out what they did to be up there.

There were the bright ones, he told them, put inside for something they might have said that somebody did not like. With their quiet words and educated ways, they changed the men without the wardens noticing. Taught them how to talk up for themselves, how to hold on to an argument. And those who could not take their minds off their women and their children were made to think of things that had never crossed their minds before. Like why cane was so cheap and they couldn't afford to buy the sugar that was made from it; why the dry season always brought with it so much rage and hardship on an island where the soil they walked on was so rich. So rich, in fact, that if a pusson dropped a needle on the ground it grew into a crowbar.

The smile left his lips, and his hands grew quiet in his lap. Now the young ones were coming, he told them, children who had no place among big men. Sent there by men who thought they owned the country. Who could not abide the impatience of these young ones who asked more questions and wanted a life that took them further than these narrow acres of bananas and sugar cane. Which was why there were more guns and soldiers now; which was why something had to break. Soon. It didn't take the edicated men to show him that. He could see it coming.

Pynter eased his head off Tan Cee's shoulder.

'An' you, Missa Birdie, if it so bad in dere, how come you like jail so much?' He didn't understand the sudden silence and the look that Deeka shot him.

Birdie raised his head and laughed, but the furrows on his brows that had not been there before made his face look different.

'You de funny one – not so? You de second-born?' Birdie said.

Tan Cee rested an arm across Pynter's shoulder and drew him in to her. 'And you the one who name we give 'im.' She smiled. 'Hi first name is your middle name. We call 'im Pynter.'

Tan Cee's words seemed to take Birdie somewhere else. His face relaxed. His eyes got soft and dreamy.

'I ferget that,' he said. 'I ferget that name. S'what happm when you got something and you never use it. Dat remind me,' he rose up like a small earthquake from the floor, 'Cynty down dere waiting.'

That night, curled up on the floor beside Peter, Pynter realised that his uncle had not answered him. His head was a hive of questions he never got to ask – why, especially, was he always thiefin things that were never really useful?

The last time the police had come for him was after he arrived in the yard with a fridge on his head and a television under his arm, even though the whole world knew that Lower Old Hope didn't have electricity. And it was a waste, because the chickens made their nest in the fridge and one of the policemen who came to take him went off with the television.

'Peter, you like Birdie?'

'Uncle Birdie,' Peter hissed.

'Uncle Birdie – you like 'im?'

'Uh-huh. And you?'

'He not well an' he don' know it.'

He felt Peter shifting in the dark. 'S'not true – Tan Cee tell you so?'

'No, I tell Tan Cee so.'

'Which part of 'im not well?' Peter said.

'You say s'not true, so I not tellin you.' He felt his brother moving towards him, felt his breath against his ear.

'Jumbie Boy – you'z a flippin liar.'

Elena Bender was smiling when she asked Pynter to come and sit with her beneath the plum tree. That was not good. His mother never smiled so early in the day. She picked up a piece of stick and began making patterns in the dust with it. A thin film of sweat had settled among the very fine hairs on her upper lip. She glanced sideways at him, briefly, tried to smile again, but he could see that she was forcing it.

'You goin to your father house from Sunday.'

'My father – Manuel Forsyth?'

'You don' call 'im Manuel Forsyth; he's your father.'

'He got another name?'

'Is the same rudeness you bring to your Uncle Birdie yesterday. You see how upset you make him? Peter know what y'all father look like. You don't think you ought to know him too?'

He didn't answer straight away, preferring to follow the flight of a pair of chicken hawks high on the wind above them. Their cries reminded him of bright sharp things – knives and nails and needles.

'He a old man,' he said. 'Ten times older'n you. Dat's what Miss Lizzie say. I not goin nowhere.'

'What else Miss Lizzie say?' She was looking at him sideways.

'Lots o' things.'

'Like what?' She was speaking but her lips were hardly moving.

A small current of uneasiness ran through him. He turned his head away from her, remembering the evening he returned from the river after Tan Cee had taken him there. During dinner, Patty the Pretty had come to sit with him. She'd asked him what had happened down there by the river. He told her, finding that he'd lowered his voice like hers. When he finished she was shaking her head and she wasn't smiling as she did most times.

'You must never tell your mother about these things, y'unnerstan? You talk to me or Tan Cee, but never your mother, y'hear me?'

He'd asked her why. She seemed to be making up her mind about something, then she touched his arm, 'Know Miss Maisie?'

He nodded.

'See that long white mark that run across she face?'

He nodded.

'Well, one time, when y'all was little baby, Maisie say something to your mother about y'all and Manuel Forsyth. Elena put you an' Peter down by the roadside and went fo' her. It take four people to pull her off. She only had time to do that to her face. Imagine if she had another coupla minutes.'

He looked across at his mother, his voice a plea this time. 'Let Peter go – I don' like 'im, Na.'

'You don' like somebody you don' know? Is you he ask for.'

'Why?'

She looked away.

'I wan' to stay with Tan.'

'What you say?'

He felt the change in her. It was as quiet as it was frightening. He jumped to his feet to run. Her hand shot out and closed around his shirt.

'Siddown!' The voice came from her throat. 'Lemme teach you something. I'll never have to do this with Peter – but you, you different. I don' know what kind o' child you is. You want to know who's your modder? Well, let me,' she shook him, 'show you,' she shook him again, 'who your modder is!'

She was loosening the buttons of her bodice with the other hand. He watched as she lifted the ends of the garment. Still staring into his eyes, she took his hand and placed it on the small bulge on the left side of her stomach. He tried to pull away. She dragged him back.

'Peter was here fo' eight months an' thirteen days. You,' she pulled his hand over to the other side, 'you was here a extra two days. This,' she forced his finger along the lines that ran like a faint network of vines around the bulges, 'is y'all signature. Is de writing dat y'all leave on me. Dis is Peter; dis is you. Me, Elena Bender, I'z your modder. So!' She shook him hard. 'Don' get renk with me, y'hear me! I not askin you, I tellin you – next week you goin live with your father.'

She pushed his hand away, got to her feet and went inside.

A couple of mornings every week, when it was still so dark even the chickens beneath the house had not begun to stir, there came the clip-clop-clipping of his father's donkey, the thud of a bag of provisions hitting the ground, then the voice, 'Elen-ooy!'

Pynter would listen to his mother in the bedroom as she got up, quickly dressed and hurried down the hill to the road.

Pynter would hear the rhythm of the donkey's hooves fading into the distance, following them in his imagination through the sea of plantation canes in the lower valleys of Old Hope, over the Déli Morne River, past the stony wastelands of Salt Fields, where they said the bamboo rose so high their branches swept the sky.

For a long time Pynter had tried to put a face to that voice.

The hands that lifted him onto the back of the donkey were big like Birdie's. A face turned back at him – brown and smooth and hairless, the eyes resting on him almost as a hand would. And then a voice, 'Is quiet where we going; you sure you want to come?'

He nodded. He liked the smell of the man.

His father's house stood on a ridge that looked down on Old Hope. From there he could see the deep green scoop of the valley winding towards the Kalivini swamps where his grandfather disappeared, and the purple-dark hills that seemed to hold back the sea from spilling over onto the canes and the people who worked in them. His father's house was smaller than his mother's and had no yard to speak of, just the lawn he was not allowed to walk on, which belonged to Miss Maddie – a greying woman whom he'd only caught a glimpse of, and who his father called his daughter.

A window with six glass panes let light into the bedroom. It was the only room with a door that was open to the day.

41

His father pointed at the back room first – a lightless doorway that stood gaping like a toothless mouth, and from which came a warm and unexpected breath – the odour of musty, nameless things. 'Don't go in there,' he said, without offering a reason. 'And leave this place alone,' he added, turning to the living room.

He'd said 'this place' as if the living room did not belong to the house. It had been abandoned to spiders and dust mites. A mahogany table, on whose surface he drew finger faces and curlicues, stood in the middle of it. The matching chairs were arranged around it strangely, as if the people who had been sitting there had suddenly got up and, without looking back, had left the room for good. Two brownish photographs hung in the gloomiest corner of the room. The smaller one was just the head of a young man, his hair cropped short, staring directly out at them. In the other, a man sat on a beautiful chair with a gaze that was direct and grave. A still-faced woman rested a gloved hand on his arm. Four children, a boy and three girls, were arranged around them like flowers in a vase.

His father gave him their names the moment he stepped through the doorway: Maddie, a sour-faced child, knock-kneed and resentful even then. To the left of her, Eileen – beautiful and dreamy. His father's voice had gone dreamy too. Eileen left the island soon'z she was old enough to travel. Never look back. Pearly was the youngest – too young then to know that she had to sit still to get a proper picture, which was why her face was no more than a smudge.

He left Gideon for last. Gideon was the only boy. 'Apart from y'all, of course. Gideon build bridges for the government.

'Gideon fifty next year. Pearly forty-seven. Eileen,' he smiled, 'she thirty-five next month.'

For a while Pynter felt that the man had forgotten he was there. The bag he'd taken off the donkey was still hanging from his shoulder. His eyes were on the photograph. A stillness had come over his face.

'Time pass. Time pass too fast, son. Time does pass too fast.' His voice had grown thick and slow. There was a sadness there that made Pynter turn his eyes up at the heavy shape against the backlight of the doorway.

Once, this shape had been no more than a sound. A voice. It used to stop his hands from whatever they were doing. His father's voice – different from the voices of all the men he'd ever heard. And now that he could see him, it was the only voice that fitted the face to which it belonged. A large face, brown like burnt ginger, not smiling, not strict, not young, not old. A face that shifted easily, like shadow over water.

Miss Lizzie's words came back to him, 'Ole Man Manuel, s'not s'pose to be.' Words that invited him to shame. Words that tried to force themselves into him the way his mother and his aunts would pin his arms against his sides, pull his head back and pour medicine down his throat. Old Man Manuel ... Peter and he were not supposed to be. Something, something must've happen. Something ...

And whatever that something was, it shone like a dark light in their eyes; in the women's laughter by the river. It was there in the silence of his mother when she pulled him and Peter close to her to inspect their hair or skin. It was there when she combed their hair or bathed them. There in the words they said that Gideon had told her. It was the reason why Gideon had tried to take them away from her before she'd even had them. It was there, always there, in his grandmother's quiet gaze.

He felt a movement from his father, more a stirring of the air about him, and then the hand, rough like bark, resting against his right brow. His father's hand moved down and cupped his chin. Pynter eased himself away.

'You'll meet Maddie tonight,' he said, swinging his head slightly at the large white concrete house a little way behind them. 'Call her Miss Maddie, y'hear me? And when Pearly come to see me, call her Sister Pearl. As for Gideon ... '

'Gideon – he – he come here?'

'Sometimes.'

'He my brother too?'

'He my son, you my child. He your brother.'

Pynter shook his head.

'Whatsimatter?' The man looked at him concerned.

'Then, den how come … ' His tongue felt heavy on the words.

'How come, what … ?'

'How come he try to kill us? Before we even born.'

As soon as he said it, he knew that something terrible had come out of his mouth. So terrible it froze the shape above him. Made it lower itself before him, reach out solid hands that closed down on his shoulders. He felt the deep ruffle of the bag just before it struck the floorboards. The vibration travelled up his feet and made his heart turn over. Now he felt his father's breath on his face.

'Who tell you that? Who tell you that!'

He feared the rage seeping out of that voice. He feared the strength he felt in those fingers.

'Nobody,' he stammered. 'Nobody tell me nothing.'

The fingers released him. 'You never use them words again, y'hear me, boy. Never lemme hear you say them words.'

'No, Pa.'

His father stood up then, spoke as if he were addressing something that lay some place far beyond the walls of the house. 'You call me Pa. I like dat. You must always call me Pa.'

Pynter nodded, swallowing hard on the soft knot in his throat.

He never asked his father who he left his rich garden to or why he gave it up as soon as his mother sent him off to live with him. Why so soon after Santay they were so quick to see him off again. Why they had chosen him instead of Peter. Why they would not tell him for how long.

'Is you your father ask for,' his mother said. But she could not hold his eyes. She couldn't put words to the other things that her tied-up lips and drifting eyes were concealing from him.

He never asked his father about the silence which sat like an accusation between Miss Maddie and himself. Why Miss Maddie looked past him the way she did from the very first morning he called out to her, made her leave her porch and cross her lawn to come over and see her lil brother.

He was not sure she saw him. Her eyes had drifted skywards, over to the Kalivini hills, up to the Mardi Gras and finally down to some point above his head. They passed briefly over their father's face and settled on the concrete steps on which they were all standing. Small eyes in a face as dark and swollen as blood-pudding.

'Uh-huh,' she grunted, and waddled back to her porch. He was sure she hadn't seen him.

Her son Paso came just when the small pre-dawn birds began to stir the early-morning stillness with their chirping, when the crickets quietened suddenly and altogether, and the silence they left behind got filled in by the humming of the ocean a couple of hills beyond and the whispery shiftings of the canes. He came like the tail end of a dream and seemed to disappear soon after, making Pynter wonder if he had ever been there at all.

'A scamp,' his father told him, 'a child of the night, that Paso. I don't remember what he look like now, becuz I don' know when last I see him. You never see him in the day.

'Not surprising when a pusson know how and where the boy was born. Maddie picked 'im up in Puerto Rico, see? Take a boat back home when she was big as a full moon. Bring the belly back with her but not the man. She didn make it back to land on time. Had him on the sea. Matter o' fact,' the old man slapped his knee and laughed, 'she had him in the middle of it. Now, a chile that come like that can't tell nobody which country he from, not so? Cuz he wasn' born in one. Now that's between me and you, y'unnerstan?'

Pynter thought about his father's words and began laughing too. The old man seemed surprised by it. "Mind me of a uncle you had – that laugh.'

'He here?'

'He out there. In the hallway. Just the picture. He not with us no more.'

'He … '

'Before you born. Sea take him.' His father passed his hand across his face as if he were washing it with air. 'Funny fella he was, your uncle. But nice. Dress like a king. Dress in black, only black. We used to call him Parlourman because of the black. Pretty face. Smooth like a star apple. Talk pretty too. Every woman he meet used to want to kill for him; but he never was interested. I could never figure 'im out. He didn have no children either. Sank with a boat between Curaçao an' Panama.'

'What dead feel like, Pa – it hurt?'

'Don' know. Why you ask?'

'Jus' want to know … '

'When it come, I s'pose the part of you that know jus' not around to know no more, y'unnerstan?' As he touched the boy's face with the meat of his hand, a chuckle rose from his chest. 'Even I don' unnerstan what I jus' tell you. Come eat some food. I glad you here.'

Over the steamed yams, sweet potatoes and fried shark that Miss Maddie had covered up and left on the steps for him, his father's eyes were on him again. This time it was a different look. It seemed impossible that the anger he'd seen there earlier could reside in eyes so soft.

'You talk kind of funny too – like him.'

'Like … ?'

'Like your Uncle Michael.'

He wanted to know more about this odd uncle that the sea had taken. To understand the nature of the quietness that came over his father when he called his name. But all he got was a promise that wasn't really one, 'P'raps I'll get the time to tell you about it one day, if I manage to find de mood.' Or a statement that was so tied up it took him many fruitless days of trying to unravel it. 'When a man put hi dog to sleep, then is sleep it have to sleep, y'unnerstan?'

'No.'

'Well, I can't explain no better.'

5

HE UNCOVERED HIS Uncle Michael in a grip in the room his father had told him not to enter. He also found his mother there.

He didn't understand why his father should forbid him to enter a room whose door was wide open. He could see, dimly, right through to the furthest wall. Mornings, he stood at the lip of that door-mouth, his head turned sideways, his father's voice like a staying hand inside his head. But the fingers of light that entered through the cracks in the board wall on the other side kept drawing him back to the gloom inside. However bright the day, the light in there was always yellow. It made burning pathways across the floor, on books and piles of paper, along the red handle of an axe, over the bunched darkness of a broom, and small piles of clothing strewn like debris thrown up on an abandoned shore.

The room had an odour, too, that spread itself throughout his father's house – the smell of things that had dried too fast to rot.

It took him days. Of tiptoeing and stopping. Of stopping and tiptoeing. Each time a step or two further in, listening to his dozing father's breathing in the room next door, mapping out the space around him with his eyes, summoning up his courage. It was a while before he noticed the grip in the corner. It was partly concealed beneath a child's small mattress. A small, deep-brown case, worn and raw at the edges, with bright brass studs at each corner. The three latches at the front were also made of brass, the handle shaped from some white-veined material that had a wondrous glasslike translucency. He laid it gently back against the mattress, wondering how it could have got there. If the sea had swallowed the boat his father's brother had been travelling on, wouldn't it have also taken this with it?

There was a small book in there. It was laid on top of the folded clothing, with pages that looked and smelled like paper money. There was a picture of a slim-faced man at the front of it, with large, light-flecked pools of eyes staring out at him, and a mouth that was soft and curved like his Auntie Patty's.

He'd seen pictures before but never one like this: the paper so smooth and shiny it seemed to preserve something of the darkness and the glow of his uncle's skin. Those eyes were really watching him, still on him when he reached beyond the little book and began to slowly lift the clothing aside. Things in there were cool to his touch even though his hands were sweating. His thumb was bleeding where he'd pulled on the catch too hard and a splinter had slipped into his flesh.

It was like reaching into a dream. The lining that ran around the box shifted like water beneath his fingers. The shirts were made of fabrics soft as soap suds. The white ones seemed to give off their own glow in the gloom. A razor folded in a soft brown square of leather. Talcum powder in a pouch that smelled like cinnamon, like the ocean, but mostly like the scent that came off the skin of limes.

Further down beneath the razor and the shirts, past the heavy grey trousers, his fingers hit on something hard. He touched its edges and it slid away from him. He could not close his hand around it. Realising what it was, he slipped his hand under and eased it out – another small book, its cover as rough as bark, its pages ragged at the edges as if they had been ripped from something else and put together by absent-minded hands. Nothing in it but small, haphazard markings like a nest of disturbed ants spilling over the edge of every page. Nothing much worth looking at apart from the photo of a boy.

Perhaps it was the smell of the fabric, the sheen of all those things in that dirty time-scratched box, that held him there.

The boy in the photograph was sitting on a step, his head thrown back as if he were in the middle of the most beautiful daydream. The houses and the people around him were bleached almost to a whiteness, but the boy wouldn't have seen them because his eyes were closed. And as Pynter used to do in his time of blindness, he shut his eyes, rubbing his thumb against the upturned face in the photograph. He found himself slipping into a happy dreaminess, and he knew that this boy, at some time in his uncle's life, had meant everything to him.

He found his mother in that room too, scribbled over the fat purple-veined leaves that people called the love leaf. Santay had shown it to him – a strange leaf that took root anywhere, even between the covers of a book, and which threw out little plants exactly like itself from the little dents around its edges. They called it love leaf because it fed on air, drank the water from itself and gave life to its children just long enough for their roots to reach the earth. The mother plant could release them only when she dried up and died. Until then, they fed on her and lived. What better love than that?

But, like his uncle's markings, his mother's made no sense to him. He'd seen those lines and curlicues of hers before, from the very first week that Santay sent him home. Peter said she'd always made them. These were different, smaller, packed tightly together, but they had the same loops and curves as those she made on the earth between her feet when she sat alone beneath the grapefruit tree, a stick in her hand, a strip of grass between her teeth, her eyes so far away she wouldn't have seen him if he'd stood in front of her and waved.

The leaves were dried up now, even their children, because, lodged as they were between the covers of the large brown book, they could not fall to earth. It smelled of earth, the book, dropped carelessly in the corner by the door, its covers riddled with the little tunnels the worms had made through it.

He found nothing else among the pages, just the leaves with those marks he'd always thought his mother made only in the dust.

The days merged into each other like the lines he marked on the steps with the bits of chalk and charcoal he found inside the room. His father rarely left the house. He would sit on the long canvas chair beside the door, muttering to himself over the Bible, solid like a slab of rock on his knees, its pages spread like wings on the altar of his palms.

They hardly talked. Pynter didn't mind. He had the room to go to.

Over the weeks, Pynter came to know the cracks that ran like little ravines in the flooring of that room, from which he'd extricate buttons, marbles, needles, rusty pins, little bits of coloured glass, a child's gold earring, three silver coins with birds on them, a small chain of beads that slipped from the crease of his palm in a glittering liquid stream, a tiny copper buckle and bits of fingernail.

Still, he felt that even if he'd entered this room, had explored every part of it with his fingers, it had not really opened up itself to him.

'Pa, I want to learn to read.'

The old man stopped the spoon before his lips and, without looking up, he said, 'I been thinkin that you'll have to soon. I'll start you off with this.' He nodded at the Bible.

By the time the man with the white shirt and the stick with the head of a lion came, Pynter had begun to make sense of all his mother's writing on those leaves. Her words, he realised, were not meant for his father. Not in the way that Uncle Michael's were meant for the boy in the photograph. She wrote them the way she talked, almost as if she were answering Miss Lizzie and the women in the river. A story which over time he slowly pieced together, ignoring the nudge of hunger in his guts, not hearing his father calling him sometimes as he sat in the gloom shuffling the leaves, sorting and re-sorting them until the words followed each other easily. A strange feeling it was too, rebuilding his and Peter's history with those dead leaves, one he now knew began long before either of them was born.

When John Seegal walk i use to wish i went with him. i use to wish i didnt have to wait no more for him to come back home. from the time he leave all I find myself doing was just waiting. i used to like Fridays by the river fridays was quiet like you dont have nobody else in the world excepting you and the river water running over stone like it want to tell you something, and the quiet wrap itself nice and safe round you. i use to like that. It feel like if the water was my thoughts running through my head.

One morning i take the washing early. i take the long way down, through the ravine that was a road when rain didnt fall and the bottom get dry.

i come to the place i like to wash because it got a flat stone there. It was big and wide like a bed, like a place you want to sleep on. The top was bleach like a sheet from all the soap that dry on it.

i like to finish wash and leave the clothes to dry so i could watch the water turn white or get dark according to what cloud pass over it. But dat time for no reason at all i get tired of just sitting down dere and I decide to walk down the river. i was talking to myself, or maybe thinking to meself i dont remember now so I didnt notice tie-tongue Sharon and she son a little way ahead of me.

i know her. she cant talk because she tongue was sew down to she mouth. is so she born. People treat her different because of that, but i never. First time i look at her close i see how pretty she is. She got the prettiest teeth anybody ever see and she got eye that look at you as if they watchin from inside a room.

i see how she say things with she face too, if you look in she eye you understand everything she cant say with words. i did always like miss sharon.

She was standing by the end of the stretch of water in front of me, and the little boy was standing up in the middle of the water with her too. They was naked as they born and she was bathing him. It dont have no words for it. *i feel sometimes that is because she cant talk words that she show so much love with them two hand she have. i remember the light too because the sun did find a place through all dem leaf and it fall on them. the little boy was shyning like if fire itself did bathing him. i could hear he voice and hear him laughing to heself sometimes and sometimes answering questions i never hear miss Sharon ask him. she was full with child, contented and full, that is what i remember. Like was them alone in the world and still them wasnt missing nobody. Not like me.*

One time she rest her hand on her belly. I see the boy face. I see how perfect and happy he was. Was like if all the question I been asking ever since my father leave get answer right there, all them question I didnt even know I want a answer for. I didnt miss my fadder John Seegal no more.

I know miss Sharon know dat I was there because after a while the two of them was lookin over where I was. I wonder to meself how come they know I there on that stone behind the bush. But then seein as I know she was watching me I get up sort of guilty.

She do the funniest thing when I stand up. She laugh.

I didnt hear her laugh but I know she laugh because she whole body do it. It shift that way and this way like she koodnt keep the funniness inside of she. I didnt want her to hold it in eider because she look nice an pretty laughing like that. I get up from where I was and walk down to her because she call me with she hand and when I reach she look in my face kind

53

of soft and deep. The little boy was pretty like her. He was slim and and smooth like guava wood.

Dat light, is de light I still remember. All dat light around dem and I was in dat light now, like if I did belong dere too.

I know she must have hear me thinking because she take my hand and rest it on she belly like i was touching the whole world with my hand or the reason for the world, or something.

I ask her how I could come like her. what I did mean was how I could be so happy and contented. She look at the boy and she understand and her body laugh. Her face and her hand tell him something dat he tell me afterwards. he say dat she say I have to be a woman first. A woman. Like that word was something that she just hand over to me.

i get impatient with de years. I get sort of fed up waitin to turn woman, sometimes. And a couple of times I try to hurry things up. I start talkin to meself too, bicause all them thoughts was running round inside my head like ants and when I couldn hold dem in, I sort of let dem roll out of me and i write dem down on anything my hand fall on. Is how they begin to think that I gone crazy. Dat my father spirit get tired of that dirty swamp down dere and seein as I was his favrite before Patty come he come back to possess me.

I know you long before you know me. I know you from de time you look down straight at me one morning, when I get up early to go to the pipe for water.

I had my bucket on my head when you reach me and I lift my eye to say Mornin Missa Manuel Forsyth. I tell myself afterwards that I shouldnt do that. I should a keep my head straight but I was remembering what Miss Sharon tell me by the river. Everything I been waitin fo ever since she tell me come back to me.

You didnt look like no old man to me. Wasnt no old fella I see when I look and wasnt what I see afterwards.

I dont know why it had to take three months of getting up early in the morning and saying Good Morning Missa Manuel befo I work meself up enough to tell you what I want. And it wasnt no old fella lookin at me when I ask you first time even if you look at me as if I mad.

I keep asking till I wear you down. After a little time I see you couldnt hide behind your age no more because all thats left was a man looking at a woman.

That was how I come to feel alright again since my father leave, because after that I was going to have something dat bilong to me.

What I never understand …

He could not find the leaf that would have told him what she never understood. Not a whole one, but fragments that, whichever way he placed them, did not fit together …

…dam fool to believe ——
—— crazy l——
——y —— mother and all th——
—— love and ——
—— chilren who is ——.
—— dam fool ——
—— hatin all ——
——nofabitch tha—

How did it end? Was it with love and —— or was it with —— hatin all ——?

Uncle Michael's words were stranger than his mother's, colliding in odd and unexpected ways.

moon over your shoulder shadow in my eyes.

Today you looked much older.

Today I made you cry.
Aruba, May 1945

And it was strange that even when he'd forgotten them, it still felt as if they'd left some part of themselves inside his head. Short words, not half as long as his mother's; sometimes a line running across a page – like a tiny ant-trail against a vast white desert.

Day yawns, cracks the egg of dawn. A coq-soleil's
sopranoing rises and circles a clean sun.
Panama, August 1947

Those words did not help him understand why his uncle never wanted children. They were like the doorway that had invited him into this abandoned room. Everything was laid out before his eyes but their messages remained hidden. A darkened room that was as full of stories as the women in the river. Only these were littered in untidy heaps across the dusty floor, and stranger to him than anything he'd ever heard before.

It going to be quiet up there, his father had told him, but it was not quiet in his head. He missed the voices of the women in the yard. The foolish and the awful things they talked about and laughed over. He missed his fights with Peter and above all he missed his auntie's hands.

Now that the dry season had come, his aunt, Tan Cee, would be down there among those tiny black dots crawling along the green edges of the never-ending fields of sugar cane. Patty the Pretty would be home because Leroy had taken her out of cane. They would no doubt be doing what his grandmother said his youngest aunt always did when Leroy was around: trying for a child.

He never wondered what that meant. It was some kind of magic between adults that involved hiding themselves away and, if he were to judge by what he saw from Patty, looking very sleepy and smiling all the time.

Tan Cee would be down there with the men, swinging her machete at the roots of the cane, his mother just behind her, gathering them in bundles, tying them and lifting them over her head onto the tractors that looked like big yellow beetles from where he stood. Home was just a walk away, but from here it seemed as if it would take an entire lifetime to reach them.

He wondered if Birdie was with them, then he remembered Tan Cee saying that Birdie only ever sweated over bread.

It was quiet up here. The quietness stretched beyond the house. At the back of it, the land ran wild for miles, all the way past the hellish quarry-land of Gaul through to Morne Bijoux on the other side of the ridge of hills that separated them from the rest of the world. Afternoons, when the heat of the day pushed the old man into a deep sleep, he left the room and retreated into the bushes, making his own little pathways among the borbook and black sage.

There was a long, narrow ravine that went down to a tall wall of plants with bright blossoms. His first few visits there, he couldn't figure out why everything seemed to be either in fruit or flowering when everything else around was dry. He had gone closer, to examine those heavy deep-scented flowers, when he felt himself falling. He landed in a tangle of wist vines, was shaken but not hurt. Sat there while his eyes adjusted to the thick green light.

He was in a gully that he would never have known existed had he not fallen through the bush that covered it like a roof. The earth was dark with dampness, though it hadn't rained for weeks. It was cool here too, like the riverbank. There were the same darkish odours of growth and fermentation.

He began picking his way through the tangle. This place puzzled him. The earth was covered with guavas. They hung thickly from the branches above his head. A slight brush of his fingers and they fell into his hands. Wherever there were guavas there were serpents. Santay had told him about the reddish ones that grew long and fat and wrapped themselves in tight knots around the branches. And sure enough he saw them, untying themselves, their heads stretched out towards him, their tongues flickering like small flames in their mouths. He made a hammock of his shirt, selected the fruits he wanted and left there quickly. Later, in the dimming light of the late evening, he sat on the steps and broke open the fruit, tasted each one tentatively before stuffing himself full.

He came back to that place often, because he could find food there. He found crayfish canes and water lemons further down the gully, and a little walk beyond that, sapodillas and star apples. Everything was growing there in that long green tunnel of light and leaves, a secret place that only he, the birds, the millipedes and serpents knew about. He called it Eden.

It was during one of his visits there that Gideon came. When Pynter returned to his father's house, he heard a new voice pitched high and fast. It sounded like an argument. His father's rumblings were soft and subdued against the other. Miss Maddie was bending over a pepper plant on the side of the house, a can of water in her hand. His father was lying back on the canvas chair. A man in a pressed blue shirt sat on a chair he had taken from the living room. His legs were close together and he was leaning forward slightly. There were papers on the bed.

The stranger turned and saw him, looked at him as if he knew him. His eyes paused on his face, then dropped to his naked feet. They stayed there a while before travelling back up to his face again. Pynter was suddenly aware that he hadn't washed his hands. Hadn't poured water on his feet and cleaned them in the grass outside. He felt an urge to go outside and do it.

'So you the one they call Half Pint?' The man was showing him his teeth. His face was strange. It was long like his father's but thinner, with all the bones showing through. His eyes were round and bright like polished marbles and when he spoke, his lips hardly moved.

'Pynter,' his father said, 'dis is Gideon, your brother.'

Gideon closed his mouth as suddenly as he'd opened it to show his teeth. He turned back to face the old man. 'So, how you gettin on, Ole Fella?'

'Don't "Ole Fella" me, I your father. Pynter?'

'Pa?'

'Say hello to your brother, Gideon.'

Gideon threw a quick sideways glance at him. 'I met the boy already.'

'Gideon hardly come to look for me,' his father said. 'The more money he make, the longer he stay away.'

Gideon protested, his stammery voice rising and falling quickly. His father chuckled. Soon Pynter was not hearing them. He stood at the doorway, his shoulder pressed against the side of it, watching the face they said his mother feared more than any other in the world, following with his eyes the hands that had almost taken Peter and him away from her. Gideon was still wearing his grey felt hat. It looked new. Everything about him looked new, even his pale blue shirt and shiny brown leather shoes.

Gideon turned his head and saw him staring. He glanced at their father, who was busy with figuring out the exact value of the farmland he'd stopped working in the far end of Old Hope. When Gideon turned back to Pynter it was with a look that reminded him of Deeka, like that time she pushed him off the top of her steps and Tan Cee came so close to striking her.

He retreated into the living room and sat on the chair closest to the bedroom door. He didn't know what was making Gideon talk so low and rapidly, but occasionally he heard the old man chuckle, and just once Manuel Forsyth's voice rose sharp and clear: 'You can't make a fool of me, Gideon. I still got my senses.

I not signing anything, specially now that I can't see too clear what I going be signing.'

Miss Maddie was still out there shuffling around the house. She was nearer the back now, uprooting grass or something. With Gideon here and Miss Maddie at the back, things made a little more sense to him. This dusty wooden house suffused with its deep and sweetish odours of wood-rot and neglect was theirs. Gideon, Miss Maddie, Sister Pearly and Eileen-in-America wouldn't have minded the shadows in the corners, the very faint odour of Canadian Healing Oil, the smell of bay leaves and black sage that grew on the windward side of the house. It was their feet that had smoothed the wooden floor. The walls had thrown their voices back at them. His father's house would never be his and Peter's the way it had been for them.

His mind must have taken him a far way off. Miss Maddie was no longer moving around the house. He got up and went to the bedroom door. 'Pa tired,' he said. 'Dat's why he not answerin you no more.'

That sudden sideways glance again. The expression was still there when Gideon laughed. ''Kay, Pops. I see you again soon.'

Gideon stood up, took out a roll of money and peeled off two brown notes and three green ones. He shoved them in his father's hand.

'Thirty-five dollars. All I have. Come, walk me to the door, Quarter Bottle.'

'My name is Pynter.'

'What's the other one call?'

'Peter. He your brother too.'

Gideon's hands were stuffed inside his pockets. Keys jangled. He pulled them out. 'How you know dat, uh?'

'Everybody know dat,' Pynter told him flatly.

Gideon brought his face down close to Pynter's. 'Look here, Half Eights.'

'Pynter!'

'Okay, Pinky! Either I lookin at a miracle or you and whatever-his-name-is is the fastest one anybody ever pull on my old man and get away with it. Jeez! And believe me dat is a miracle, cuz he never was nobody fool. I don' see no part of us in you.'

'Me neither!' Pynter said, and he turned to run back in, but Gideon's hand had closed around his collar. He could have cried out, let his father know, but he didn't want to. He spun round, stared into the man's face, putting the weight of all the memories of all the things the women by the river had said behind his words. 'I don' like you, Gideon. I never like you since before I born. An' long as I live, I never goin to like you.'

Gideon stiffened. Pynter thought he was about to hit him. But something in Pynter had changed from the night when Coxy had pinned his back against a tree and looked into his eyes. He would never let a man lay his hands on him again. He closed his fingers around Gideon's wrist and had twisted his shoulders to sink his teeth into his arm when a voice came suddenly between them, 'Let the little fella go, Gidiot.'

Gideon stepped back. Pynter turned his head to see a young man leaning against the house. He had both hands in his pockets and his legs were crossed. His eyes were like Miss Elaine's – large and wide and bright. There was no collar on his white shirt. A small book with a blue cover peeked out of one of his pockets.

'What the hell you want?' Gideon squeezed the words out through his teeth.

'Pick on somebody your size – you flippin thug.'

'Lissen, Mister Pretty Pants – watch your … '

The young man's movement cut Gideon's words short. He'd pushed himself off the wall so quickly, so unexpectedly, that Pynter felt his heart flip over.

Gideon stepped closer. 'You try anything, I give what you got coming to you.'

'Not from you. For sure. And don't forget, you beating up a child and threatening me in my mother yard.'

The man mumbled something under his breath and turned to leave.

Paso smiled. 'Say what you thinking, Big Fella.'

'You and your mother won' like it.'

Paso curled a beckoning finger at Pynter. 'Come this side,' he said. He was looking at Gideon sideways. 'That's bad blood there. Sour blood.'

'At least I'm a man.'

'You say that again, I make you sorry.'

Their voices had drawn Miss Maddie out onto the porch. Gideon saw her, straightened up and strolled out of the yard.

The youth stared down at Pynter, smiling. 'First time you meet that dog?'

Pynter nodded.

'Don't go near 'im. He'll bite anything that move. When he come, jus' give 'im space.' He stepped back, playfully almost, as if he were dancing. 'So you my mother brother? I hear a lot 'bout y'all. People round here talk! He thumbed his mother's house. 'Call me Paso, and you – you Paul – no, Peter. Not so?'

'I Pynter. Peter home.'

Paso reached for his hand and shook it. 'So how I must call you – Uncle?'

'Pynter.'

'Pynter, okay – nuh, I think I'll stick with Uncle. It got a certain, uhm, ring, nuh resonance to it. See you around, Big Fella.'

He winked and strolled away. Pynter watched him walk towards the porch, watched him until he stepped behind his mother and seemed miraculously to be swallowed up by her bulk.

Later in the evening, when dusk had just begun to sprinkle the foothills with that creeping ash that would thicken into night,

Paso appeared again, this time with Manuel Forsyth's food. He had changed his trousers but not his shirt.

'Still there, Uncle?'

Pynter nodded. He'd spent most of the afternoon waiting to catch a glimpse of Paso again.

Paso placed the plate on the step beside his foot. 'I tell the Madre to put a little extra in for you – not just this time, but every time. You been inside that lil room yet?'

The question caught him unawares. Paso dropped questions the way a person threw a punch when the other was least expecting it.

'Which room?' Pynter asked.

'The dark one.' He winked.

'Uh-huh.'

'Find what I find in there?'

Pynter turned his head and shrugged. Paso laughed.

'Take me a coupla days and a bottle of the Madre cooking oil to grease them hinges. The Old Fella used to keep it locked. He shouldn't ha' tell me not to go in there. S'like an open invitation, s'far as I concern. I leave it open so he could know I was in there. He never close it back.'

'Where you go to every night-time?'

The smile left his nephew's face, but only briefly. In less than a heartbeat it returned. 'Wherever night-time want me. Ever hear this one?

The road is long, the night is deep,
I got promises to keep, and miles to go before I sleep.

'Uncle Michael?'

'Nuh, Merican fella name Robbie Frost – with all the warmth from me, of course.'

He was fingering the little blue book in his shirt pocket. 'Know any poetry?'

'Wozzat?'

'You serious?'

Pynter nodded.

'You been reading Mikey's stuff – and … ' He laughed, looked at Pynter closely and laughed again.

'Jeezas, man! Moon over your shoulder.'

'Shadow in me eye,' Pynter cut in. The words had come almost despite himself.

'You been reading Mikey stuff and you don' know what it call? Listen to this … ' His fingers slid the little notebook from his shirt. He held it up before him. The way Missa Geoffrey sometimes held Miss Tilina's face.

> *In the morning dark*
> *my people walk to the time of clocks*
> *whose hands*
> *have spanned*
> *so many nights*

His voice was as soft as Missa Geoffrey's too, and it was as if he were talking to himself from a bellyful of sadness.

Paso stopped, looked up. He didn't smile. Pynter shifted under his stare and before he lost the courage, before it became impossible to say what had been sitting on his heart from the moment his fingers retrieved that strange little book from his uncle's grip, he turned up his face at Paso.

'I wan' to make wuds like dat too, I want … I … ' Something desperate and quiet fluttered in his heart. He turned his head away.

Paso steered him towards the steps and sat him down. 'That book was the most interesting thing you find in there, not so?'

Pynter nodded.

'Why?'

'Don' know.'

'I tell you something. Once, it cross my mind to take it. Yunno – copy all of it over to this lil book and make meself believe is mine. I start doing it. But then, that same night, I had a dream. I was walking down some kinda road. Long road. I couldn' see the end of it. The more I walk, the more I see road in front of me. When I was close to givin up, I realise I had somebody walking beside me. It wasn' Michael. It was hi friend, the boy.' Paso threw a sideways glance at him. 'Yunno what that young fella was to 'im?'

Pynter shook his head.

'One day it will come to you. Right now nothing in life ain't prepare you for that kind of … of awareness. Mebbe you'll never work it out. Don' know … Anyway, that fella say something to me that I wake up with in me head. It come like a realisation. I can't forget it. Now I going to pass it on to you. "Find your own words" – that's what he say to me. "You done have all of dem inside you; you just got to take dem out and put dem in de order that make your living and your thinking and your feelings make sense." Y'unnerstan?'

Pynter nodded, even though he wasn't sure he did.

'When you try to steal a pusson words, s'like you trying to steal their soul. You want to make words work like that? Then feel with your eye and see with your heart.' He elbowed Pynter gently. 'Now tell me, Uncle – what is the colour of my eye?'

Pynter looked at him, a shy sideways glance. 'Black.'

Paso shook his head, worked his mouth as if he'd just munched on something awful.

'Nuh! That's seeing with your eye, not feeling with it. Now feel – turn your mind to all the things the old man must ha' tell you about me. Talk to me, fella, jus' … '

'Night.'

'Wha'?'

Pynter smiled, tentatively. 'De colour of your eye is night.'

'You sure?'

'Uh-huh.'

'The colour of yours is water. History too – a lot o' things looking out at me from dem eyes o' yours. What's the taste of cane? Think of your mother, think of all your people down there. What's the taste of cane?'

Pynter lifted dreamy eyes up at the Mardi Gras. 'Bitter. Cane is bitter. An' dat mountain up dere is ah old, old man, quarrellin with God.'

He felt Paso's eyes on him. 'Them your words?'

'Dem my words,' Pynter told him.

'Well, dem is words – y'hear me, Uncle?'

They laughed out loud together.

For the second time that day, Pynter watched his nephew walk away. So strange. So different, so, so ... bee-yoo-tee-ful.

The next morning Pynter's sister called him to collect the old man's breakfast. He came out and took the plate. He noticed an extra helping of sweet potatoes. The food was also warm. He didn't trust her smile. The rest of her face wasn't smiling.

'Gideon stay with y'all a long while,' she said.

'Yes, Miss Maddie, with Pa not with me.'

'First time you meet him?'

'Yes, Miss Maddie.'

'He talk about a lot o' tings?'

'Fink so.'

'You think so – you didn't hear what he say?'

'Culatral,' he said.

'What?'

'Culatral, o' something like that.'

'Collateral – the sonuva ... ' Her voice retreated into her throat and kept rumbling in there. 'He say for what?'

'Say what fo' what?'

'Collateral – he say collateral fo' what?'

'Don' know.'

'Is the land, right?'

'Which land?'

'Never mind, you hear de word "land" come from deir mouth?'

'Who mouth?'

'Paso say you smart – I wondering which part o' you he find the smartness, cuz … ' She sucked her teeth and began walking back towards the house.

'Thanks for de two extra piece o' fry potato,' he called after her, remembering his manners.

She stopped short, shook her head and continued walking.

6

WHENEVER GIDEON CAME, Pynter left the house for the gully. Now he knew he shared Eden with two people. They came from the other side of the hill, where a cluster of small, brightly painted houses were huddled beneath a line of corse trees whose branches swept the sky.

They arrived together, the woman holding the front of her dress high above the water grass and crestles. The man was the colour of the mahogany chairs inside his father's house. His hair rested on his shoulders. The woman stepped onto the boulder so that she was like a giant butterfly above the water grass, and called his name.

'Geoffrey!' she said, and the words came out like a bird call, like the beginning of a song.

He called her Petal, sometimes P, or Tilina, and from where he sat in the nest of elephant grass, Pynter gathered that her father's name was Pastor Greenway, and that Geoffrey herded sheep somewhere in the valley beneath Morne Bijoux. He spoke of his sheep the way the women in the river spoke of their children. He learned that Pastor Greenway would kill Miss Petalina if he knew she ran away to meet Geoffrey here. The fear was there on her face when she arrived, coming off her like the perfume she was wearing.

Pynter always got there before they did. He would listen to the man sing to himself with that heavy bullfrog voice, watch him gather leaves before Miss P arrived. Sometimes he would close his eyes and feel the man's low thunder vibrate deep inside his head – a rich voice, dark and thick as molasses, bouncing around the gully.

He liked to watch Miss Lina coming across the sprays of light pouring through the undergrowth, falling over her yellow dress, making her look pretty as an okra flower. She would come to rest beside Geoffrey on the nest of leaves he'd made for them both.

Pynter waited until their wrestling was over, until her chirpings had subsided, and Geoffrey's croakings had grown low. And then he crept away.

Back at the house, with Gideon gone, he would find his father quiet. He knew it was a kind of war between them – a battle in which his father was struggling to hold on to something that Gideon wanted badly. It left the old man sleepy and exhausted. Pynter would reach for the large black book, lower himself on the floor, his toes resting lightly on the old man's feet, and begin to read for him.

Pynter loved this time of quietness, when the last of the evening light poured into the room and settled like honey on the bed, on the wood of the long canvas chair and on his father's arms. He loved the feeling of lightness that rose in him when he knew that Gideon would not come again for another week.

But a shadow had crept into these moments, something his father had been keeping from him and Gideon. It was there in the way the old man avoided signing the papers brought to him each week, how he passed his hands across his face more and more these days. Their father was going blind. Pynter saw it approaching the way night crept down the slopes of the Mardi Gras. He saw it wrap itself around the old man like a caul and settle him back against the canvas chair. He saw how it made his gestures smoother, softer and less certain. How it steadied his head and made his body slow and unsure of the spaces it had been so accustomed to.

There were times when the old man spoke to Pynter of his days on ships in Panama, his journeying through the forests of Guyana searching for gold in riverbeds and streams, and his time in tunnels that ran like intestines in the belly of the earth. It was down there in one of those mines that he'd walked into a metal rod and damaged his left eye, had lived with that injury most of his life – a small white scar like a tiny worm against the black of his left eye that had suddenly come alive.

The questions his father asked him now were always the same. What was it like before Miss Santay gave him back his eyes? How did he manage when he needed something and no one was there to help him? How would he have felt if he had had to live his whole life with nothing out there to see? And so Pynter taught the old man not to fear the coming darkness. He told him about his own time of darkness, when, for him, the world was just a roar at first, how he'd come to use the sounds around him, how he'd learnt to recognise the things that touched his skin.

It was the other way around for him, his father said, for while he was heading into darkness with a clear picture of the world inside his head, Pynter, having just emerged from it, had only light and colour to look forward to.

'Not all of it goin to be pretty,' his father said. 'But it can't have pretty without ugly. It can't have bright without dark.'

He was silent for a long time and so still it was as if he'd gone to sleep. When he spoke again, it was with an emotion that Pynter did not recognise.

'One thing I'll carry in my head to the end of my days is the first time y'all mother bring y'all to me. I didn know she was comin. I was weeding corn. I lift my head and see her walkin through my garden with two bundle in she hand, one on eider side. When she reach, she didn say a word, she just hand y'all over to me. She didn have to say nothin, you see? Was the way she do it. Like she was sayin, "Look, I givin you what's yours."'

He passed his hand across his face.

'Gideon – as far as he concern, my funeral done happm and now is time to hand everyting over to him. Like y'all don't count. Like y'all come from nowhere. Like somebody pick y'all off a tree. But when the time right, I got a nasty shock for him. Let's hope that he kin take it.'

7

Pynter couldn't figure out how a person's clothes could remain so smooth and perfectly pleated. It was as if the khaki shirt and trousers of the little man had just been taken still steaming from a hot iron and gently placed on him. He wasn't walking up the hill – not as normal people did – he tiptoed as if he hated the idea of touching the ground with the soles of his glistening leather shoes. Pynter caught glimpses of his white socks as he lifted his shoes and carefully set them down on the patches of grass that dotted the concrete road. The man carried a little brown case under his arm. It matched his jacket and trousers exactly. In the other hand he swung a beautiful stick with a curved silver top. Despite the heat, he was not sweating.

'Is there a Mister Manuel Forsyth living here?'

'What you want my father for?'

'That's his place?' A fat little finger shot out before him.

Pynter didn't answer at first, but then asked the man to follow him.

The man walked across Miss Maddie's yard and straight into his father's house. He entered the bedroom as if he visited every day. His father sensed the stranger's presence as soon as he stepped in.

'Who's it?' he grumbled.

'Mister Manuel Forsyth?'

'I is he. Who you and what you want?'

'My name is Jonathan, Mister J. Uriah Bostin, Schools Inspector for the parish of San Andrews – urban and suburban, that is – as well as the, er, outer peripheries.'

'A what?'

'Schools Inspector, Jonathan U. Bostin.'

The old man's body relaxed, his face became vacant. 'I name Manuel. Shake my hand.'

The man seemed to be thinking over the invitation. He stepped forward quickly and stretched out his right hand. Pynter's father felt the air and got hold of it, his hand almost swallowing the man's. He seemed to be examining the man's wrist with his fingers. The stranger didn't like it. He made an attempt to get his hand back, his large eyes bulging.

'You short!' Manuel Forsyth said, letting go. 'You short-breed people. What you say you name was?'

'J. U. Bostin.'

'Those Bostins from Saint Divine – you one of dem?'

'There is a connection there, I think. I'm here to see you about the boy.'

'What happen, you not sure?'

'Well, er, my father is from there – Saint Divine, I mean.'

'And you?'

'Well, I was born there, er, if you don't mind, Mister Forsyth, I am very pressed by the matter at hand. This boy here, your, er, er…' He frowned at the sheet of paper he'd slid out of the case. 'It says here that he is your son. Sorry, a typing mishap, I should think.'

'You shouldn't think. He my son. What he done?'

'Turned truant, I believe, aided and abetted by yourself.'

'Pynter, get a chair for 'im.'

Bostin placed the brown case on the seat of the chair and the stick beside it. Pynter could see that the silver handle on the stick was the head of a lion. Bostin reached into his right pocket and pulled out a white handkerchief. He wiped not just the seat of the chair but also the back. Finally, with a smooth and curious side-ways movement, he took up his things and slid onto the chair.

'Well, er, yes. It has been brought to my attention that in relation to the education of this boy, and you might be quite unaware of it, you are contravening the law.'

'Which law?' His father seemed almost pleased with the man.

Bostin creased his forehead. 'The law of the land, Mister, er, Forsyth. The one that bequeaths me the powers to bring this matter to your attention and to take the necessary action if my recommendations are not adhered to by yourself and …'

'Which law you talkin 'bout, passed when, by who, under which sub-section of which article of which Act?'

'Well, er, we don't have an Education Act, per se, but …'

'Then we don't have no law which kin force me to send my child to school. That is why you come – not so?'

'You kin say so.'

'Is so or is not so?'

'Depends on how you interpret the matter.' The man lifted his case and placed it on his lap.

'You a very frustratin fella, y'know dat?' Manuel Forsyth had pushed himself forward in the chair. 'You come here to tell me I breakin a law dat don't exist an' threaten me in my own house. I have a mind to report you to the head pusson in your place an' make you lose your job!'

'I am the head person, Mister Forsyth. You'll have to, er, report my misdemeanours to me!'

'Good. I'll make you fire yourself then. You finish your business with me?'

'No, sir.' The man slipped his hand into his case and eased out a green notebook. He studied it for a moment. 'Truancy is a punishable offence in, er, the, er,' the notebook moved closer to his face, 'in the case where parents have been informed and they persist in, er, withholding the subject of the enquiry from going to school.'

His father laughed. 'Tell me, Bostin, what is de definition of truancy?'

'Pardon me?' Bostin wiped his brow.

'Define truancy fo' me.' Manuel Forsyth was directing a kindly gaze in his direction.

Bostin folded the handerkerchief and dropped it on his lap. 'I don' wan' no argument, sah! I jus' doin my job, okay? Is confusion I tryin to avoid right now.'

'Truancy occur in instances where – you lissenin?'

Missa Bostin nodded, sourly.

'He lissenin, Pa,' Pynter cut in gently.

'Good! Truancy is when a child, for any kind o' reason, decide not to go to school. An act of will on de part o' de child. It imply an unwillingness to learn on the part o' de child – a voluntary act of self-deprivation. You agree?'

'I hearin you.'

'Well, let me inform you that Pynter don't need to go to no school. It is I who decide not to send 'im.'

'Can you say that again?'

'Pa, he writing down what you say in a lil green book.'

'Let 'im write! I got a lot more for Mister Bostin to write down. I hope your book big enough. Tell dem fools who send you that de purpose of schoolin is to learn – to be educated. It don't have no other reason for goin to school. Now once I kin prove dat Pynter here is not missing out on his education, you don't have no case in a court of law against me. In fact, I would like for you to take me to court so'z I kin make a fool of every single one of you. Then I will take y'all to court for taking me to court and causing me a whole heap of stress I didn ask for. You out of place to come here in my house and call my child a truant. What I really want to know is who report me to you. Who do it?'

'I cannot expose that, sir.'

'I hope to God dat is not who I think it is. Pynter, get me the Bible. You a believer, Bostin?'

'A regular churchgoer and a family man, sir.'

'Well, listen to the boy read and be blessed at de same time. C'mon, Pynter – Matthew, chapter uh, lemme see, seven. Yep! Matthew, chapter seven – start from verse three.'

Pynter took the book and threw the man a sympathetic glance. He began to read. '"And why beholdest thou the mote that is in thy brother's eye, but considerest not the beam that is in thine own eye?"'

'Skip verse four,' his father said. 'Jump to five and six.'

'"Thou hypocrite,"' Pynter continued, '"first cast out the beam out of thine own eye; and then shalt thou see clearly to cast out the mote out of thy brother's eye. Give not that which is holy unto the dogs, neither cast ye your pearls before swine, lest they trample them under their feet, and turn again and rend you."'

'Good.' Manuel Forsyth smacked his lips. 'You see my boy can read and with feeling besides.'

Mister Bostin pulled out his handkerchief and sopped his forehead. He gave Pynter a hard sideways glance. 'You numerate?'

'Yes, he kin count,' Manuel Forsyth said.

Mister Bostin turned the back of his right hand towards his face and examined his fingers. The nails were cut very low, except the little finger, which sprouted a long and curving outgrowth that he was clearly proud of.

'Well, I'm reasonably satisfied that he's doing something. I must refer the matter, though. A daily diet of the Bible may be just the, er, thing – morally, that is – but to school the boy must go. That's what my job dictate.'

'You mean, I waste all this time arguing with you?'

The man got up. For the first time he smiled. Pynter was surprised at the brightness of it. 'That's for you to decide, sir.'

'I'll fight every one o' you in court.'

'You'll hear from me, Mister Forsyth. Follow me, boy.'

'Half-edicated jackass.'

Pynter looked quickly at the man and then back at his father. His lips were moving angrily. Bostin paused as if he were about to say something. He thought better of it and tiptoed out of the bedroom.

The man turned to face Pynter on the steps. His voice was almost a whisper. 'Talk the truth now, lil fella, you really want to go on like that? The truth!'

'For now.'

'You sure?'

'Yup.'

'How come?'

'Iz all he got right now.'

The man nodded. 'How old you say you is?'

'I didn say how old I is. I almos' ten.'

'Ten?'

'Almos'.'

'Ten, you say?'

'Yup, ten. Almos'.'

'Look, son, it have a lot more, er, there is much more to school than reading books and counting fingers. You got to go to school, y'unnerstan?'

'Pa say I don't have to.'

'What you going to do when he gone?'

'He not going nowhere.'

'Everybody got to go somewhere. He ought to be preparing you for that.'

'Don' unnerstan.'

'S'all right. Tell me, where's your modder?'

'Home.'

'Home where?'

'Where she live.'

He pulled a page out of his notebook and wrote quickly.

'Give this to her. It got my name, place of employ and the name of the person – Miss Lucas, the headmistress in Saint

Divine Catholic School. Come September, I want her to take you to that school and give this paper to her. It got to be September. Or you'll miss your chance.'

'What chance?'

'The one I would have given my eye teeth for. Promise me you going give her.'

'Okay.'

'Come September, I'll be checking up on you pussnally.'

'Who call you to come here – Miss Maddie?'

Mister Bostin rested puzzled eyes on him. 'S'far as I could tell, 'twasn't a woman. He say that you his uncle.'

Department of Education
Division of the Ministry of Internal and Related Affairs
San Andrews
12th July 1965

Mr. Manuel Forsyth
Upper Old Hope
Parish of Old Hope
San Andrews

Dear Sir,
This is to confirm our conversation at your residence on
May 15th of this year in which you stated your decision to
keep your son and minor …

'Pa, what minor mean?'

'Go on, read the letter.'

…your son and minor Pynter Bender from school. After
much deliberation I have decided …

'He decide! Who he think he is?'

I have decided that it is not in the best interest of the child in question to be exposed solely to the literature available at your residence.

'He goin to burn in hell fo' that. Condemning God word!'

In view of the above observation and consistent with the powers vested in me, Jonathan Uriah Bostin, Schools Inspector, San Andrews Division of the Associated State and its environs…

'If fancy title was money, he would be a rich man. Read that part again fo' me!'
'It long!'
'Read it, boy!'

In view of the above observation …

'Pure wind! Fart – that's what it is. Read de rest fo' me.'

…I have agreed with the relevant authority to enrol the minor, Pynter Bender …

'Pa, what's a minor?'
'You.'
'What it mean?'
'A lil boy.'
'And how you call a lil girl?'
'A minor. Finish de letter, child!'

…to enrol the minor, Pynter Bender, in the Saint Divine Catholic …

'And he claim to be a man o' God!'

…Catholic School from first September. Failing which and without valid reasons, said authority reserves the right to proceed legally against you.

'You mus' never learn to write like that man, y'hear me?'
'Why?'
'S'not natural.'
'Why?'
'Say what you have to say and finish it. Always.'
'Why?'
'It help to keep life simple.'
'How?'
'Stop bothering me, boy.'

8

THE NEXT MORNING he got up and told his father he dreamt of screaming people.

'You wasn' dreaming,' his father muttered, 'I hear them too last night – Harris and Marlo.' The old man's face was thoughtful. 'Only Harris I was hearing, though. And Harris the one you never hear at all.'

Harris and Marlo lived in a two-roomed house at the bottom of his father's hill.

Fridays especially, nights in Upper Old Hope were reduced to a small room and Marlo was the hurricane inside it. Pynter had quickly grown accustomed to these weekly brawls, although the first time he'd heard Marlo he couldn't bring himself to sleep. No reply ever came from Harris. And if, as his father told him that first time, it was a case of one man warring with himself, he used to wonder at the sense of it.

A few times, after a particularly violent night, he woke early, crept out of the house and sneaked down to the road.

Harris eventually came out, saw him standing there and, without breaking stride, waved his hat at him, 'Hello, young fellow. How's the Old Bull?'

'Not bad,' he answered as he watched the tall man's body follow his feet up the road till he disappeared around the corner.

Pynter wished he would grow tall enough to be able to step out of his own little house like that, stretch out his long legs like Harris and sway, not from side to side, but in a kind of roundabout way, as if the rest of his body were fighting to keep up with his feet.

Harris was the tallest man he'd ever seen – the highest in the world. Always in the same loose khaki trousers and shirt that had been so bleached by wear and washing they were almost white. He wore his felt hat slanted down over his greying eyebrows, though it was never low enough to throw a shadow on his smile.

Harris was one of those men who'd travelled to the oil refineries in Aruba and returned a couple of weeks later to tell Old Hope how he'd taken a fall and got tangled up among the vast spiderweb of steaming pipes there. He would have died, had actually died in fact, when a pair of hands to which he had never been able to put a face had reached through the steel and dragged him out. That night he cut through the high fences that locked in the thousands of working island men, 'borrowed' a rowing boat and, without water, food or sleep, spent *months* ploughing a passage through all kinds of high dark seas and hurricanes to his little house in Old Hope.

'Look at the height of the man,' Manuel Forsyth laughed. 'What you expect from Harris – not tall tales?'

But these stories only made Harris taller in Pynter's eyes, so that sometimes on mornings, just when the night chill lifted itself off the valley floor and seeped like drizzle through his thin blue shirt, he would creep out of his father's house and tiptoe down the hill to receive that special early-morning greeting.

For this – just the sight of Harris, the rolling head, the long windmilling arms, the big yellow grin, the pale felt hat bobbing like a wind-rushed flame above the tops of the rhododendrons at the roadside – for all this, the early-morning coldness nibbling at the skin of his back and arms was more than worth it. Even standing in the rain.

It was raining the morning the slight quiver in his chest was replaced by something else – a smell and something more. A sensation on his skin.

Coming out of the house, he saw something squeezing itself through the doorway. It took a while before he realised it was a man. He did not move, not even when the great boxlike head lifted with some effort and swivelled towards him. Not even when the small red eyes fell on him and narrowed, and the man's lips – purple-dark and thin – seemed to curl themselves around a curse.

The heavy hands drifted to the dirty leather scabbard at his side. Just then Pynter caught the scent of the man. He began backing up the hill.

Marlo's eyes did not release him until he reached the top of his father's road. He lowered himself on the steps, struggling with his breathing and the sudden urge to cry.

'Dat's Butcherman Marlo.' Manuel Forsyth pulled his lips in slowly. 'Don't go near 'im, y'hear me?'

From then on, those mornings became a gamble. Pynter did not know who would come out first and it didn't occur to him to wait for Harris after Marlo. In fact, he never saw Harris come out after Marlo, so that sometimes he imagined it was the same man that the night had transformed into something else.

If it were Marlo, he would hold his ground for as long as his thumping heart allowed him. He would keep his breath in while the dark, knuckle-curled head lifted and skewed itself around. Then his legs would propel him up the hill to the safety of his father's steps.

He knew now that the thick red man with the curly hair and bloodshot eyes was the father of all butchers. That the abattoir in San Andrews left the biggest bulls to him: the frothing, red-eyed animals that chewed through their ropes and broke their chains and routed San Andrews with their rage. When that happened, they sent for Marlo.

And if, from time to time, someone decided to leave one of those animals too loosely tethered, or deliberately forgot to draw the bolts of the steel pen, it was so that they could watch the town take to the top of walls and barricade itself behind the closed glass doors of stores while Marlo placed his back against some building on the Esplanade, or planted his legs like tree trunks in the middle of the market square, his head lowered like the animal's, his shoulders twitching, his right elbow bent so that his finger barely grazed the leather at his side as the animal charged. And at the very last moment, with a movement that the men would recall over dinner in words that would disgust their women and thrill their children, Marlo would call the length of sharpened steel to his palm. He never missed an animal's heart whenever he reached for it with that knife.

'Men like blood,' his father told him quietly. 'Some o' them jus' don' know it.'

'I don' like blood,' Pynter answered earnestly, staring at the milkiness in the old man's eye.

'That's becuz you not a man yet,' his father muttered softly.

'Rain fall last night too. Dry-season rain. Mean a lot more heat to come. It still wet outside?' His father's voice pulled him out of his thoughts. Through the window he could see that it was drizzling, but he said he was going outside to check.

There were people gathered by the roadside when Pynter got down there. Harris's house looked tired and rain-sogged against the giant bois-canot tree that supported it. The door was partly open and the window facing the road hung on a single hinge. He stood on the wet grass, listening to the lowered voices, the grunts of disbelief, the quiet shock, subdued like the drone of bees. He didn't think they had seen him. They were lost in talking their thoughts out to each other

' … such a nice fella.'

' … in hi own house.'

' … never do nobody no harm.'

'An' Marlo gone an' done dat to him.'

' … a piece o' bread … '

84

' ... murder ... '

' ... worse than murder.'

A rough wind shook the trees above them. The water that had settled on the leaves came down in a cold shower on their heads. He shuddered, began wondering what his father was doing now. Soon he would have to collect his breakfast from the steps before the chickens got to it.

No one knew who called the ambulance. Although it was still very early, it had come and gone long before most of them were there. More people were arriving, some from as far up as the foothills of Mont Airy. A tall, slim-faced woman with a white head-wrap kept repeating the story to them of what had happened – Marlo had disappeared, and the police were somewhere up there in the bushes at the foot of the Mardi Gras with their dogs; they were sure to find him before the day was over, she said.

Pynter wiped his eyes and looked up at the Mardi Gras, its head buried in the greyness of the flat, soggy morning. He could hear the dogs barking. He didn't like dogs. Dogs didn't like him either. He could have told the police or the dogs that they were not going to find him up there in the forest. Marlo could hardly walk, far less climb a hill or run.

He left them by the side of the road, scratching, shifting and murmuring among themselves, their hands moving aimlessly about them, as if they were rummaging the air for something they'd forgotten or misplaced. He criss-crossed his way back up the hill.

Miss Maddie was on her porch, craning her neck towards the road while still managing to keep her eyes on him.

'Boy!'

He lifted his face at her.

'What happenin down there?' It was the first time he'd ever seen her smile.

'Don' know,' he said, not even bothering to break his stride.

Her smile went out like a light.

'Is true what I hear about those two down there?'

'Don' know, Miss Maddie.'

'You don' know and you just come from down there?'

He shrugged.

'I ask you a question, boy!' Her tone had hardened.

'And I answer you,' he replied, and broke into a run.

He waited till his father had finished eating and then he told him all that he had just heard from the mouths of the people by the roadside.

When his father found his voice, he asked, 'You sure?'

''Bout what?'

The old man passed the heel of his hand across his face. 'Why?'

'Uh?'

'Why he done it?'

'Missa Marlo?'

'Yes, why?'

'Don' know, Pa, don' know. For piece o' bread, Miss Tooksie say. For a piece o' Missa Marlo bread dat Missa Harris take becuz he was hungry. A piece o' bread, Pa. Marlo rip hi guts out fo' a piece o' bread.'

'Pynter! Don't talk like that. Don't talk like that!'

Pynter leaned his head against the bedroom door and stared at the ceiling.

9

THEY CALLED IT Rainbow Weather – that time during the dry season when the sun was bright above their heads and a drizzle came down from the Mardi Gras and covered the valley with a spray so fine it was almost as if the air were filled with talcum powder. There were rainbows everywhere, some of them as faint as washed-out ribbons, but there was always the one they called The Mother. It curved high and glowing above their heads, its foot planted in the water somewhere behind the hills that kept the ocean back.

A gardener might catch a glimpse of it, straighten up and lean against his machete, suddenly aware of the flowering okras, the pigeon peas and the amazing likeness of their blossoms to little yellow butterflies. He might see the manioc differently, how their shiny, dark-limbed trunks resembled the skin of a well-greased child. And he would feel a tiny tug of sadness in his heart that a day would come when he would no longer be there to see all this. A woman would stop mid-laugh and for some reason turn her mind to the children she did not have. Or another would sketch a private smile, remembering the time when Dreena's little girl-chile – now a woman who worked the canes with them – tried to follow a Mother Rainbow to where she thought its root was planted in the sea. Dreena's lil girl returned to her mother's yard exhausted and in tears because, however far she walked, it never got any closer.

Rainbows reminded Pynter of the strap that Paso wore around his waist for a belt. It reminded him of the wish that Deeka carried in her eyes, and then when it faded he took the track to Eden.

Earlier that morning and most of the afternoon, the dogs had been searching the foothills for Marlo, but Pynter could no longer hear them; they must have given up. Men with guns had arrived, their Land Rovers came roaring down the road. He had heard the slamming of doors and the thud of feet on asphalt. But they too had left a couple of hours later. And soon after the sound of their engines had faded in the distance, Gideon's white Opel came gunning up the hill.

Pynter had forgotten that his father had told him that Gideon was coming. His father also said that he should go to see his mother. But he didn't feel like it. He wanted this to be one of his by-himself days, and so he was down here at Eden, where it was quiet, even the birds were silent for once. And where Missa Geoffrey made his leaf bed for Miss Petalina, the earth was bare and brown. Maybe they'd found another place. P'raps Pastor Greenway found out and killed Miss Petalina. Everybody was killin everybody these days. For no flippin reason a pusson could understand. But if Pastor Greenway really done that to his best an' p'raps only daughter, news didn reach nobody yet. And he better not, because he, Pynter Bender, would pussnally ask Birdie to bus' his arse real bad when Pastor Greenway got sent to jail.

Pynter wondered what Peter was doing now. What would he say when he told him about Marlo and Harris? He sat on the earth, not bothering to settle himself down in his hideaway in the elephant grass. He wanted a stick to make markings like his mother on the ground. He wanted words to make all of it make sense.

He saw the man the instant his hand reached out to pull a twig – a shadow at the corner of his eye almost as if one of the trees had moved. He was on his feet before he'd even thought of it. Felt the wet grass give way beneath him and his shoulder hit the trunk of the guava tree in front of him. He heard a grunt, felt the tree heave. A shower of guavas hit the grass. A hand closed around his ankle. He kept moving. He kept moving because Tan Cee had told him to. He couldn't remember how long ago, or how many times she'd said it to him and Peter. He'd forgotten where he was or exactly when she'd said so, but now her voice was like a whisper at the back of his ear. 'If a pusson get hold of you, and you know dat they don't mean you no good, you don't jus' stand up there. You move, you kick, you bite, you make a whole heap o' noise.You don' tell yourself you weak, you don' tell yourself you finish, you never tell yourself you lose. You keep movin, even if they lock you down, you never stop movin, y'hear me? Jus' move … '

The hand slipped off his ankle. He swung himself away and in that single eye-blink of a turn he caught a glimpse of Marlo's fleshy face, the leather scabbard at his side and his bulk against the guava trees. And then there came a shout from another man nearby.

'Ayyy! What de hell goin on 'cross dere?'

Pynter found his back pressed against Missa Geoffrey's stomach, the man's hand holding him firmly there. Missa Geoffrey's chin was lifted high, his body rigid. He held a large stone firmly in his free hand.

There was a crash of trees, branches breaking, and suddenly Marlo was no longer there.

Missa Geoffrey stepped away from him – with his light brown eyes and a tiny brown moustache. 'Who de hell is you, and what bring you here?'

'Pynter – I'z Pynter.'

'You know who dat was?' Missa Geoffrey lifted his chin at the bushes beyond them.

Pynter nodded.

'You know what could've happen if it didn cross my mind to come here now?' His face was hard and unsmiling.

Pynter nodded again. He realised his knees were shaking slightly. Missa Geoffrey was there beside him, yet he sounded as if he were speaking from a far way off.

Missa Geoffrey dropped the stone. He looked about him. His face and shoulders were twitching. 'Why dat murderer had to come here, eh? Dat sonuvabitch could ha' gone everywhere else, but is here he had to come. I have to report this now, not so?' He gestured at the bushes. 'An' what happm when I get out o' here and call police? Next thing you know, this place full up of all kind o' people.' He looked about him again as if the gully were his house. Pynter thought the man was going to cry.

'And you,' he turned brown accusing eyes on Pynter, 'what de hell bring you down here? This look like place for chilren?'

'I come here when I hungry,' Pynter told him.

'Come here when you – you playin de arse wit' me, not so?' The man was staring at him closely. His eyes narrowing down to slits.

'I don' look, Missa Geoffrey. Not all de time.'

'Don' look – look at what? Look, you say?' Geoffrey moved his lips to say something else but coughed and rubbed his chest instead. He swung his head around as if expecting all of Old Hope to be there. He brought his hand up to the side of his face and coughed again.

Missa Geoffrey looked around him. 'Look? What de hell it got down here to look at? Dem guava? Dem serpent over yuh head?'

Pynter found himself replying in his father's flat irritated tone. 'A pusson not blind, yunno.'

His words stopped Missa Geoffrey short. Left him openmouthed and confused. He kept smoothing the hair back from his forehead and then he coughed a very distressed cough.

'Lissen, lil fella,' his voice rumbled out of him deep and low exactly as it did with Miss Petalina, 'I just save your life. You know what dat mean?'

'Nuh.'

'It mean,' he dropped his voice to a half-whisper, 'it mean you owe me a life.'

'I don' have no life to give back.'

'I don' want no life back, man. You tell anybody 'bout … ?'

'You an' Miss Tilina? Nuh.'

'Me an' Miss – Jeezas, man. Jeezas! Then you keep it so – okay? You keep it so, cuz … '

Pynter nodded. 'A life fo' a life.'

'Eh?'

'Pastor Greenway goin kill 'er if he get to know.'

Missa Geoffrey sat back on the wet grass. 'You prepare to swear on de Bible?'

Pynter nodded.

Missa Geoffrey slapped his pockets with both hands. He pulled out something bright and red and shiny and held it out to Pynter. 'Look – look, I want to give you this.' It was a small penknife. 'Dis mean me an' you'z friend. Dis mean you can't tell nobody nothing. Dis mean me an' you agree man to man, y'unnerstan?'

Pynter took the knife.

'Okay fella, we settle then.' Missa Geoffrey looked up as if suddenly alerted to something. 'Come, let's get outta here. And don't come back again, y'hear me. Is my land.'

'Is not.'

'You hear what I say?'

'Yessir.'

When Pynter reached the yard, it was raining again. Warm dry-season rain, the kind that fell with all the violence of a flashstorm and lasted just a short while. Pynter wondered if Gideon had left yet. He was trembling, but he wasn't cold and he didn't want to go inside if Gideon were still there.

He stooped between the pillars of the house and watched the rain come down.

10

'GIDEON TAKE MY father,' Pynter said.

Elena shook her head. She didn't understand him.

'I come from Eden. I shelter under de house and when I went in he wasn' there.'

His mother shook her head again. She still didn't understand him. 'You look in dem other room?'

'Gideon take my father,' he repeated.

'Where he gone to?'

He heaved his shoulders and turned his face away.

'Where...' She stopped herself short. The cloth that she was drying her hands with dropped softly on the floor. She brought her face down close to his. She touched his cheek and looked into his eyes. 'Gideon take your father where?'

He heaved his shoulders again. 'Gideon come and take 'im when I wasn' there.'

'You get wet,' she said. 'Your head soakin wet. You couldn shelter from the rain?' She began unbuttoning his shirt.

He was staring at the wall behind her head.

'Pynter,' she said.

He did not answer. She peeled the shirt from his shoulders. 'You must learn to cry. Y'unnerstan?'

She touched his cheeks again. Her face was working. 'When you feel like this, when you feel like you feeling now, you must try to cry. Y'hear me? You have to learn to cry.'

She wiped her eyes with the back of her hand and pulled him close to her.

He did not tell her everything – how he'd gone to Miss Maddie's house to ask her where his father was. How she had looked away from him as if she didn't want to answer, her eyes red. And all she had said was that she wished Paso had been there when Gideon came. She had stood him in the kitchen and wiped the rain off him. She'd done it the way Tan Cee or his mother would have done, pausing every now and then to examine him. She'd stretched his arms out and slid her fingers along the bones all the way down to his wrists. Had turned his palms up towards her and examined them under the gaslight in the kitchen. She'd passed her fingers along the small drain at the back of his neck, followed the fissure all the way down to his spine. She had come closer to his ear as if she were about to whisper something, traced the shape of his lobes with her fingers, and spent a long time over his feet. She'd gone to the fridge and offered him some food. He didn't want anything to eat. She'd left him for a while and come back with a towel. She had tried to smile. He had seen that she had three gold teeth. She had told him the towel was hers, spent a long time wiping his hair dry.

'You got feet like Paso,' she had said. 'An' them fine little hairs on your back same like all my father children.'

'Miss Maddie,' he had turned his head to look up at her, 'you could tell me where Gideon live?'

He could not make out the expression on her face because the evening had thickened into night. He had only her voice to go by.

'You shouldn't think of goin there.'

'Tell me where he live.'

'He's not a good man. He my brother, but I have to say it.'

'If you don' tell me, I'll still find him.'

She had nodded. 'Take one o' your people with you. He got dogs.'

'Where he live?'

93

'Westerpoint. Take your family with you.'

'G'night, Miss Maddie.'

'Y'hear me!'

'G'night.'

She had placed two mangoes in his hands and told him she was sorry.

He didn't tell his mother either that he knew now why they'd chosen him instead of Peter to go to live with Manuel Forsyth.

11

PREPARING FOR GIDEON meant standing in the sun on Glory Cedar Rise and staring into the distance. It meant lifting his vision above the canes, beyond the far green weave of bamboos that made a tunnel over the river.

There, past the festering swamps that his grandfather had walked into, at the foot of five pale low-lying hills, sat the big white houses of Westerpoint, scattered at the end of the long concrete road like bleached seashells against the blue heave of the ocean.

Gideon had come along that road one day to enter Lower Old Hope for the first time. The rumour of a cane girl carrying his father's seed had brought him to their place one morning. He found the cane girl waiting her turn at the standpipe by the road. He'd called her name, and when she turned he began striking her with the sawed-off piece of piping he'd brought along with him. And all she could do was curl her body down away from him, offer him her shoulders and save the children she was carrying for his father. Elena saved herself by playing dead.

Two years later, Birdie's woman told him of these things the very first night he returned from prison. He left Cynty's bed, forgetting the loving he had come for, and walked back to the yard. He sat on the stone that John Seegal had placed there for himself and which Deeka would not have anyone else sit on apart from God and Birdie. He'd looked into his sister's face and asked her if the things that Cynty had just told him were true. He was close to tears, they said, not because she did not answer him, not even because she knocked his hand off when he reached out and touched her shoulder, but because he understood then why she'd given his middle name to Pynter: the difficult one, the strange one, the one born blind, the child not born to live. Not as a way to please him, but as an accusation.

Preparing himself for Gideon meant reminding himself of all these things – recalling the words of the women in the river and learning, while he did so, the way the days unfolded in that place at the edge of the sea.

He sat there until night settled over the long, flat piece of land that stretched itself out like a tongue into the sea, and then with a tightening of the brows he slowly made his way back home.

'Y'awright?' Tan Cee's eyes were steady on his face.

He smiled at her and nodded.

Birdie was stoking wood into the fireplace. Peter stood beside him. He'd missed watching Birdie chopping wood. His uncle did not cook with sticks and bramble; Birdie preferred trees. He brought large portions of their trunks down from the foothills and dumped them against the grapefruit tree. Mid-mornings he took out the axe, shed his shirt and laid into them. The sound of his chopping reached the foothills and bounced right back in their faces. It drew boys to their yard, small crowds that stood and watched in flinching circles. It paused the women on the road below and turned their eyes up towards him, standing there, rigid as a tree and half as tall as God, his legs straddling the wood, the axe coming down and rising, down again and rising, with the sweat and sunlight glistening on his back like grease.

Tonight they would have man food, large portions of everything: wild yams the size of logs that Birdie had also brought down from the foothills, dasheen he'd dug up from the banks of Old Hope River, dumplings, of course, and every kind of meat his uncle could lay his hands on. During the day people passed and dropped lengths of pigtail, a bag of sweet potatoes, or something surprising like pink-fleshed pum-pum yams, or a bowl of dried peas that they'd been hoarding for the hard, dry times like these. Half of Old Hope would turn up later, drawn by the giddying smell of Birdie's cooking. Elena and Patty got out the plates, the calabashes and bowls. They served the smaller children first, then the bigger ones and finally the adults, whose silence lasted longer than their words these days, whose gazes, while they ate, were always turned away and downwards towards the darkness where the canes were.

These nights Birdie left with Peter. And as the dryness and the heat dug in, they would return later and later, with Birdie sometimes carrying the sleeping boy on one shoulder, a bag of provisions slung over the other. Birdie would lay Peter down so tenderly his brother barely stirred.

There grew a creeping uneasiness about these night-time journeys that saw his uncle and his brother returning to the yard closer to morning every time. Pynter saw it in his mother's face, in Tan Cee's glances at Patty, in their wordless avoidance of Birdie's greeting when they got back. His uncle began to bring home a different kind of food, fat chickens and beautifully tended vegetables and fruit. Their avoidance of Birdie turned to whisperings in the dark, the mutterings of Patty and Tan Cee in his mother's ear. Pynter knew that whatever it was that was nibbling away at their ease required them to say something to Birdie, and those muttered words were a way of talking themselves into a kind of urgency. A way of making whatever they had to say to Birdie come out of them more easily.

If his uncle sensed this, he did not show it. Hard times had changed him. He laughed less, frowned more, would pass his fingers thoughtfully through his beard. There was a temper there too – tight and uneasy behind the passing smiles he would throw at them.

As if to ease her mind of all these things, Tan Cee played a game with Pynter. Nights, she came and placed presents in his hands while he slept: seashells, seeds, sweets; marbles, strange beans and buttons; dark blue pebbles veined with streaks of glowing white; flakes of crystals that winked at him like tiny eyes. Pynter would unfold his fingers in the morning and find them there.

The morning he left for Gideon's place, Pynter was smiling inwardly. A little way down the road, he saw Tan Cee's blue headscarf and his heart flipped over. She was sitting on a culvert on the side of the road, chewing on a stick of cinnamon and trying to smile at the same time. He pretended not to see her.

'Taking a walk, Featherplum?' She stepped out in front of him and placed an arm across his shoulders. 'Whapm, fowl pick yuh tongue? Not talking to me this morning?'

She placed more of her weight on him. It slowed him down. 'Take Peter with you,' she said. The smile had left her voice.

He glanced quickly up at her. 'Take Peter where with me?'

'Wherever you goin.'

'I not goin nowhere.'

'Then take him nowhere too. In fact,' her face twitched as if she were about to sneeze, 'he and Birdie waiting fo' you 'cross the river. That the way you goin, not so?'

She glanced at his face and burst out laughing. She was shaking with it, like a joke she had been holding in for years. Her eyes fell on his face again and a louder burst came out of her. People must have heard her at the top end of Old Hope.

Pynter rolled his shoulders violently in an effort to shake off her arm. Her laughter was nettling his temper.

'Gimme the gun,' she said, pointing at his pocket.

'What gun? Somebody gotta gun? It got gun round here? Which gun?'

Her hand darted into his pocket and pulled out his catapult. She tied the rubber straps around her wrist, leaned back from him, shaking her head.

'I watch you knock a coupla bird outta the sky with this last week, an' I tell myself, God help the fool who cross you. All that hatin. You full of it. You been full of it from the time you come home from your father. You been feedin yourself on it. Look how it make you magga-bone and dry! See what hatin done to your grandmother? You want to 'come like her?'

He lifted blazing eyes at her. 'You better don't come round me no more. You better don't – specially when I sleepin, cuz…'

'Cuz what, pretty boy? You goin beat me up? You have to be awake to do dat.'

He searched his head for words to throw back at her but he couldn't find them, so he stomped off, complaining long and loudly to himself. Her laughter followed him all the way down to the river.

Birdie grunted when he arrived. He'd taken to having his woman plait his hair but today he'd loosened it. It stood up like small clumps of cus-cus grass from his head and made his eyes seem larger. He carried two bags on his shoulders, the big bottomless one he made his night-time forays with and the long canvas sack he'd brought with him from prison.

He was looking down at Pynter. The gold tooth at the front of his mouth glittered like a little flame. There was an expression on his uncle's face which he did not understand, the look of someone trying to see into the distance while the sun was in their eyes. He shifted the bags on his shoulder, rested a hand on Peter's head and pushed him gently forward. 'Go 'head o' me. I meet y'all down there.'

Down there was a walk through the cane plantation, past the collapsed windmill around which giant cogged wheels were scattered like the teeth of a decaying monster. Wheels which Tan Cee told Pynter used to be turned by mules when there was no wind. When they looked back, they could not see Birdie. The mud had forced Peter to take off his shoes. They'd greased his brother's feet and fitted him with a new pair of rubber sandals. Pynter could see that Peter was tense and distressed, almost tearful. As the gleaming houses with their tall cast-iron gates came up,

Peter's eyes turned more and more urgently behind, looking for Birdie, who now could not be seen.

They walked until suddenly there was the ocean rearing up ahead of them. The concrete road glistened like a silver bracelet. It was all sky and water and wind, and the gusts that came off the sea seemed to want to push them back along the road they'd just travelled.

Even if Miss Maddie hadn't told him that Gideon's house had a big yellow door and light-blue blinds, he would have found it anyway. Gideon was sitting on the wall of his veranda. Two women were on chairs. They held glasses in their hands and were nodding while he spoke.

He was bringing a glass to his lips when he saw them standing against his gate. His hand came down and he got slowly to his feet.

Pynter knew that sideways look of Gideon's, but Peter didn't. His brother began shuffling backwards. Pynter didn't move. Gideon came down the steps, his eyes no longer on the two of them but on the three Alsatians chained to the concrete pillar. They had been quiet when they arrived, but now that Gideon was approaching them they began peeling back their lips and barking. Pynter saw Peter against the gate of the house behind them and smelled his brother's fear. He had been counting on his slingshot. Would have blinded Gideon from the moment he came down those steps. Would have done that first to him and then the dogs. He'd been practising for months. But then he heard Peter's cry behind him, shrill and high like a gull's. Then the sound of pounding feet. Saw Gideon straighten up. Felt himself dragged backwards. Saw the fear twist Gideon's face into something dark and tight and ugly as Birdie stepped inside the gate.

Pynter felt a sudden tightening in his throat, didn't know what sound came out of him, but whatever it was, it halted his uncle and brought Gideon's hands down from his face.

Birdie swung his eyes back round to Gideon.

'Jus' touch dem…' he said, slowly, with a terrible gentleness. Gideon stumbled away from the lunging dogs, his eyes on Birdie.

Birdie lowered himself to the grass and laid the axe across his legs.

'Gwone, fellas,' he said. 'I relaxin out here.'

Pynter did not know what he expected, but not the sight of the old man spread out on a clean white sheet with all that light and wind coming through the window above his head.

The young woman was there with him. She was sitting on the edge of the bed, holding his hand. She looked up anxiously at them, smiled and said that Grandad had been expecting them. He realised that his father knew nothing of the trouble outside, which was strange because he should have heard the dogs. The young woman smiled again and got up to leave.

Pynter did not return her smile. Peter was looking at the way her skirt swished about her feet as she walked out of the room. 'She nice,' he whispered.

'Patty nicer,' Pynter grunted.

Manuel Forsyth seemed to have been expecting them. Not on that day exactly, but any day soon. And it was clear that, lying there with the light from the window on his face and neck, it was all that he had been doing.

'What take y'all so long?' he muttered.

His father lifted his hand and Pynter nudged his brother forward. Those hands had spent a long time knowing Pynter, but in all these years their father had hardly ever laid his hands on Peter.

'Peter?' the old man said softly, his eyes switching from side to side. Pynter noticed how thin and drawn he looked. His father traced Peter's arms with the tips of his fingers, passed his palms across his back and waist, his face still turned up towards the window, almost as if he were listening with his hand.

'Pynter will grow taller. You goin make a broader man. Solid.' The old man chuckled. 'You, Peto – you carry me inside you.'

In the silence that followed, all Pynter could hear was the sea. He wondered where Gideon had gone, whether Birdie was still on the grass out there. Their father's voice came to him as if it were floating down from the ceiling.

'I wasn't always good to y'all mother. Y'all know that?'

'Yes,' Pynter answered softly.

The old man didn't seem to hear him. He smacked his lips and stirred. 'Have children. Remember me. Remember me to dem. Y'all hear me?'

Peter mumbled something. Pynter glanced at him.

'A lawyer will come to y'all one day when time right. He'll hand y'all papers and ask both o' you to sign them. Sign them. Y'hear me? Pynter, you goin read fo' me?'

'Which part?'

'Any part. Just wan' to hear your voice.' That seemed to turn the old man's mind to something else. 'Paso come to see me last time, Pynter.' Pynter nodded and slid his hands beneath the covers of the book. The leather sighed against the skin of his palms. Its weight was familiar; its smell was like much-used money, and now something else hung over the pale yellow pages: the smell of the woman who had just left the room.

His mind shifted back to those evenings in that empty house, so crowded with the memories and ghosts of other people – other lives that the old man said was family. And with Peter beside him, the shuffle of feet outside the door, the waves coughing against the rocks outside, he started reading.

'"And if I go and prepare a place for you, I will come again…"'

He lifted his head. Peter's eyes were on the gulls wheeling in the air outside and his father was snoring softly. When they came outside, Birdie was where they had left him. Gideon had disappeared and his dogs were lying on the grass with their jaws resting on their forelegs. The woman was leaning out from the veranda as if she wanted to place her lips against their ears.

'Y'all not – y'all not goin meet him again like…like…'

'I know.' Peter looked back at him with a little surprised smile. They'd both said it at the same time.

In the light of the decaying evening, the large concrete houses were no more than shapes against the sky. He didn't realise that they had been that long inside Gideon's house. He looked inland in the direction from which they had come. He could see no houses, not even the canes, just the ash-blue hills that squatted like children at the foot of the towering Mardi Gras. The concrete road was now a wide grey snake cut out against the side of the sea cliffs, threatening, it seemed, to slip into the ocean at any time.

Birdie placed his big hands on their shoulders. He was looking straight ahead at the road, his head pulled back, listening it seemed to something that was somewhere beyond their hearing.

'Life's a lil bit like dat, fellas,' he said finally, his voice a rumble above their heads. 'A pusson have to walk it. Ain't got no choice. And a time mus' come when dem have to stop cuz dem can't go on no more.'

He was silent for a while and when he spoke again his voice was different. The thunder was no longer in it.

'Do me a favour, fellas. Tell y'all mother I really beat that man up. Tell 'er I beat 'im bad. Tell 'er that for me. Go 'head o' me. I meet y'all at home.'

12

HIS FATHER'S WORDS – *Remember me* – were like the drumming of fingers in Pynter's head. He patterned his walking to the rhythm of their syllables, searching those two words for the meaning he knew was hidden there. And with the passing of the months, they fleshed themselves out with all the things that people said around him.

It amazed him that even when he'd listened, he'd never heard what Deeka was really saying when she loosened her hair and talked; that beneath her words there lived another story – one that sat at the back of almost everything the adults said, especially when they spoke of those who had come before them and those who would come after.

This new thing that his father's last words taught him: that in the villages above the canes people did not die. As long as memory lived they did not. They passed. Leaving always something of themselves behind. John Seegal, their grandfather, had passed most of himself over to Birdie, except for the thieving ways, o' course, which came from a great-grand-uncle whose name Deeka refused to say. And the long-gone aunts, the grandmothers, the uncles were there with them right now. They were scattered among the children the way the leaves of a forest tree became the flesh of other plants around it. They were there in the curve of a young man's spine, the turn of a girl-child's head, the way their lips shifted from their teeth in a grimace or a smile.

There too in the shape of a baby's feet or the quickness of its temper. There even in the flavours they preferred, and the things their bodies asked for.

For wasn't it true that Columbus, John Seegal's only brother, had passed on his singing voice to all the Benders that came after? And where did that shine-eye beauty of Patty come from, if not from the very best parts of all those cane-tall Bender women who knew how to unravel dreams and turn their hands to medicines; and who, sometimes just for the sake of it, created new and marvellous things from rope and thread and fabric? And what about those children born with a wisdom older than their age? Did that come from nowhere, eh?

It explained, at least, the querying hands of those adults who, like his father, mapped the bones of children and sought to read their futures and their past there. And it explained why the idea that his body was a house to a man who had lived long before his time made perfect sense to Deeka Bender, his grandmother.

Her problem was the way he had come. Not a little while after Peter. Not even later in the evening. But two days after his brother. She who had brought him out still talked of the way he'd fought her. For all of two bright dry-season days when, with the whole world living life outside, night hadn't left that birth room. And that cry, when he'd finally released his death hold on her daughter – that cry wasn't the cry of a child at all, but the raging of a young man. And then, of course, they saw the eyes, or what hid the world from them.

It was not so, Tan Cee told him. Not as Deeka said it. She did not remember it that way. In their first few years, Deeka didn't remember it that way either. But remembering was like that. Remembering was like life, like people: it got better or worse with time. There were women like Deeka, she said, who tied their lives to a man's so tight they forget they ever owned one. And when that man got up and walked, it was not just his life he took, he went with theirs as well.

'So what left for them to do after?' She smiled dreamily at him. 'They look for something they kin blame. And you – you the one your granny pick.'

He'd asked her what John Seegal looked like, because even if they'd said he looked like Birdie, he could not make an image in his mind. Just a shape – a scattered force that inhabited his grandmother and the children he had left with her. He used to imagine him within the stones he'd used to build the yard, especially the large flat rock beside the steps which they said he used to sit on.

He wasn't sure that Tan Cee heard his question. Her eyes were on her husband, off again, he'd told her, to start work on a house somewhere in the south. He would be away a coupla days.

She took her eyes off Coxy, adjusted her skirt and sighed. 'Some things have to … ' She stopped short, considered what she was about to say and smiled quietly at him.

'Your granny always talk 'bout how she meet John Seegal. She never talk 'bout how he left. She never say much 'bout Anita either. Y'ever wonder why?'

She told him of a morning her mother was sweeping the yard when a child arrived and called her by her real name. He stood at the edge of the yard, his stomach exposed, his thin legs crossing and uncrossing, his hands small and thin like a bird's, moving around his face as if he were washing it with air.

Deeka asked him what he wanted. He told her that he wanted nothing. She asked him why he came then. He said his father sent him with some news. She told him that men never sent their children anywhere with news. And a woman wouldn't have sent him because she would bring the news herself. And so she turned her back on him.

But he was still there at the corner of her eye. Still washing his face with his hands. And then, when she was least expecting it, his voice came across the yard as clear as if he was standing right next to her.

He told her that her husband Big John Seegal had wagered her, his house and his three girl-children that he was going to cross the Kalivini swamps in the early hours of the morning and emerge from it alive.

Deeka smiled at the joke at first, found herself remembering it throughout the rest of the day and laughing. But by late evening, when she heard her husband's footsteps coming up the path, the words of that boy seemed somehow less ridiculous.

He came home full of his own thunder. Sat on the steps stinking of the rum he'd despised all his life. Sat there working up a murderous argument with himself. He raised his hand at Deeka and told her for the first time what he really thought of her and the four children she had given him. And at the end of it he stretched himself out in the yard and would not look at them.

Deeka gathered the children around her and told them what their father was about to do. Down there, she told them, way past cane, there is a place where the Old Hope River meets the sea. The river does not die there; it becomes something else: a stinking, bubbling tangle of mangrove where the sharks swim in on the early-morning tides to feed on all the things the land rejected. She told them that their father, overtaken by some demon for which there was no accounting, had decided to cross that place in the small hours of the morning.

Deeka fought all night to keep him: I ever give you cause to feel you not a man? That you less than another woman man? What about the children? Eh? What about them? They not healthy? They not yours? You want somebody to tell you sorry for something they didn do to you? Okay then, I sorry. If me, the children or anybody do anything to push you to where you is, to make you come like you come home tonight, I want to tell you sorry.

She turned to the girls with a deadly, soft-voiced rage. I want every one of you to tell y'all father sorry. Tan Cee, the eldest, was more temper than tears. Elena fixed him with an unblinking, tight-lipped gaze. And Patty the Pretty, his last, his youngest, the dark-skinned miracle he'd named himself, Patty who could stop her father in mid-stride, who could melt his anger with a touch, the muttering of his name, even Patty could not turn him. And Birdie, the son who looked like him and had the strength to hold him down or tie him against a post or tree or something solid till he came back to his senses – Birdie was in jail.

By the morning, they had grown quiet, the girls starved of sleep, and Deeka just too tired to be tearful any more. Defeated also by a realisation that had come to her during all those hours of pleading. That there was something in John Seegal's decision that went beyond his drunkenness. That it had not been made over a glass of rum, but over time. So that in the still grey hours of that morning, even while she stood on the top of Glory Cedar Rise and called out his name as they watched him walking down Old Hope Road, watched and called until the canes and distance swallowed him, she knew that all the pleading in the world would not make him turn around.

She went back to her house, pulled the trouser leg from under the mattress they'd conceived their children on, emptied the contents on the floor, counted the money she had placed there over the years and began preparing for his wake. And while she prepared she cursed the canes. She blamed this shallow valley she had come to from the north, this long, blue gorge of sighing, coughing, whistling grass which consumed their men so casually.

'But you can't beat cane,' Tan Cee muttered. 'You can't do much to hurt it back.' Which was why, she said, Deeka retreated into a dark-eyed, watchful bitterness and kept reminding them of the miracle their father used to be.

'And soon after,' Tan Cee sighed and got to her feet, 'Elena body start changin with y'all.'

'And de baby girl – Anita?'

'She wasn' no baby girl de time de trouble start. I got a coupla things to look after.' She dusted her skirt and walked away.

13

THE FOOD THAT Birdie brought back now was meant to last them longer. Peter confided that he'd even tried to bring along a cow but it wasn't to be persuaded. Besides, the cow had horns that were long enough and sharp enough to win the argument.

Peter talked with a look of puzzlement that brought the laughter out of them, all the more because he couldn't understand what they were laughing at. Couldn't see the joke either when Birdie sneaked off during the day and returned home with ridiculous things: a couple of giant plants sitting in heavy, white stone pots; an iron gate; three beach chairs; an aluminium oar; the two back wheels of a car; a child's plastic bicycle.

The women seemed to recognise this change in Birdie. They responded strangely: they touched him more, kept back the best of everything for him; made difficult dishes like cornki and farine which took them two days to prepare, and sat and watched him while he ate.

He held their gifts of food between his fingers and brought them to his mouth as though the pleasure was not just his to have but also theirs.

And during these nights of bright moon and still air, when voices and laughter travelled down the foothills to their yard, riding it seemed on the achingly sweet fragrance of the lady-of-the-night, he repeated the stories of his time in prison.

It was only Peter who did not understand this ritual. Not even when his uncle tried to make him know by almost saying so. By leaving him at home without an explanation, by the quick flushes of irritation that left Peter tearful and ill-tempered, by not having time for him these days. Perhaps the women had spoken to Birdie. Perhaps he'd read their worry all along and was doing something about it now. Pynter wasn't sure.

And then one night Birdie took Peter away. It was close to morning when Birdie returned – a night of lashing rain and the kind of cloth-thick darkness that made it impossible to see ahead – but he did not have Peter with him. Birdie dropped his bag, pulled off his boots, took the cloth that Deeka held out to him and began wiping himself dry. He sat amongst them without a word.

For a while there was silence, only the snoring of the valley, the rain dripping from the trees and the rising babble of the river below.

Elena turned on Birdie with quiet, unblinking eyes. 'Where my chile?' Her lips were twitching and she was studying his face as if he were a stranger.

Birdie held her eyes, his face gone soft, held her gaze as if his life depended on it. 'Out there,' he answered. 'I had to do something.'

A sound escaped Elena – soft, deep-chested – a cross between a chuckle and a cough. She sat on the floor, crossed her legs, her eyes hard and bright as nails on her brother's face.

The whistle of the sugar factory in the south had already released the night shift when Pynter eased himself up on his elbow and muttered at the ceiling, 'Peter coming.'

They barely recognised him when he got home, mud-soaked and exhausted. Elena reached for him but he rushed past her and threw himself at Birdie. He struck out wildly, blindly at his uncle's face; sobbed and cursed him at the same time. And when Birdie had judged it was enough, he caught Peter's swinging arms and pinned them against his sides.

Tan Cee and Elena exchanged glances, nodded briefly at each other. Patty sneaked a smile at Birdie.

Not long after, Birdie staggered up the hill carrying a log of wood and dropped it near the giant iron platter at the end of the yard. They thought nothing of it until he dragged the log out to the middle of the yard, stripped it of its bark and propped it upright between a couple of stones.

The wood was pink as flesh and gummy to the touch. And where the axe had left its broad tooth marks it seeped a milky fluid. He left it there for a week, covering it with plastic when it rained and placing it in the middle of the yard when the sun came out.

The day he brought his axe to it they observed him under lidded eyes. Watched him move around the wood, his muscles roused and rippling, as if they weren't there. And even from the safety of the house, with the rise and falling of that axe, they all felt exposed.

'What you makin, Birdie?'

Birdie leaned the axe against his leg, spread his hands at Elena and grinned.

'A flyin machine.

'A poor man plane.

'A thunder maker.

'A wood bullet with steel boots.

'God shoe – just one side. De middle one!'

He lifted the axe and tapped the log.

By the following week, the sun had dried the outer surface white and the wood was bleeding no more.

It took a while before they guessed his intention. For it seemed at first that all he wanted from that round, solid piece of wood was a plank. Seemed so much like a waste of effort, since he might have bought or stolen one.

But then one morning he climbed the slopes of the Mardi Gras and came back with a length of guava wood. The following day he brought home a handful of four-inch nails, a couple of blocks of wood and knelt before the plank.

He left the wheels for last. Two of them were identical, but the third was almost twice as large as the rest. It took another day for the machine to be ready.

By then the news had travelled across the valley, so that by the time he'd fixed the wheels onto the axles, the yard was packed with boys standing at respectful distances examining the machine that Birdie said would fly.

'Okay,' he said finally, 'I want de best hill on dis island. Show me de steepest, highest, smoothest, longest hill and I will show y'all how to fly.'

And with hardly a word between them, they left the yard and headed for Man Arthur's Fall.

Man Arthur's Fall was a ridge that ran between two valleys. It was the place where Old Hope Road briefly lost its footing against the hillside and plunged down towards an old iron bridge that protected vehicles, animals and drunks from falling onto the boulders of the ravine below. It carried the name of the man who had thrown himself down its slope because he owed the estate more money than he could pay back with his labour in a lifetime.

From up there – where the man smell of the ocean reached them; where, ranged against the sky, they could see neither the bridge nor the gully where Arthur Sullivan fell – the road swept down and away from them in a massive, suicidal curve.

Birdie held the thing aloft. The wood was as white as dough now and smelt of a deep and feral musk. And because they did not know what it was, or did exactly, apart from what Birdie Bender told them, his power over them was total.

He placed a couple of heavy, flat stones on the plank and made the steering rigid with a length of rope he'd brought along with him. He attached another piece of rope to the rear axle then eased it over the edge of the hill, his muscles straining as if they were about to burst the skin. Then he let it go.

The machine rolled off with a low, impatient rumble, the sound of it seeming to rise from the bowels of the earth. They knew it would not get to the bottom of the hill, but it had a good long stretch of road ahead.

Halfway down, it began chewing up the asphalt, the sound of its metal wheels rising quickly to a wail. And then the machine struck the bank, spun several times in the air and landed on the asphalt with a terrible crash.

Oslo and Arilon ran off after it, their shirt tails trailing behind them like wings. They returned running and placed the machine at Birdie's feet.

One of the boys looked up earnestly into Birdie's face. 'It can't fly, Missa Birdie.'

'How you know dat?' Birdie smiled.

'Cuz it didn,' Oslo said.

Birdie's gold tooth flashed. For the first time he seemed unsure. 'Didn, yes! Not can't! Now, fellas, y'all see how short that road is. Besides, dat scooter didn have no rider. God shoe got to have a foot to make it run.' He spoke briskly, irritably. 'Y'all ever see a plane take off? Or a chicken hawk?'

'It take speed firs'?' Pynter offered.

Birdie lifted a triumphant finger. 'So! If plane and chicken hawk take speed to fly, what make y'all think it different wid dat scooter dere?'

Birdie placed the tip of his boot under the machine and flipped it over on its back. Turned belly-up to the hot afternoon sky, the metal wheels burned with the brightness of the reflected sun.

'Speed, fellas,' Birdie chuckled happily, having regained their faith. 'Dat's what's goin to make y'all fly.'

He wiped his forehead, lifted the scooter, turned to Peter and laid it at his feet. 'Peter Sweeter, I make it for you,' he said.

Peter stared at him, then at Pynter and then at all the others, and gradually his face softened. Envy travelled like a shot of liquor through the gathering. For a moment it also blinded

Pynter, then just as suddenly he felt relieved. For his brother's pain – which he'd carried in his eyes and in his silence during all that week – had suddenly been lifted.

They knelt before the machine and felt the wood, assessed its weight, its size. They would not forget the way it had charged down the hill, and that instant just before it struck the bank, when the grumble of the wheels became a wail and then a scream. And there, in all its mute and disconcerting newness, it seemed impossible that this bit of wood and metal should do what Birdie had set out to make it do: to take to the air and fly.

If Pynter allowed himself to believe his uncle, it was because he knew that Birdie never lied, not really, not even when he joked. Not even when he'd asked them to tell his mother how badly he'd beaten up Gideon. It wasn't a lie. Hadn't Pynter himself, on looking down on Westerpoint from Glory Cedar Rise, blinded Gideon a thousand times with that catapult he'd made? Birdie must have done the same or worse to Gideon every day in jail.

Besides, there were different ways in which a person could believe something. Like those times he imagined that his kites were messages, which, when he cut them loose, took with them some part of his longing to see the world. Perhaps that was what his uncle meant by flying, since Birdie had also told them on the very first night he sat and talked about the men he'd left in prison that anything that took your mind off pain, anything that made you lose yourself, even for a little while, anything could make you fly.

14

Scents which everyone else told Pynter weren't there. People shapes that walked with him in darkness. Shuffling feet, like the whisperings of the canes. Presences that touched him softly, like the brush of clothing on the skin. Whimperings that came up from the canes on mornings. Muffled struggles in the houses that he passed at night. Voices. Things he was afraid to speak of because they would call him Jumbie Boy. Like the heaviness that Birdie carried inside himself which the loudest of his thunder-laughter could not hide. Like those early-morning dreams in which his Uncle Michael stood in the middle of the road calling him, a long brown coat flowing down his shoulders like dark water. Like the stirrings of the baby that his mother was now carrying for the man he smelt on her. He could have even told them that this man was foreign to these parts. A stranger who left the smell of nutmeg, sweat and cinnamon on his mother's skin. That that man would come to their yard one day and may never go away. He knew this by the urgency with which his mother left hours before the others stirred, the tiredness she no longer carried when she returned much later than the rest. The distance of her gaze even when her eyes were on them. He could have told them this weeks before Santay came and said it. But they would have called him Jumbie Boy.

Pynter was also the first to see the five men emerge from the yellow car and walk up the hill to their yard. He pointed them out to Peter who ran inside and called the women. Deeka waited for them with her hands planted on her hips like the handles of a jug.

'G'mornin, Miss Dee. Long time no see.'

'Five years, two months and a coupla days, Chilway,' Deeka said to the man who greeted her. He had a very large stomach and was breathing heavily from the climb. He pushed his right hand towards Deeka, from which she selected just his thumb and shook it briefly.

'Where's that nice fella who come with you last time?' She did not seem to expect an answer, she just needed something to say while the yard adjusted to their presence.

'You mean Layto?' the man answered pleasantly.

'No – de tall one wid de nice smile,' Deeka said.

'Layto, Miss Dee. He gone back to Kara Isle. Married a woman from dere. Left a lot of other wimmen deprive o' dat sugar smile of his.' He laughed.

'Nice fella – we can't afford for Birdie to go.' She'd slipped in the last words hastily. They caught the man off-guard. He stared at her as if he'd just been cheated.

'Wha you say, Miss Dee?'

Deeka offered him a quick, dry smile. 'Y'hear me first time.'

'The watchmen bawling murder on Crosshatch estate becuz they losing provision every night, Miss Dee.'

'What make them think Birdie take dem provision?'

Chilway smiled. 'One catch sight of 'im, Miss Dee. They threaten to poison every bunch o' banana in sight. And dat,' he looked with mock alarm around the yard, 'dat can't be good fo' nobody.'

'Poison don' pick out poor from rich,' Deeka answered drily. 'Missa watchman might poison hi boss instead. Times rough and Birdie do what Birdie got to do to ease de time.'

'Times rough fo' everybody, mam.'

'Den how come roughness don' rough y'all up same way?'

Chilway laughed out loud. 'Is jus' cool we coolin him off, Miss Dee. Soon as de pressure ease, we send 'im back. Besides,' Chilway lowered his voice and nodded in Peter's direction, 'I hope you notice we didn't even mention 'im!'

'If is trouble you want den go ahead an' mention 'im.'

'No-no-no-no-no! What you take me for?' The man looked genuinely hurt. 'I never mention 'im. He's a boy, not so? A juvenile who's acting under, er, influence and...' He splayed his fingers as if he were about to count them. 'Duress – yes – a juvenile acting under duress.'

He dragged a large green handkerchief from his pocket and mopped his neck and throat. He squinted angrily at the sun as if to lodge a protest against the heat. 'Dat's worth at least ah extra coupla years, Miss Dee. In fact, a malicious magistrate could make dat – lemme see – three or four, or even five.

'And I not even mentioning all de thiefin yet. So is generous I definitely is today, mam, cuz I not includin influence-an'-duress. What you say, fellas? We not includin influence-an'-duress, right?'

The fellas smiled.

'Yuh see, Miss Dee – we tryin we best becuz we jus' de servant of all dem law deh. Not so, fellas?'

The fellas nodded.

By then Birdie had come out. The big boots he'd arrived in from prison were unlaced, their canvas tongues hanging out as if they too found the heat insupportable. 'What y'all want?' he grumbled.

'C'mon, Big Bird. I wan' to make dis quiet.' Chilway's voice had hardened.

'What de hell y'all come here for?'

'Gwone, boy!' Deeka shouted. She seemed angry now, impatient for him to leave.

'I not goin nowhere!'

117

'Yuh better go an' put on some decent clothes! Cuz you not leavin my yard like dat.'

'I not!'

'Gwone, boy!'

'I not no boy. I'z a big man an' I not…'

'Birdie, yuh do what dem warders say befo' dey influence-an'-duress y'arse in jail, y'hear me?'

For a moment Birdie stood on the steps glaring at the men. Deeka was the only one who looked at him directly with that same still-water detachment she had greeted him with when he first arrived from jail. Birdie turned abruptly and slammed the door. The house quaked under his weight. They heard the table slam against the partition inside, chairs rattling, something heavy hitting the floor. When he came out he was dressed in the khaki shirt with the faded number below the breast pocket and the cotton trousers Tan Cee had given him. He had even combed his hair.

Chilway rested his hand on Birdie's shoulder. 'Look at you,' he said. 'Big man like you! You think we like to come here and embarrass weself like dis?'

Birdie blew his nose into his sleeve and wiped his eyes.

One of the men rested his hand on Birdie's, tentatively. 'We didn bring de van,' he told him softly. 'Nobody will hardly know we come to take the Bird.'

Peter began to cry. He wept as if he needed air. Shut his eyes while he stood there gasping. Patty was wiping her eyes and Tan Cee had turned her back on them.

They'd stuffed Birdie's bag with fruits and what remained of the delicacies they'd prepared for him. The wardens gave them time to get to Glory Cedar Rise, and from there they waved and shouted at the yellow car until it disappeared.

Pynter turned to Deeka Bender. 'How long he gone for dis time?'

Her head averted slightly, the words seemed to drop out of the corner of her mouth. 'Not as long as de last.'

It occurred to Pynter that she'd been waiting all her life – waiting not just for John Seegal, but also for Birdie. Not like Miss Cynty, who at least filled her life with something in between while Birdie was away. Deeka existed like the dry season, many unbroken years of it, holding on for a man who came as scarce as rain, and another who would never return to her. And then he thought of Miss Lizzie quarrelling with life itself for the child they said she would never have, Patty the Pretty always trying, Miss Maddie holding on each night for Paso, Tan Cee watching Coxy Levid walk away from her every Wednesday night. Perhaps that was what all women did – wait.

'Desert!' he mumbled, which was all his grandmother heard, which touched, barely, on what was turning in his mind. But she'd caught enough of his tone to sense his meaning and it made her turn those too-steady, too-dark eyes on him.

Hers was one of the few faces that could frighten him, for it carried so openly his condemnation, as though every time she looked at him she was passing sentence. Which was why he often felt he hated her. He was sure she knew this, because she rarely said a word to him, and sometimes when she thought he was not looking, she licked her finger and made the sign of the cross above his head.

'Watch out, you!' she said.

'S'what I always do,' he replied, his tone like hers exactly, intense and murderous.

For the rest of the day his grandmother stalked him with her eyes.

It lasted months – that quiet, dark-eyed gaze. That surreptitious crossing of the hands above his head. That shadowy prowl around him. Tan Cee had taken to sleeping in the hallway beside him. She told him it was because she had to edicate him about the ways of the high-falutin, low-fartin school he'd just won a scholarship to in San Andrews. Still, she spent hours talking into his ear about the kinds of food he must never eat from anyone's hands, especially his grandmother's, and why his granny was the way she was with him.

In that time of Pynter sheltering from his grandmother's malice, and the yard trying not to remember Birdie, the Mardi Gras gave them special days near the closing of the year when the yam shoots eased themselves out of the earth and the purple-yellow blossoms of pigeon peas gave way to tiny hairy pods that would replace the meat Old Hope wouldn't have during the months to come.

Sorrel hung like drops of blood from the stems of plants that looked as if they'd soaked up all the pain the earth had ever borne. The blossoming corns stirred their hair in little winds with the fussiness of foreign women, and a new chill came off the ocean and crept along the valley floor at nights, leaving drifting skeins of mist and a heavy sprinkling of dew in the mornings.

·This was the time when the mountain reminded them that it was there, had always been, and that this valley in which the canes they worked in grew and thrived was as much a part of itself as the crown of mist that swirled around its head. It sent rain down its slopes like drunken marching armies and made Old Hope a dripping, tapping, drumming water orchestra. The canes were silent then, their whisperings replaced by the growling of the little river below, grown fat and fast and muscular from the water it was feeding on.

And amidst all that wetness the first wonder arrived. It came like a present, like something the night had created and left in the yard for them, so that first thing in the morning it drew their eyes to it. A gloria lily. A flower-flame. Large as the head of a child and impossibly round, it stood among the stones, the raindrops hanging off its petals like jewellery; the flesh of its stem the colour and sheen of ivory. It had been sleeping in the darkness all year long and now the late November rains had called it out.

The women leaned out of their windows, their eyes on their children. They would observe the ones that backed away from all that beauty and those that moved towards it with quiet, wide-eyed wonder. One or two would stoop and run a finger up the stem, hesitating only when they reached the bright cold flame. Another might even become tearful. And always, always there would be one among the little crowd whose hand reached out and broke it from the earth. There would be no irritation when that happened, no anger at the killing of a thing so beautiful and strange, since something just as precious would have come out of it – a glimpse into the deeper natures of their children.

And anyway, if the gloria lily did survive the children, it would live only for a day; would begin to die before their eyes by early evening.

This, Deeka Bender reminded them, was the time of little miracles, the time they called the halfway season. It was when Elena 'took up' Manuel Forsyth's twins (and she wasn' saying dat 'twas a proper thing to do). Fact was, strange things happened to a young pusson's feelings, so parents with part-grown girls and mannish lil boys had to be specially watchful because babies appeared from nowhere.

And true enough, in these flat grey days when it was easy to believe that they would never see a purple sky again, little miracles happened. A tiny slit in the clouds opened up one morning like the parting of a pair of lips. The light came down thin and sharp like a blade, tapering out just wide enough to hit a single flowering tree at the foot of the Mardi Gras. A shout from someone somewhere brought them out into their yards to stand there staring at the burning immortelle that made the hillside look as if it had just sprouted a wound.

It happened again later in the evening with night already hemming the foothills: another parting of the heavy dam of clouds. A different light this time. Syrupy and glowing, it settled on the high and slender branches of a dandacayo tree, turning it all metal – a living, shimmering thing against the darkness of the hillside.

'It have hope in that,' Tan Cee said, lowering her chin on Pynter's head. 'It have a lotta hope in that.'

It turned Deeka Bender's mind to John Seegal's only brother, the one her children never got to meet – Columbus of the mis-shapen head and big soft eyes.

He was larger than Birdie, she told them, and still growing when she came to Old Hope. Had the shoulders of a giant but couldn't shift a stone because his hands would not allow it. He was not meant to be born that way, but made so by the hands of a young English doctor who didn't know what he was doing.

She could see him now: that heavy walk of his. A forest tree on two legs. Columbus never stop growing. Never got accustomed to the body he born in. A lil boy, that's what he was, a lil boy struggling to free himself of all that flesh that held him down.

Talked as he walked too! Heavy and slow and not-so-certain. A pusson listen to him speak and 'twas easy to believe that all he did was mumble to himself.

But same way that light come through and hit that tree, God left a lot of light in him. A lotta light becuz nobody could pick a petal off a flower as gentle as Columbus. Nobody 'ceptin he would think of holding a living insect up against the light to make everybody see the colours they never thought it had. He could thread a needle without looking, pick a mosquito off a pusson eyelash. Big as he was, he had hands and eyes for things almost too small to see and touch.

God take away hi talking voice and gave him something better. God fill hi mouth with song. Used to sing like a girl, a voice so pretty it raised the hairs on a pusson arms. Was the only part of himself he'd passed down through the family, and proof of that fact was that there wasn't a Bender, except one p'raps, who couldn sweeten a pusson ear with song.

Used to have a man in Old Hope name Josiah. Short fella. Hardly talk to nobody. He hate chilren. Hate man too. Hate woman more. Hate turn flesh was what he was. Never laugh in all hi life. Once a week he come. Don't say hello to nobody. Don't look at nobody. He come an' sit in John Seegal yard and ask Columbus to sing for 'im. He sit with hi head point up in the air an' lissen to Columbus sing. And when Columbus finish he get up, put a dollar in Columbus shirt pocket and walk off. No hello; no ba-bye; no thank-yuh. The dog!

Deeka brought her hand up to her headwrap and untied it. The hair fell loose. Now they could barely see her face.

He didn only use to sing, he used to cry too, a big belly-cry. A man swimmin in a whole heap o' misery. Nothing worse than a man trap inside a body he don' know what to do with. You could hear him struggling with himself, raging against all that flesh that wasn' serving him. John Seegal used to leave the yard an' come back next morning cuz he couldn take it.

Santay must ha' heard him from all that way up there. One mornin she come here vex as hell an' tell John Seegal, 'He want a woman. Dat's what he want.'

'What make you think he want a woman?' my husban' say.

'A time does come when every man want something to lose 'imself inside,' she say.

'Don't have no woman goin to want my brother,' John Seegal tell her. And he damn vex too becuz he don' like the way that woman talk to him.

'Then show him how,' she say. 'You a man an' he a man – show 'im how to ease 'imself.' And she walk off.

Lord ha' mercy! I never see a man so upset like my husband. He upset for days. But then time pass an' Columbus didn make dat noise no more. In fact he got so quiet, a pusson used to forget that he was there. The only pusson that didn like de change was Josiah, cuz Columbus didn sing for him no more.

Now, I come to the part I want to tell y'all about. Yuh see, the same happiness that make 'im stop singin used to send 'im up in the bushes above my house whole day, 'mongst the nettles, comfortable as you please gathering insect and mumblin to himself. Yunno, holding out hi hand to spider, crickets and whatever else.

One evening he was up there and the sun, after it hide itself away all day, just come out in a big yellow blaze the way it do a lil while ago.

I don' know what make me look up. Mebbe it was something John Seegal was saying to me and he stop sorta sudden. Anyway, I look up and see Columbus up there in the middle of all that sun with a heap o' butterflies flying an' dancing around 'im like a million little candle. An' it bring to mind what long-time people used to say: dat it have a little piece of every yooman soul inside every living thing that crawl or creep or fly. My granny used to say that. She used to say that every one of us got a lil piece of weself inside some creature. A part of we that is not we – like water, like food, like fam'ly. And y'all better don't ask me to explain dat, cuz I jus' tellin y'all what she say.

Is the only part of us that really free, she say. So I figure that if that lil part of Columbus was in a hundred million butterfly 'twas because hi soul did need more light an' air than most of us.

Elena reminded them of the time that she'd taken Peter to the river and he was surrounded by a host of dragonflies. Hers, she said, were ants. She could stand in a nest all day and never get stung by one.

Patty recalled the rain-birds that sang like a Sunday choir on the days Birdie came home, even though he'd gone to jail so often they got fed up with praising his return and went off somewhere to rest for good. That raised a convulsion of laughter from them. Tan Cee's were iguanas – the ones that stood their ground and nodded at her toes like a crowd of wizened old men.

Pynter stirred and turned expectant eyes on them, 'And mine? What'z mine?'

Deeka reached out and stirred the fire. As if prompted by the gesture, Patty did the same. Coxy, who hardly ever spoke, commented on the moon: how round it was, and white like a plate of rice, which made Tan Cee turn and look at him with deep, expressionless eyes.

His grandmother inspected the smoking end of the stick. It seemed to be an extension of her finger. 'Well, I don' see none o' yours tonight. Yuh see ... '

'Watch your mouth, woman!' Tan Cee's back was turned towards the fire.

'Nobody don' know what I was goin to say.'

'Nobody don' want to know. Cuz whatever it was, it wasn' goin to be good.'

Pynter narrowed his eyes and looked up at the sky. He came to his feet. Tan Cee's voice reached over their heads to him, 'S'awright, Sugar. Yours will come to you.'

He stepped out into the night.

He didn't know why he returned straight after, except that he'd looked up at the Mardi Gras often enough to know that bad weather always broke. Deeka was bad weather. Tan Cee knew it. His Aunt Patty did too, and her words to him were strange these days. She too had offered to come to sleep beside him because she didn't like what she was feeling.

He saw the way they moved around him like a pair of shadows, always between himself and the larger, darker shadow of his grandmother. If his mother was concerned, she didn't show it. She was sitting by the fire now, her head in the air, working her mouth around a chicken bone. Her eyes were never on him and Deeka. They were on the stranger that she went to every morning.

Patty lifted her chin at him. His eyes paused on her. Light loved her skin. Like now, it gave a glow to her legs and arms and face. Tan Cee didn't notice him; she was staring at her husband.

Pynter crossed the yard and sat on John Seegal's stone.

Deeka hadn't looked at him till then. The words died in her mouth and something in her nature changed. There was a piece of iron near the steps on which they tethered cockerels when they were harassing the hens too much. He'd often combined his efforts with Peter to try to pull it out, but they could never manage to. Deeka did so with a single movement of the hand.

Tan Cee was on her feet from the moment Deeka moved. It was as if she had felt the tremors in her mother and her body had responded. It was more glide than run that brought her in front of him, her arms spread away from her body as if she were preparing to fly.

He'd risen to his feet much as he would after finishing his dinner. He followed Deeka's movement towards him with a kind of interest and when she halted, the iron uplifted in the air, he had somehow placed himself in front of Tan Cee, his gaze on his grandmother's face as if he'd seen something there that he wanted to get closer to.

It was his mother who stopped the hard, dark shape bearing down on him. It was the movement that Deeka saw at the edge of her vision that made her drop the piece of metal piping on the stones and turn round to face her daughter. For Elena had moved her arm just once – in what looked like a casual, absent-minded gesture – for the old metal bucket they used for scooping out the ashes of the fireside on mornings. Had just as casually reached into the heart of the fire with the empty bucket and scooped it full of burning coals.

The bucket swung on its handle from her right hand, the smoke swirling up and around her arms and spreading itself about her face so that all they saw from the shoulders up was a smoking, shimmering woman shape.

Something – a sound, a choke, a gurgle – issued from Deeka's throat. Her body seemed to drag her away towards one side of the house. Elena, her eyes still on her mother, convulsed her arm and the coals poured out of the bucket in a hissing amber gush back into the fire. She sat down again and crossed her legs – her mouth working around the chicken bone she hadn't paused from chewing.

'Something happm to you in yuh father place. What happm t'you up dere?' Tan Cee was standing over him and breathing hard.

'Nothing happm, Tan.'

'Don't lie fo' me, y'hear me? What happm in your fadder place?' She closed her hand around the flesh of his waist and spun him round. He thought she was going to strike him. He did not understand her rage. Couldn't make sense of her questions.

'You left this yard a different child. What happm to you in Manuel Forsyth place?'

Pynter shook his head, dodging the words she was throwing at him. Elena had come out briefly to take her washing off the stones and gone straight back in. Peter sat on the step, staring at them with a finger in his mouth.

'That woman – yuh granmodder,' Tan Cee's teeth clamped down on the last word as if it were something she was biting into, 'she was coming at you last night. And you – you start walkin towards 'er! Dat make sense? Eh? You think your brodder there would do a thing like that? You know anybody apart from foolish you who do chupidness like that? How come you lose your 'fraid? Why? What happm to you up there?'

She was close to shouting now. 'This,' she said, tightening her hand around his waist, 'is flesh. Flesh is nothing without feeling. Y'hear me? The less you feel, the less flesh you is. The less flesh you is, the more you 'come the spirit yuh granny say you is. Look at me!'

He lifted his eyes and held hers. They were moist and that surprised him. 'You have to learn to feel, y'unnerstan? You have to … ' Her hand released him.

'Tan,' he said, a quiet desperation tugging at his heart. She'd placed herself so far away from him it filled him with a kind of panic. He leaned into her. Stared into her face, his eyes following the curve of her forehead, the way the light settled on her cheek-bones and her chin, the star-apple darkness of her lips. She did not pull away. She did not move to touch him either. 'I feel,' he told her quietly. 'I feel all de time.'

15

FROM THE TIME Elena destroyed John Seegal's stone, it changed something in Deeka Bender. It was as if her daughter had reached a hand inside of her and crushed a wick. And Pynter honestly could not decide which was worse – the breaking of the slab of granite his grandfather used to sit on, or the memory that Deeka carried now, of her own daughter preparing to kill her.

It was the way she was going to do it, Patty said, the certainty of it too: with a bucket of fire in her hand and a gaze so quiet and so terrible it had crept into Patty's dreams and stayed with her, even in her waking. It was the only thing she remembered afterwards, she said – that, and the fact that Elena did not only stop Deeka Bender hard, she almost stopped her dead.

But what a pusson expect? When you kill a pusson for good reason or no reason, you add their weight to yours. Did he know that? For what remained of your life, you carry that pusson weight with you. To kill a child was worse. You add that child's weight ten times over. Why so?

His auntie reached out a hand as if she were rummaging the air for words. Well, for the woman or man that child would ha' become. For each of the children they would ha' given to the world. For the fact that a yooman been could even think of it, far less lift a hand to do it. So that his mother, Elena, reaching for the fire with which to set alight their mother in order to save him, was not a pretty thing to think about o' talk about, but in a way 'twas saving his grandmother from a worse and different kind o' death.

His mother's hammering had dragged them out of sleep next morning. She'd brought a pillow out into the yard, had tied a strap of cloth under her stomach and sat on the earth with the slab of granite between her legs. And with her body curved over it as if she were in prayer, she'd taken the hammer and the chisel that John Seegal left behind, and slowly begun to break it.

The sound of her hammering had followed them throughout the day and far into the night, and then close to morning, with only the fluttering yellow of a masantorch to see by. A slow sound, hollow as a heartbeat, that left Deeka Bender curled up on her bed with her hands wrapped around her stomach as if her daughter were chipping away at her insides.

Pynter had lain with his head pressed against the floorboards, staring beyond the ceiling, his mind drifting past the sound to the memory of the old woman bearing down on him, a metal rod held high, her hand beginning to make a hard dark arc towards his head.

He could still see his aunt, Tan Cee, gliding over the stones with her arms spread wide – like the picture of Christ that Patty the Pretty kept above her bedhead – to place herself before him. He remembered the fizzing in his blood, the tightness in his throat that had pushed his body past her. And the calmness that had come over him, just after. And then Deeka halting suddenly, as if she'd collided with a wall of air, her eyes on the smoking bucket in her daughter's hand; her body dragged towards one side of the house by something more terrible than fear. And suddenly that movement of his mother's hand.

The awful thing he saw in Deeka's eyes had placed a question in his mind. It lived in his head every day until Patty the Pretty offered him an answer. She told him it was love.

'Love?' he said quietly.

There wasn't another word for it, she said. Or if there was, it was too big a word to fit inside a single person's head, which was why it was so simple. The smile was there, as always, on her face.

'Love.' He'd worked his lips around the word as if to get beneath the sound and taste its meaning.

It was one of his mother's last words in her leaf letters to Pa. She'd written it just once, carefully, properly – scratched along the spine of a desiccated leaf. A fragment. A little island on its own without other words to lean against and give it sense.

Love. He'd heard that same word differently in Eden. That time it came leaping from Miss Petalina's throat, stronger than the thunderings of Missa Geoffrey: a scream that was a sob, that was a sigh, that was a laugh, that was also none of these. It had come out of her so high and bright it made him think of dragonflies taking to the air.

That word had also brought to mind one of Uncle Michael's poems, its five lines stacked one on top of the other like the fingers of a hand.

> *where will this loving lead us?*
> *on my left soft breasts of sand*
> *at my feet the dark rocks stand*
> *splitting the teeth*
> *of breakers*

It made him think of his grandmother, Deeka Bender, standing with her three daughters on the top of Glory Cedar Rise, calling out his grandfather's name as he walked towards the dark waters of the swamps. It tugged at the edges of the sadness he felt on Wednesday nights when his auntie's husband, Coxy Levid, got to his feet, slipped his fingers across his crotch and left her sitting in the yard, staring at her knees.

'Love?' He angled his head away from Patty, his eyes sliding over to the place where John Seegal's stone used to be. 'Then – then, who, who love more, Tan Patty? Somebody prepare to kill fo' you or somebody prepare to dead fo' you?'

She looked at him strangely, her face gone still, her eyes glowing in the evening sun like strips of glass. 'Which is de better love? That what you mean?'

'Don' know what I mean,' he said.

Her hand shot out and pulled a leaf. She held it in the flat of her palm in front of him. Her fingers were trembling slightly. 'This,' she said, slipping her thumb along the surface, 'is your Aunt Tan Cee, and this … ' She flipped the leaf over. Now he could see the darkly veined underside, a deeper green. 'This is your modder. Same leaf, come from de same tree. Love to kill for, love to dead for – same love.'

She placed a finger against the hollow of his throat, looked into his eyes. 'That not what you really askin, though. Not so?'

He did not answer her because the word was not enough. It did not explain his mother leaving secretly on mornings to go to the stranger in that place down by the river. It could not explain the rage that slept beneath her skin, which had always been there, like a hole in the middle of the yard that they'd grown so accustomed to they'd learned to step around it without thinking. That sleeping anger made him think of the serpents he used to look up at in Eden, their slow uncoiling, the blind flickering at the air with tongues as bright as flames as they eased their dark lengths towards the lizard or the bird they were about to consume. When they struck, it was always fast and hard and frightening. His grandmother had forgotten this, and look … Look what nearly happm … Forgettin' almos' kill 'er. Which was why he could never tell his mother that he knew the place she went to early mornings. That even if he hadn't met the stranger she went to, he was certain that he wasn't from these parts. That he was slimmer than the men of Old Hope. Could make things with his hands that were just as strange and beautiful as what Patty made from straw and bits of coloured cloth. That when he, Pynter, looked at her sometimes and felt the stirrings of the stranger's child in her, it reminded him of the sea.

It puzzled him that the other women in the yard could not see these things: how slowly his mother walked these days, how carefully she sat down on her stone now; how she combed her growing hair more often. The way she sang to herself throughout the day, and whistled like a bird. Her skin had changed the way the leaves of a candlebush did over time: smoother, shinier, almost as pretty as Patty's. And from time to time, without thinking, she lifted her hand to touch the little throbbing vein at the base of her throat, which hadn't been there before.

A couple of mornings ago, he'd raised his head to look at her and found her large, quiet eyes settled on his face with the softness of a moth. He also saw the trembling sadness in his mother's face, because now she was dead in Deeka's mind.

Mornings, she made a cup of cocoa, covered it with a saucer and placed it beside his grandmother. It sat on the step till afternoon, curdling at the top as the heat got sucked out of it. At the end of the day, Elena would go to the step, lift the cup and stare at the contents as if she were hoping it would speak to her. Then she would go to the back of the house and tip it into the soil. She hung there a while, looking down at the moisture at her feet before sighing heavily and walking back into the house.

Dinnertimes, she served her mother first, her hand bringing the end of her cotton dress to the enamel of the bowl and polishing it till it threw the flames back at them.

Deeka would not take the outstretched bowl of food. She watched them eat, her body a soft shape against the steps. Then, if she felt like it, she would strip a square of banana leaf from the tree beside the house, bend over the pot and serve herself.

It did not change his mother's gestures. It did not modify the stillness in her eyes, now down-turned all the time, her face fuller than they'd ever seen it, her shoulders lower than she'd ever held them.

She did these same things every day: the cup of steaming cocoa, the brightly polished bowl of food, the tireless, wordless gestures. And when she spoke, she addressed her mother softly, as if she were trying to ease her out of an awful dream.

Sundays were worse. His mother's hands were restless from the time she woke. For she'd been washing and braiding Deeka's hair since she was a girl. The task had fallen to her, they said, for reasons no one cared to remember. And anyway, it wasn't that which mattered now. What mattered was that after all these years, grooming her mother's hair had become more than habit. It had become a knowledge that had settled in her body. For Elena understood her mother's head of hair far better than she did her own. Her fingers had pulled at the very first strands of grey there. Deeka had blamed her in part for it, pointing to the time she'd brought her 'belly' home and would not name the father. And with the passing of the years, the rest of Deeka's hair had whitened beneath Elena's fingers.

Come Sundays, without Deeka's bony shoulders against her stomach, without the small pressure of her mother's head against her chest, it left Elena Bender with a hollowness and empty gestures. Her hands still did the things they'd always done on Sundays: the same slow downward strokes, the straightening and the parting; the plaiting and the oiling; the raising of the shine with coconut oil mixed with cinnamon grass and mint. Come Sundays, his mother's hands had nothing solid to hold on to.

Pynter had seen this before: the way his father in his blindness would reach for his Bible, or turn his eyes towards something he expected to see. He remembered in his own self the way he sometimes turned his ear towards a voice, or leaned his head away from it, the better to know its owner – forgetting that he possessed eyes.

The body remembered things the head had long forgotten. He knew that now. The body felt things it did not even know it did. Like his mother's inside-crying; like her fingers combing the empty air before her. Like what not grooming his grandmother's hair reminded them of now: that they carried another blood. First People blood. The blood of strangers who'd once resided on the small blue hills above the Kalivini Sea; who used to live on fish and leaves and fruits; and whose voices, Deeka told them once, still carried across the sleepy waters of lagoons. They'd left nothing of themselves behind apart from the pieces of patterned clay he sometimes found lying at the edges of the sea. That and the length and glow of his grandmother's plaited hair.

Evenings, they looked down at their plates or found their eyes wandering across the silence towards the soft dark question mark that was Deeka's shape against the steps. Not expectant, not even sorrowful or upset, just wondering what a pusson was s'posed to do after dinner done. Deeka Bender's voice had filled in all their after-dinner silences from as far back as their minds could take them; and further still if they 'lowed themselves to think about it.

Make it worse, in the silence that she'd left them with, something secretive and wordless had crept in and taken over. Or maybe it had always been there; but now there was nothing else to turn a pusson mind away from it: that tense, uneasy thing between his aunt, Tan Cee, and her husband, Coxy Levid, which lived at the back of every word they said to each other, especially on Wednesday nights.

These evenings, his auntie no longer brought her hands down to the hem of her dress to pull at the threads that weren't there when her husband told her he was walking. She did not shift her eyes beyond him and flick her tongue across her lips to moisten them. Instead, she would stir, look up at him and raise her voice loud enough for all to hear her.

'People buildin houses in de night?'

The first time she spoke that way, her words had stopped the cigarette halfway to her husband's mouth.

He didn't turn to look at her, but even from his end of the yard, Pynter felt the rush of anger in the man. It never reached his face though. It never got that far. He was looking down at her and smiling. And the words he spoke slipped through the small gap that his smile made.

'P'raps in the place where dis man going, people do,' he said.

He'd closed his lips down on the cigarette and turned to leave. But her voice came at him again, steady and soft and stroking. 'Ain't got no night-time where you going, then?'

Patty's hands left her knees and began tugging at her ear lobes. His mother reached for a stick and poked it into the fire. She pulled it back and turned the burning tip towards her face. Held it there a while, meditating on the living amber at the tip. Then she tossed the whole thing back into the fire.

'How far you goin dis time, den?' Tan Cee coaxed.

'S'far as man foot take him.'

'And how far'z dat?'

The frown lines on his face got deeper. There was a glitter in his eyes. It sent Pynter's mind back to that night when those eyes had looked into his face. When the long brown fingers now stroking the red box of Phoenix cigarettes had closed around his throat; had pinned his back against a tree and made him know how easy killing was.

Now, though, his auntie's voice seemed to match her husband's face exactly. It raised the hairs on his arms because it was so soft, so steady, came so easily out of her.

She'd turned her chin up towards him, the firelight like yellow water dancing on her throat. It hollowed out her eyes and filled in the rest of her face so that she was a different person altogether. And there was a small smile on her lips.

'So you ain't got no time, then? That what you sayin?'

Coxy didn't answer her.

She lowered her face then, turned her gaze down to the stones. 'Watch how you walkin, fella. Just watch yuh step.' But Coxy Levid didn't hear her, he was halfway down the hill.

The gradual hardening in his aunt, Tan Cee; the sleepy desperation Patty the Pretty carried; the smell that crept into his nostrils, reminding him of the odours of the swamplands his grandfather had walked into; the dream he had been having every night for weeks in which he watched the darkening of the Mardi Gras mountain by the shadow of a bird. If he ever said these things, it would prove he was a Jumbie Boy, prove that he was like Santay, the woman who had given him back his eyes and was here now to see him.

The sight of her had raised the hairs on Pynter's arms. Santay walked over to him, reached a hand towards his face.

'S'awright, Osan,' she had said, 'you been on my mind.'

His mother went inside the house, came out with a bowl of unshelled peas and began to pick at them. Santay talked of weather, corn and cane, and the new illnesses that Old Hope women had been bringing her. The New Year had something to do with it, she said. Didn they see how it begin? Nice an' bright, like a basin full of promise – her eyes rested briefly on his mother – but when that basin finally tipped over, what did it give them? Politics. But she didn come to talk about no politics, she said. Wasn't that which bring her here. She been sent here by a dream. In her dreams, she said, one of Deeka Bender's daughters was sitting on John Seegal's stone. And on that stone there were birds and watermelons and the daughter's feet were in a puddle of rainwater. Trouble was, the daughter's back was towards her and she couldn't figure out which one of them it was, even if that dream came back to her four nights in a row.

Santay fixed the women with dark, interrogating eyes. A pus-son didn't mean to look inside nobody business, but was any of them with child?

His mother's fingers were busy with the bowl of peas that she was picking clean of chaff. Patty the Pretty's hands drifted down towards her stomach. Her eyes grew soft and large and something like a smile spread across her body. 'Oh God,' Patty muttered softly and sat down on the steps.

Tan Cee muttered something, or perhaps it was her lips that trembled slightly, and Deeka Bender, who'd greeted the woman with a silent, flat-eyed gaze, turned her back on them and walked into the house. They could hear the brushing of her feet against the floorboards.

Yes, the woman said, resting her eyes on Patty. Santay's fingers reached for the knot of her headtie and loosened it. Tan Cee's hand reached out and fingered the flattened plaits and she began to unplait her hair.

Water was woman, Santay said. The child was going to be a girl. And that child ought to bring a lot of light into their days. The birds around the woman's feet told her that.

And one more thing. She shifted her head away from Tan Cee's hand. Call the baby anything but … Her voice trailed off, and there was something new and different in her eyes. Would it be askin too much to add Adiola to the baby's name? It was her name, she said, an old name, one that her mother had passed on to her. Every girl-chile in her family had carried it from time, and though she never used it, she did not want that name to die. Was that askin too much?

Patty shook her head and smiled. The lines around the woman's mouth relaxed. Tan Cee touched Patty's arm. 'Lordy,' Patty said, and again more softly, 'Lord ha' mercy, girl – I … '

Patty's chuckle cut across her words like the tinkling of bracelets.

16

THERE WERE THOSE February evenings when night settled like a sheet over the valley; when the darkness was so thick it felt like something a person could wade into. The air was quiet and chilly, brittle like glass. They could hear the river in the valley below slipping over every pebble. If bad weather was about to break, the suck and surge of waves forcing themselves through the caves along the seashore would reach them as if they were just there, butting against their doorsteps.

Hemmed by the after-dinner fires, with the darkness rising up towards them, it was easy to believe that they were sitting on a raft and what lay below them was a tossing, living ocean licking at their feet.

It was the only time that Deeka Bender talked to them of things that were not about John Seegal. She spoke of the glittering black sand beaches of the north where she came from, of Atlantic breakers as tall as ships, collapsing at the feet of cliffs so high their foam looked like white lacing on a deep-blue dress. It was from the lip of one of those precipices that the pure-blood of her people – the first humans on these islands – had launched themselves and left the earth for good.

She would wonder at the puzzling and unnameable things that traversed the world: roads that ran beneath the earth and carried cars and people; machines that sat on air the way a man would sit on solid earth; buildings so tall a pusson could stand on one, reach up and stir a cloud. And as the evening folded its skirts around them, her talk returned to Old Hope.

She would tell them of the year the snakes arrived – snakes that didn have no right or reason to spoil a proper New-Years-After-Christmas season. It didn't make no sense. In the season of parched corn and smoked ham, of sorrel and hard-dough bread, and black cakes so packed with fruit and rum a pusson got drunk just from smelling them, it was the last thing that a pusson expected.

And 'twas not as if a pusson didn do what they was s'posed to do. They'd greeted the New Year with fresh curtains. They'd laid the floors with sheets of linoleum as bright as flower gardens. They'd stained and polished the mahogany chairs they rarely ever sat on. Had indulged the children with sips of the dark sweet wine smuggled in from Kara Isle, and laughed their heads off as the spirits took hold of the lil ones and threw them about the yard, grinning foolishly at everyone while they fought to reclaim their limbs.

But still them snakes came! The first sign of them in Old Hope was the part of themselves they left behind: shimmering silvery stockings as delicate as a child's communion veil. A pusson found these stockings everywhere: in tight tangles between the grasses, fluttering high on branches where the wind hung them up for all to see. At the door-mouths to their houses.

And 'twas all right to watch those flimsy white stockings blowing everywhere, until a pusson find out which snake they belong to. Crebeaux – those night-dark creatures that most yoomans live a lifetime without seeing, that didn live on trees like any decent-minded snake ought to, but in the twisted arteries of the earth, in the lightless hollows under stones and forest-root, in the dampness of ravines that never felt a direct ray of sun. Snakes that didn crawl but flowed away from them like oil.

And, of course, they started killing them.

But then the girl arrived, if a girl is what she was. She was short and muscled like a man, with a yellow ring around the iris of each eye, exactly like a bird's. They remembered how she placed herself before the machete-swinging arms of men and would not let them kill these creatures, how she slipped an arm beneath the snakes and guided their heads towards the holes and crevices they came from, the way they flowed along the skin of her arms as if she were pouring them out of herself. And word of her presence in Old Hope had stopped the men from raising their machetes, for she'd spread something far deeper than fear or panic in their hearts.

She'd made them ask themselves: what if 'twas someone somewhere in Old Hope who'd done or dreamed up something awful that had given shape to her? What if she might be some woman living right here 'mongst them and some wicked deed had reshaped her?

You see, Deeka said, there were birds and creatures with wings as wide as sails amongst them. There were Old Hope men, as ancient as the canes, who became balls of living fire in the night, crept through the cracks of houses and sipped the blood from the softest parts of women's thighs. There were cakes a pusson found in the middle of Old Hope Road some time between midnight and no-time. You saw them there, laid out nice as any wedding cake, with icing too-besides. They smelt like cakes; they looked like cakes. But you cut them and drew blood.

There were people who were so fed up of dying, she said, they discarded their bodies like old clothing and took over those of youngsters. And a pusson wouldn't even mention them long-dressed wimmen of the night who waited for drunken, drifting men at crossroads. A fella saw her back first, curved like a spoon, then her hair spilling down her shoulders like dark water. She cooed his name. He followed her. And that jackass would not see her cloven hoof until she raised a leg to kick him down a precipice. In fact, a lotta man who walk when night-time come don't end up overseas. Is precipice they get kick over, which is why you never hear from them again.

And what about the unborn children that the wimmen of these cane valleys refused to bring into this world? You listened hard enough at night, you heard these half-borns whispering against the doorways of all the childless wimmen. And then there were those who had no right to be amongst them, who sneaked their way into the world behind a true-born. But God make it so their time was never long with yoomans.

It was what people said that raised the agitation in Deeka's voice, this shu-shuing, these river-wimmen whisperings, this fly-buzz of ugly words that had attached themselves to the Bender name about children with eyes like flames. Who walked the night when the world outside was quietest. Who needed no light to see by, becuz them eyes carry their own inside-shining. They conversed with ghosts, spoke the language of bats and owls and, according to the talk, knew of things before they happened.

Matter o' fact, those who lived in houses beside the road said they often heard them in the deepest, darkest of all nights. Nights a lil bit like this one, in fact. They hear them whistling – soft an' pretty – like a rain-bird calling down the clouds. And if a pusson brave enough to put one eye against a crack in their house wall, they sometimes saw the white glow of a shirt, but they never heard the footsteps.

Pynter's feet took him down towards the river. In his head he carried Patty's laughter, his mother's hand over the basin of pigeon peas, and the parting words that Santay whispered in his ear.

When she'd finished talking to the women, she'd come over to him. This time he'd allowed her thumbs to pull against his lower lids. His eyes, she said, were getting darker now. Was he eating the things she'd told him to? Was he still partial to fish? Then she'd brought her lips closer to his ear and her voice turned cocoa-dark and soft inside his head. 'Watch that face o' yours, Osan. It don' know how to lie.'

He knew where he was going; he hadn't worked out why. He did not know what he would say to the stranger his mother met down there. He did not know what he looked like, apart from the print his body had made on the bed of leaves he'd left there. A slim man, heavier than his size suggested, a man who had placed a caul of secrecy over his mother. Who'd brought on a furtiveness in her that he could not understand.

He hadn't been looking. He hadn't followed her. His mother wouldn't believe him when he told her that. He'd been following his eyes.

There was a dark patch of green that began where the cane fields ended. His feet had taken him there because, whatever the time of day, and however bright the sunlight, it never seemed to change.

It was much further than he thought and when he arrived it was cool and strange. The trees laid their shadows along the riverbank the way the women spread their clothing on the river stones. He'd found himself standing at the mouth of a long leaf cavern through which the river slowed then slipped like a snake entering its hole.

It was not like Eden. Here the light made him think of smoke, not water. The earth was softer too, and darker. The riverbank yielded to his weight as if to ease him down into itself. And the oddest of all things, he could smell the sea as if it were right at his feet.

He'd stood for a long time at the mouth of that river tunnel, expecting something but not knowing exactly what. Finally, beneath the tick-ticking of dry leaves, the shifting of the branches above his head, the sighing of the water at his feet, he heard then saw what moved about him: crabs – blue as fallen fragments of sky, their finned legs flat and white like those that lived beside the sea. He watched them slip sideways into the water and swim away like fish. Flat-tailed iguanas nodded at him from branches. The silver backs of fish – long and sleek as conger eels – ghosted past his eyes. Flies bright as sparks were settling on his naked arms and nibbling at his skin; and crayfish, large and transparent as the glasses in his mother's cabinet, drifted along the edges of the water.

It had taken him a long time just standing on the soft mud bank to work it out. That in this little forest, so far away from the shoreline, the sea was also present. That it had crept into these animals and changed them, the way yeast did Uncle Birdie's bread. The way his mother's secret child was changing her.

It suddenly came to him that this land, this valley, this place he was born in, carried more secrets than all the washerwomen in all the rivers in the world. And he found himself laughing – at what he did not know. He stood on the water's edge and shouted down the long leaf gloom, shouted Birdie's name and then his Uncle Michael's. He said everything he wanted to say to Deeka Bender, including what a bad-minded, wicked so-an'-so she was. He called John Seegal Bender a son-a-va-biiitch and liked the sound of it so much he said it eight more times. And still he wasn't satisfied, so he told John Seegal what a foolish fool he was to walk, and lose 'imself in swamp mud, and leave his wimmen with so much don'-know-what-dey-want-to-do confusion. He'd cackled at the dark ahead of him and stuck his tongue out at Old Hope, danced and stomped on the riverbank and dared the soft, wet mud to suck him in. Then he'd called his father's name and felt himself go quiet.

He was tired when he left, and so pleased with the puzzle that place had left him with he decided that he would take it to Peter just to watch his brother's face go funny-an'-twist-up when he told him that the sea was not just water, the sea was also soil.

He'd taken the shorter walk back home through the bamboo forest. It was one of those days when the bamboos talked amongst themselves, sounding as if they were grumbling to each other. And it was there, just above the river, at the far end of the high leaf houses the bamboo made, that he found the little room.

The stranger wasn't there but he'd left his smell of cinnamon and cloves and the print of his body on the leaves where he slept.

The traces of his mother were there too – not love leaves this time but the yellow vines that did not grow on soil but tied themselves around the canes and suckled on their sap. She'd made her curlicues and scratches almost like the signatures that he and Peter had left on her stomach. Against the trunk of a bamboo, just where he thought the man would place his head to sleep, was a string of beads. They were spotted black in places, like little ladybirds. He'd picked them up and brought them to his nostrils, and knew at once that the hands of the man had made them.

His mother was standing over the fire when he returned. She lifted her head to say something to him, but her lips froze over the words. Her eyes were on the chain of ladybirds around his neck.

He expected her to come at him straight away. He did not expect the quiet turning back towards her cooking, the casual sideways glances thrown at him from time to time; the gradual hardening of her movements with the pot spoon. It didn't look like anger; it did not look like any emotion that he knew.

He was oiling the wheels of Peter's scooter when her shadow fell over him. He hadn't heard her coming. His head was still turned down, his hand spinning the metal wheels, when he felt her hand brush his collar. When he looked up, the beads were in her fist and she was staring hard into his face.

He stood up, wiped the grease on his trousers and faced her. Something in her eyes retreated briefly; but then she leaned in suddenly towards him.

'You! You! What wrong with you?' It came out as a whisper. Like a secret they were sharing.

'Not me,' he said, his voice tight and urgent, and strange to his own ears. The thing that had stuffed his throat all morning, that had sent him down to the river to that leafy room, that had made him place the string of beads around his neck, seemed suddenly

145

to free itself. He stepped back from her; looked over to Patty, sleepy-eyed and smiling, with her chin on Leroy's shoulder. 'Look,' he said, 'look what you gone and done.'

He looked into her eyes and held her gaze, did it because Tan Cee always told him that to hold an adult's gaze like that was downright freshness. He curled his lips around the words, and what came out of him was more air than sound. 'Who you tink you foolin, eh?'

He felt her movement before she struck him, felt his head go dizzy, but he did not drop his gaze. She hit him again, and because he did not move, because he did not run away from her like Tan Cee told him he was s'posed to, the flat of her hand exploded against his face again.

His mother was breathing hard. She was staring at her hands now, and shaking her head as if she'd just discovered them. And when she lifted her eyes, her mouth was working around words that did not come. She dropped the beads. She said something. She called his name. Called his name again. Reached out an open hand towards him. He stepped back. Kept stepping back from her. And when he could step back no further, he turned around and ran.

17

WHAT COULD MAKE a pusson hit a child so hard that they could make them blind again? Where all dat wickedness come from, eh? And what about the nice new school that he jus' begin to go to? What left for him to do? How come God always givin chilren to people who does maltreat dem so bad? Eh?

A pusson want to know dat. A pusson want to know how come and why?

Patty's crying came from some further, darker place inside herself. That was what it felt like when she came down to the yard next morning. The song in her voice had dried up. She'd gone deaf to Leroy's pleading to come home and rest herself. She greeted no one. She aimed her questions at the air.

She said these same words over and over again, in different ways, her voice coming from every corner of the yard. His young aunt's words seemed to push Elena towards him – slowly, awkwardly like a child that did not trust its feet. He would feel the heaviness she carried now; the fumbling uncertainty with which his mother tried to speak to him or touch him. But Patty always drove her back with words.

What she wan' to touch 'im for?

Is hit she goin hit 'im again?

Is beat she goin beat 'im up again?

She wan' to murder 'im this time?

His mother left the yard and did not return till evening. Pynter heard the dragging of her feet on the asphalt road below before it went so quiet it felt as if he were the only person left in Old Hope.

After his mother struck him, he'd taken his rage all the way down to the river. He'd returned to that place of crayfish and iguanas where the sea had crept into the soil and changed them. His head was still throbbing from the blow. His mother had thrown her weight behind it; and something in his head had been knocked back hard and it had not righted itself. His body told him so. On his way down to the river, he'd tried to walk in a straight line and found he could not do it. The road beneath his feet seemed to want to shake him off. He'd stood on the bank and looked down into the darkness of the long leaf tunnel that hung over the water, and when he looked back towards the bamboos and the light, the world had suddenly dimmed and he could hear the hollow snoring of the winds above the Mardi Gras.

The sun still hot on his skin, and his limbs feeling even looser now, he'd drifted back to the yard. He'd sat on his stone, brought his hand to his face and stared at it. His mother's hand had sent him blind again.

All he could think of was his friend Arilon and the moon. Old Hope used to call Ari Crab-Hands until he, Pynter, made him change the way he used them. When they asked his friend to stretch out his fingers, Arilon would refuse. He hadn't always been like that. Arilon became that way after his mother left their pretty red and blue house one early Saturday morning. She told him she was going shopping in San Andrews with her new man-friend, and ended up in Trinidad.

There was going to be a full moon tonight. He would have gone up to Glory Cedar Rise with Arilon, sat on the fallen tree up there and watched it rise and burst above the Mardi Gras. They would have looked up at the dark shapes on the branches of the glory cedar trees and argued over the amount of birds there were above their heads. They would have talked about Gideon, Paso and Miss Maddie – Paso's mother – the old woman who was s'posed to be his and Peter's sister. He would have told Arilon about his Uncle Michael, who'd drowned and left all of his inside-self between the pages of a ragged book. Pynter would have recited the words of Michael's poems, wanting his friend to also live that part of the life that his brother Peter had never had with their father.

Arilon would have asked him about the new school he'd won the scholarship to in San Andrews, and he would have told him again of the building that sat on a small hill just above the mouth of a volcano which the ocean had flowed into and made into a lagoon, which was why o' course that lagoon had no bottom.

Arilon liked to hear him talk about the yachts coming in on evenings, with pale half-naked men and women whose eyes were exactly like his own – yachts slipping along the path of light the sun made, like giant white-winged birds. He would have told his friend about the lady teacher who leaned so closely into him he could smell her armpits. If they'd gone up there, with a full moon over them, he would have pointed at the silver rope that was the horizon along the far edge of the ocean.

He would not let them touch him. Not even Tan Cee. He did not want Santay to take him to her house again.

He asked for noni leaves and candlebush, and the sap of aloe vera. He fed himself on fruits, and the leaves of the plants he described to Arilon. He sat through whole nights in the yard, went in to lie down on the floor on mornings. And when he woke, Arilon would be out there waiting on the steps. Pynter would sit with him for most of the day, talking of the things they were going to do when he started to see again.

And with the passing of the time, Pynter slept less, ate more of the oily, soft-fleshed fish he asked for, brought the sap of aloe vera to his eyes less often. He came out of the house earlier each evening, and wanted to know when there was going to be a moon.

They moved around him like a crowd of drifting ghosts. Nights, he heard the footsteps of Tan Cee on the stones before she lowered herself beside him and placed her lips against his left ear. And with a voice so tobacco-dark and soft he barely recognised it, his aunt said that if he loved himself half as much as she did him, he would stay with them, with her. If she had her way, she would pour all the remaining life she had into him. Did he know that? Did he? Did he know that when he came she'd lost the wish for children? She could've done like his mother, Elena, if she wanted to. Could've gone off and proved the fault was not with her. Same way that 'twas not with Patty either. It was the men that life had brought them. That was why a pusson couldn't blame Elena for doing it a different way. God gave her eyes for men who carried life inside their loins.

She'd spoken of her husband, and of a kind of loving that sounded more like hate. The tearing that the men who walked at night always left behind them. Until a woman couldn take the tearin no more. Like Miss Anna-Jo, who made a powder of the bottle that her baby drank from, mixed it in her cookin and fed her man to death because all dis night-time walkin, this leavin and returnin in the mornin with the smell of some other woman on him, all this been strippin her down, strippin her right to the bone.

And did he know why? Becuz wimmen like Miss Anna-Jo was different. They was like Deeka, like Miss Edwina who went crazy coupla months ago. They was like her, Tan Cee. They couldn't find a way to let a man inside themself then let him out so easy. He become part of what make blood-an'-bone – lovin 'im so hard same time that you hatin 'im for the hold he got on you. For findin the kind o' comfort in some other woman he make you feel you can't provide. For feelin that woman you never seen in the movement of his body, specially them hardly-come-at-all times when he reach out a hand and turn you over.

It didn't always use to be like that, she whispered. There were those early days of slipping through the back window of her father's house at night; of concealing their night-time meetings from John Seegal – the terror and the trembling while waiting in the shadow of some roadside tree for Coxy Levid, before the lightness and the lift that came from just seeing him arrive.

Coxy Levid didn't build houses. He made them. The way a careful child would shape a spinning top; the way Patty brought a bit of broken bottle to a piece of wood and made a perfect face with it. In fact, it was Coxy Levid's way with wood that first drew her eyes to him.

It was that house she'd seen on her way to the canes at the lower end of Old Hope. It appeared on a hill above the road one morning, just so, and began to take shape at the hands of a man who sat way up there astride the frame, his back against the sky, a cigarette glued to his lips, cutting, measuring, driving nails.

After a while he noticed her. She knew because he made his measuring more deliberate, his way with wood more precious. It made perfect sense that she should begin to want him, because by then a certainty had settled in her heart that no man could build a house so perfect if he wasn't like that inside.

They married in their own way. Just Coxy and her: he smiling all the time; she gripped stiff with the fear of her father, even if John Seegal would never have found them in that quiet lil bay in the shadow of a cliff that people called The Silent, with the seagulls as their witness and the waves their congregation.

She remembered the light. Remembered the way it came down from the sky and settled on the water: pink, like the inside of a conch shell. Like the colour of church windows. She'd taken his hand in marriage but she never took his name. And it was exactly a year before her secret slipped from her. She said it to her mother and her sisters two days after they stood on Glory Cedar Rise and watched John Seegal walk into the Kalivini swamplands.

Tan Cee said the same things to him every night, her agitation beating against his ear like the flutterings of a moth, and at the end of it, she would lean away from him, preparing herself for those last words she always left him with. She wanted his understanding in advance, for this thing her mind kept turning her towards. This growin, worryin thing that gone and creep inside her head and would not go away because it did not want to. And if, if he could not give her his understanding, at least, she wanted his forgiveness in advance.

A thin skein of drizzle was drifting down the Mardi Gras the morning they saw Pynter rise to his feet. The water had settled on the soft matting of his hair. His skin was glistening like the bark of a June-plum tree. Holy Rain they called it, this God-spray – this feathering of water from the mountain that fanned the sunlight out above their heads, softened the shapes of rocks and trees and left a glow on everything.

They followed his climb up to Glory Cedar Rise, all legs and arms and shifting torso, his slingshot slung around his neck like a rubber noose. They watched until he was no more than a shape against all that sky up there, lifting the Y of his catapult, his left arm flexing and unflexing, his whole body a living arrow with a single barb.

Tan Cee called them up there later. The shudder in her voice was all they needed to send them hurrying after her. Up there they could look down and see everything that lay beyond Old Hope. The wind was strong enough to snatch away a person's voice and fling it down the hillside. Strewn across the carpet of decaying glory cedar leaves – like a scattering of feathered fruits – were birds: hill doves, brown and soft as innocence, johnny birds and pipirits and pikayoos. Ramiers – normally made grey by flight and distance – now glistened like polished slate around their feet. Cattle egrets, so white their wings threw back the light like mirrors, hummingbirds – little scraps of fallen rainbow – and cee-cee birds and johnny-heads and blackbirds. Each of them knocked out of the sky. Each of them lying on the earth with shattered eyes.

Deeka made a hammock of her skirt and sat amongst the carcasses, shaking her head. Did they know? Did they know that long-time people, her people, used to believe that birds were the eyes of God? Did they know that? Eh?

She turned her gaze up at the glory cedar trees, their dark wind-hardened branches arched by age and time. 'He must've hear me say it,' she muttered. 'But I – I don' remember sayin it. I don' ... '

She came to her feet and brushed the dead leaves off her dress. She turned towards Elena, taking in her daughter's swelling shape, her eyes gone dull with malice. 'You won't touch 'im again,' she said. The words bubbled out of Deeka's throat like oil. 'He come through you; but he never was your child.'

She turned her face up to the trees again, placed a toe against a bird and turned it over with her foot. 'He vex,' she breathed. 'He vex to kill.' And then, softly, wonderingly, 'S'like he know hi time comin soon. So he quarrellin wit' God.'

BOOK TWO

Hands

18

THE CANE-CUTTING season, the long, hot months they called the Stretch, brought with it the kind of labour that deadened the eyes and numbed the tongue. All Tan Cee's night-time whisperings in Pynter's ear, after his mother's hand had sent him blind again, were sopped away by tiredness.

It was two years since Birdie had left and these were the months they missed him most. They were the months of lowered voices and half-said things, when children tiptoed around the tempers of their parents. Evenings were reduced to grunts and gestures, and that smouldering far-eyed gaze that fixed itself on nothing in particular.

They came home each evening smelling of the heat and straw down there. They would try to wash the day away with bucketfuls of water tipped from high above their heads, scrubbing and scrubbing, but the day would remain with them. It stuck to their breaths and came out in their utterings over dinner. There was Lana's man who was about to walk and, hard as he tried, that long-face dog could not hide it. All a pusson had to do was watch the way he didn laugh with nobody no more. And that new-and-fancy sweetman walk he practising, never mind the crossing and uncrossing of them bow legs of his. As if a pusson didn know that he watchin 'imself in some fancy, freeze-up place in England or America. As if!

And right now in the middle of the Stretch, Pinny found herself with child. And her trouble was the trouble of every woman who ever worked the canes – to lift the heavy bundles above her head and hand them to the loaders as if the baby was not there. There was no other way to do it, no easier way to carry cane. It would mean that in a coupla weeks, it really wouldn be there no more. Or she could make the choice that was hardly one at all: leave the canes, live on less or nuffing, and let the baby live. And did they notice that that McKinley foreman fella was makin eyes at Myna's girl-chile, who body only just begin to say things that she herself don' unnerstan? They must keep their eyes on her as often as the work allowed. But like all them years before, however close they kept to her, McKinley was sure to find some way. Knowing she didn have no father or brother or uncle there to make him feel the hard part of a machete. Knowing that as long as this valley shifted under the weight of cane and he counted their money every week, he would get away with murder.

They talked as if it were their fault; as if it were for them to find the answer to this botheration they'd been carrying all their lives. And this year there was more trouble. They hadn't realised it then, but it had started with the man who came to them a couple of years before, dressed in brightly polished leather shoes and a nicely ironed shirt. He'd arrived in a jeep and given them a different way to plant the canes. He wanted them to place the rows much closer than it made sense to do. He'd lost his temper when they told him what this meant: more borer worms, more of the skin-eating cow-itch plants making beds of themselves in there. And certainly more of the useless love vines that looked like flames and fed on the sap of canes. He didn't even allow them time to mention the trouble they would have cutting through the tangle.

They'd planted more sugar cane on less soil. And with the land they were left with, they were told to cut more roads. Later in the year, when the plants were shoulder-high, the truck with chemicals came to kill the borer worms and the flaming yellow vines. But it was when the green machines with wheels that turned like mills arrived at the start of the cutting season that they understood the reason for those roads. They replaced the men. They spat out the canes in mutilated heaps behind them. Now everyone was struggling to keep up with the thundering machines, while the men stood by and watched them kill off in half an hour the job it took them all of a day to do. The machines cut, a few men trimmed, the women packed and lifted. McKinley argued it was less work. At the end of each week, he looked at the heaps, turned his eyes up at the sky, guessed the exact amount of sugar that must be lost given the heat of the sun that day, the amount of rain that didn't fall and whatever else his mood or mind came up with. Then he cut their pay accordingly.

Pynter looked up from his dinner one evening, uncrossed his legs and glanced over at Peter. His brother was humming to himself while eating. 'Tomorrow,' Pynter said, 'you come to Top Hill wiv me?'

Peter threw a sideways glance at him. 'Fuh what?'

'When you come, I show you.'

'S'awright.'

'S'awright, no; or s'awright, yes – which one?'

'It depend.' His brother licked his fingers and resumed his humming.

Peter was as their father had said he would be: broader hands and a fuller body, with muscles that had already begun to fill his shoulders.

'Depend on what?' Pynter felt the irritation rising in his throat. He swallowed hard on it.

During all these evenings of the women returning home, preparing dinner and handing them their plates, he'd been wanting something different from his brother. He wanted to offer him a feeling – an emotion that nobody in the world apart from their nephew, Paso, had been able to put the proper words to. He wanted to let him have that portion of the ache and desperation that was due him. To have Peter also put his hand around this thing his teacher told him in his school above the ocean.

Pynter slipped his hand behind him, unstuck the handle of his slingshot from his waist and dropped it at his brother's feet. 'You come wiv me, I give you this.'

Night was already settling like a fine coating of dust on the furthest slopes, but here where they stood on the summit of Top Hill, the last of the evening sun still left daubs of honey on leaves and bark and branches. They could see the foothills, and the villages encircling the hillside, and, below them, the greying emptiness that had replaced the canes.

He pointed out to Peter all the places his brother already knew. Told him also what it was like beneath the gatherings of trees that hugged the hollows in the hillsides like the bunched hairs of an armpit; the overhangs of rocks and the far, fragmented patches of grey where the coconuts rose like tall upstanding brooms and swept the sky. He kept talking because he wanted to keep his brother distracted until the foreman's whistle came.

The sound reached across the valley like a stricken bird-cry and released their people. It turned his brother's gaze down towards the valley. Pynter fell silent, his eyes on Peter's face.

His brother brought his finger to his mouth. The catapult hung loosely in his other hand. Pynter pointed at the long meandering line that began spilling onto the white dust road – a wavering thread of stick shapes, thin as drought, with the dying sun glancing off the angles of their limbs like blades.

'Show me our modder,' he said to Peter. Pynter paused a while, then pitched his voice more urgently at Peter. 'Show me Tan Cee.'

His brother was leaning further forward and away from him. His eyes narrowed down to slits.

'Show me Deeka,' Pynter said.

Peter looked up. He shook his head. 'I can't make them out, Pynto,' he said, his voice stuck somewhere between bewilderment and panic. 'I can't.' He passed his arm across his face.

Pynter told his brother what he remembered of Paso's words –
'In the evenin dark, my people walk to the time of clocks, whose
hands have spanned so many years … ' – and how those words
had changed the way he looked at cane. Spoilt it in a way.

Their nephew must have seen this, he said. He must have
stood on one of these hills and looked down on the fermenting
valley and watched that long grey line of men and women dragging their shadows behind them like an extra weight, with the
dust of the old cane road frothing around their feet.

Paso had to have watched the way night gathered around
them, seen the darker mounds of canes piled high behind them,
stretching all the way down to the darkness that was the sea.

And he too must have let this enter him and settle there; must
have lived this quiet desperation, this helplessness that was so
much like the way he, Pynter, used to feel when he watched their
father fumbling about him for all the familiar things that he
could no longer see.

'Dat's why I goin to burn it, Peter,' he told his brother softly.
'Everything. S'why I goin to kill cane. For good. Don' know
when. But before I dead I do it.'

Peter must have told Patty about his decision to set fire to Old
Hope, because she had her eyes on him.

Evenings, he returned from school, spread his books out on
the floor and began murmuring over the pages. He would lift his
head from time to time and glimpse his youngest aunt hovering
at the edges of his vision. She never looked straight at him,
always seemed to be studying a cloud or something when he
raised his eyes at her. It bothered him, this sly-eyed shyness, this
not-watching-while-you-saw-everything expression on her face,
and he felt a lift of relief when she walked into the house one
Friday and lowered herself beside him.

She looked down at his book, slipped a sideways glance at him
and smiled. She didn't touch his face or tug at his ear lobes or call

him Sugarboy this time. Just sat there shifting her large eyes from the pages to his face and back again. He eased himself up from his elbows. She rested a hand on him, a gentle staying touch.

'What you reading?' she said.

He tried to figure out a fast way to tell her, realised he couldn't, shrugged and said, 'Don' fink you'll unnerstan.'

She rose to her feet, paused briefly at the doorway and walked away. And all he could think of afterwards was that quick last glance of hers. That dark-eyed flash of hurt.

She missed dinner that evening. She had never done that before. Leroy came, nodded at no one in particular and took away some food. She didn't come the next day either.

Patty's absence left a scooped-out hole in the yard – a hollowness that entered him and settled in his stomach. He found he couldn't clear his mind of the little smile that had briefly creased her face.

He noticed something different about the women's conversations. They no longer spoke about their time down in the valley. Words came from them in fragments, like half-formed thoughts; got picked up by the others; were left aside and returned to later. Short sentences, partly said, never finished by the one who started talking. As if they were helping each other remember things they thought they'd long forgotten.

But with the passing evenings and Patty's space still vacant, he eventually worked out the pattern of their talk, and marvelled. It was a kind of weaving. It was what Patty did with bits of thread and cloth: words and thoughts, and little bits of meaning they looped around each other, the way they plaited hair.

They were remembering a child whose name they did not mention. Her mother had carried her not nine but ten months and a half. Her mother was not worried, it had happened in the family before. And when that baby came, they saw that her limbs were longer than any other in the family. Her ear lobes were darker than the children who had come before her and she did not cry. She did not talk either, not for eighteen months. And the first word they ever heard from her was 'nice'. As if she was noticing the world for the first time and found favour with it.

It took her just as long to walk. When she rose to her feet, people looked on her and thought of things that flowed: bamboo, vines and rivers. Her father regretted the name he'd given her, always said that he should have called her Grace, because of the way she walked and the way that girl-chile changed him.

He carried her everywhere. A man rough as the stones he'd worked in all his life would stop to notice flowers, to fondle the smoothness of a pebble, the patterns on a leaf or tree trunk. Like she was teaching him another way – a better way to be.

He carved little things for her – animals and human shapes that looked like people they knew. He taught himself to braid her hair. He would've killed the man, or dog, or insect that dared to upset her. She brought a sweetness on this rough-hewn man, a softness he did not know he possessed. A gentleness that surprised him.

All this meant she did not go to the lil infant school on Senna Hill, to recite all dem multiplyin tables-an'-chairs, an' alphabeticals like his children who came before her. He did not want the world to touch her, didn't want her stained. Sometimes too much love don't feel like love. Sometimes too much love is prison. And if – if … a pusson didn …

Pynter left his unfinished bowl of food beside his stone. He could still hear their murmurings when his feet hit the asphalt road. He would walk tonight. He wanted to walk. He would take the old cane road along the river and go towards the sea. He would sit on one of the hills above the bay and think about their secrets: all the things they never said, which stared out at him from the back of their eyes. All the things they held back about John Seegal. And why, why when he thought he was so close to understanding it; when he thought he saw the answer right there in front of him, he could never close his hands around it. Why it was so difficult to grab hold of the thing that really made his grandfather walk.

Patty was still on his mind when he started hiding the dollar his mother gave him every morning, in the little nest he'd made for his slingshot beneath the house. He left home early and walked the eight miles to and from his school above the ocean. Walking gave him time to think about Patty, and the woman teacher who had stepped into their class the year before, dropped her black leather bag on the floor beside her desk and begun talking about mirrors. She'd heard about their mother's little mirrors that they brought to school and rested on the floor, she said, so that women teachers could walk over without knowing, which was why she'd decided to wear trousers. It made better sense than causing irrecoverable injury to the little fool stupid enough to try it. She'd paused and offered the class a twisted little smile. And by the way, she was not there to educate anybody. She was getting paid to teach. If they didn't understand the difference, they had no reason to be sitting there in front of her.

The San Andrews boys, whose parents dropped them off at school in bright new cars, did not like her words. They didn't like the way she looked: her hair cut low like a boy's; a loose unironed shirt hanging carelessly over a pair of olive green dungarees that didn't match the shirt. And a gaze so direct and sure of itself they found themselves shifting in their seats and throwing glances at each other.

She'd paused for a while and seemed to be counting them, her body leaning slightly forward, a pencil pressed against her lips.

But there seemed to be no logic in the movements of her head, no pattern in her counting, and it took a while before Pynter realised what she was doing. She saw the understanding in his eyes, moved as if to say something, then changed her mind.

She straightened up and called their names, pausing over each to stare into their faces. Then she snapped the register shut, gave the class a last, dry smile and left them sitting there.

They waited until they heard the hard, flat slap of her sandals on the concrete courtyard before turning round to stare, realising with a kind of panic that she hadn't even told them her name.

'Lordy, Pynter Bendup!' Marlis Tillock said, breathless, bright-eyed with a grin as broad as a beach. 'That 'ooman is war!'

And it was Marlis Tillock himself who started it with what looked like a shrug.

By then, they'd grown accustomed to her abruptness. The bright, short-lived smiles. The sullen, red-eyed days when she stared at them and did not talk. The evenings she held them in detention and worked them hard for all the times she came into class and did nothing at all.

Marlis – short, quiet, with the shoulders of a man – was leaning over an equation with Pynter, their heads pressed against each other like two sides of a swing bridge. They were arguing about the quickest way to arrive at an answer that she'd already given them.

A San Andrews boy had leaned over and whispered something in Marlis's ear. Marlis didn't look up. He lifted his elbow. Kept muttering over the numbers even after Mikky Coker hit the floor and stayed there. Marlis placed his pencil on the desk and, with a voice that was soft and almost kindly, said, 'Pynter Bend-up? I tell dat town boy twice already, don' call me cocoa-monkey.'

He rose to his feet, picked up his bag. He didn't make it to the door. The teacher was there ahead of him, her back against the door, her eyes still and wide and hostile.

'Where you going?' she said.

Marlis moved his hand to say something.

She cut him short. 'Go to your seat. Right now!'

She gestured at the groaning boy and they helped him off the floor. 'I don't know what you said,' she told him, staring at Coker with narrowed eyes, 'but I know you said something.'

She faced the class, lifted her hand and stared down it as if it were the barrel of a gun. 'You,' she said, 'you, you, you – remain here after school. The rest of you will leave.'

Twelve had to stay behind and Pynter was one of them. She made them bring their seats together as closely as the desks allowed. She bolted the door and sat on a desk before them. She looked at her watch, threw a quick glance at the window and leaned forward.

'Fifteen minutes,' she said. 'No responses; no questions. Put this in your heads. Burn it in.'

She was counting them again, to make sure that they were all there; then she sat back on the desk.

She wanted to know if they knew how long it took for them to get to this school above the ocean. The answer she gave surprised them. More than a hundred years, she said. And they shouldn't fool themselves; they didn't start that walk. Which was why she wanted to know why Marlis Tillock had decided to make leaving so easy.

Marlis wiped his sweating face with his palms and hunched in his shoulders. Pynter felt a rush of sympathy for the suffering boy.

'What is it that finally brought y'all here? Why now?' she said. 'Why not before?' It wasn't the riots and the burnings and the jail, she said. It was something she was going to show them. She bent down to lift her bag, then straightened up suddenly, the large silver hoops of her earrings tossing against her jawline. 'No,' she said, 'I have a better idea.'

When she reached for her bag this time, her hand came out with something. Pynter heard the soft intakes of breath around him, felt his heart flip over. For the pen she was holding up before them had the creamy gloss of Patty's Sunday earrings. The clip on the cover was a tapering gold arrow pointing downwards at the nib, which glowed in the window light like a drop of liquid fire.

'Bring the answer to me,' she said. 'I'll give you this. The first who comes with it, of course.'

She left for last what she'd really called them there to tell them.

'Some of you will poison the roots you grew from. You'll walk like them.' A group of boys were strolling across the courtyard. They were swinging tennis rackets at each other, and laughing. 'You'll

166

talk like them. You'll make yourself believe you're them. You won't look back. A few of you might stop just long enough to say thank you to the people that you came from before you walk away to anywhere that is not here. None of you will carry them with you.'

They stepped out into the empty courtyard. The white concrete – blindingly bright by day – had been darkened by the shadow of the school which the evening sun had thrown across it.

They did not speak to each other. Normally, Marlis would have turned to Pynter, waved a hand and offered him a parting grin. Now he was drifting along the concrete verge, his body angled forward as if he were pushing against a wind. Pynter also felt the sluggishness that had settled in his limbs. He glanced back at the classroom to see the upper half of Sislyn Chappel leaning out of the window, her elbows on the sill – much as his mother would do at home. She nodded and Pynter looked away.

All Pynter could think of on the journey back to Old Hope was who this woman was whose eyes so often tried to hold his own, and navigated his body openly, differently – not as Deeka did; not as Tan Cee or his mother either. Not in any way he understood. And as he tried to push those last words of hers away, he felt them settling in his heart like stones.

Scraps of scripture. Lines from the songs the radio played. Pieces of poems. Pictures of places, and faces cut out from magazines and newspapers tossed in the bins of the sprawling white houses that lined the road up to his school. It took him a week to gather them. And at the end of it, he walked into his grandmother's house, dropped his canvas bag on the floor and said quietly to Peter, 'Tell Tan Patty to come.'

He laid a coloured sheet of Bristol board across the floor. It was the shade of purple that Patty liked. He placed two red and yellow crayons prettily against each other, sat on the floor and waited.

When his aunt arrived, she saw that he'd prepared for her. She lowered herself beside him much as she'd done that first evening she came to him, and leaned her shoulder against his.

All he wanted to do for this first time was talk, he said. He showed her letters, not as he had learned them from his father but as he had worked them out on his morning walks to school. He told her that each letter was like a little person. It had a shape and size and sound that belonged only to itself. And that sound was its voice, which was different from the voices of all the others. And in the same way that people came together and were family, these letters came together and were words. Then he spread before her the pictures he'd collected, the bits of scripture and the poems, read them to her, and then they argued over what they meant.

The next day he did not send to call her. Patty came high-stepping down the hill, broke off a bit of the sugar-cake she was chewing on, popped a piece into his mouth and admired with him the foliated iris of the large marble she had brought him. But she was worried and he sensed it. He let her talk, and while she did, he took the marker off the floor and wrote.

'Copy this,' he said.

She took the pen, fixing it between her fingers exactly as she'd seen him do, threw a quick uncertain glance at him before leaning over the page. She straightened up. He saw that her wrist was trembling. He smiled at her and nodded.

'What I writing?' she asked, a little lost, a little worried.

He pointed at the letters.

He could have told her what occurred to him those mornings on his way to school: that she'd been writing all her life and did not know it. That those long curved lines she made in the dust with sticks when her thoughts were resting on the baby she could not have with Leroy – that was a form of writing. And the little birds, the insects and the butterflies she stitched into those bits of pretty cloth, and the patterns she made in his mother's hair when she combed and plaited it. If what his father had told him once was true, if writing was nothing more than making marks that meant something, then all the women in Old Hope were writing without knowing it.

Patty leaned forward again, her fingers steadier now. He watched the curve of her back, her hair, thick as Deeka's, pulled back from her forehead in a lazy pile, the creeping of her hand across the page.

When she finished, Patty lifted her head as if she'd just emerged from under water. She blinked at him. He reached out his hand and slipped his thumb along the ridges of her lips, as she so often did with him. 'You just write your name.' He smiled.

She pointed at the paper; shook her head as if she did not understand him.

'Uh-huh, right there – "Patty Bender".'

She rose to her feet then, gathering up the paper with her. It crackled in her hands like firewood. Patty was looking down at him now, and even with all that light from the doorway behind her, he could still see her eyes. She stepped out of the door, stopped there a while. Then she was kneeling beside him, her fingers brushing against his throat. He felt the little pendant of the thin gold chain she'd just taken from around her neck grow warm against his skin.

They both said nothing. Pynter watched her swaying back for a while, then stretched himself out on the floor. He closed his eyes and could hear the dull heartbeat of someone chopping trees up in the foothills. Halfway down Old Hope, Miss Muriel was singing, 'Roooock oof Aaaages' – the only song she ever sang. Missa Ram's white jackass was kicking up a rhythm on the road below. And just outside, Patty's pretty laughter rising, bright and rapid like light over fast water.

They shifted the cooking to later in the evening. Mornings, his mother, Elena, got up even earlier and prepared 'a lil in-between somefing in advance', which he chewed on while he sat with Patty.

Elena had moved from peeling the provisions in the yard to finding a lil space on the step, because it was more comfortable, she said. Tan Cee came and sat beside her. And his grandmother wanted to know why they gone an' decide all-of-a-sudden-so to take up the space that was hers by right since she was the one who always sat there.

By then Patty was reading on her own and getting better fast. Now she was practising to be A Lady, which meant not eating with her fingers any more, chewing very, very slowly even when she told them she was starving, and walking a little more upright than she already did, with a daintier smile, a slightly stiffer neck, and making every word she said sound as though her mouth was stuffed with bread. Till Deeka, in a flush of irritation, raised a finger at her one evening, wanting to know if she was practising for a stroke.

Patty didn't see the joke, but for the rest of the week they couldn't look at her without breaking into laughter.

Wait, she told them, wait and see who'll be skinnin their teeth and laughin, when she got her job in one of them pretty department stores in San Andrews.

Pynter did not know exactly when or why he started talking. Perhaps it was this sense he had each evening of their waiting without words, the knowledge that these days, after work, they had created a little room of silence which they were expecting him to fill. Perhaps it was the last few words that Miss Sislyn had left them with when she'd kept them in that first time. Perhaps it was all of them that came together in his mind the evening he eased himself up off his elbow, picked up a book and made a rolling fan of the pages with his fingers. The movement took their gazes off his face, but only briefly.

His mother's hands stopped rummaging the rice. Patty shifted her weight and moved closer to him. He couldn't work out Deeka's expression. She'd lowered her head and was staring at him from an angle.

He began talking the way his father used to, with his head pressed against the partition, his eyes half-closed, his voice dark and thick and slightly weary.

He told them the story of a whisper – how a little rumour that some wicked so-an'-so name Iago pass on to Missa Othello and make that fella destroy his wife and then 'imself because of it. And what about that old fella who call 'imself a king, the so-an'-so gave his daughters all his land and money in exchange for words. Just words – just for telling 'im they love 'im even if they didn. And the trouble that he caused the child who didn lie; becuz she tell 'im that she love 'im only in the way a daughter ought to. No wonder he went crazy.

There was also that time of other gods, and not-so-different men, when an old man was compelled to roll a boulder up a steep hill. It never reached the top becuz as soon as he almost got there, the stone slipped from him, and he had to begin all over again. He didn even have his own death to look forward to, becuz that old fella was cursed to live for ever.

'A helluva thing,' Tan Cee said, quietly appalled. 'Day make a pusson tired. At the end of it they sleep, not so? Same way with life. At the end of it a yooman been expect a decent rest!'

And always when Pynter finished he felt the change in them: the stillness with which his mother sat with the rice bowl on her knees; that new look in his grandmother's eyes, as if he were no longer the stranger she'd always made him out to be. And Tan Cee there, her eyes gone vacant, a smile on her face which was not meant for him, because she was still in that place that his words had taken them to.

But Peter did not miss his urgency – the soft-voiced rage that lay behind his words. His brother's body said so. Said that it was sensing the thing that he, Pynter, was talking them towards each evening.

He was always there, Peter, in the middle of the yard, his hands folded around each other, his eyes drifting to and from the faces of the women as if he were hearing something different from the rest of them which he did not trust. And as the cutting season crept to a close and the tractors began to climb out of the valley, Pynter felt his brother's eyes settling on his hands as he thumbed the pages of his books more thoughtfully – more and more selectively.

The evening came when Patty picked up the little brown book Pynter always placed beside him in case he needed to refer to it.

'Aunty-gone,' she said.

'An-ti-gon-e,' he corrected. 'Name of a girl.'

'Which girl?' Deeka's voice surprised him.

'Jus' a girl,' he said.

'What about 'er?' his mother said.

They wouldn't have believed him if he told them how he came by the little book. He'd found it in a plastic bag against one of the roadside bins he raided for magazines. A woman had watched him from a nearby house, through the slit in a yellow curtain. There were rumours about that house. She was a doctor-woman, they said, chased across the Atlantic by some disgrace a pusson could only guess at, to this rotting place above the road on which he travelled to his school.

This little brown book – he would keep the worst parts back: the bits that they would call an abomination, like what Missa Laius did to Pelops's son. Like the curse that followed Laius afterwards. Like the thing it made him do to his boy-chile. He would skip those bits. Would start instead with this old fella name Oedipus who owned the lives of all the people under him, in the same way that the man who ruled this island felt he owned the lives of everybody on it. He would start with Teiresias (and if they wanted to know exactly who Teiresias was, he would make them think of Santay) and what Teiresias said to him.

'He tell Missa Oedipus that one day he goin kill his father, get married to his mother and give her children. Part of the problem was he didn know who his mother was, becuz soonz he born she pass him over to somebody else. She didn want him. She thought that he was a curse. He meet a woman one day. He like 'er. She nice. He like 'er a lot. He married 'er. She give 'im four chilren – two boys and two girls. And 'twas awright until he find out that woman was his mother. Just thinkin about it nearly kill 'im. He so shame he blind 'imself. Take out hi two eye; lef' the country to his brother. And from then on he start to walk. He make 'imself a beggar. Left his chilren wiv his brother. He never stop walkin. He never look back. Shame – shame eating him up so much cuz he couldn live with 'imself no more. He just get up an' left one day an' never come back.'

It was quiet after he finished the story and then his mother spoke. 'They teach you 'bout dem wickedness in school?'

He did not answer her. For some reason he was distracted by the smell of the grapefruit tree beside the house. It was in blossom. It never bore fruit. It suddenly reminded him of something.

'And the girl?' Patty asked, irritably, urgently. 'What about the girl?' She was hugging herself, her eyes on the cover of the book as if she expected it to answer her.

'Antigone was hi daughter.' Pynter pushed himself up off the floor. 'We not eatin tonight? I hungry.'

He stepped out into the yard.

Deeka had eaten quickly, nervously. She'd spent most of the evening poking at the fire. Pynter felt the turbulence in his grandmother. He'd watched it take hold of her from the time she left the steps. The abrupt reaching of her hand behind her head to loosen the coils of hair had confirmed it for him.

His mother and his aunts sat with their heads together. He could barely hear their whisperings.

Peter came to sit beside him. Pynter moved over and gave his brother space.

'Why yuh have to talk like dat, Pynter?'

'Like how?'

'Nobody in this yard don' talk like that. Even Deeka never talk like dat.'

'How Deeka talk?'

'I don' know … Bad tings,' Peter said. His voice had risen. It made their mother look over at them. 'It don' make a pusson feel good afterwards.'

Peter swung himself around. Pynter felt his brother's breath on his face. 'It sound like if you wan' to … '

Peter didn't get to say the rest. Deeka's voice surprised them. For she hadn't spoken during all these months. Not really; not properly. Every evening, without so much as a word or gesture, she'd reminded them of the reason: that her daughter, Elena, had filled a bucket of burning coals to throw at her. The very idea, the very thought of it, had killed the stories in her.

Tan Cee's hand paused with the bit of yam she was about to place in her mouth. She inspected it and dropped it back into her bowl. Elena shifted the baby on her shoulder. The eyes she rested on Deeka were deep and almost fearful.

'Is twenty years,' Deeka said, her voice trailing away like smoke. 'Next month make it twenty.'

She was leaning against the wall of rock at the top end of the yard. She'd crossed her arms and she was looking straight at them. 'What – what make a mother love a child different from the other? Better than the other? Eh?'

It could be anyting, she told them. 'Could be because dat baby got some weakness that the others don't have. Or it replace a pusson who come before. O' p'raps it ease some hurtin or achin or sorrow.'

She'd given John Seegal the children he'd asked for, she said. Tan Cee first, then Elena, then Birdie. Patty was the last. Patty came as a present. A surprise. He'd taken to them in a way most fathers in these parts didn't have the smallest idea how to. He roped them in so tight with all that lovin. They hardly had their own pussnal air to breathe.

'It didn have no space inside that rope for Anita. And she know she never goin to have none. She was a growin girl and my husband wasn' blind to it. Ain't got nothing more revealin than a man pretendin dat he blind to something hi two eye can't avoid. I see de quiet that come over 'im when she pass in front of 'im. I see the struggle in 'im. I see de fever dat take hold of 'im. I see it and I didn know what to do with it. I don' know what happm between them. I didn wan' to know. I still don' wan' to know. She had to go.'

Deeka stood before them as if all her age had settled on her shoulders. But her head was up, her words deliberate and clear as if, now that she'd decided to tell, she needed them to hear it all.

'I didn have to tell her, becuz dat lil 'ooman learn soon enough dat it have different kind o' lovin and not all of it worth havin. Not all of it is good. I didn have to make her go. She went anyway. The first time police bring 'er back, they say they find 'er halfway up the island. Walkin. All day walkin. They ask 'er where she goin. She say she going to meet 'er father. Don' know how she know. I never told her. My husband must ha' told her. Next time she went, she didn even go lookin for no father. She just went lookin. Is twenty years now. I – I believe she lookin still.'

Pynter glanced at his mother and his aunts, their shoulders stilled, not so much by Deeka's words (for he was sure that they already knew these things) as by the fact that she'd finally said the one thing she had been holding back in all their years of listening to her. And it was good that his grandmother had finally said it. For wasn't it Deeka herself who had told them once that even things that rotted needed air? To dry up properly, and then disappear – and even if they didn't disappear, they became at least more bearable.

His grandmother's words had delivered something else to him. The thought had settled on his mind that during all this time it was not John Seegal they were missing, it was this girl whose name they never said unless they had to.

Peter was right about those stories. All he wanted was to drive the grandfather he'd never seen back to the swamps he'd decided to walk into, and have him stay there. To be able to live their lives without carrying a dead man's weight with them for what remained of their time above this valley of heat and hurt. To kill him off, properly. For good. Only then, perhaps, would it be possible for Anita to come back.

Now his grandmother was looking at him directly. She was talking as if he were the only person there with her. 'Shame,' she said, 'shame could be so strong it … it make a man get up, leave everyting he own behind – an, an … '

She didn't finish. She climbed the steps and went inside.

Pynter felt his brother's elbow grind against his ribcage.

'Dat's why Deeka say you born for trouble!' Peter said.

'Dat's not all she say,' said Pynter. 'She say I born to dead too. And what you say?'

'I say – I say you'z a flippin dog.'

'That make you one too. We got same mother, not so?'

'But I born first.'

'Then you born a dog befo' me.'

'You sonuvabitch.'

'You call 'Lena a bitch? Cuz she my mother too.'

'I didn say dat.'

'If you call her a bitch again, I tell her, you … '

'I didn say dat!'

'Yes, you say so! By flippin implication.'

'By wha? You flippin long-word, word-a-mouth show-off. I different. I'z not like you, I … '

'What you like then, eh?' said Pynter. 'You small-word, no-word, dry-mouth, long-mouth sonuvabitch!'

19

OLD HOPE WAS a place of roads – a spider's web of tracks that could take a person anywhere.

There were the everyday roads that children learned the way they learned to read. They were made to travel them so often they became as familiar as the markings in their hands.

There were other kinds of roads. Some took a person to the edge of a cliff and seemed to leave them there. The rest of that road lay far below, joined to the spot on which they stood by the snaking root of a dandacayo tree, or wist vines stripped naked of their thorns.

There were the desperate roads, the hardly-talked-about roads, the roads of last resort. They were there only to carry messages in an emergency. These were the little paths that followed the rise of rocks, of fallen trees and roots, with little cuttings made in them, just large enough to fit the feet and hands of a young one. The children would outgrow them the way they outgrew clothing.

There were the never-talked-about roads – secret tracks that took a running Old Hope man to a hill above some trees. He would have headed there because he knew which of those trees below would take the weight of a leaping adult, and which would deliver him to the bed of rocks beneath them.

There were places where the trees tied their branches in tunnels that lasted miles. A person could slip into that green night in the early hours of a morning and surface at the far end of some place further north to find the sun going down.

And then there were the ghost roads – the hidden travel-ways left there by the Old Ones, water paths and rock trails designed to cover flight, where the sunlight filtered in so faintly a person navigated by the shape of things. The whisper was that people still followed them: the soft-walkers, the self-talkers, the strange-borns. The loners with an appetite for puzzles who sought meaning in the shapes of roots, in the unusual curve of branches. They passed each other in the half-light, treading softly, ghosts on roads so old and faint they were hardly there at all.

Which was why when trouble came to Old Hope, Deeka Bender turned to Pynter.

He was telling Peter about planets and stars, and numbers and distances so far-an'-futile the yooman mind could never hold them in; and did he know that there was a time when that moon up there used to be a lantern, before some bad-minded, too-curious Eye-talian fella name Galileo Galilei looked up at the moon through a piece of glass one night and from then on it got reduced to a lil piece o' rock? Pynter was about to tell him what a foolish-fool Christopher Columbus was and why, when he paused, made a little circle with his head and muttered softly, disbelievingly, 'Birdie?'

Peter stirred and looked at him.

'Bread,' Pynter said. 'Bread jus' cross my mind – that's all.'

But that was not all. There was also the tincture of man sweat that was only Birdie's. Mebbe it wasn't a smell at all; mebbe 'twas just a thought.

Peter was staring up at the moon through a bit of broken glass. 'Another year to go an' you dead, Jumbie Boy,' he said.

Pynter pulled his shirt around him and eased his back down on the stones. Jumbie Boy. He shaped his lips around the name. It had been said so many times he hardly heard it any more, unless it came from Peter. He'd tried everything to kill that name in Peter's mouth but still his brother said it: the first morning he left the yard for his new school in San Andrews; the evening he'd returned. And when his head was down and his mind was so far inside a book that he did not hear Peter's feet approaching, his brother would place his lips against his ear and breathe those words.

He'd tried to make Peter understand it – this way of being sure sometimes. Of knowing without thinking. He'd asked him to imagine one of the women by the river gathering up her basin full of clothing before heading home. Each piece of washing had its own colour, not so? And it didn't matter how much that woman washed it; it still carried the odour of the man or child who wore it. P'raps if Miss Maisie closed her eyes and brought it to her nose, she would know its owner straight away. He – he didn't have to do that. He could stand on a stone a lil way up the river, call out to her and tell her.

'Is what I is,' he'd said. 'Is so I come.'

His mother's voice pushed its way into his thoughts. It came so sharp and urgent it made his heart flip over. She was looking at Peter. His brother was staring past the grapefruit tree into the dark.

'What happm?' Elena said. She spun round suddenly, prepared to fight off whatever it was that held Peter there so rigid and wild-eyed.

Nothing happened; not for a while. Not until a large dark shape detached itself from the stool of bananas at the back end of the house. Tan Cee stood up with that strange smoothness of movement which always made it look as if she was helped up by some force outside of her.

Pynter felt a new heat in his brother. Smelt the fear too. He turned to tell him not to worry cuz it was only Birdie, but his brother was no longer there. He glimpsed the pale shirt disappearing up the hill into the night, listened to the stiff thumping of Peter's heels on the earth, before silence returned and settled on the yard.

Birdie did not speak.

With a movement that was almost as abrupt as Peter's, Elena shifted the baby on her shoulder and a sound came out of her.

Tan Cee ran out of the yard. She returned almost as soon as she'd left with the shirt and the pair of trousers that she always kept for Birdie.

Birdie remained where he was, his back against the darkness. He seemed to be waiting for something from them – some sound or gesture that would fill out the solid block of shadow that he was and make him flesh and blood. And when it came it was almost tearful. 'Come, son,' Deeka said. 'Come, tell me.'

Tan Cee held up a chunk of burning wood before her as if it were an offering. They noticed the dark mixture of mud and blood that ran all the way down Birdie's shoulders to his fingers; the ripped trousers and khaki shirt hanging off him like torn banana leaves; the mud-caked pair of canvas shoes; the gold tooth glimmering through half-opened lips; his eyes just as large and luminous as Patty's.

Deeka reached out and took Elena's child from her. 'Hot some water,' she said. 'Get a cloth. Bathe him.'

Now, the words that passed between the women were soft and taut and urgent. Pynter did not need to know what lay behind the small grunts from his aunt, the little cries of anger and surprise from Patty, the heavy silence of his mother. He listened to the water crashing down his uncle's body, turned his head up at the moon and wondered where Peter had gone to.

Tan Cee called his name. Pynter rose to his feet and went to her. He did not look at his uncle's nakedness. He did not look at his mother either. From this aunt of his – who sat over him at nights and listened to him dreaming; who placed marbles in his hands and whispered unspeakable secrets in his ears; whose smell of eucalyptus oil and cinnamon was as much a part of her as the knife she carried somewhere on her person – he would learn what the trouble was. Not the details yet, but something of

180

its magnitude and weight. And it would not be from what she said, but from the adjustments in her breathing, and all the things her hands and eyes were doing.

'Stay out here.' Tan Cee's gesture embraced Old Hope. He understood that whatever the trouble his uncle had brought home to them, he, Pynter, must not sleep tonight. He listened to the shuffle of the women's footsteps on the floorboards. Felt the slight change of pressure as the house adjusted to his uncle's weight. Stay out here. From as far back as he could remember, it had been this way. The awful things that had no name or words to them – the women always kept them to themselves.

The Mardi Gras was a hulking shape against the sky above them. There was no mist up there tonight. He could see the shape of the summit, curved like the head of a chicken hawk and, lower down, that puzzling scooped-out hollow that was so much like the mouth of a man opened wide in what could just as easily be a roll of endless laughter or a scream that had no end to it.

Birdie knew something about his mother that the others didn't. Maybe he used to listen to her stories differently and so had discovered a part of Deeka Bender that she had never shown her daughters. Else why didn't he do what so many of the men who'd broken out of prison did: run to the hills, or climb to the top of the Mardi Gras and bury themselves amongst the mists and ferns up there? Until, of course, the dogs were sent to drag them down.

Instead, Birdie came running to his mother.

Pynter imagined his uncle sprinting through the little back roads that stood between the prison and Old Hope. His desperation was there in the cuts and bruises on his skin, the stripped down shirt and knee-cut trousers. The wildness in his eyes was no doubt placed there by his fear of the Rottweilers and Alsatians Birdie thought were just behind him.

Pynter had no idea how much time Peter had passed out there on his own or how long the women and Birdie had been inside talking. When his brother returned, Pynter found himself hurrying over the stones towards him. But Peter did not see him. Whatever it was his brother had returned with from the dark had stiffened his head and shoulders, and thinned his lips down to a thread-line.

Peter climbed the steps and threw his weight against the door. The chair the women had placed behind it crashed against the floor. Pynter followed him inside.

Birdie was sitting on the only chair that would hold him up, one he'd built and fortified himself. His elbows were on his knees, his hands propping up his chin. The women were sitting at his feet. He'd curved the bulk of his body forward over them like the outcrop of a cliff. Four pairs of eyes, bright and yellowed by the lamplight, settled on their faces. Birdie did not look up at them.

A thin film of sweat glazed Peter's face. His lips were working and his eyes were on the window behind their uncle. The women's still-eyed condemnation changed to puzzlement and then concern. For they too had not seen this agitation in Peter before. Peter – the first-born, the one who laughed so easily, who preferred to stay at home and drift around them, who hummed hymns and love songs all the time, danced in the yard to the radio and made them chuckle at his foolishness.

Their mother pushed her weight up off the floor. Her movement prompted a gesture from Peter – one so abrupt and violent she sat back down. Now he was lifting his finger at Deeka, 'If – if yuh send 'im back … '

He dropped his hand, his lips still working, his sweat-glazed face glistening in the lamplight. 'If – if he go back…'

'They'll kill 'im,' Pynter cut in softly.

He followed his brother out of the door.

Elena came out after them. She stood amongst the stones with her hands dangling down her sides. There was a small smile on her face. 'You sure?' She flicked her wrist at Pynter.

'Is Peter words,' he said.

'But you…'

'Is Peter words; you don' unnerstan dat?' His ferocity surprised him.

Their mother was looking at them both, her hands still hanging at her sides – that smile that wasn't a smile at all still tugging at her mouth. They stood side by side, staring at her.

A little cough escaped Elena. Her right hand drifted up and rested on her stomach. Her lips moved around some words. She turned and went inside.

Peter began humming to himself. He swung his head from side to side, curling his tongue around each rhyme so that the words came out the funny way that Jim Reeves's did.

Pynter felt a sudden pulse of sympathy for him. A desire too, to play the game they'd invented a couple of years before, where they stood back to back and tried to guess exactly what the other was seeing. They never cheated; they never lied; they never argued over what the other said he saw.

He took his eyes off Peter and lifted his face to the hills. It was up there, some way below the tall fall of vines, just beneath the ridge of white cedar and bamboo, that Miss Maddie and Miss Pearly – another sister whom he'd met just once – had laid their father. He'd gone to Miss Maddie's house and told her that this was what their father Manuel Forsyth said he wanted: a place that overlooked his garden, his children and Old Hope. He did not tell her that he'd dreamt this a couple of weeks before their father passed.

Pynter sniffed at the air and caught the faint smell of early-morning rain. He placed his lips against Peter's ear and breathed softly, happily, 'Jumbie Boy!'

He laughed so loud it made Patty push her head out of the door and stare at them with depthless eyes.

What Peter said made the movements of the women sharper. It shortened their words. It made their footsteps heavier. It was as if their grandmother was unravelling a ball of thread that Peter had thrown at her.

They knew now that Birdie had blocked the butt of a soldier's gun from breaking the face of one of those discontented youths he'd talked about the last time he came home. The soldiers lifted them off the roadside every day now for talking too much and too loudly; for cursing the name of the man who believed he owned the island; for asking questions they were not s'posed to ask about the unnecessary price of necessary things; about the labouring that crippled or killed their parents early. About the thieving and the waste.

Birdie had made a wall of his body and placed it between the soldiers and the youth. He'd lifted all seven of them like useless bits of debris and knocked their heads against those old stone walls that locked him in. There was an eighth who'd stepped back to aim the muzzle of his gun at him. What Birdie did to that one – he would not say.

That was why Chilway would not come for him this time, Deeka said. It would be small men with bodies as slim and hard as whips, and eyes that hardly blinked. They would not be the ones he'd half-killed, o' course, and they would not come to Old Hope night-time. Chilway would've warned them about Old Hope people and the night!

They would arrive quietly in the early hours of the morning, their rifles held across their chests, their fingers on the trigger. They would not argue or make sweet talk with Deeka, or splay their fingers before offering her a handshake. They would not make a joke of Patty's loveliness. They would look up at the giant that her son was, see the size of his arms, the muscles that rippled like a river down them, the hull that was his shoulders, the hands that made an axe look like a matchstick. They would not think of the bread he made with those hands, the laughing ease with which he lifted his sisters to those shoulders. They would miss the softness in his eyes.

S'matter o' fact, for her boy, they would need no reason other than the fact of what he was. A stronger man. A bigger man. A man who was more man than they was. And when little men find they can't measure up to something bigger than they was – what they do? Eh?

She spat the question at the night, waited for the answer, and when it came she was the only one who heard it. But they saw the way it straightened her spine and pulled her shoulders back.

'They do what all man do, from time. They try to own it or cut it down to size. And if they find they can't do either, if they can't make it the same like them or less, they pull it apart. They break it. They turn it into something useless.'

But no man of hers was ever going to go like that. Not so easy. Not so foolish. Not for nothing. Not again.

Not even for God.

It was as if, by giving voice to all these awful things, by making them happen before, with words, his grandmother was obviating what was to come tomorrow. But there was something more and Pynter knew they had to wait for it. He knew that all this was grand-move, a voose – a rain dance of words. It was the old woman's way of stepping out ahead of them to some place they had never been to before; and she needed to be there first to see what it was like before she called them over. And whether they welcomed it or not, it would determine what was to become of all of them.

When it came, it was so quick and simple it caught them unawares.

Deeka brought her hands up to her headscarf and tightened it. She swung her shoulders round and said to Tan Cee, 'Go call that man you call your husband.'

'Take your child to Maisie house and leave it there,' she told Elena.

She paused at Patty, looked her youngest daughter up and down with a dry, assessing gaze. 'Go change your clothes. This is not no short-skirt time.'

Now she was leaning towards Pynter and all he could see was the high curve of her forehead and the patterns of the firelight on the right side of her face – and those eyes that had always revealed that she cursed his birth.

'You know de night,' she said. 'I askin you to go to every door in Old Hope. Tell dem … ' She straightened up, gathering breath to say the words. 'Tell dem that Victor soldiers coming to kill my son tomorrow.'

She turned to Coxy Levid, who'd arrived by then, pulling on a cigarette and smiling.

'Go wiv him.'

'I go alone,' Pynter told her. 'Else I don't go.'

Pynter pushed a hand beneath the boards and pulled out his slingshot. He leaned further in, brought out a little sack of ball bearings and tipped it over. The steel marbles glittered in his palm like drops of water. He eased the handle of the weapon down the waist of his trousers, threw Coxy a last hard glance. 'Don' wan' nobody falla me,' he said softly, mockingly, and slipped into the night.

Coxy took the cigarette from his lips, spat on the flaming tip and dropped it on the stones.

20

IT WAS CLEAR from the time the blue Land Rover entered Old Hope the next day that Victor's soldiers knew nothing about the place.

Foolish! So foolish! Enough to make a pusson shake their head and laugh.

Chilway would have known – he would have known that men would never gather by the standpipe at the roadside to hold no low-voice conversations with plastic buckets at their feet, becuz that was children's business. Cane men didn stoop in groups to fill up potholes in the road with stones the size of children's heads, becuz that was government business. And at the height of the cutting season every house in Old Hope should be empty ... and those children wouldn be down there in the cane fields doing their parents' work.

Chilway would have known – and what Chilway didn't know for sure he would have scratched his head about. Like why Muriel chose to climb to the top of Glory Cedar Rise at that time in the morning to sing 'Rock of Ages' with a voice that carried to the far end of Old Hope. And when she stopped so sudden in the middle of the song – well, that would have had him thinking.

Word of the soldiers' coming had passed along those houses high above the twisting road. And in places where the distance between them would have made shouting necessary, the words were handed over to a child who took them running to a household further on. So that when the vehicle turned the corner,

Deeka and her daughters were waiting at the roadside. They already knew that there were ten men in the jeep – eight at the back, the driver and another who sat beside him. They also knew that each carried a rifle, except the man who sat beside the driver. That the cap he wore was a darker blue than the rest of them and the silver watch on his left hand had a greenish face on it.

The driver got out first, followed by the others. They were as Deeka had imagined them, unsmiling, underfed young men balancing .404 rifles in their hands. They looked up the hill towards Deeka's yard because they heard men's voices up there. And by the laughter that reached the road, these Old Hope men were having a whale of a time. They saw that those who had been at the standpipe were now sitting on the grass verge a little way behind them. They too were talking amongst themselves.

They looked further up beyond John Seegal's house and saw small gatherings of youths spread out along the top, their bodies still as stonework against the bright skyline.

The man who stepped out from amongst the soldiers looked older than the others. His face was smooth as a child's. His eyes were red, as if they needed sleep.

'Birdie Bender,' he said. 'He belong to y'all?' He was looking into Patty's face, and something in his gaze made her back away from him, her large eyes shifting in a kind of panic towards her mother.

Tan Cee moved to answer but Deeka stayed her with a movement of her head.

She was staring at the men. As soon as they arrived she'd begun squinting at their faces, pausing briefly on each one with rapid movements of her eyes. When she spoke, her voice was not what Pynter expected. There was no anger there. No irritation. No trembling or fear. The words bubbled out of her like oil.

'Send Chilway,' she said.

'Is I come for him, not Chilway.' The soldier's voice crackled above their heads like parched leaves.

'Chilway,' Deeka repeated. It was as if she hadn't heard him. 'Let Chilway come.'

'You didn hear me firs' time. Is I dat here to take him.'

'And how you goin to do dat?' Deeka asked. She sounded as though she really wanted to know.

'Yuh trying to play de arse wiv me?' They watched the irritation tighten the man's face and change it into something stiff and ugly. He moved then: a twist of the head, a fast glance at the men behind him. Pynter saw the stiffening in the Old Hope men, the quick adjustment of their hands. The change that came over his grandmother was much quieter. She seemed to be drifting towards the men.

'Look up there,' Deeka said, pointing at the shapes against the skyline. 'Listen.' She raised a hand above her head. 'You kin take all of us with you? You fink you kin manage dat?'

Now she was pointing a finger at one of the young men. He wore his cap differently from the rest, the peak pulled sideways. The way he held the gun was odd too – his fingers wrapped around the metal of the muzzle, not the stock.

'You – you a Skinner, not so? You from up dere?' She raised a hand at one of the hills on the other side of the valley. 'You got de Skinner head an' mouth. Your modder got de same-shape face as you. Is you who show dem where we live; not so?'

The young man did not answer her. He threw a quick glance at the Old Hope men behind him; not at their faces, but at the machetes in their hands.

'But you didn tell dem why you look so 'fraid? Eh?'

Deeka started backing away, her finger still levelled at the young man's face. Her voice rose high and bright and sudden. It startled the man; it made Pynter's heart trip faster. It silenced the laughter in their yard and brought the men on the grass verge to their feet.

'Well, Missa Skinner, tell dat fella here dat if he make any of you just lif' dem ting, none of you goin live long enough to hear one o' dem go off! Tell dat sonuvabitch for me. Tell 'im! Make 'im know dat is why I ask 'im nice-an'-polite to send Chilway for Birdie. Tell 'im!'

Deeka turned round with a rush of air and began striding up the hill, the bottom of her dress flapping around her heels like wings.

The Old Hope men that the soldiers hadn't seen began appearing on the road. They came from everywhere. They slipped down the banks from the bushes that overlooked the road. They emerged from the backs of houses. Deep-chested men with sugar-sack shoulders and dark-water eyes. A couple nodded at the strangers standing in a tight bunch with their guns. Some even grunted a greeting.

Sloco, tall, rum-eyed, always smelling of molasses, and as unsteady as a cane stalk, cocked an eye at them. 'North-woman,' he explained, lifting his chin up the track where Deeka and her daughters had just disappeared. 'Do what de lady say, fellas. When north-woman want a man, you send de one she ask for, y'unnerstan?'

He adjusted the machete on his shoulders. 'An' if y'all tink she bad-an'-ugly, y'all should ha' meet de husband.'

He cackled at his own joke. Thought about what he'd just said and laughed again.

The arrival of the soldiers and the intention in the eyes of their leader had so shaken Patty she'd placed her back against the house to steady herself. A stillness had settled over the yard which even the chickens seemed to sense. For as soon as Deeka returned from her confrontation with the soldiers in the road, they'd retired with panicked chuckling noises to the knotted clumps of pine grass at the back of the house.

His mother cooked in darkness – not on firewood this time but over a nest of smokeless charcoal whose steady glow reddened the stones of the yard. Deeka went into the house and brought out a bowl of flour. She said Birdie's name. He came out on the steps and she handed him the bowl. She gave him a cup of salted water and placed the little brown bag of corn flour beside his feet. He raised his head at them, the tendons switching at the sides of his neck like ropes – his eyes pausing, it seemed, on each of them in turn. It was not the gaze of a frightened man. The shaky desperation with which he had arrived had left his body now. It was a look Pynter remembered – the one he'd given Peter all those years ago on their way to Gideon's house, when he'd sent both of them ahead of him and promised he would be just behind.

Pynter studied Birdie's kneading hands and rolling shoulders – solid as the boulders on the bank above the house – and he could not imagine his uncle the way Deeka had talked of him the night before, crushed at the hands of these men who'd come with guns to take him. And for the first time since his uncle arrived, Pynter felt the tightness in his chest relax.

Last night he'd done as Deeka asked. He'd gone out there and tossed a pebble at every door, passing on his grandmother's words to the hand that pulled a blind, the eyes that studied him from a crack in the wall of the wooden houses or the head that popped out from a window.

Tonight, Old Hope would not sleep. Nobody had to tell him that. They would be attentive to the barking of their dogs. Every footfall on the road would be listened to and made to match its owner. And in all this watching silence there hung a statement, as certain as the whispering canes beneath them, as solid as the hills that overlooked this valley: that Deeka and her family needed to use this time to find a way out for Birdie.

But as Deeka told them earlier, there was no straight road to anywhere. In fact, there was no road at all when a pusson didn know exactly where they off to, or where they s'posed to go.

One thing was certain, though: north was the only way to go. She'd spoken as if 'north' was a destination. She'd argued her way to the upper end of the island and it was only on her way back down that she'd settled on Kanvi – a village full of straight-back wimmen and tight-lip men, who'd stared at the ocean so long, she said, they carried a portion of it in their eyes.

There was a woman there named Ada Bowen. She was family. Birdie must go to her and tell her Deeka's name. She would take him past the scattering of islands that stood between their place and the world. She would leave him on the last one, Kara Isle, which – little and useless as it looked – was the doorway to everywhere. Englan' was on the right of it, a long-long way away; Cuba was on the left; Trinidad sat a little way behind him. America was straight ahead.

America was easy. A pusson just travel the curve of islands, play hopscotch with them. That route been always there, old as time, old as her people who'd discovered it, who'd learned that the surest way to get there was to follow the flight of birds, the ones that arrived and rested here at the tail end of the year: the yellowthroats, the blue-head' buntins, the blood-throat doctorbird, the tanagers and warblers. The swallows an' swifts an' nighthawks; the raptors and the thrushes; parulas and sandpipers. Plovers, terns and catbirds. Each one of them could take him to that place that looked so much like a whiteman nose hangin above a shoutin mouth. They called it Florida these days. It had lost the name her people gave it.

That was the easy part, Deeka said. The hardest part was getting him out of Old Hope. The Old Hope men who, that very day, had been prepared to face the soldiers' guns for Birdie would not take him out to sea. These were cane men. Give them a machete to clear the foothills with, give them a hoe to make a garden all the way up to the top of the Mardi Gras, bring all of Victor's soldiers to Old Hope and line them up before them, they'll stand their ground and face them with only a coupla stones between them. But they knew nothing about sea.

The sea turn them into lil boys. It frighten them.

And it had always been a puzzle to her why so many of these island men, who could stand on any hill and see the ocean almos' touchin their eyelashes, were so terrified of it. Perhaps it was the way they had arrived, she said. Perhaps they still carried the memory in their bones.

For her people – for the Old Ones – the sea used to be a road to everywhere.

Deeka cleared her throat. She tightened the knot of her head-tie. She reached for the kerosene lamp and turned up the wick. Birdie would have to take his chances on the road – all fifteen miles of it. He would have to travel like the thief he was and always keep in mind that soon as night-time reach, the road belong to Victor soldiers.

Pynter followed not so much the details of their worrying as the broad outlines of it. It felt more like standing on a hill and watching the curve of a meandering road below him. He'd been thinking about trees, about Birdie's strength and something he would have liked to do, though he might never have his uncle's stamina or the desperation it required.

Deeka's worrying finally brought her to a dead end. The women's exhaustion surrounded him now like a rancid towel; the air was stale with it – that and the smell of Birdie's fear.

His mother's gaze shifted to and from the moths that stumbled down the hot glass funnel of the lamp and became charred bits of nothing in the flames. Patty's eyes were still and wide and staring, while Tan Cee leaned against the open window. Made restless by the fretting of the women, Peter had stepped out into the yard.

Footfalls, faint like padded heartbeats, slipped into the silence.

'Somebody,' Pynter said, rising from the floor and reaching for his slingshot.

'Cynty,' Tan Cee answered, her head still out of the window.

The name made Birdie shift his weight on the chair. His hand came up and crept towards his forehead.

Cynty brought something new into the room. Her presence made Pynter feel as if all the worrying they had been doing before she arrived had been for nothing. And that puzzled and amazed Pynter since nothing had really changed. Perhaps it was her size, the dark solidity and steadiness of this woman in the doorway whom all of Old Hope puzzled over. Cynty smiled more than she talked; in fact, she hardly ever talked, and large as she was, whenever she said something, her voice was barely above a whisper.

She walked across the floor and lowered herself beside Birdie so that her left shoulder rested against his right leg. She offered the room a brief smile then she turned her face towards Birdie.

Peter came back in after her. He stood in the middle of the room with a finger pressed against his lips as if he did not trust what might come out of them. Pynter followed his brother's gaze and he too did not want to take his eyes off Cynty. She was half as tall as Birdie and almost as wide, with the miraculous darkness of skin that even now made her bare arms shimmer in the lamplight.

Miss Cynty reminded him of tight-skinned fruits: avocados, watermelons, star apples and plums. She was looking into Birdie's face and smiling – a slow upward curling at the corners of her mouth that ended in a tiny trembling, and her expressions were changing all the time. They slipped across her face like a soft wind over water.

He'd seen how Miss Cynty halted the talk of men whenever she walked past them, the way she froze their gesturing hands, the slipping of their eyes along her body and the way those eyes rested on her shifting hips. He wondered if they ever saw what lay behind her eyes.

Now she was talking to Birdie with that whispery, liquid voice of hers. Birdie brought his ear down towards her lips; and what seemed to come out of her was a low and endless thrumming. His uncle dropped his right hand down the side of Cynty's face so that his fingers grazed her collarbone.

Pynter watched his uncle's fingers talk: stiffening from time to time, describing little circles beneath her jawline, brushing the softness there. Once, a sound came out of him, a rumble that was also a sigh. His uncle rolled his head. Another sound came out of him deeper still, and all the anguish and the trembling he'd so far hidden from them came out in his breathing while Cynty kept her lips flush against his ear. The only sign of life was the soft throbbing of her throat and the air that hummed around her.

Pynter had never seen Birdie like this before; never seen beyond the heaviness, the laughter and the thunder. He lifted his head, conscious of his own breathing, the throbbing in his throat, and realised that now he was the only one in the room with them. The others had left so quietly he hadn't felt a single movement of the floorboards. He rose quickly and tiptoed out of the door.

Outside, the women stood in a small huddle. They were murmuring amongst themselves. Patty made a flapping gesture with her arms. A chuckle escaped Tan Cee which she cut short with her hand. Deeka's bony shoulders stood above theirs like the flat of a broad-bladed oar.

Pynter felt as if he were looking at them from some place much further off, that none of this had anything to do with him. He looked past their shoulders. The night felt sonorous and endless. He felt the familiar urge to slip into it and walk, perhaps to his little rock above the sea. To sit at the very end of it with his feet over the waves and think of nothing in particular, or perhaps the father of his mother's last child, Lindy, whom she was so certain would arrive one day, soon. It was always soon – even after ten months, as if for this man especially, she did not measure time in days but by the strength of the conviction that she carried in her.

'What troubling you now, Ole Fella?' Tan Cee had broken away from the others and come over to him. Her voice was gruff and mocking, her hand warm against his neck. She was looking into his face with the narrow-eyed intentness he had grown accustomed to.

'You growin,' she said, nodding in that far-eyed, private way of hers and smiling. And it was true that in these, the hardest, most unforgiving months of the year, his body had surprised them. Now Tan Cee and his mother had to lift their chins to look him in the eyes.

He rubbed his head and looked up at the window, gaping like a tongueless mouth out at the night. 'They quarrellin,' he said.

'At least you catch that part.'

'They arguin. They ... '

'That what itchin you?' She was laughing at his confusion and he was in no mood for that. He was about to turn away and leave her there when he felt her hand around his shirt tail. She drew him towards the steps.

'What make you feel you got to know everyting, Pynto Benduh?' There was no trace of humour in her tone now.

She released his shirt, grabbed his arm and pulled him down beside her. 'She telling 'im to let her go. She want to hear 'im say it. Y'unnerstan dat?'

'No.'

He'd said it coldly, irritably, and that raised the irritation in her too. 'Well, you de edicated one – work it out yourself.' She'd made as if to get up, but changed her mind. She pressed her back against the upper rung of the step, slanted her head away from him and said nothing more.

Her hand came up and cupped his ear. It was one of her tricks. She hadn't done it for a long time. He closed his eyes and rested his weight against her. His mind drifted back to Birdie and Cynty and their wordless struggle in the house. He thought of Birdie's hands washing Cynty's face with air, her half-closed eyes, the throaty whispers pouring from her lips.

This love they said started when they were children. Their mothers had brought them to the river one Saturday morning and had raised their heads to see them holding hands – two children staring at each other so ignorant-an'-confuse a pusson didn have the heart to chastise them.

It was not attraction, they were too small for that; and love was not the name for it, they said. Not at that age. It was what happened to a pusson not looking for somethin and findin what they always want. A kind of recognizin. The difference was, it happened to them from childhood. And in a way, those two had never unlinked their hands from that very first time they met in the river.

Cynty was tiny, they said, with limbs that told them she was going to be small-boned like her mother. Her limbs had lied. It was as if her body had decided to ignore itself and go along with Birdie's. His chest deepened, and she'd fleshed out straight away. And wasn't it true that Cynty was the only woman in Old Hope who fitted Birdie's embrace?

It was an old love, Deeka told them once. Gloria lily love. The kind every yooman been was afraid of and yet longed for at the same time, for it could not be killed by absences or distance, Birdie's rolling in and out of jail for so much of their lives was proof enough of that. A kind o' love that was so certain of itself it put no emphasis on claiming. Which was why in all them years he was away, Birdie allowed Cynty to have whatever man she wanted, but she must never bear his seed.

A little fella named Tobias filled those absences. Cynty had brought him to Old Hope from somewhere else. And he was everything that Birdie was not. A small man, so small, in fact, she could lift him with one hand and cradle him in her arms. When Birdie arrived from jail, he retreated beneath the house, sat there with his elbows on his knees while the little house rocked above his head. After that first time he disappeared, returning only when Birdie went off again to jail.

There had been a joke in all of that. A little story. The small atrocious things they'd done to Tobias during Birdie's absences. For a start, Old Hope did not see him. Even when he said hello and smiled at them, Tobias wasn't there. For in this village above the canes, to laugh with a man was another way to embrace him.

Besides, he was half a man. His body said so. Imagining him with Cynty jus' didn make no sense. It bothered them. It left Old Hope men with an itch they wanted to satisfy. Which was why he shouldn't have trusted Gordon Coray's invitation to join them at the rum shop. He should have noticed the eyes behind the smiles of the men sitting on the wooden stools. Should never have gone past the first glass of rum they handed him.

He was strong they said, his body fought the liquor. It took a while before it seeped into his limbs and turned them to rubber. The rest was easy. Gordon placed his hands beneath his armpits and lifted him as easy as a lil sack of sugar. They slipped his trousers off.

Rumour was, the laughter reached the houses on Top Hill. It turned the women's heads down towards the rum shop, for they'd heard in it the devil in their men. At least he'd woken up in Cynty's bed. She'd known where Tobias had gone to and that very same laughter had made her leave her house and walk towards the shop. She never told Tobias about it, and he did not remember anything; or if he did he never showed it. He said the same hello to everyone and seemed a happier fella when they winked at him and grinned.

Pynter raised his head. He was startled to see Tan Cee's eyes on him. She'd remained so still she might have fallen asleep. He wondered how long she'd been looking at him that way.

'Make sense,' he said.

'What make sense?' She folded her arms around her stomach and leaned forward. He caught the smell of cinnamon.

'Is not jail this time,' he said. 'Is a different kind o' leavin – not knowin where a pusson off to; not sure they comin back.'

She said nothing for a while. She seemed to be looking past him at some far thing overhead. 'Yes,' she breathed, finally. 'Heart feed on hope, Pynto. You starve de heart of hope, it die. Birdie have to unnerstan that.'

He came to his feet before her, reached out a hand and pulled her up. Now they were standing exactly as they had been earlier. He slipped his arm around her shoulder. He felt her stiffen. He did not drop his arm.

She was looking up at the window. 'The kind o' thing they got between them, breakin loose is not de same. Birdie have to make it easy fo' Cynty. He have to tell 'er go.'

'Tan,' he said. 'I know a way to go. I know a way dat's not down there.' He pointed at the road below.

He thought she hadn't heard him.

'Tan, I ... '

'Fo' true?' She kept looking away from him.

'For true.'

He felt her move against him. 'You carry so much hate fo' 'im – an' a pusson don' know why. You behave like if he done you something. You fink you don' know dat? You fink ... ' Whatever she was about to add, she choked on it.

He looked up past the foothills towards the flake of moon that had risen above the valley – bright white like a half-closed eye. It crossed his mind that he had never seen Tan Cee cry.

'S'not me,' he said. 'He the one behave like if y'all done him something.'

She did not catch his meaning. But the tone of his voice must have told her that she wouldn't like what he was about to say. But right now, he told himself, he didn't give a damn. All this trouble with Birdie had left him with a flippin headache. Tan Cee was giving him one of those tight-lipped, sideways looks.

'What Birdie always runnin from? Eh? An' don't tell me is John Seegal. Cuz is a long time since John Seegal gone. What kind o' pusson prefer jail to family, Tan?'

'Watch yuh mouth, Pynto. Y'hear me.' She'd stepped back from him. She'd closed her fist and was holding it up before her like a warning.

He grinned at her and raised his voice a pitch. 'S'not you, s'not Patty, s'not my modder. S'not even Deeka. S'all of y'all put together. Don' matter what Birdie make y'all believe. Don' matter what happenin in there right now.' He pushed a thumb at the house. 'He don' like wimmen. Dey frighten 'im. He prefer the company o' fellas. Man! And de sonuvabitch should say so, becuz ... '

He saw the hand coming towards his head. He leaned away from it, ducked the second swing and jumped away from her, blowing her a kiss as he ran off.

21

A DEAD MAN had shown him the other way out of Old Hope. That was what he wanted to say to Deeka. He wanted his grandmother to know that he was Zed Bender born again, Zed Bender who'd fled the canes with a girl named Essa and got caught and killed somewhere up there in the foothills, under a tree that he, Pynter, had finally discovered. He'd wanted to go past the place where Zed Bender had fallen and find out, not what he and Essa had been running from, but the thing they had been running towards.

He was finding the 'ghost roads' all the time. It was easy when a pusson knew how. You ask yuhself: in Zed Bender time, what mus' a runnin pusson do to get 'way from Bull Bender and his dogs? And suddenly the landscape rearranged itself before you. Something adjusted in your head and the way you saw things changed. You saw the cleavage between boulders, like the space between two thighs, become a little passageway; you noticed the trees that hugged a particular hillside, at the top of which a narrow plateau ran. You noticed the way a branch was made to grow, and the large, flat stones that pointed to a gully.

He sat on the floor with his legs folded under him. Patty brought the lamp down over the sheet of paper. He took her purple marker and began to draw, while Birdie's bulk leaned over him like the shadow of a storm cloud.

He told them that the island was like a lizard with a shortened tail that lay belly-down on the ocean. Up there, behind the Mardi

Gras, if a pusson climbed past it, they would see the receding ash-dark humps that were the lizard's spine. It was those humps Birdie should be heading for.

Travelling up to it was like climbing through the seasons. A pusson leave the simmering heat of the flatlands, go past the cooler, wetter belt of cocoa, bananas and fruit trees, until they meet the forest that had always been there. You step over streams that never make it to the sea. And from there, the climbing gets much harder because the soil is never dry.

Up there is a different country – a bone-deep chill and unforgiving winds. The trees are short; their branches hug the earth. The spaces between them are almost as wide as a road. On moonlit nights you see the ocean on the left below you. And when there is no moon, there is just an arcing void of darkness.

You run north like Deeka say; keep runnin until you see a gatherin of lights below you; a brighter patch of sea. You swing left there, and down towards Kanvi.

Pynter dropped the pen. It landed with a soft plok on the paper. The movement seemed to startle them.

He avoided their gazes and sprang off the floor. 'I go wiv 'im part-way,' he said.

The factory whistle had not yet sounded across the valley when Chilway arrived. The air was chill and damp, with the kind of morning stillness that made even the furthest sound seem as if it were next door. They'd fed the fire in the yard with long-burning wild-pine wood. Patty had thrown a few handfuls of nutmeg shells into the blaze to suffuse the early morning air and make the waiting easier.

Deeka had ordered them to place two masantorches in the yard. She'd even planted two along the path that led up from the road. Patty complained she felt exposed. Deeka retorted that she should go put on more clothes.

Chilway had replaced the yellow Austin Farina with a white Land Rover. They noticed his hair was much whiter than it was the last time he came for Birdie and he was wearing spectacles. The four men who usually walked behind him were now at his side.

Deeka was dressed as if she'd prepared herself for church. She'd swept the house too, and spent a good part of the night clearing the yard of leaves. She'd even broken a bunch of hibiscus and dropped it in a bottle on the table in the hallway.

Chilway nodded at them all and offered Deeka a hand. She did not take his thumb this time. Her fingers wrapped around his completely. The four men helped him to the steps. From there he looked across at Patty and what passed across his face could just as easily have been a grimace or a smile.

'You want a drink?' Deeka said.

'What you got?' He gestured at the men who backed away from him. These were tall men – greying at the temples – whose faded khaki shirts and trousers were always beautifully ironed. The dark-brown polished leather belts they wore and the batons which hung down from their sides seemed as aged and well-kept as they were. These were men with wives and children, Deeka had said. They returned to the same bed every night; they comforted their children, they were fussy about their food, they tended their women's flower gardens. They'd seen their women bleed. Things like these made all the difference between a warden and a soldier.

Deeka splayed her fingers and counted as she listed for Chilway, 'I got Jack Iron, Mountain Dew, Sea Moon – and I have a drop o' special.'

'Everything, Miss Deeka. Mix them. What can't kill will fatten. Is mix-up-ness I want today. Is confusion I courtin. Put it in a cup inside the house. An' when you bring it out, pretend like if is water.'

Deeka went into the house, returned with the drink and placed it in Chilway's hand.

He gestured at the men again and they stepped further back from him. He brought the cup to his lips and lifted his eyes at Deeka over the rim. Chilway didn't shift his gaze until the cup was empty.

'When last you see a doctor?' Deeka said.

'Fuh what? For him to tell me what I know already?'

The men were looking at him with the same interest that Deeka was. They kept shifting their eyes between Chilway and the house. Chilway didn't seem to notice them. 'Kinda quiet here,' he said.

'We quiet people,' Deeka said.

'That wasn't what got report to me.' A laugh broke out of him.

'Foolish,' he said. 'Foolish.' He fluttered a wrist at his men. 'I keep telling y'all, fellas, is not gun that make you smart, is brains. When Sylus come and tell me – mad like hell – that Miss Dee send for me, y'all remember what I tell him?'

The fellas nodded.

'I say to him, I say, "Sergeant Sylus, you telling me what Miss Dee say, not what she mean."'

Another laugh escaped him. It ended in a fit of coughing that pulled his body forward. Deeka took the cup from his hand.

'Because, fellas, if y'all don't realise it yet,' Chilway stretched out his legs and leaned his back against the steps, 'Birdie not here. Birdie gone.'

He kept his finger in the air as if to say that there was more to come. 'I'll tell y'all something else, fellas: Miss Dee wasn't askin for me; Miss Dee was askin for time. Now, in the interest of procedure and because we, the servants of Her Majesty and all them law deh, have to be seen to be performing we duties in accordance with them self-same law deh, I ordering y'all to proceed inside Miss Deeka house and search, with the caveat of course that none o' y'all don't turn the lady place upside down or destroy her possessions. Else y'all will pay for everything y'all break. Now please proceed, then come back and report to me.'

Chilway seemed very pleased with his own words. Deeka's eyes flitted over him the way she had done with the soldiers when they came. He was smiling too much; was too relaxed. He was not the kind of man to make a joke of trouble. She handed him the cup of rum and topped it up.

They could barely hear the feet of his men on the floorboards. They were conversing in whispers. When they finally came out they said nothing to Chilway. Or if they did it was not with words. Chilway simply looked at them and smiled.

'I tell y'all something else,' he said. He eased himself forward, slipped his hand into the back of his trousers and brought out a radio. 'I figure I could stop him. I figure I know exactly where Birdie going. The way I work it out, Miss Dee, I still got time – two hours for the most.' Chilway rested the radio on the steps. 'Lemme tell you how I work it out.'

The man patted the walkie-talkie and then turned his face upwards and away from them. The firelight didn't seem to settle on his face so much as slide off it.

'Ain't no way Birdie goin be runnin up dat freezin mountain up there. Birdie like comfort. You won't find him 'mongst those cane-an'-bush down there either. He remember the dogs; he remember how patch-up and piecemeal those felons, that those dogs retrieve, look when they come back. He take the river. He wouldn leave the water till he get to the end of it. Now when Birdie reach the end of that river, he got just two ways to go: through the swamp or round it.

'But,' Chilway looked into their faces and smiled, 'he won't go through that swamp, he know what's inside there. Is worse than you can imagine, Miss Dee – what Birdie see inside that swamp. You won' believe 'twas just his father he see in there when he start bad-dreaming and bawling. So I rule that out. I rule that out completely. He heading for the biggest, widest door in all God world. He heading there.'

The man pointed at a cleft in the hills. It was too early to see the white, glittering heave that was the sea between it. 'Kalivini Bay,' he said. He sipped from the cup and rubbed his chest. 'It still dark, Miss Dee. A coupla fellas down there waiting for him. A few more come to see him off. Is not a big boat. What people round here know is cane, not sea. Is the kinda boat you play around the bay with. Is a little boat. Is a fly in the mouth of the sea. But they like Birdie, everybody like Birdie, even them dogs we got like Birdie. In fact, Sylus try to send them dogs after him and they got confuse. He put Birdie clothes in front of them and they start to wag their tail. Sylus's order didn't make no sense to them. Yuh see, Miss Dee – is a very stupid dog that bite the man that feed it.'

Chilway pushed back his head and laughed, carefully, tentatively, as if he were tiptoeing his way around the fit of coughing that was just behind it.

'Yes,' he said. 'We reach the bay, not so? Somebody will take him out, but one thing they won't do – they won't go south. That boat too small for all that bad water down there. They heading north. North, Miss Dee. North because Birdie want a bigger boat. Birdie need a boat that know tall water. A boat that understand the sea. Now, fellas, I know only three places on this island where he could find a boat like that. On the top of the island, where Miss Dee come from. That make sense. He got family up there, and family is blood. But that place too far. It too far, fellas. Birdie know that. Miss Dee here know that. I know that. Besides, Mister Boatman tired. San Andrews is the second place. But San Andrews fisherman don't have no heart. All he think about is his family and himself. If he see a man running, he want to know what that man running from before he even look at him. Now if Birdie tell him that he beat up some soldiers real bad. If he say is eight of them that he mash up. He don't even need to add that one of them is critical in hospital and chances is he never goin walk an' talk again. That fisherman not going nowhere. S'matter o' fact, he running to call the police. So that leave just one place.'

Chilway rested the cup on the step. 'How I doin, Miss Dee?'
'You talkin, sir; I lissenin.'

During all this time they'd hardly changed position. Tan Cee was still there, with a hand resting on her hip like the handle of a cup. Patty looked as if she were about to cry. Pynter's mother had become like Deeka, even in the way she stood. The plum tree was taking all of Peter's weight. He didn't appear to be listening to Chilway. His eyes were on the radio.

'That leave Kanvi. They got everything that Birdie want there. They got twenty-footer boat that know the ocean the way you fellas ought to know your bed. Kanvi people have a different law. They judge a man by what they think they see inside him. It don't matter what he done, once it wasn' done to them. If they like him, they'll take him anywhere for nothing; if they don't, it don't matter if he offer them ten new boat and a coupla aeroplanes, they'll turn their back and, excuse me, ladies, they'll leave him in his shite. Now, this is the interesting part.'

Deeka moved to fill Chilway's cup, but the man raised a staying hand. His eyes were slightly redder but his voice remained steady.

'You see, it don't matter what time Birdie left here. He could've gone to his woman house and spend a coupla hours tryin to make up for all the times he never had with her, and all the times he never going to have with her. Or he could've left straight away. It don't matter. It don't make a single difference to the time Birdie goin hop off this island. Yuh see, man is a beast of habit. And that is why,' Chilway looked at his watch and slid a finger across the glass, 'for the next hour or so, Birdie still belong to us. Yuh see, somebody will take him, but they'll take him in their own time. They'll get up in the morning, just after four, like they always do. They'll eat the fish an' provisions their woman fry or cook for them. They'll go down to the beach and prepare their boat. They'll boil a lil coffee there. They'll check the water and the weather and what kinda fish God make available today. After that, they'll double-check with one another and agree who goin be fishing which patch of sea today. Then just after the sun come up and hit the water, they'll prepare to leave. Right, Miss Dee?'

Chilway handed her the cup. He leaned forward and reached for the walkie-talkie. He unclipped the leather flap that kept it in the holster and slipped it out. It settled in his hand much as a pistol would.

'I had a choice between the gun they offer me and this, Miss Dee. I take this. Is new. Englishman invention. Scotland Yard.' He turned it over in his hand. 'That van down there is like a lil radio station. I switch this on ... ' His thumb slid across the silver button. The thing came alive and began hissing like a little metal hive. He studied the object for a while and then looked up.

'Now, Miss Dee – I'z cognizant of the fact that I been procrastinatin here. I been giving y'all my prognosis when duty behooves me to ... '

'What he say?' Deeka's face could have been cut out of the stones that packed the yard.

Pynter looked at the man and a quiver ran through him. For despite the rum-reddened eyes, the dry white lips, the tired, ash-grey face that seemed to have been charred to the bone by illness, the brain that lived under the cotton-white head of hair was as active as live coals.

'He say he wastin time wiv all dis ole-talk,' Pynter said.

Chilway's head jerked sideways at him. He rested the radio on his lap and grinned.

'Ah! A lil epistemologist. Secondary?'

Deeka nodded, her eyes on the man's hand.

The pleats on Chilway's forehead deepened. He was leaning forward now, his hand adjusting his glasses. 'Birdie never tell me 'bout this one. He yours?'

'He ours. He was here last time you come. He grow. We call 'im Pynto. He got Birdie second name. He de first in de family. First in Ole Hope.' She opened her palms at Chilway. 'And the way he goin, yunno ... '

'I know,' Chilway cut in. 'The rest round here will follow after him. He show them that is possible. Now, Miss Dee.' The man's eyes were holding Deeka's and the expression on his face was strange. A hardness resided in his eyes now. His voice had also changed. 'Gimme one good reason why I shouldn keep my finger on dis switch an' put my mouth to it. Make me unnerstan why me – big man like me – who been doin this job fo' thirty years, who never lose a man, why I should spoil my name for Birdie.'

The words had issued from the corners of his mouth – flat, emptied of the humour he had greeted them with when he arrived.

Deeka cleared her throat. Her hand drifted in the direction of her daughters. 'We, we the cane, Missa Chilway. We take the heat. Y'unnerstan? Dey,' she gestured at Pynter, 'de children, dey what come out of it. Of us. They the rum, the sugar, the … ' Deeka shook her head, as if to clear it of some pain. 'We bring dem in de worl'; we not s'posed to see them go before we go. Else, what sense it make in livin – in livin like we live? Tell me, Missa Chilway, then what's de use o' cane?'

A tear slipped down her face. She turned her back and cleared it.

Chilway rose to his feet, the little machine still in his hand, still turned on, the crackly voices coming from it. He flicked the switch. The machine died. Peter eased his back off the plum tree and began humming to himself.

Morning had just begun to streak the peaks of the Mardi Gras. It hadn't reached them yet. Wouldn't for another half-hour or so.

Deeka fed them fried fish and bread and cups of scalding cocoa. Pynter went off and returned with a shirtful of water lemons, and guavas whose flesh the five men sniffed and marvelled at.

And Patty, only for that morning, became the dream she knew that Chilway always wished for: she brought his plate to him, she poured his cup of cocoa, brushed the breadcrumbs off his shirt, and when he finished eating she brought him the water to wash his hands, and poured. The man looked up at her, his face gone soft and vulnerable as a boy's, and said in a low, unsteady voice, 'What's the opposite of death, Miss Pretty?'

'Life,' she told him, smiling.

He shook his head. 'Everybody get it wrong,' he said. 'The whole world get it wrong. The opposite of death is beauty.'

Then, as if he'd just been reminded of something, he looked across at Pynter. 'And you, Missa Secondary? What you say?'

Pynter had been allowing his mind to drift along the top of the island, the high inscrutable places of wind and silence that looked down on the villages. He'd been thinking about a name that had been said to him which was supposed to mean something. He blinked at the man and shrugged. 'Ain't got no opposite,' he said, 'jus' … '

'Just?'

'Difference.'

The man rested his elbows on his knees and leaned forward. The frown lines deepened on his forehead. 'And how you work that out, young fella?'

Pynter lifted his shoulders again. He felt his mother's eyes on him, glanced at her and caught her quick cautioning gaze. He sensed the sudden wariness in the women too. He felt his mouth go dry.

'Talk to me, young fella,' Chilway said, his voice gone whispery and impatient.

Pynter was suddenly afraid too – that whatever he might say now, this man who was looking at him so steadily, so strangely, might find something in his words that would send his hand reaching for his radio.

Pynter licked his lips. 'Stone blunt; knife sharp. You – you kill somefing wiv a stone, or you kill it wiv a knife – same – same intention, same result. Ain't – ain't got no opposite.'

Chilway nodded. 'Just difference.' He split a guava and scooped out the soft flesh with a thumb. He held it up before him then placed it in his mouth. 'How old you say you was?'

'I didn say how old I was.'

'He twelve,' Elena said, her voice strident with a warning for him and an apology for the man.

Chilway smiled at her. 'They teach you that in Secondary?'

Pynter shook his head. 'S'what I think, Missa Chilway. And – and if it got a opposite to death, is not no life.'

'Is?'

'Knowin.'

'Knowing?'

'Uh-huh.'

'Don' know what wrong wiv 'im,' Elena cut in, her voice pitched even higher. 'Dis – dis boooy!'

'Yuh miss the point,' Chilway told her sharply, irritably. 'And that mean,' he held a rigid finger up at her, 'you miss the problem. Cuz Missa Secondary here jus' show you whaaz frightening this whole country right now, and why they want all of 'em in jail.' The man jabbed a finger at his head. 'The mind they got belong to them, and they don' give a damn who know it.'

He was breathing heavily. The rum had loosened his jaw and from time to time he lifted his shoulders and dropped them as if he were trying to shake off the drunkenness.

'Times change, Miss Dee. The job turning into something different. Things gone upside down. Everything.' He looked at the radio in his hand. 'I wish everybody had one o' these so I could talk in it just once and make them understand that. Used to be a time when they send me for a fella like Birdie. I'll take two or three of my men with me. If I know him well, if he is a regular, I'll go alone. I remind him that if he take a farmer goat and cook oil-down with it, without that farmer consent, is tantamount to theft, no matter how much his children starving. So he should expect me to come for him. He unnerstan that. His woman might start bawlin becuz life just got a lil harder for her and the children that he leave her with. I bring him in whole. A coupla years later he come back out in one piece. Okay, not all the time. I not a perfect man and some o' them does try me patience so I have to bus' dem arse. A coupla blows with this,' he pointed at his baton, 'is enough to turn them into angels. Is not the same as picking up a coupla schoolchilren and telling them they guilty of dissent and dissatisfaction. It don't have no – no,' he looked angrily about him, 'no elegance in that. I can't hold that up in front of a magistrate and say, "Your Honour, take a look at the quantity and the size of dissatisfaction this young fella here commit and see for yourself what a criminal he is."'

For a moment Patty's fingering of her earrings arrested him.

'You give a man a gun, is not just a weapon that you hand him. You give him permission to find out how it work. One day he goin to use it on somebody, if only to make it do what it s'posed to do. Is the only way he know that is really what they say it is. Is the only way he know that is for real, y'unnerstan? The trouble is it got a kind of man who never satisfy with one time. He do it over and over again. He don't need no provocation. S'like he need reminding all the time what killing really feel like. That's Sylus, Miss Dee. That's the fella you shame yesterday. He'll come again, when y'all not even looking. He done it before.'

He wagged a chin at Peter first and then at Pynter. 'Watch out for y'all children. Is the children that they after.'

One of his men reached down and helped him to his feet.

Chilway stood at the edge of the yard looking about him as if he'd forgotten what he'd come for. He cocked a finger at Deeka.

'I hope you never have to ask yuhself if saving Birdie was worth all the trouble he left y'all with.'

They watched the fellas help him down the path.

22

SIX MONTHS AFTER Birdie left, they climbed the foothills to watch the tractors leave – a slow, juddering procession of dirty steel, trundling eastwards towards the cleft between the hills that marked the beginning of the Drylands. They did not return home until evening, not until the thundering far off in the distance died completely and the smell of trees and the river replaced the fetor of machine oil.

The tractors had left a sloping expanse of wasted straw behind them and the smell of exposed soil. They'd taken what remained of the dry season with them also, for the furnace of the valley cooled soon after, and now Old Hopers were turning up their heads to the softer skies of another halfway season.

This was their time, Tan Cee said, these days of quiet air, and light as brittle and pure as glass, when the moisture that the hills released was cool on the skin, when bananas bloomed momentously – the curved head of their single, elongated flower straining to lick the earth like giant scarlet tongues. And silk-cotton trees buried deep inside the climbing forests floated fertility messages on the wind – tiny seeds wrapped in bolls of cotton that were so thin and light it was like catching bits of solid air.

If Deeka noticed this change, she did not show it. From the night that Birdie left them, she'd been searching for signs of his arrival somewhere. She studied the spiralling fall of leaves, the flutterings of the perishing moths inside the lampshade, the

213

unsteady flight of seagulls – as if there ought to be some meaning in the rapid scribblings of their wings on the winds that drove them inland.

She hardly ate. She hoped aloud that Birdie had escaped to a country where he at least understood the language, which o' course meant Englan' o' America.

Just when Pynter thought there would be no end to this grumbling, sour-faced vigil, the evening came when he watched his grandmother follow the flight of a single cattle egret that lifted itself from the gloom of the valley floor. It rose fast and steady, in a dazzling arc, like a streak of light against the smoke green of the hillside. It looped high and hard, seemed to hit a sudden wind up there above their heads, then it began descending in a dizzying whorl towards them. Deeka brought the palms of her hands together. She held them before her, her body pushed forward in a nervous, aching prayer. The bird settled like a fluttering fragment of tissue on the tres-beau mango tree above the house.

His grandmother spread her arms and smiled. 'Birdie awright,' she said. 'Leasways, I feel so now.'

Pynter turned towards his scooter, smiling, because his mother and his aunts had already begun to remember Birdie differently.

Evenings, Patty became Chilway, while Tan Cee and Elena took turns pretending to be Deeka. And because it sweetened the jokes a lot more, Peter walked and talked like Birdie. And it did not matter what his grandmother said or did to kill the fun, they made a fool of Birdie over dinner and laughed about his chupidness.

Now, with Deeka's mind at ease, Patty remembered aloud the time when Birdie stole a whiteman's dog and Chilway came for him. Patty high-stepped to the middle of the yard, her bowl of soup cradled under one arm. She pulled down the sides of her mouth, half-closed one eye, dropped her shoulders and leaned her head like Chilway.

'Miss Dee,' she croaked, prodding her stomach and turning to Elena, who'd put on the dark-eyed, tight-lipped face of Deeka. 'Miss Dee, I got something growing in here dat no doctor could cure and I know fo' sure is not no chile.'

Patty adjusted the bowl and made a face at Deeka's back. 'Now, I want to ask you, Miss Dee: how long I been comin here to pick up Birdie? What's de longest time I keep 'im 'way from you? A hundred years, right? Not three, not four, just one. Only one lil hundred. An' dat, Miss Dee, is only becuz he thief dat whiteman dog, and it ain't got no way you kin thief a whiteman dog an' prove is yours in court. Cuz Englishman not like we. English people an' deir dog does talk.'

Elena was still mimicking Deeka's expression but she had trouble holding it. Tan Cee's shoulders were twitching.

'So, when dat Englishman call hi dog – dat Birdie say is his – in front of everybody in court and tell de dog to turn round an' jump up an' smile, an' every time de dog wag it tail an' do it,' Patty lifted a finger limply in the air, 'it ain't got no way a judge from Englan' not goin to charge Birdie for abduction. F'twas a local dog, or in fact a local judge, Birdie would only get charge fo' thiefin. But,' the finger wagged, 'Englishman dog get treat like people. An' accordin to Judge Crichlow, you don' thief people, you abduct dem, an' dat's de same as thiefin a Englishman dog. So you see, Miss Dee … '

Patty didn't finish the joke. Deeka came after her with a bowlful of water. They ran rings around the house while the others staggered about the yard, so drunk with laughter they could barely stand.

Patty's new way with words sent ripples of pleasure and surprise through Pynter. It was as if his youngest aunt had found the handle of a door that took her further into herself.

The week before, he'd been muttering words that Miss Sislyn told his class to memorise. Words, she said, that were going to speak more and more directly to them of the coming times. He turned his head and realised that Patty had been listening. Her eyes were wide and she'd frozen the yellow comb above her head.

'Say dat again, Pynto.'

' "In the dark you call my ... " '

Her hand released the plait of hair. 'Say it like you just say it.'

' "I have told you ... " '

'Nuh! Not so!' She jerked her head, sharply, pettishly, as if he were about to deprive her of something that belonged to her. 'Say it like you say it firs' time.'

> *In the dark you call my name*
> *I have told you, child*
> *Outside is not the same*
> *Hard heels crash against the night*
> *And our streets run red with tears ...*

When he'd finished, she sat with her head cocked at an angle as if she were still hearing him. After a while she stirred. 'Them your wuds?'

Nuh, he told her, they'd come from the mouth of a jailbird and a drunkard. And suddenly he wanted to tell her more. 'They more dan words, Tan Pat. Is the trouble an' the danger dat dey carrying inside dem.'

He paused, finding pleasure in the way he'd just described it. He told himself that he was going to put it that way to Miss Sislyn.

But he was not sure that Patty understood him. He thought for a while, then offered her an image. 'Take cane, Tan Pat. Cut it, break it, crush it, strain it. Boil all the water and the nonsense out of it. What you got left?'

She curved her neck and laughed. 'Syrup, Sugarboy. Pure syrup.'

'Uh-huh,' he said. 'Same like these words.'

She pulled at her hair with a sharp movement of the comb. It made her wince. As if prompted by the pain, Patty lifted her head and held his eyes. Her voice dropped to a whisper and only her lips moved when she spoke. 'I comin after you, Pynto. I breakin out of here. It don' matter what I have to do, you not leavin me behin', y'unnerstan?' She turned away from him.

He remembered staring at her back and nodding, wanting to ask her where she intended to follow him to.

Now there she was, shrieking and laughing at the back of the house. His grandmother's chuckles came like the crackling of firewood. He knew exactly where Deeka was holding Patty to make her laugh like that.

After her rough play with Deeka, Patty slipped away from them. She lifted a finger at Pynter and winked. He pretended he did not see her. When she returned, her arrival killed the women's conversations and brought them to their feet. She stood amongst them in a blue dress – the colour of a halfway season's sky.

Pynter looked across at her and smiled. He'd been holding Patty's secret all week and was tiring of it.

The very morning after she told him that he was not leaving her behind, she'd met him halfway up Old Hope Road. He'd seen her in the distance and for a moment he could not believe that it was Patty, for she hardly left the yard except to go to the cinema in San Andrews once a month with Leroy.

She'd spoken to him in whispers. Handed him a roll of dollar bills and told him to buy a dress for her. A nice one, she said. One worth all the money she was handing him. And by the way she said it, he understood she wanted something that would make sense of the past few months of labouring in the canes. He told her he knew nothing about dresses. Dat's awright, she said, and passed him a reel of sewing thread. Made him run lengths of it across her shoulders and around her waist. She pulled the string along an arm, broke it when it reached her wrist and gave the string to him. She anchored the thread to the nape of her neck with one finger and dropped the reel, then instructed him to break it off just under her calves. He took out his ruler, measured each piece of thread and wrote the numbers down. One more thing, she told him. She slipped a dollar into his shirt pocket and said it was for him. She was smiling when she finished.

She pointed at the numbers on the paper. 'I want a dress like dat,' she said. 'A proper one, y'hear me?'

Later, he chose one without sleeves, spent a long time fingering the fabrics in the store until he felt the exact softness that he wanted.

His heart had stepped up a pace when he brought the bag and handed it to her behind the house.

She didn't take it straight away. She'd dropped her hands to her sides. They were trembling slightly. The trembling was also in her voice when she looked at him and asked, 'It goin gemme de job?'

'Which job?' he said, before suddenly remembering.

For a moment he did not know what to tell her. He lifted his shoulders and dropped them. 'A pusson have to do, Tan Pat,' he said. 'S'long as dey live dey have to do. Else do will get up an' do them.'

'Them your wuds?' she said. She took the bag.

'My fadder words,' he told her.

Now there she was standing in the dress as if she were clothed in seawater. It hugged the length of her body all the way down to her calves.

Tan Cee and his mother were inspecting her, not with their eyes but with fingers which slipped quickly under the sleeves and hemline, adjusting the curve of the collar, pausing over the downward curve of Patty's shoulders, the flare of her hips. As if, with those caresses and pats and pauses, they were not only measuring the way the blue dress fitted with the matching shoes Patty had borrowed from Miss Elaine, but were tracing the shape of what was to come tomorrow.

And yes, they told her finally. Right there. Just as she was in front of them. Like that. Just so!

The way she stan' up an' look down she nose at them. Uh-huh. It didn have no doubt 'bout it. She was a proper front-store girl. Not no shop-front girl! No! Store-front! A department one – wiv glass-wall an' pretty-shiny-counter, an' 'lectric light an' everyting in between.

S'matter o' fact, she was more proper than all them proper store-front girls in San Andrews. It didn make no flippin' difference if she get de job or not.

If Leroy had raised his head from staring at the stones, he might have caught Deeka's eyes on him – a gaze that took in all of Patty's man in rapid little passes. The way she'd looked at the faces of the soldiers when they came for Birdie.

And while the women teased and fondled Patty, Deeka did not take her eyes off Leroy. She prodded her headwrap, moved her lips and nodded as if a thought had just occurred to her. She gave him a final sideways glance before turning back to her daughters.

Pynter could not remember a time when Deeka spoke to any of her daughters' men directly. When they were sent with something for her, she did not take it from their hands. She pointed to the table or the steps and busied herself with something else. She pretended not to hear them when they greeted her. And the few times that she chose to answer, it was with a grunt.

Word was, she used to be much worse with his and Peter's father. She'd almost taken a machete to Manuel Forsyth once, they said, but his mother had stopped her.

Leroy was still looking across at Patty. He'd crossed his legs and stuffed both hands down his pockets. And Pynter knew that it was not the chill that had risen up from the valley this evening that made him pull up the collar of his white shirt until the up-pointed ends were brushing against his ears. Pynter thought he also knew what his grandmother had been thinking when she looked at him. In fact, she'd said it the evening after Birdie left. Men, she'd told them, carried trouble inside them the way their wimmen carried their seed. It grew in them to bursting, till they couldn hold it in no more. Difference was, when they delivered it, they left the trouble behind and walked.

It crossed his mind that perhaps Deeka had been lying to them all along. Perhaps it wasn't John Seegal who didn have time for men, who did nothing at all for the only son he fathered. Perhaps it was Deeka who'd managed to slip all that flippin' bad-mindedness into his head. S'matter of fact, might ha' been one of the things that killed him.

Pynter liked the thought. He liked it so much he was still carrying it with him the next day on his way down to the river.

His passing paused the conversations of the women. A few lifted a hand and waved. Miss Elaine flicked her fingers and smiled. Lizzie acknowledged him on the little road above them by stiffening her spine.

There was a small precipice up there above the river where he spent his weekends. Directly under him, there was the deep blue pool people called Young Sea. Even from the height he sat above it, he would feel its rising coolness brushing the soles of his feet, the water glittering through the leaves below, like eyes. Beyond that, there wasn't much to look at apart from the brighter patch of green that marked the course of Old Hope River towards the sea.

There weren't any boys this morning. They would be fishing further up the river since they never went beyond Young Sea. They knew nothing of the creatures that lived in the leaf tunnels which began just after it.

News of what was there would reach the other Old Hope boys and they would return with their fathers' machetes, with lengths of wood and kerosene. They would chop their way through the tangle, and put fire to anything that burned. They would kill the living things they set their eyes on, carry them in sacks up to the roadside and scatter them along it, so that the rest of Old Hope could marvel at the strangeness they had discovered and destroyed.

If he'd met them on the way there he would feel their eyes on him, especially Oslo, brown and upright as one of Birdie's breads, his bright white eyes forbidding him to join them. A couple might call out his name, or mumble something they thought he couldn't hear. One of them might beckon, Frigo perhaps, or, if Arilon was with them, he would detach himself from the group of boys, come over to him and rest a hand across his shoulders.

He marvelled at the distance that a pusson eyes could place you, even when that pusson was smiling in yuh face. Then his thoughts fell back on what Birdie said to him the night he'd taken him up to the top of the island and left him there. A name. A single word that his uncle had thrown over his shoulder almost as a person might toss a careless coin, before his footsteps faded like a dying heartbeat in the night.

Slimmer, he'd said, ask yuh people about Slimmer. Y'hear me?

He was still wondering what a name he'd never heard before had to do with him, o' anybody fo' that matter, when, ahead of him, a figure detached itself from the overhang of rocks that stood over the cane track. He slowed down. He switched his plastic bag of books over to his left hand and pulled out his slingshot.

His grandmother was coming towards him with that quick hill-woman stride of hers. The tail of her dress was flapping around her legs as if she were pushing against a high wind. She was holding her machete in her hand.

He folded a ball bearing into the tongue of the weapon, halted in the middle of the track and waited.

As she approached, he thought that there must have been a lot of truth in what she said she was like as a young woman. That if she were Patty's age and it was at all possible for someone to place them side by side, a pusson would only have eyes for Deeka.

Purpose gave his grandmother height. Anger made her larger. Although, right now, he could not decide which emotion was propelling her towards him. He dropped the bag of books beside his feet and kept his eyes on the machete. Deeka stopped abruptly a little way off from him. She looked down at the slingshot, then at his face. Then with a movement that seemed both sudden and contrite, she dropped the machete in the grass beside her.

And in this quiet afternoon, on this little track above the river, it felt odd that he should come face to face with his grandmother for the first time. Until now, he'd never stood anywhere with her alone.

The rubber straps of the catapult felt clammy in his hands. He felt his body turning sideways, his chin lowering itself, almost as if his body had taken over from his mind. Now he was looking back at her along the line of his right shoulder.

Deeka cleared her throat. She pushed out a hand towards him. A bright red packet of something was sitting in her palm.

'S'for you,' she said.

He shook his head, stepped further back from her. And yet when he looked up, the distance between them seemed the same.

'Take it,' she said. Her shoulder convulsed slightly. She took a small step towards him.

The sweat had gathered at her brows and on the top of her upper lip.

'S'for you,' she said.

He heard footsteps behind him. They were coming fast. He did not look round. He knew who those footfalls belonged to.

Deeka broke her gaze from him. She looked even taller now. The sweat had broken the dam of her brows. It ran down her cheeks. She did not seem to notice.

He heard his name.

Tan Cee's steps became slow and hesitant behind him. Her words seemed to reach him from a distance. 'Take it, Pynto.'

Her voice came like a release. It gave him something to hold on to.

'I don' want it,' he said. 'Whatever it is.'

He turned to face his aunt and what he saw surprised him. He expected irritation, even anger, but not the tearfulness, not the pleading on her face.

'You don' know what it is,' she said. 'Take it, Pynto. Fo' me.'

'Don' matter – I don' want it.'

A shuffle of feet turned his head back towards Deeka, but she was already striding back towards the rocks from which she'd seemed to emerge so miraculously.

Tan Cee doubled her knees and picked up the little red ball. She lifted the tail of her dress and brushed the dust off it. He saw that a string was looped around it.

His auntie straightened up and lifted it towards the light, as if it were an offering, not to him, but to whatever she was feeling for her mother.

'She hurt,' she said. 'She hurt bad.' For a while, her hands took over from her words.

'I come runnin,' she said. 'Peter tell me you lef' a lil while back and he see Deeka leave right after. He didn tell your modder. God bless 'im. He know better than to tell Elena dat Deeka gone after you wiv a cutlass in she hand.' She glanced down at the slingshot in his hand. 'I don' know my own modder mind, Pynto. But I know enough o' yours.'

Her gaze felt like an accusation.

'Deeka been tryin to tell you somethin.' The way she said this, he knew that the hurt was also hers.

'She can't make de wuds. She can't.' Tan Cee gave him a brief, agitated smile. 'She feel she owe you a life. Birdie life. And this … '

She held up the little red bag. It sat like a fat droplet of blood in her palm. She brought it closer to his face. He caught the scent of strangeness and pulled back.

It contained oils, she said, saps and gums and barks from plants that grew only in the mountains of the north. There were the essences of seeds and shellfish in there, secretions from the rocks that hid the sulphur springs in the heart-part of the island.

Hard-to-find things a pusson wear in a lil bag against the skin. It made old men remain fertile; kept the skin of wimmen young throughout their lives. It purified the blood of children. And whether a pusson believed it or not, fact was it take the best part of a lifetime to bring all of it together in that lil red bag.

And all he could think of while she talked was that it would have been better if Deeka had really come to harm him with the machete she'd left lying in the grass. You can't fight the hateful gazes that been following you all yuh life. A pusson can't reply to twisted lips or half-said words that shaped the spite you never hear. Eyes that never met yours, that always saw above, around or past you. You can't aim a slingshot at that.

'He ours,' she'd said to Chilway to save that thiefin son of hers who murder a man and make a couple of others useless. He ours, my arse. How come? For who? Since when? When she said it, he was thinking, No! I not. Not me. Cuz I'z the one that you want dead from time. Not so? I'z this Zed Bender fella born again to give y'all a whole heap of hell. I de one who s'pose to dead next year.

And what happm if is so? Eh? S'pose I'z really he? S'pose I got jus' one more year to go? Is I who make meself? I ask y'all to bring me back? Eh? How come y'all don' blame my modder? How come is only me?

And it was not true what Tan Cee said about Deeka not knowing a way to talk to him. She had found a different language, that was all.

She'd been placing little presents beside the stone he sat on every evening. Hard-to-find things: shells which Peter told him she'd walked to the bay and collected herself. A few days ago she'd returned from the foothills with a plant whose leaves were also flowers – cream and soft like a tongue, with bright purple edges. Last night she laid a beetle on the floor where he did his homework – so iridescent in the lamplight its carapace seemed to spark. And it made his body twitch with irritation, because there were never any words from her, just these offerings of shapes and colours and patterns, which Peter took up and examined as if they were meant for him.

Tan Cee looked away. 'You still believe she want you dead? That what you feel?'

A child's voice, bright as a blade, came up from the river. The chattering of others further up joined in. The babble faded just as suddenly.

Tan Cee was quieter when she turned back to him. 'Hate an' love, Pynto – sometimes dey hardly different. Either way, is feel-ins. Either way a pusson carry you inside dem. S'why hate-an'-love does exchange place so easy.'

Perhaps it was not the words but the little wave of sadness that crossed her face which made him think of Coxy. He raised the tail of his shirt, reached out and brushed the sweat from her forehead. Now she was looking at him strangely.

'Wimmen funny,' she breathed, a small smile tugging at her mouth. 'We always love de bad ones more. S'a gift from yuh granmodder, Pynto. S'a proper gift.'

'S'not enough,' he said again.

He took up his bag of books; paused over Deeka's small machete. It lay flat and dull like a petrified snake in the grass. He took it up and handed it to Tan Cee.

'Time, yunno – a lil more of it. Thaa'z all.' He was not sure why he said that. Didn't know exactly what he meant by it. He straightened up and stared down at the river.

'Let's go home,' he said. 'I hungry.'

23

THESE MORNINGS the women's eyes searched his face, striving to read the things he was not telling them. Walk more carefully, they said. He would be fifteen soon – a dangerous time for young people. In the evenings, on the way back from his school above the ocean, he should remember to turn to face each vehicle he heard coming up behind him. If it were full of soldiers, never look them in the eye. Force a smile – at least it would soften the sourness of that face of his, if nothing else.

A fast way home was anywhere that was not the road; it was the slopes that rose above San Andrews, the high hill gardens that overlooked the mansions just beyond them. The brutal heave of trees and mud tracks that stood between him and Old Hope.

His mother would reach up and pat his collar for the hundredth time, her eyes fixed on his face. And if, she said, her advice didn make no sense to him, just remember lil Jordan.

Lunchtimes, he reached into his bag and felt his slingshot lodged against his books, folded with the same care with which she wrapped his sandwiches. The rubber straps felt fragile between his fingers. His grandmother never forgot to place it there before he left for school, her way, perhaps, of reminding him too of Jordan. And it was true that every time his fingers brushed those straps, it stirred in him the memory of that boy, with his dangling arms, and eyes so glazed and distant it reminded Pynter of his father's. The steady, staring eyes of Jordan which could no longer recognise the place he was born in. Jordan, standing at the side of Old Hope Road where Sylus and his men had dropped him, gazing into his mother's face and not knowing who she was.

Jordan's mother blamed it on Birdie. It was the scooter Birdie had left them all those years ago. It was the madness that this bit of wood and metal had sneaked into their children's blood. The memory of their uncle standing on the top of Man Arthur's Fall, tall as God, with his flying machine, had never left them. It had taken Birdie an evening to build it; a moment to show them what it did; no time at all to tell them how it would make them fly.

In the quiet of that evening, as soon as his uncle had left for Cynty's house, he and the other boys had sat in a tight group by the roadside and talked about the machine Birdie had built Peter. It was not Birdie's fault that it did not fly. It was the haste with which he'd built it. Becuz serious tings need serious time. And a jailbird like Birdie never have nuff time. Which meant, of course, they had to build themselves the machine he intended.

News of the carcasses of cars and trucks sent them walking the island with lengths of iron and crowbars across their shoulders. They invented new tools, the better to reach inside the engines and prise the bearings out. It took them months – which proved their point about Birdie's hastiness – of building and rebuilding, of breaking and remaking, of adjusting wheels and wood and axles. Of launching themselves from Man Arthur's Fall, their minds still fizzing with the memory of that first time Birdie Bender tied a stone on a flesh-coloured plank of wood and told them it could fly.

Pynter remembered the first time that he tried himself, lying flat on his stomach, watching the road slip by in a swift grey river, half an inch below his face. The sense of being lifted out of his own skin, the weightlessness as they raced down Man Arthur's hill, filling up the world with thunder. For there was no sound on earth like the wail of sixty metal wheels on asphalt, no sensation like the dizzying delirium of jittering bone and blood. No certainty as chilling as the one that emptied their heads of everything and held them to the slipping road. All there was between the safe side of the shaky iron bridge and the rocks below on which Man Arthur threw himself was a simple twist of the wrist.

Right here at this desk in his school above the ocean, he'd wondered what it would be like to hold a steady line between the wheel-span of a tractor, to go clean under it and come out the other end unbruised. He'd worked it out and done it, with the others watching from the top of Man Arthur's Fall, with Peter screaming his name so loud that, despite the tractor up ahead and the grinding of his own machine, he could hear the terror in his brother's voice. By then they had trimmed their machines down to nothing, so that all that lay between them and the road were three ball bearings and a strip of wood half the width of their bodies. They had so terrified the drivers that, in the closing months of the cutting season, they'd reduced the flow of sugar cane to the factory to a nervous trickle.

It was two years since Chilway had come to Deeka's yard and warned them about the trouble to come, so they'd forgotten the warden's warning. These April days when Old Hope Valley felt hollowed out and calm and the air that drifted in from the sea brought ground doves down to earth to feed beside the road, they'd forgotten the threat of a soldier named Sylus.

No one missed Jordan until his mother began calling out to him that evening, patiently at first, then more urgently as night began to fill the valley. Her keening, high-pitched calls finally urging them out of their yards.

They found Jordan's machine lying in the middle of the road, its wheels turned up towards the sky. They had no way of finding out what had happened until Tobias said to Cynty that the soldiers had him. The men wanted to hear it from Tobias themselves. He stood before them, grinning, his large eyes rolling in his head, and told them he knew nothing more. The men stepped away from him to observe what his hands and eyes were doing while he talked. They adjusted their machetes, nodded at each other and agreed that there was nothing to do but wait.

And in that time of waiting, the boys hid their machines in gullies and ravines, between the branches of high trees, wherever the adults could not lay their hands on them.

On the third day after Jordan disappeared, a long blue van arrived quietly, so quietly Old Hope did not hear the engine and if it wasn't for Lizzie collecting water from the standpipe they would not have known that Jordan had been returned.

The van was speeding up the road by the time Lizzie started shouting.

Jordan, he used to be the mildest-mannered boy they knew: a long, smooth face and eyes so dark it was as if there was no limit to their depth. Thick-haired, tall and healthy, with the prettiest smile Old Hope had ever seen. Almost too pretty to be a boy, and so gentle with it a person hardly heard him when he spoke.

The sounding out of Jordan's name tumbled them onto the road, a shuffling, hustling thunder of feet stretching from the small hill-rise of Hinter to the crotch of Old Hope Valley.

Jooordan come back! Dey bring back Joooordan!

He was just standing there in the middle of Old Hope Road, staring at all that grinning, laughing, jostling confusion.

Jooordaan! Jordan?

But he looked lost. 'Jordan not dere at all,' Deeka said. He looked frightened, and when he tried to speak, the words got all squashed up in his mouth. That was what Pynter remembered now: a quick boy gone slow. It broke the heart to watch him force his lips to shape words.

Not remembering was best sometimes, Tan Cee said. It was something that the heart knew. It pull a pusson in, far back into demself. And nobody could bring them out again until they cured an' ready to face de worl'.

But it seemed to Pynter that Sylus had done something worse to Jordan. He'd reached inside of Jordan and crushed him up in there.

Deeka was in the yard when they returned, leaning against the mud bank with her lips pulled together in a knot. She lifted her head at them, wanting to know who the hell Muriel thought she was to wrap her sour mouth around her son like that? What the hell Muriel take Birdie for?

That was the trouble with Old Hope. That was the problem with this whole island. People forget. They make themself forget. They clear their heads of rememberin, like how some fussy wimmen clear their yard of leaves.

And she was certain that a time goin come when they won't remember Jordan. Not as they saw him standing by the road this evening. They would make themselves remember what he used to be before Victor soldiers lay their hands on 'im. The same way, during all these years, they choose to remember the man who believe he own the island, that was until this evening, when he reach his hand inside this lil cane valley, lift a young-fella off the road and bring 'im back so confuse he didn know hi own mother.

It wasn' Birdie who did that. 'Twasn't even the soldiers. It was the man that all of them decide to make a Christ of. And Muriel will never think to point at him.

What did they remember of the man who believed he own the island, eh?

Elena placed her back against a house post. She sat cross-legged, with the sleeping child across her lap, and made small, caressing circles with her fingers in its hair. Tan Cee leaned, quiet and far-eyed, against the grapefruit tree. Peter came and stretched himself out on the stones beside Pynter.

Down there, Deeka said, pointing at the strips of cane land beyond which the stones began. There used to be a time when the soil between those stones was payment for their labouring in the canes; not the soil itself but the food they made come out of it. But food rot, she said. You can't take part of it, wrap it in a bit of cloth and leave it somewhere safe. You can't decide not to use it. You can't hold on to food and make it add up to something more. You can't break it into smaller pieces of itself, use some of it and leave the rest for as long as you make yuhself believe that you don't need it.

Money was not the name for what Victor gave them. That word didn say nothing about the choices it allowed them: to save little parts of what they earned, to starve themselves so that the chilren who come after could break away from cane.

That night, she told them of a man who walked. What made him different was that he came back. A young-fella, beautiful to look at, with the dark-skinned loveliness of Patty and a tongue that wrapped the ugliest words in syrup.

Victor used to stand by the roadside too and talk, and it was there beside the road that he made them understand why food was less important than a wage and all of the things that tied them and their children to this land.

Men had lifted him off the road too. Did they know that? Did they? They came in tall skyscrapin ships with guns that looked like cocoa-rods, with sharp knives at the end of them. They had eyes like Pynter, the colour of the sea between those hills. Eyes that looked upon them with the coldness of the place that they arrived from. She remembered their eyes. Remembered the wall of bodies she was part of, standing between Victor and these strangers, on that curve of concrete in San Andrews that overlooked the sea.

For they would have done anything to preserve the life of this man who pointed out for them a better way to be; who gave them a picture of their children long after their time. Who made them unnerstan that the future was not something a pusson hope for, it was something they made.

It was like waking an emotion in a lover that made them yours for life. Truth was, Victor break the thing that tie them to the strips of land down there. And in a way he make it possible for every man-an'-woman in Ole Hope to walk. And Victor gave them something else, she said, something the whole island had forgotten. He'd stumbled on their taste for it, on a memory they'd put to sleep. Fire.

Fire was the one thing their people used to turn to when nothing else would do. He reminded them that fire was the hottest whore and she cost nothing. Fire was a red-hair woman with the walk of giants. Her skirt was de wind. She fan herself wiv it. She grow tall in it an' stronger. And like the harlot that she was, she wrap her scorchin legs round anyfing an' take it in completely.

Deeka laughed at the memory. She laughed louder at the discomfort of her daughters. And her madness made her beautiful and frightening in Pynter's eyes.

It was their fault, she said. Victor was their fault.

What happm to a man who receive so much lovin from so much people all de time? Eh? What happm when he look in the eyes o' people and realise they value hi life above their own? That they'll give him anything he fancy just to keep remindin dem that they worth something too? It change the way he listen, not so? He grow bigger in his own eyes. He mistake their thanks for prayers. He become the man they make him out to be. He start believing that he God.

And like Missa-Moses-in-de-Bible say, God don' give up the thing he feel belong to 'im. He prefer to destroy it.

Pynter's mind had gone into a drift. He was thinking about a white shirt and a classroom full of empty chairs when something in his grandmother's speaking brought him back. She hadn't raised her voice, but it seemed to come from further down her throat; so that now he could hear the breath around each word. He looked up quickly, not sure at all that it was her.

She was cursing them. She'd separated herself from all of them – her daughters, the yard, even John Seegal – and was curling up her lips at Old Hope. She was laughing at their foolishness. For not makin sense of the thing that was right there in their faces all the time.

'Them fields down dere, dey angry,' she said, pointing at the canes. 'Dey vex. And de chilren know it. Dey feel it. S'what all dis scooter nonsense is about. Cuz chilren don' just inherit the blood an' bones o' parents. Dey inherit somefing from dis land too.'

Deeka rested the back of one hand in the palm of the other. They knew that cupping gesture and the kind of words that always followed it. His mother came to her feet, made a staying motion with her hand. 'Not my children, not dem,' she said.

Deeka's retort was hollow and mocking. 'You can't stop storm, Elena. You can't raise yuh hand at rain an' tell it not to come.' She jerked a thumb in his and Peter's direction. 'Trouble come here to trouble y'all and y'all got no place to run to. So do what y'all have to do. Throw the trouble back in trouble face. Put fire in Victor arse. Show de sonuvabitch what hell look like. P'raps ... ' She'd cocked her head in Pynter's direction. 'P'raps dat's really what yuh come back here for. P'raps ... '

Deeka took up a handful of bramble, broke them in the middle, doubled them up and broke them again.

She tossed them in the fire.

What Pynter did not tell them at home was that here, in his school above the ocean, their headmaster, John Coker, was saying the same things as Deeka. He hid his urgings behind words, disguised his raging with a voice that fell on Pynter's ears like the tinkling of copper bells. Every morning, they said, their headmaster received a phone call from a man with a beautiful voice somewhere in San Andrews. It ordered him to hold his boys in. To lock the gates and keep them there. To guarantee their best behaviour to and from his school. Because his pupils had been standing on oil drums and boxes beside the road, hot with hate. They had no fear of guns. The man in San Andrews wanted to know the source of this new recklessness, which had them shouting curses even as they were lifted into long blue vans.

John Coker used to be cruel. He would take a piss-soaked strip of leather to a boy's naked behind for nothing. The wickedness had been there on his face for all to see: the quick pink tongue which slipped across his lips like a flame, tasting their nervousness, savouring their fear of him.

It was Marlis Tillock, who Coker had once hated, who had taught him love. It was the only way Pynter could put it, though he would never have said this to Marlis. Coker never mentioned Marlis knocking out his son all those years ago. But from that time on, the headmaster seemed to know him. He punished him for everything: the loudness of his voice; the shabbiness of his shoes; a missing button on his shirt; the dirt beneath his fingernails. For strolling when the bell rang; for running when he was supposed to walk. For talking with his mouth stuffed.

Perhaps Marlis had softened the headmaster with his shamelessness. Perhaps John Coker got so tired of chastising him he'd lost the joy in it. They became accustomed to the sight of Tillock sitting on the rails of the veranda, his legs swinging with the regularity of twin pendulums, while Coker leaned against the door frame of his office and read to him or talked. Their conversations after school lasted hours, more often than not with Coker's finger somewhere on the pages of a large book and Tillock leaning over it, looking up at him from time to time and nodding. It was a conversation that seemed to have no end to it.

John Coker was there against the doorway of his office with a book in his hand during the lunch break, with a little smile on his face, when word reached the school that Tillock had been lifted off the road. Sislyn returned to the staff room, sat at her desk making circles in the air with the pencil in her hand.

The school went silent. Their eyes were on the white shirt in the office, the hard, dark curve of the telephone pressed against John Coker's ear, the rapid rise and fall of his arms. His voice came high and sharp just once before subsiding into something softer. And then there came the sense of frozen time as the headmaster stepped out of his office, reached for the bell and rang it.

He told them to go home.

Pynter watched the boys file out of the courtyard, their humming mixing with the drumming of the sea below. Now he sat alone and watched Coker, his shoulders squared and stiffened, the sleeves of his white shirt rolled up past his elbow. He'd dropped the bell on the chair beside the doorway, brought the palm of his hands up to his hair and brushed it vigorously. It was a Marlis Tillock gesture. And for no reason that Pynter could point to, he felt his heart flip over. Coker rested his elbow on the railings and stared out into the empty yard. Now he seemed almost at ease, as if the troubles of this morning had never really happened.

Pynter pulled his books together and stepped into the courtyard. It was early. He didn't want to go home. He might walk over to Patty's store and spend some time with her.

A flash of white at the corner of his eye made him raise his head.

Coker was on the veranda above him, looking down as if he'd never seen him before. And then the voice, relaxed, matter-of-fact. 'Tillock, he was, er?'

'In my class, sir.'

'And you're, er?'

'Pynter Bender, sir.'

'Yes,' he said, as if the name was so obvious it was foolish of him to ask.

'Uhm, Painter Brenda? You remember what Hegel said about, er, cabbages and, er, death?'

'Don' know nobody name no Hegel, sir.'

'Pardon me?'

'I'm not aware of the existence of anyone called Hegel, sir.'

'French Revolution?' Coker cocked a chin at him. 'The coldest, shallowest of, er … '

'I still don' know, sir.'

Coker stroked his head. 'Tillock would have known,' he said. He walked into his office and closed the door behind him.

The next day they were chewing on their lunches when the bell rang. The school already knew that the night before Coker had travelled to Marlis's home. Whatever he met there was still in his eyes when he stood before them, haggard, his white shirt a pale bloom against the gloom of the large hallway. From now onwards, he said, they were going to leave the chair of every missing boy in every classroom empty. No one would use those chairs. There was also a small blackboard beside the door of his office with a mark on it for every one of them who, for reasons other than delinquency or truancy, did not return. Word of this slight modification in school policy must not go beyond these gates, of course. Did they understand that?

He rested his elbow on the edge of the stage. He'd been thinking about Troy and the early days of Christendom, he said. He'd been thinking about the Seven Ages of the World and the Ravishing of Lucretia, all worth talking about in some detail, of course, but it wasn't the point of this assembly. He'd been wondering, you see, not so much about the marvellous things that Jason of the Argonauts did, as about why so many of his men, certain of the death he was taking them to, still wanted to follow him.

They should think about that, he said. That was worth thinking about.

And in this glass-walled hall, the images of blood and fire Coker fed them seemed to meld with the layering hum of the boys and the sound of the sea thrashing against the rocks below.

Outside, their teachers were standing in small groups when they left the hall. They seemed as sober and adrift as Coker. Sislyn curled a finger at Pynter. He followed her to the back of the school. She sat on the grass above the lagoon and patted the earth beside her. He sat down and pulled up his knees.

'You wrote this?' She held up a sheet of paper.

> *Something the sea says*
> *Deep in my night of blood*
> *Of some coarse pain the ocean moans*
> *Some hollow rhythm, slow …*

'They my words, miss.'

'What's all this end-of-the-world-o'-God-my-belly-hurtin thing with you? And you so young for all o' that? Eh?' She waved the paper at him.

Pynter kept his eyes on a schooner in the distance. The mast was leaning low, the bottom of the boat turned halfway up towards the sky. Sislyn followed his gaze. For a while she too seemed to be absorbed by the struggles of the boat. She folded the paper and rested it on her lap.

'I like your mind. I like your restlessness. I always did. And I don't like that. I don't like looking at you when I'm not supposed to. I'm a teacher. There are boundaries. You think you special, but you not. You … '

'You like the poem, miss?'

A current of irritation flashed across her face, and then she laughed. 'Well – "the clashing of wet shackles" – that's not bad. The rest, well … the rest is history. You been doing this a long time?'

'Since Jordan.'

'Since … ?'

He told her about Jordan. He was not sure that she was listening to him. She'd lifted her chin and seemed preoccupied with the thrashing of the rocks against the water below them.

'Methuselah gone mad,' she said as soon as he finished. 'Old men – Victor and the people who surround him. In this country old men don't give way to the young. They rather consume them. I don't like old men.' She turned towards him, her forehead knotted in a tight frown. 'Promise me one thing, Bender. Stay as you are. Keep your cool. Watch your words. Don't do anything reckless. I listen to Coker stuffing y'all head with those, those … you know what a trope is?'

He shook his head.

'Meme or theme or motif – it's all the same. Nations respond to tropes. In some places it's rape; in others it's their flag. Fire, darkness, land – whatever their history makes them desire or fear the most. Use it in a certain way, you can make a country go to war or wreck itself. Clever politicians know this.'

'What's ours?'

'What's what?'

'Meme or trope or … '

'Listen to Coker – he's using it on y'all. Anyway, you know it. You're full of it, you just don't realise it.' She flicked the paper in the air. 'This is the only thing I've read from you where I see no sign of it.'

Sislyn glanced at her watch and got up. She plunged a hand into her bag and brought out the pen she'd held up to the class the first year they arrived.

He was surprised she still had it. He could barely remember the question she'd asked them; he'd never forgotten the pen. It glowed like a stick of honey in her outstretched hand.

'A present from a man who didn't want me to forget him,' she said. 'I didn't. I wanted to have his children.' Sislyn looked away briefly, then angled her face towards him. 'Y'unnerstand that?' She was looking at him closely.

He nodded.

'He went home to fight a war that didn't need him. Y'know anything about Angola?'

Pynter shook his head.

'Anyway, I promised. I wanted to. I thought returning here would make the waiting easier. It's five years now and between that place and here – it's not just that.' She pointed at the sea.

'It's – it's a whole heap of silence. Problem is,' Sislyn pulled her feet together and wrapped her arms around her knees, 'waiting can become a habit.' She stuck the pen in his shirt pocket and got up. 'I'll tell you what I told him the night before he left. I told him war is not a place for poets. And for what I believe is coming, I hope to God you prove me wrong.'

Over the years, he had come to know her face – the expressions that flowed across it – almost as well as he knew Tan Cee's. The pupils were her project, she said. Which was why she'd 'owned' every class they had progressed to. He was eleven when he first walked through the gates of this school. Now he was fifteen. In those four years of watching her and listening past all the things she said, he'd realised that Sislyn was always crying, even when they managed to make her laugh.

Pynter reached into his pocket and handed her a bit of paper. 'S'for you,' he said. 'S'how – s'how I feel.'

She looked at the paper in his hand, then at his face. She shook her head. Her voice dropped almost to a whisper.

'I can't take it, Pynter. I'm not s'posed to and I won't.'

He watched her shifting shoulders as she strolled across the courtyard.

It was the first time she had ever called by him by his first name.

He went to meet Patty at the store in the hope she would lighten his mood. He was doing this almost every day now, since Marlis Tillock was no longer there to sit on the wall of the courthouse above the town and have long arguments with him.

Pynter leaned cross-legged against the building on the other side of the street, watching his aunt through the moving gaps in the traffic. She was chatting with three young women at the counter and making dainty arcs above their heads with her hands. Her store-girl friends were prodding each other and laughing. From here, with the grating of the traffic making a wall of sound around him, and the chattering of gulls over the far end of the street, Patty looked as if she'd always been a store-girl.

She looked up once and saw him; waited for a gap in the traffic then fluttered a hand at him.

Over the months, his aunt had replaced her hill-woman walk with small, high-stepping movements that reined in the swing of her hips, stiffened her spine some more and pushed her chin up further. Patty jingled when she walked. She'd taken to gold bracelets and earrings, until one morning she asked him how she looked. He said that silver would suit her better. She'd soured her face at him. So, to show her what he meant, he went into the house, brought out the little bag he kept his steel marbles in and dropped some water on it.

'Rainwater on dark velvet,' he said. 'Same like silver on yuh skin.'

She'd looked at him, a strange expression on her face. 'Lord ha' mercy, Pynto! No wonder … ' She'd shaken her head and left.

He did not go over to Patty straight away. At the bottom of the street he stood on, the sea had taken on the colour of a burst pawpaw; and above him and the market square, the courthouse was glowing like a wedding cake. It was up there, on the brink of the hill that led down to the centre of the town, that he had often parted company with Tillock.

His aunt stepped out of the shop. She winked at him, then looked up and down the street. 'Come,' she said. 'We getting a ride part-way.'

He followed her to a courtyard at the back of the building. There were seven cars, parked one beside the other. Patty leaned into the one nearest to the exit.

Dark-brown eyes in a light-brown face looked up at him. Slim arms in long white sleeves rested on the steering wheel. Pynter pretended not to notice the man's brief smile.

'Richard,' Patty said. 'He offer to drop us off. Richard is the boss.'

Richard mumbled something and Patty swung her head back towards him. The man said something again and Patty flicked a finger at his ear and laughed.

Pynter pressed his back against the seat and stared at Patty's bobbing earrings. He listened to her new laugh. He studied the hands of the man describing little circles above the steering wheel, rarely ever gripping it, except when they turned a corner.

Once, Richard looked into the rear-view mirror, as if he suddenly remembered him there. A smile hovered around the man's lips. It faded when Pynter's eyes met his and held it.

The man offered to take them all the way. Patty shook her head and said she wanted to walk a lil bit.

The car swung round at Cross Gap Junction. His aunt fingered Richard's shoulder as she eased out of the vehicle.

The man waved at him.

Pynter nodded.

He listened to the clicking of Patty's heels on the road. She smelled of something wonderful and foreign. From time to time he felt her eyes on him.

'Talk to me, Pynto.'

''Bout what?'

''Bout anyfing. Tell me what you finking.'

'Right now, I not finking.' He glanced at her and shrugged.

'Tell me 'bout the trouble with the fellas in your school – what happenin 'cross dere?'

''Cross dere? You make it sound like if is overseas.' He was surprised that she knew about Marlis Tillock and the others.

'Deeka been watchin you, Pynto. She see something buildin up inside o' you, she say, an' it goin to break out soon. And,' Patty put some of Deeka's gravel in her voice, 'God help Ole Hope when it break out, y'all hear me?' His aunt prodded him and laughed. 'What you plan to do to us, Pynto?'

'Deeka talk too much,' he said.

She threw him another quick glance. 'See dat girl on the counter next to me – Nincy? She look at you like if she want to eat you whole. An' I tell 'er, tall as you is – as you, erm, are – you still a boy. I tell 'er … '

He smelt her perfume again – and the nervousness beneath it. Both her hands were holding the clasp of her shiny blue bag, which hung down from her shoulder.

'S'not my business, Tan Pat, y'unnerstan?'

'What you sayin?' she said. She'd turned her head away from him.

'Don' gimme no "what-you-sayin". I look like if I stupid?'

'Don' talk to me like dat, boy.'

'Don' boy me neider! And don' take me for no chupidee.'

She turned on him abruptly and leaned into his face.

'Pynto! Don' talk to me like dat. You talk to me like dat again I cuff you, y'unnerstan? Right now! Cuz I your flippin aunt and I want to know where *all* yuh respect gone!'

Her voice had risen with her hand. He was sure she could be heard several houses away. She was wide-eyed and close to tears. Patty would never strike him, he knew that. And she knew he knew. What he had wanted to tell her as soon as they'd closed the door of Richard's car was that he did not want to hold on to anything for anyone which could not be said. He wanted no part of secrets. They were the worst kind of lie, specially when they concerned the people you were close to. Becuz a pusson live with you believin somefing different from what really is the case.

What he didn't like about the people of Old Hope was the way the women made tight circles around the awful things that happened so that their children would never witness them, the language of blood and blades that the men of this valley had invented for themselves with their vocabulary of nods and winks and gestures that kept everyone out but themselves. The stories they kept buried in dark places in this valley, of which Zed Bender was just a small part.

Now Patty looked hurt. She hadn't taken it the way he meant it and he was too upset to explain. He watched his aunt slip off her shoes and dust the soles. Her hands were trembling slightly as she placed them in her bag. She'd painted her nails. He hadn't noticed until now the small silver chain around her left ankle.

'Tan Patty,' he said. 'I don' wan' nothing to happm to you, dat's all. I don' know what I'll do.' He was surprised at the knot in his throat, and this new and quiet fear that had come to settle in his heart. He had never imagined a world without them, could not think of any of them not being there.

She reached out a hand and touched his shoulder. She beat her fingers – like the fluttering of a bird against his ear.

Patty did that with her fingers when she was wrestling with words. He could see her trying to shape them in her head. 'S'like a lil hill, Pynto – dis job. You climb a lil way – you see better what's ahead o' you. A pusson realise dey got a few more road to choose from. Dey want de one dat take dem furthest. Dat my fault? Dat not natural?' She looked at him as if she really wanted to know. 'I meet people, Pynto. Dey nice; dey different. Now I … I find … ' She made a little frightened sound. 'I find dat love is not enough. I find … '

Patty placed a hand against her mouth.

A young man passed and sang out her name. Patty glanced across at him and waved. She straightened up as if the voice had dragged her from a daydream. They started walking.

Pynter reached into his bag, pulled out a book and handed it to her.

Patty scanned the cover. 'Mar-tin Car-ter. Fo' me?'

He nodded. 'Got the poem you like in it: "I come from … " '

'Nuh-nuh, lemme say it.'

She was excited now, the words slipping from her lips in short cascades, her hand making solemn, chopping arcs in the air.

He lengthened his stride to keep up with her. And while he listened and laughed, it occurred to him that even if there had never been Leroy, she would always insist that Richard drop her off at Cross Gap Junction.

Patty stopped at the beginning of the track that took them up to the yard. The nervousness had returned to her hands. 'Pynto?'

'Won't say nuffing,' he said.

His words did not relax her. 'Leroy,' she said. 'Y'all don' know how he is. If y'all know how he could be, then … '

Later that evening Patty would not look at him. She sat with his mother and Tan Cee joking about the ole-fella who stood at the storefront every lunchtime to stare at the girls at the counter. Sometimes she fell quiet, her fingers worrying the silver hoops that hung down from her ears. And when their meal was over, and the night-time chill crept in and made their conversation sparse, Patty still sat with them, her small talk peppering their silence in little fitful bursts.

She got up when Leroy came. He said good evening and hovered at the edge of the yard with a small flashlight in his hand. Pynter felt Patty's eyes on him. He looked up at her and smiled. The women followed the uphill meandering of the blade of light until it disappeared. Tan Cee sighed and muttered something to Elena. His mother did not answer her. Deeka went to the steps, made a hammock of her dress and leaned forward, one hand propping up her chin, the other fingering her ear lobe exactly as Patty had been doing.

Pynter folded the paper he'd been scribbling on, stuffed it down his pocket.

'I takin a walk,' he said.

24

THE FADING BLUE of jacarandas and the frothing blooms of tamarind and damsons – that was what they expected from October. A milder, cooler time. Not this.

October had stolen the heat of August and July, wrapped it up in a parcel and thrown the whole lot at Old Hope. It had already turned good soil to ashes, deprived the canes of all hope of growth and left shimmering heat-ghosts over the road.

Still, a pusson didn't mind the funny weather too much. It was all the trouble that was playing hide-an'-seek behind it.

A hurricane was better, Deeka said. At least it announced itself before it hit. It came from a place a pusson could lift a hand and point to. It did what hurricanes were s'posed to do: it flattened the island, took some careless lives wiv it and left. People's hands would go back to doing what they always did: mend the wreckage, put the pieces back in place. Becuz life was like that. Life never lost its way for long. But this creeping silence to which a pusson could not put a name – it bothered them.

Rumours started to travel down the western coast and put Deeka in a mood. Someone from the village Birdie had run to – that place of slow-talking men and quick-tempered women, who walked the length of the island selling the fish their men brought back from the ocean – said that an old man named Skido had watched a soldier shoot a young man over an argument the soldier was losing. The boy's blood had spilled in the old man's drink. Deeka said it was not true. Rumours like these came with the seasons and went away with them. Over the years there had been so many – so preposterous and wonderful – they became entertainment. Like all the rumours that came before, this one would go away.

But this one stayed. It fed on the wind and grew fat as it travelled southwards, so that by the time it reached San Andrews it was not one soldier but twenty of Victor's henchmen who had shot a running child for nothing.

Every day Pynter returned from school with different versions. The boys collected them and swapped them. They examined each one for imperfections, brushed it up a bit and passed it on, much as they would with marbles. But unlike Deeka, they never doubted. They simply selected the one they wanted to believe and kept it in their heads.

Talk of the shooting, and the curfew which followed it straight after, arrived at a time when the voices of Birdie's educated prison men began to reach them from behind the thick stone walls on Edmund Hill. Young men who'd served their time were returning to their yards. They had stronger voices and prison had made them less afraid.

Besides, Old Hope had not recovered from Jordan. His mother sat him like an accusation on the step to her house. From morning, she left him there tangling and untangling his fingers, until she brought him in at night. And the sight of Jordan quietened Old Hope. It made this village above the canes exchange words in hushed tones.

It couldn't last. Something had to give. So in a funny way when Leroy brought his hand to Patty's face it came as a brief release.

Leroy couldn't have chosen a worse time. That Sunday morning, Tan Cee sat wringing the tail end of her dress and staring into air. Elena had little Lindy across her lap, and was stroking the child's curls with hands that had been restless from the night before. Peter was oiling the wheels of his scooter somewhere behind the house, while Pynter lay on the floor with a book on his chest and Sislyn's pen between the pages.

The sound of Patty crying killed his thoughts and brought him to his feet. When he got outside, Peter was already in the middle of the yard.

Leroy was strolling down the hill behind Patty, one hand in his pocket, the other dangling beside him, and he was saying something in a gruff voice to their aunt.

Patty was trying to ignore him. She had one hand against the right side of her face and was moving the other about her in wrathful, fluttering agitation. Leroy halted on the little mound of rocks just above the yard. Patty hung there, a little way from him, her palm still pressed against her face, her shoulders shuddering from time to time.

Pynter found himself beside Peter, and, like his brother, he couldn't keep his gaze from switching between Patty and the women. Tan Cee was staring calmly up at the foothills. Deeka looked as though she was searching about her for something and she could not remember what it was. His mother was holding up a bottle to the baby's mouth. There was no expression on her face. His mother left the baby propped up against some pillows in the doorway and went inside the house. Deeka strolled across the yard and placed an arm across Peter's shoulder. His grandmother mumbled something in his brother's ear, urging him backwards while she spoke, towards the grapefruit tree, her voice light and throaty almost as if she were telling him a joke. Deeka stopped with Peter under the tree. Her hands followed the drop of his arms and lightly folded themselves around his stomach. She placed her chin against his cheek and kept talking in his brother's ear.

Pynter felt a hand on his elbow. Tan Cee was smiling up at him. She'd been speaking; he hadn't heard most of what she said. ' ... Somefing I have to tell you.'

Tan Cee squeezed his arm and led him towards the steps. And then Deeka's voice cut a path across the yard, dull and flat like a rusted blade. 'What de sonuvabitch done to yuh, Patty?'

Patty uncovered the side of her face and they saw the swollen eye, the inflated cheek. There was a thread of blood at the corner of her mouth.

Deeka heaved with Peter, pulling her weight backwards, her chin snapping down, the tendons twitching along her arms like cables.

Pynter had also surged forward, so certain of exactly what he was going to do to Leroy he already saw him dead. But Tan Cee had locked her legs around his feet. And suddenly her chin came down and hit the hollow between his neck and shoulder. He dropped back against her. And while he lay trapped and weakened against his aunt, he saw his mother coming down the steps.

Elena had changed her clothes. She was wearing the rough brown cotton trousers she worked the canes with. She'd rolled the legs up to her knees, gathered one end of her khaki shirt and knotted it at the side. She walked over to Patty and stood in front of her. She eased Patty's hand off her face and brushed the swollen shininess with a thumb. Then she lifted her chin at Leroy and narrowed down her eyelids.

Tan Cee said afterwards that Leroy should have hurried away then. He should have forgotten he was a man and turned his back and run. But there were too many things he did not know about Elena. He didn't work the canes, so this tall, pretty-face fella, muscled like a campeche tree, who paraded as a watchman and a driver for one of those rich landowners further east, had never seen how the people in the cane fields softened their walk around Elena. He didn't realise that they had seen this coming, from the time Patty got that store job in San Andrews. You add to this the rememberin a man name Gideon who she never forgive for almos' takin away her two boy-chilren a coupla months before they born. You add that again to watchin a useless brother waste most of hi life in jail – what else? – and all the troubles with the foreman and them young girls in the cane down there. And now, of course, seein Patty pretty face gone ugly with a slap. Well, 'twas all of that she hit Leroy with.

And 'twas not even a fist. It was just the heel of Elena hand he got.

The shock of it sent Leroy stumbling backwards. The impertinence of it. Becuz Elena a woman and woman not s'posed to hit a man like that. Not so bold-face. Not so hard. Not in front of other people. Cuz he a man. He bigger than she. He stronger. He goin slap her down, like he just done slap down Patty. Only worse.

She's not in a hurry, Elena. She's not even bothered about the baby in the doorway fretting after her. She's chewing on a piece of coconut and taking her time with Leroy. She wants him to recover; to straighten 'imself up, to organise 'imself and fight her back, becuz, like John Seegal used to tell them, that is the only truly lasting way to make a fella unnerstan that he should never touch a Bender woman, unless she ask him to.

Leroy swings at her. She bends an arm and brings it up. His wrist connects with her elbow. He clamps his lips down on the pain; and with all that hurting, he forgets that he is going to slap her down. He makes a fist of his other hand. Doesn't even have time to raise it. She hits him hard. Tosses the rest of the coconut into her mouth and hits him again.

Patty stopped her crying. She was out there beating the air with her hands and calling out to Elena in a voice fluttering with panic. She might have gone to save Leroy had Deeka not pinned her right there with her eyes.

Leroy was covering his face with one hand, the other stretched out before him in a swaying, staying motion. Elena turned her back on him and began to walk away. Now Deeka was running towards Elena with Tan Cee hurrying after her, because Elena was wrestling a small boulder out of the ground. The two women threw themselves on her but Elena shook them off. They threw themselves at her again. Now they were gesturing to Peter and Pynter to come help them hold her back. And even as he got there, even with Deeka and Tan Cee between himself and his mother, Pynter felt her enormous strength.

That evening, Pynter felt the floorboards shift under her weight, looked up to see Elena standing over him.

'What troublin you?' she said.

He saw no trace of the anger with which she'd brought her fists to Leroy that morning. Pynter pulled his legs together and sat up. Elena lowered herself beside him and handed him the baby. He loved this child and they knew it. They called her by the name he'd given her, Lindy the Lovely. Supple as a vine and long-limbed, with hair that was curled and black, which he'd taught himself to braid. A dougla girl.

Lindy looked into his face with her glistening eyes, prodded his lips with her fingers, nuzzled her head under his neck and promptly went to sleep. They'd told him this child should have been his twin, not Peter. She had his moods and temper. Cried for the same things that he used to as a child. So 'twasn't a hard thing to believe that, big as he was, lil Linny was the woman part of Pynto.

Elena lifted the book from the floor. She took the pen, held it in her hand and weighed it. Then she brought it to her nose. All the while her eyes were on him.

'Who the woman, Pynto?'

'Woman? Which woman! You see any woman round here?'

'Tuesday gone – you come home smellin of her. Las' week Friday an' yesterday – same thing.' She brought the pen to her nose again. 'Who the woman?'

'She a friend,' he said.

'A friend? She a teacher?'

'Uh-huh.'

'She know you got famly?'

250

'Uh-huh.'

'But she don' know de kinda family you got, not so?'

'Nuh.'

'You mus' tell 'er. Tell 'er de kinda family you got. Tell 'er 'bout me. Y'unnerstan? Cuz, big as you is, you still a boy an' … '

'I don' know whaaat yuh tryin to say. Cuz nothin not happenin and … '

'I knooow dat.' She gave the pen a quick, dry smile and spoke again as if she were addressing it. 'You fink I don' know that? But … ' She adjusted the dress on the sleeping child. 'I sure you don' wan me to come to no fancy school o' yours, dress-down just like how I dress-down now,' she pointed at her work clothes, 'to ask no high-falutin 'ooman-teacher what she got wiv my son.'

She rested the pen on the floor beside him and got up. 'S'a nice pen though.' She stopped at the doorway and looked back at him over her shoulder. 'All I sayin t'you, young-fella, is dat 'ooman is a ocean; you swim in 'er too soon, you drown.'

Outside, he could hear her whispering with Tan Cee. These days, they were like the canes – they whispered all the time. There was no end to it. They muttered about the new things they were learning about Patty and the trouble she was heading for if she was not careful; about the way his and Peter's bodies had changed over the year; Peter's edginess around him; the buried grief of his mother for a man she'd handed her heart to; the quietness of Old Hope men over what happened to Jordan.

The night before, his mother's irritation with Tan Cee had seeped through the floorboards. She wanted to know what Tan Cee was doing 'bout Coxy. When would she find the heart to break 'way from that dog she call her husband? How much mo' hell she waiting for him to bring her? And when Tan Cee replied, her voice had been like a girl's – thin and tremulous and so uncertain it had brought a lump to Pynter's throat. Tan Cee said something about love. It couldn't be, his mother said. Whatever it was, 'twasn't love. Love don' make a pusson feel so useless.

Pynter knew what this was about – this mouth-running-like-a-river talking of the women. They had been heaping up all the worries. They'd been collecting and sorting them in little piles, preparing themselves for their visit to Santay.

It was the beginning of the hurricane season. Crabs, flushed from their holes by the first rains, brought flocks of little children down to the river with pointed sticks and bags. Men were uprooting wild yams from the foothills, callaloo and crestles from the river, and were cooking tall butter tins of 'man-food' which they left for anyone to fill themselves with. They were putting their shoulders together and rebuilding or straightening houses in preparation for the storms. Girls, chattering like gulls, made sieves from tins, rolled their skirts up to their thighs and walked the waters of the river, harvesting migrating swarms of chi-chi-ri, the tiny silver fish so densely shoaled they looked like underwater rain.

They'd also put off the proper naming of their babies for this time. Up there, in Santay's place, where only women and young children were allowed, they would give the baby the name they'd argued over and agreed on at home. And at some time when it suited them, they would take it to the priest in the Catholic church at Cross Gap, pretend the name had just occurred to them, and have him sign the papers.

This year was different. For the first time the women of Old Hope wanted men up there in Santay's yard. But they had to wait. The first hours were for them and their business alone. It was for Patty and her troubles with Leroy; for the promise that a man had left his mother holding on to, which she refused to let go of. For Birdie and the way he left them and the way Deeka secretly feared he might return. For Miss Lizzie's strivings for a child, and all the things that required the stripping of a woman or a young girl to fix what had gone wrong with her.

Pynter sat with Peter in the darkness of the yard, watching the dancing masantorches – a climbing thread of fire that marked out the turnings of the track that led up to Santay's house. Up there, this night, small miracles would happen. And they'd prepared themselves for them. They'd left with bamboo poles and flags, calabashes and coloured candles, bottles of grated nutmegs mixed with olive oil and mint; crushed cinnamon and garlic, flakes of asafoetida, unsalted rice, a bottle or two of methylated spirits; a couple of live chickens, the seeds and sap of plants, and the best of everything they'd grown and reaped and kept for this time. They'd waited for the moon, and now that it had presented itself – bright like a one-eyed god on the crest of the Mardi Gras – they'd lifted their children onto their shoulders and, with a masantorch in one hand, climbed up to Santay's house.

When, later, Pynter joined them up there, the light from the torches was so thick the women seemed to be wading in it. They were moving across the open space like giant night-time butterflies. Miss Meena was all snake and grace and water. Rough earth had become air beneath Tan Cee's feet, the stones of the yard an oil slick for his mother, and Patty was thrusting a blade of bamboo at the throat of the world. Deeka stood tall above them all, rocking like a palm frond in a hurricane.

With his back against a tree, his head on Peter's shoulder, Pynter followed Miss Maisie, Miss Lizzie and Miss Anna-Jo – their shoulders fused, their palms parallel to the earth, journeying around the edges of the yard, as if their bodies were propelled only by the oaring of their arms.

This agitation, the touching of the four corners of the earth, the stammering of the drum in Santay's lap and the strange words slipping from their lips like pebbles – Eshu, Yemanja, Olokun, Oba, Orissa – were for Jordan. For the week before, the demons that Sylus and his soldiers had placed inside Jordan's head had finally consumed him. They would send his soul off dancing. They would urge him on with a tripping rhythm which Jordan, being the kind of boy he used to be, might just decide to dance to.

Peter shook his shoulders and woke him. Pynter opened his eyes and saw that night had begun to roll out of the valley. He caught the morning smell of the river down below. The first birds had begun to stir the air with song. Having danced their way past Babylon and Zion – and all the rivers and mountains in between – the long and arduous journey back to this hill above Old Hope had left the women stern-faced and exhausted.

'Had a dream,' Pynter said.

His brother shook him off and came to his feet. Peter looked as clear-eyed as if he'd just arrived.

'Serious,' Pynter said. ''Twas one helluva dream.'

'I know.' Peter scratched his head and looked away. 'Everybody hear you.' He lifted his chin at Santay. 'She tell me not to wake you, Jumbie Boy!'

Soft as Peter's voice was, Santay seemed to hear him, or if she hadn't, his brother's movement must have caught her eye.

Santay lifted a hand and called him over. She looked into his face and smiled. 'Lord ha' mercy, Osan! You gone tall-an'-smooth like cane. An' you still wiv us.'

She reached out and hugged him.

'Dis mornin,' she said, her face closing down again abruptly, 'you goin spend a lil time wiv me.'

The night had left a sheet of mist on the vegetation where the river was. He watched the sunlight reach down and peel it off, until the exposed parts of the river became glittering pools of silver. Santay waved the women off. They drifted down the hill, the reds and blues and yellows of their clothing a multi-coloured blaze amongst the greenery.

He wondered what she wanted to tell him this time. Tan Cee told him once that the secret to this woman lay in a language that she still possessed, a language so bloated with old memories of those who came before them that the people of this island had decided to let it die. It was the language forced on them by the Frenchmen who destroyed Deeka's people. But you couldn't make a pusson chew on stones. You can't compel the tongue to make words it had no taste for. So they'd changed that language and remade it, until it became their own.

But every death deprives the world of something useful. Did he know that? Even wicked people had their bit to offer. For that language also carried the knowledge of the people of Zed Bender's time: the plants they used to cure themselves with; the secret pathways out of cane; the songs they sang to lift themselves above the hurtin. The knowledge of how to fly.

Pynter was conscious of Santay's eyes assessing him like his mother. She went into her house, brought out a coal pot and lit it on the step. It was strange that here, right now, standing as he was in the middle of her yard, he felt completely at ease with her.

She handed him a cup of cocoa. He held it before his face and drew in his breath. Nutmeg and earth and cinnamon and all-spice. He glanced at her and smiled. She had baby's eyes – the whites pure as the albumen of boiled eggs, her pupils depthless like Lindy's. He remembered a time when he stood on this very spot with her, a boy-chile then, to whom the world had suddenly become a new place.

'Osan, how long you got to … ?'

'Two,' he said.

She smiled. She was testing him. She would say or ask him something else, just to make sure he was with her.

'And de lady … she from … ?'

'Englan'. But she born here.'

'Yuh sleep wid yuh head on yuh brother las' night. You love 'im,' she said, glancing up at him, 'but he – he not so sure 'bout you.'

'I know,' he said.

'He goin be a good man,' she said.

He wondered again what it was she really wanted to say to him. He followed her gaze along the valley to the hills beyond. They could see more of the ocean from here. And nearer still, the bright, tapering peninsula, pointing northwards.

'Dat bother you sometimes – jus' knowin like you know?'

'Uh-huh.'

Her hands fiddled with her headwrap for a while. 'De way I see it, Osan, some people same like bucket. Some collect more water. Dey don' look no different to de odders, dey jus' gather more of whatever it got out there to gather – and all of it make sense to dem a lot quicker. S'not worth de trouble tryin to work out how dat come to be. Is so it is – daa'z all.'

'Is so,' he muttered, turning his gaze towards the old dust road that led towards the canes. It was white now in the morning sun, and curving like a noose around the old stone mill.

'It ever cross yuh mind, Osan, dat mebbe a long-long time from now, p'raps a young-fella an' a lil ole lady might be standin right here on dis same hill with dat same river down dere. An' them cane … '

'Won't be no more cane,' he said. The words had slipped out of him despite himself.

Santay looked up sharply and held his gaze for a long while. 'What about them?' she said, gesturing at the valley as if the place itself were people. But then she lifted her shoulders and dropped them, answering her own question better than he could have. 'Life is a river runnin, son. It always find anodder way.'

Santay took the empty cup from him, walked to the pot and filled it. She sat on the steps and held it out to him.

'I been wantin to ask you, Osan. You a tall-for-sixteen fella, not so?'

'Sixteen an' four months,' he said.

'Elaine got somefing wiv you?'

He shifted his weight and looked away.

'Yes,' she said, 'I been askin meself what keep a big-woman lookin so hard at a sleepin young-fella dat she forget de plate of food in she hand and drop it every time? Keep lookin at 'im an' droppin tings. So, later on, jus' to make sure, I make 'er say your name, so I could hear de way she say it. I let her know dat if she make you lay down wiv 'er, your modder goin to kill 'er. Dat's one ting that I sure about. It got woman like dat. Young as you is, dey'll have yuh seed to have yuh.' Santay gestured at the valley. 'Your Patty Pree and dat Elaine – dey hardly different. They born inside o' this. But they not make for it. They the same like corn. Corn can't grow proper in a field o' stones. Miss Patty know it, Elaine know it. Dey know it from the time they born. S'like half o' dem still sleepin, and the lil part dat 'wake still cage up inside a house that they never step outside of. They see all dat sun and brightness out dere wastin.'

She touched his arm, and he knew it was her way of asking him to trust her words.

'Anyfing dat's a lil different. Anyfing dey fink could bring a bit o' what's outside to them … dey want it. Dat's why … '

Pynter barely heard the rest of what she said. His mind had drifted to a morning by the river. Elaine had come down early to do her washing and had already covered the stones around her with a dazzling shoal of red and blue and yellow skirts and dresses. And there, with the bamboo making a fluttering green arch above her head, and the yellow spots of sunlight slipping along her naked arms and neck like a rain of yellow coins, he'd simply stood and stared. She looked up and saw him watching her. And in that moment, when all there was between them was the humming of the bamboo and the river, the yellow morning air, and the pulsing in his throat, she'd dropped the coil of purple cloth and raised her chin at him. Her voice travelled across the water and the stones.

'Same fo' me, young-fella. You nice.' She'd lifted a hand as if to flick an insect off her shoulder. Then she turned back to her washing, her voice coming to him now from over her shoulders. 'But Time an' God an' dem wimmen dat you belong to never goin allow it.'

He'd left her there, knowing that she would never allow his eyes to rest on her like that again.

And there he was, believing that he was the only one who knew this, that Miss Elaine was, for him, what Patty had been for Chilway. Something beautiful and strange and distant that a pusson wanted to sit beside and touch, although he'd never been able to understand it: the fullness and the fear, the melting warmth that clogged his throat whenever he saw Miss Elaine. His father had told him once that people needed this – to reach for things they could neither have nor understand. The miracle was, he said, that sometimes they actually got what they desired.

'That what you make me stay to tell me?' said Pynter.

'Nuh,' she said, and took the empty cup from him. He was surprised to see her smiling. 'Careful how you carry it.'

25

THEY SAT ON the hill in darkness with their scooters lying on their sides beside them. They talked about Jordan, not what he became, but the way he used to be, how like a god he rode his blue machine, the little tricks he taught them, especially the way he could leap off it and land on his feet and turn around to face them laughing. They credited him with everything they ever learned about the tricks of scootering. The memory of Jordan sat on their hearts like an itch their fingers could not get at.

Some evenings, a man made his boy-chile walk the length of Old Hope Road, all on his own. They announced the fact by setting fire to something at the same time, urging the smoke and flames to rise above the foothills. Nights, they lined the road with masantorches from Man Arthur's Fall all the way down to the iron bridge, and with their stomachs pressed hard against the wood of their machines, Pynter and the others launched themselves from up there.

The curfews which had been creeping down the island from the north had finally reached San Andrews. But they ignored Old Hope. The nearest they got to them was Cross Gap Junction. And that was a problem, until a voice cut across the music on their little plastic radios and reminded them that gatherings were banned. From seven o'clock on evenings until further notice, all roads must remain clear.

Guy Fawkes Night used to be a game. Men and children from the villages above the canes came together at Cross Gap Junction and threw burning balls of tar-soaked rags in each other's direction, and it had always been something to watch and laugh at.

When Tan Cee brought Coxy to Old Hope, he soon became one of the gang of revellers. They were like a secret society, with rules and a language of signs and gestures that only meant something to themselves. And when, over the years, they'd won enough battles against the villages above the canes to earn themselves a reputation, they called themselves the Fire-Flyers, and elected Coxy as Pilot. The fireballs became bigger, they started mixing the tar and slow-burn oil with fuel, and the fireballs became dangerous. It was these new fireballs that sparked the war between Old Hope and the villages above the foothills. For there was that night, some years before, when a beautiful youth from Déli Morne danced and laughed and burned.

The game had changed from then, with the men of Déli Morne wanting a life back as repayment and Coxy and his Fire-Flyers daring them to take it.

Pynter had no memory of the time before this war. He had grown accustomed to it, and like all the little boys, he'd drawn a kind of energy from it. These were the men, the real soldiers, that every boy-chile wanted to become, whose battle was not so much with other men as with the one thing that Old Hope turned to when nothing else would do: fire. For, like Deeka Bender said, fire was better than a friend. It was the enemy of cane.

But Deeka would never forgive Coxy for corrupting the beauty of these men. Their slaps and sighs quickened the pulses of the village as Guy Fawkes evening closed in and, one by one, their torches came to life. Then the whole world would be ablaze and he, Pynter, and every other child in Old Hope would be right there amongst the men who had put the torch to it.

The hours it would take them to cover themselves with strips of sacking soaked in a stinking fluid that prevented them from becoming living torches were a time of transformation. At some point close to midnight the magic would be complete. An army of padded zombies would leave their yard for Cross Gap, chanting:

> *Somebody goin burn,*
> *Somebody goin burn tonight,*
> *Somebody backside goin see de glory,*
> *Somebody goin burn ...*

By the time they got to Cross Gap Junction, the procession would be worked up into a frenzy. But this year, something in the men had changed. Perhaps their women had caused it. Perhaps they had resurrected in the heads of their men the memory of Coxy Levid's best friend who, one Guy Fawkes Night, danced and laughed and burned. Perhaps they were finally saying out loud what they whispered in the river: about the part that Coxy had played in it. Maybe these men had listened to the worrying of their women, that to have Guy Fawkes Night at this time was like opening up Old Hope to all of Victor's army. So now, a week before Guy Fawkes Night, they sat in ruminative circles in the rum shop, flushing glasses of spirits down their throats and waiting for their women to come and take them home.

'Don' got no way to make Guy Fawkes Night happm this year,' Oslo said. He was a dark shape on the roadside amongst his friends. Pynter leaned against the bank on the other side of the road. Arilon detached himself from the group of boys and came to stand beside him. Peter had already left for home.

'I goin to make it happm,' Pynter said.

A single chuckle from Oslo. 'Can't happm.'

'I make it happm,' Pynter said.

'Cuz Coxy yuh auntie man?'

'Nuh, cuz I say so.'

'An' how you goin do dat, Jumbie Boy?'

261

Pynter felt Arilon straighten up. 'You call me by dat name again, I stop you,' he said. 'I give you two occasions. Count this as de first one.'

Oslo threw the name at him again.

'I say two occasions, fella; I didn say two times.'

Pynter heeled his machine, grabbed the axle and walked off. But he'd roused something in Oslo, and he followed Pynter down the hill, making a rhythm and a joke of the name. At the bottom of the road, on the iron bridge, Pynter swung his head around and smiled. And then he was at the back of the boy with an arm around his neck and keeling him over.

Birdie told him something once. His uncle had taken him and Peter behind the house a couple of days before Chilway came to take him off to prison. He had said he wanted to leave them with a present, just in case they found themselves 'up dere'. Becuz in that place 'up dere', men are themselves. They own things, including other men. They search for the weakness in a fella and close their hands around it. There is a cure for that, Birdie had said. You show the fella how easily he can die.

Oslo toppled backwards. Pynter's knee connected with his spine the way Birdie had shown them. Oslo screamed and hit the road.

In the darkness Pynter turned to face the others.

'Call me by my name,' he said, 'or don' bother callin me. Next Sunday, Guy Fawkes Night goin happm.'

Arilon dropped a hand on Pynter's shoulder. He shook him hard. 'Jeezas, Benderboy – yuh full o' surprise!'

Pynter shrugged off Arilon's hand and said nothing. He was grateful for the friendship of this quiet youth who walked with a straight back, hardly talked and kept the others at a distance with his gaze. He believed that Arilon would stand with him whatever the size of the trouble ahead, as he had stood by Arilon when his mother left him on his own all those years ago. Old Hope women had tidied the house for him until he could do it on his own. They reminded him to sweep the yard. From time to time their men stopped by and changed a post, or fixed whatever needed fixing. Arilon ate in whichever yard he chose to. He carried buckets of water and bundles of firewood for anyone who asked him, but he always slept at home.

They were children when Arilon had taken him up to Glory Cedar Rise one morning. He'd made a kite and said he wanted to send it up. But when they got there, he'd left it on the ground. He was frowning at the kite when he asked Pynter what it felt like to have a brother.

Pynter looked into his friend's face and saw the question which Arilon was too proud to put in words.

'I'll be yuh brother,' Pynter had said. 'If you don' keep holdin dem hands o' yours like crab-foot.'

They went on the hill again the next day. This time there was a wind. Arilon sent the kite up and tied the string around a stone. He sat on the root of the glory cedar tree above them. 'You serious?' he said.

''Bout what?'

''Bout me an' you. Brodder … yunno.'

'Uh-huh.'

Arilon had stood up, brought his hands in front of him and tied his fingers together like a girl.

'I kin sing,' he said. 'I do a song fo' you.' And even then, Pynter knew that this was an offer of repayment. For Arilon never took anything from anyone without finding some way to pay back.

'We own song,' Pynter said.

'We own,' the boy nodded.

Pynter had put the words together and Arilon added the music to it. And by the time they left the hill, he'd looked at Arilon and wished he really was his brother.

That evening, while chewing on his food, Arilon began to hum their song; then gradually the words started slipping out of him.

Be a bird on a wind an' fly
Be de heart of a chile dat smile
Be a bee, be a bird, be a butterfly
Be all of a mornin sky

Arilon didn't notice that Patty had stopped eating; that Elena had straightened up from the fire and was looking down on the boy's head as if she were about to break into tears. His voice was like clean water; it poured out of him. Sometimes it fluttered against his throat like a hummingbird that wanted to break loose.

Be de note from a rain-bird throat
Be de flood dat float Noah boat
Be a flute, be a song, be a pretty note
Be de colour of Joseph coat

The adults did not believe it was their song. They never did. It was like the offer he'd made to Arilon so many years ago, up there on Glory Cedar Rise. They were the only ones who knew.

Arilon still made things with his hands: tables and chairs and bedheads, with mahogany so highly polished the wood shone like metal in the sun. He said he had no need for inches because he measured with his eyes. S'matter o' fact, the only reason he'd ever touched a ruler was to make a better one for Pynter when he started his school above the ocean.

He walked with the height and gaze of a man now, said he was happy living on his own. But his mother's bed was rumpled the same way she had left it. Her nightdress hung above the mirror opposite the window. Her home-shoes sat on the old fibre mat near the doorway where she'd left them.

'You don' believe I kin do it,' Pynter said.

'Do what, fella?'

'Make Guy Fawkes Night happm.'

Arilon rubbed his head. 'S'not dat, fella. Is how!'
'Easy,' Pynter said. 'Jus' watch.'

A pusson did not need to look at Coxy Levid's face to know what he was thinking. They watched his hands. Smiling came too easily, even when the rest of him was tight with anger.

Coxy had the kind of hands you followed with your eyes. He'd perched the tobacco tin on one knee, dipping without looking into the tin, pulling out filaments of the brown stuff and sprinkling them on the flimsy square of paper in his palm. It did not require his attention; his eyes were always somewhere else, set deep, slow-sliding in a long, burnt-mahogany face, his fingers going about their business with that mindless delicacy that was so attractive to Old Hope men, for whom smoking only became interesting when they saw the way Coxy Levid rolled his cigarettes.

There was that other trick he did too: the quick flick of his wrist; the small explosion of a match against the box; the casual curving of his elbow, the glittering brown eyes looking past the flames as the widening curl of smoke rose up from his mouth and hid his face completely.

And just when the smoke cleared, a pusson forgot his fingers and his eyes because they found themselves staring at the flame crawling down the matchstick, till it hovered above his fingernails like a wounded butterfly. They couldn't help staring at that flame until it finally curled in on itself, dying a tiny, quivering death at the very tips of his fingers.

Pynter remembered the hardness of those fingers around his throat and the voice that went with it the night he had followed Coxy to the far side of Morne Bijoux.

Used to be times when Coxy looked at him – a passing glance, a smudge of a smile – and chided himself for not closing those fingers all the way. Over the years theirs had been a simmering, wordless attrition. From that time, Pynter had never spoken to this man who still came and went as he pleased, who, from as far

265

back as he could remember, had left his auntie tugging at the hem of her skirt on Wednesday night until he returned the following morning, his whole bearing exuding a quiet laid-back certainty that, however much he filled her up with hurting, Tan Cee would never leave him. A pusson looked at him and knew that he was full of secrets. He talked that way too – his voice barely raised above a murmur, which, despite its softness, easily gathered Old Hope men around him. It made them nod and do the things he said. They gave Coxy Levid names, although the only one he responded to was Easy. Or the name that Deeka and the villages above the foothills hated, the name every man in Old Hope called him the first week in November: Pilot. Every year, the name cropped up the same way Carnival or Christmas did.

He was sitting cross-legged at the edge of the yard. Pynter walked over and sat beside him. Coxy's fingers paused over the cigarette he was folding. He lifted the tobacco tin off his knee, snapped it shut and dropped it on the stone beside him. He turned brown, unblinking eyes on Pynter.

Pynter ignored the tightening in his stomach. 'No Guy Fawkes next week?' he said.

'So?' Coxy dropped his hand as if he were about to return to what he was doing.

'Then I run Guy Fawkes Night.'

That stopped Coxy's hands. He sat up. Pynter felt his heart flip, even as he held the man's eyes.

'S'man bizness,' Coxy said. He'd curled his lips around the words and turned again towards his tin.

'Look like man 'fraid of 'iz own bizness, then. So I goin run it.'

'Den go get kill.' Coxy tipped the paper over, flicked the strips of tobacco from it and began to rebuild the cigarette.

Pynter walked to the middle of the yard and turned his scooter over with his feet. He glanced at Peter. His brother crossed his legs and turned his head away.

Over the next few days, word spread across the valley then spilled out beyond it that Old Hope was going to do battle at the crossroads. That whether or not the men of Déli Morne were brave enough to leave their homes and face them, Old Hope – the smallest village above the canes – was going to be there. And to hell with the curfew and the soldiers and everything else.

They'd gathered the wads of mud-soaked sacking to protect themselves, and gallons of tar and pitch-oil. They'd dug a pond at Cross Gap Junction, half filled it with water and laid a few large stones around the edges.

Coxy Levid sat in the middle of all the preparations, a cigarette smouldering between his fingers, nodding at the sheets of canvas and hessian the men passed over to him. He dipped a finger in the fuel mix and smelled it. He crouched over the things they pulled from sacks and shielded them from the view of curious eyes, flicking his ash and smiling.

Sunday brought with it the sullen-faced anger of the women. There were quarrels everywhere across the valley – tearful voices overridden by the edgy belligerence of men.

Late evening, Pynter went to the back of the house, stripped and tipped two buckets of water over himself. He turned round to reach for his clothing and saw Tan Cee standing in front of him. She'd made a thin line of her lips. Her eyes were red and staring.

'You sempteen soon,' she said.

'Thought 'twas only Deeka believe dat,' he said. 'Thought 'twas only … '

'Didn say I believe it. I want you to stay home, dat's all I sayin.'

He ignored the square of cloth she was holding out for him to dry himself with. He began pulling on his clothes. They were the loosest he could lay his hands on. He'd also taken his pair of running shoes.

'S'why I have to go,' he said.

He felt the tremoring in Tan Cee's shoulders as he brushed past her.

He took the mud track down to the river through the canes.

The clearing he stepped into was like the inside of a church, the tangled arch of leaves a fluttering weave of light above him. The smell of the place had changed – a mix of mould and mint – and there was no longer the print of a man's body on the leaves. The light was bottle-green and shimmering like liquid.

Arilon and Frigo were waiting at the entrance. In the fading light, they climbed the foothills up through the high forests then down again, pausing briefly amongst the wild breadfruit plantations of a dismal valley that Old Hope called The Stoop. Frigo had drawn his shirt close. Arilon was wiping his sweating neck with his bare hands. 'What you fink goin happm, Pynter?'

Pynter turned and headed towards the voices and torches at Cross Gap Junction. He could tell them, even before they joined the throbbing, wavering mass of people there, that if they survived the night, neither they nor Old Hope was going to be the same again.

'Y'all know how dis Guy-Fox-burnin' come 'bout?' Frigo said.

'Tell us,' Arilon said.

'Well, Guy Fawkes was one of us, yunno. A blackfella from dese parts, one o' dem man who walk. He had a lil bizness wiv de Queen-in-Englan'. How you call dat, Paintuh?'

'Love affair?'

'Uh-huh! She was married to the King, you see, and he was de cook. So it had to be a love affair an' nuffing mo', y'unnerstan? Problem was de fella never satisfy. He feel dat since he the one to make de Queen feel good, he should get promote from cook to King. An' 'twasn't even as if he could cook proper food. S'only man food he could cook. Anyway, he get rude. He start makin fuss. He want mo' consideration. He don' wan' to cook nobody no mo' food. Is he dem s'pose to cook for. So guess what happm?'

'What happm?' Arilon said.

'He challenge de King fo' a fight. Well,' Frigo shrugged, 'de King bus' his arse an' jail de fella fo' life.'

'Thought dey burn 'im,' Pynter said.

Frigo shook his head. 'Nuh! Is Old Hope people burn 'im. Every year we burn de fella fo' de embarrassment he cause us. Fo' de bad name he give to Ole Hope man.'

Arilon dropped a hand on Frigo's shoulder. 'S'awright, fella; you get yuh revenge tonight.'

Dusk had begun to smudge the leaves by the time they got to Cross Gap. It had taken them an hour to descend the foothills and another to make their way around the tiny village of Bayo above the southern valleys, where the river flowed away in a giddy haze towards the swamplands and the sea.

The men had already lined up drums of fuel. At either end, dousers stood around a large metal tank of water, so that they could kill the runaway fires and stray flames which, unattended, would chew into the woodwork of the nearby houses and nibble at the dead leaves of the cocoa plantation and turn the night into a blazing disaster.

There was a buzz in the crowd which seemed to rise up from the bowels of the earth and fill the air with a quivering expectancy. A voice just in front of them rose above the din.

'Kelo, you sonuvabitch – go burn your wife.'

'Nice night for burning all kind o' wickedness,' came the reply.

'Perfect.' The men hugged and laughed, then lost themselves amongst the suck and surge of bodies.

The two sides faced each other. The fighting men from Déli Morne had been coming year after year to try and wrest control of the celebration, so that Old Hope could be reminded of the youth called Solomon who danced and burned on Guy Fawkes Night in '56, and the part that Coxy Levid played in it. They were there to rip that big red star from Coxy Levid's padded crotch and crush it, the star on which Coxy would flick the match that would lick the wick that would make the flame that would pass the fire to the drum of tar and petrol.

People began to rush away and Pynter moved with them, his hand on Arilon's shoulder. He knew that the seconds it took

Coxy to dip his hand into his drum and raise it with a fireball for the first explosive throw was all the time they had to find themselves some cover. They sheltered in the shadows of the cocoa trees that leaned over the road. From time to time Pynter scanned the edges of the crowd, his heart a hammer in his chest.

'No soldiers?' Frigo said, his forehead glistening in the gloom. Pynter did not answer him.

A rain of fireballs brightened the night. A sudden uproar as one of the men caught fire, was dragged to earth, doused with water, then rolled rapidly in the dust.

'Supposin?'

Pynter lifted a staying hand at Frigo. Something in the sound, in the feel of the crowd, had changed. A woman pulled her stall of roasted corn from the path of the flow of people. Her torch toppled over and became a bright, amber bloom as it struck the asphalt.

Pynter said, 'They here.'

The vehicles had rolled in silently. He had not heard the sound of engines in the distance. Frigo ducked into the crowd, disappeared a while before resurfacing beside him. 'Twelve Lan' Rover,' he said. 'Mebbe more. Dey cut off de engine. Dey push dem in.'

The jeeps emerged like submarines from the mass of milling bodies. They stopped a little way ahead of Pynter and his friend, blocking the road from their end. Then, as if the soldiers had rehearsed it, the engines and the headlamps were switched on. The glare cancelled the yellow flickering glow of the masantorches and hardened the shadows on the faces of the padded men standing with their shoulders fused together.

Perhaps the soldiers had not expected this: the padded men, so much larger than they really were. The oil drums filled with flames behind them. The steady gazes. Perhaps their months of warring with the people of the north had taught them something about this sudden quiet. That all of this – the slow circling of the crowd, the mild-mannered question from a woman somewhere in the crowd, 'Which one o' you deh murder lil Jordan?' – was no less than their first step on the gentle road to hell. The soldiers froze and looked back at their vehicles.

A shout rose up from somewhere, then a gasp – as if the air itself above them heaved. A streak of yellow turned their heads towards the sky.

An effigy was sailing down from the coconut tree above the road. Veins of living orange had already begun to spread through the white jacket and trousers and consume the arms and legs. They recognised the figure of Victor, and felt the hurl of laughter hit the air. Two soldiers rushed forward to beat out the fire. The effigy exploded and sent them scuttling backwards. Now hands were pointing at the crab of a figure skittering down the tree.

'Kicker,' Frigo shouted. It was Jordan's little brother.

Three men in plain clothes leapt out of the crowd, almost as if they'd been spat out by the mass of milling bodies. Pynter launched himself after them, dodging the arm that shot out to drag him down. His eyes met the soldier's briefly. He brought up his elbow, caught him on the jaw just below the ear. The man's feet folded under him, his windmilling arms bringing down the other just ahead of him. The other man was bearing down on Kicker, but the boy reached the ground before he could get to him and scuttled off on all fours. Pynter had just about caught up with the soldier when all of a sudden the soldier seemed to be in a pool of yellow flames. He was alight from the moment the fireball struck him.

Now the shouting stopped. Pynter grabbed the man and pulled him down. He rolled him on the earth, kept rolling him until a shock of water struck them. Then he was up, swinging right then left, as another figure lunged towards him.

He allowed the soldier to catch hold of his shirt. And then he pulled the trick that every child in Old Hope knew from the time they learned to walk. He tore his shirt front open and slipped the garment off his shoulders, leaving the man standing with only the torn shirt in his hands.

A sky-splitting roar swept him up as he plunged into the night.

26

FOOTFALLS ON the road below too smudged to make much sense of. The far-off soughing of the canes like a low receding tide. A woman's laugher, then a girl's, that were foreign to Old Hope. In this gloom, even the sounds of the house were different. The humming of the roof was harsher. The eaves protested in the wind. The floorboards creaked in ways they had not done before.

Deeka's face was above him. He lifted a hand, touched her, and it was real. When he looked again she was no longer there.

This was not his mother's bed. It smelled of camphor, Vaporub and methylated spirits. Deeka was a high dark shape above him again. She said something, and a hustle of feet rushed in and filled the room. His mother was holding a lamp in front of her. He could not read the expression on his brother's face. Or that of the girl who stood beside him, with hair tumbling down the side of her face like black water.

Deeka placed a finger on his chest and prodded him. He looked at her hands and nodded without knowing why. The girl stepped forward and rested a hand on his as if she'd always known him.

'Pynto,' Patty said.

The girl pushed back her hair and smiled. She leaned over and stared into his eyes, switched her gaze to Peter then back to him.

'I'z Windy,' she whispered. She turned her head up at the women. 'He – he …'

'He awright now,' Elena said. The girl straightened up and stepped back.

Patty took the lamp from Elena's hand and pushed them all out of the room. She sat on the bed beside him. She folded his hand into a fist, then cupped both her hands around it.

'We thought … we thought you gone,' she said. Her voice fluttered in her throat. She brought his hand up to her cheek and held it there.

'Deeka bring you back,' she said. 'Yuh granny fight. She…' Patty shook her head. 'Now I know she de only one dat could ha' bring you back.'

He wanted to ask her from where.

'We, we been movin you round Old Hope. You in my house now.'

'How come?' he said. His voice surprised him. Patty brought her hand to her mouth. A chuckle slipped out between her fingers.

'Lordy,' she said. 'Yuh voice break in yuh sleep?'

She moved to get up. He shook his head. Patty sat back.

'Where's Tan?' he said.

'S'not Tan Cee, Pynto; is Deeka bring you back, y'unnerstan?'

He shook his head. 'Tan not here?'

'She gone get something for you. S'Deeka…'

'Who de girl?'

He felt the hesitation in her hand. 'She yuh cousin.'

Patty looked down at him, her eyes glistening in the lamplight. 'Anita come home.'

His aunt said nothing for a while. She'd turned up her chin at the ceiling and seemed to be daydreaming.

'Las' Friday, Cross Gap people bring you home,' she said. 'An' then…' The bed quaked under her shifting weight. 'What happm t'you from school, Pynto?'

He took her hand. He closed his eyes. 'Nuffing,' he said.

They had examined his body, she said. They bathed him and found nothing wrong with him. There was no sign of hurtin anywhere. He looked perfect except for the sleep they could not wake him out of. And then he'd started slipping away – as if he'd decided to abandon them. As if he owed them nothing and they did not matter any more.

His mother brought the baby to him, thinking perhaps that if anything could bring him back it had to be all dat love he got for lil Lindy, cuz it didn feel or look like illness to nobody. The baby cried. Lindy would not stay with him. The chile behave like if she never know him.

Santay refused to come. But Tan Cee would not leave her yard until the woman told her what to do.

'Make war wiv 'im,' the woman said. 'Upset de sonuvabitch. Make 'im vex.'

That didn make no sense. An' besides, a pusson didn have de heart. Only Deeka did.

Patty unfolded his fingers and laid her palm flat against his. She widened her eyes and chuckled.

'She curse you, Pynto. She call you every dog-an'-sonuvabitch in Ole Hope and de rest o' de world. She roll you on de bed like one of Birdie dumplin'. An' what happm?' A laugh broke out of Patty. 'Is not fight you start to fight 'er back? An' dat mean you ferget dat is dead you was deadin o' something; not so? Three days, nobody get no proper sleep becuz of you. Boy! You really a dog for true.'

There were terrifying moments when they thought they'd really lost him, when he seemed to be clawing himself out of the earth. He'd said unrepeatable things to Deeka that had no right or place in a decent yooman mouth. He'd argued with a woman whose name he did not call. And who was this uncle named Michael whose hands had been so freezing it paled his skin to ashes and shivered his limbs so much? They'd had to hold him down.

Patty spoke as if the people he'd met in that place that the illness had taken him to were real. She was laughing now as if he'd just played the biggest joke in the world on them.

He watched his aunt patting his hand, arcing her neck, smiling at the ceiling and the lamp, so taken by the story she was shaping with her hands it seemed to matter little whether he was listening or not.

He remembered drifting down Old Hope Road, the houses a brown unsteady blur on either side, and people floating past like smudgy ghosts. Somewhere along the road a woman's voice said his grandfather's name and straight after that he wasn't walking any more. Hands were holding him and he was travelling through air.

Pynter closed his eyes and tried to recollect the days he'd lost. The morning after Guy Fawkes Night, Old Hope was buzzing with his name. Coxy came down early to the yard, cocked a thumb at him and smiled. And by the time Pynter stepped on the road for school, he learned that he had the fastest feet on earth. He was the young-fella who ran and danced on wind, who slipped between the fingers of a hundred of Victor's soldiers and left a coupla buttons from his shirt in their murderin-an'-killin hands. All of it, to deliver Muriel last lil boy from their terrible killin ways.

Miss Muriel was waiting for him by the side of the road with a small paper bag of sugar apples. She gave it to him. This, he knew, would go on for a while until they'd wrung the last little bit of joy from what he had done. Eventually they would have to face up to what really happened the night before at Cross Gap Junction, and what was sure to come. And what was to come would be no Guy Fawkes make-believe.

Sylus didn't come. Instead, he'd sent men who were the off-spring of friends or relatives further up the foothills. They'd burnt the jeeps. They'd ragged up the ones who'd chased after him and lil Kicker. They'd told these young soldiers it was nothing personal, and sent them walking home.

Sylus and his men would arrive when he was ready, and Pynter thought he knew how they would come. It would be the way they'd taken Marlis Tillock, the way they did it in the north, in the quietest hours of the night, sometime close to morning. They would not announce themselves. They would enter a house, hold a torch to faces, select the youth they wanted and leave as quietly as they came.

He'd gone into school that morning and leaned against the wire fence in the courtyard. Sislyn saw him from the staff room and came out to him.

'What's wrong?' she said.

He did not answer her. She followed him to their place above the lagoon.

'I leavin school,' he said.

She sat down. She didn't look at him. 'That's what you bring me back here to tell me?'

'Don' have no choice.'

'Don' tell me that!' His words had brought her to her feet. Now she was in his face.

'Listen, young man. Don' tell me I waste my time with you, y'hear me? Don't tell me I waste my … my … ' She choked on the words, brought a fist up to her mouth as if she wanted to stuff the words back down her throat. She pulled her shoulders back and sucked in a lungful of air. When she looked at him again her face was calm. 'Sorry – I have no right. I fool myself. I think I have. I don't.'

'I know you leavin too,' he said.

She looked at him quickly. 'Where you get that from?' Her brows came suddenly together. 'Is that why…'

'No, miss.'

'How did you…'

'I feel it.'

She was staring out to sea. A stiff breeze was kicking up the water below. It was one of those mornings when the light followed the curve of things and did not leave a shadow.

'I have a doctorate to return to,' she said. 'England – I need to.'

Pynter shook his head. 'Not Englan', miss.'

'Follow me,' she said, striding ahead of him.

He could barely keep up with her. At the entrance of the small library, Sislyn stopped abruptly and turned around to face him. Now only her lips were moving. 'I won't ask you why, Bender. I don't want to know. But I want my pound of flesh; I'm holding you to something.' She flicked her fingers quickly before her. 'Ten months – that's what you've got. In ten months' time, you come back here and do the exams. It's all you've got to look forward to.'

She stepped up onto a stool and began pulling books off the shelves. The desk shuddered under the weight of the armful she dropped on it.

'I'll have those replaced.' She returned to the shelves. 'Conway wants you for Economics. Edwina says you're born for Biology. And God knows who else wants you for whatever else to make them feel that they've been teaching.' She dropped another armful on the table, jumped off the stool and looked him in the eyes. 'I'm signing you up for these: the history, the language, the literature. That's you. Read what they say, see if you agree and either way, work out some damn good reasons why, then come back here and sit the exams.'

She emptied her bag on the floor and chucked it at him.

He did not take it. Sislyn raised fighting eyes at him.

'Dat's a woman bag,' he said. 'A fella can't…'

'Walk the public road with it? That's not my problem. Take it!'

She walked him to the gate. They stood there a while staring at the little road that led straight down.

'Don' know what to say,' he said.

'Don't say anything, then. Tell me, Bender, and this is purely academic – can a woman love two fellas at the same time?'

'Not only two, miss – a whole heap of them,' he said.

She rocked back with laughter.

'Go,' she said.

'Remember me,' he said.

She nodded and turned away.

'What you thinkin?' Patty said. He didn't know when she'd stopped talking.

'I lef' school,' he said. He felt tired. He wanted to sleep.

Patty got up and pushed the window wide open. He looked up at the light. Out there, a patch of purple sky, the top of the tres-beau mango tree, a slice of the hill above it – a bright truncated world.

'In ten months I go back,' he said.

Patty was silent for a while. And when she spoke she sounded almost frightened. 'Ten months – s'a long time, not so?'

His aunt seemed to be reminded suddenly of something. 'Arilon say a fella come a coupla times askin after you.' She furrowed her brows at him. 'An' de fella look more like you dan Peter. Dey won' tell 'im where to find you. He say he goin come again.'

Pynter said nothing; instead, he lifted her hand and rested it on her stomach. He held her gaze. She read the question in his eyes. She looked down at both their hands and nodded.

'Pynto?' she said, her voice dropping to a whisper. 'How – how come you know dese tings, Pynto?'

He winked at her and smiled.

Later, he emerged from Patty's house to find Anita standing with her daughter in the yard. A red woman in a sea-blue dress, fuller-fleshed than all her sisters, her brown hair rolling down her thick shoulders in coils. Her back was turned to him but as soon as he reached the doorway, she stiffened.

Anita did not turn to face him. She looked over her shoulders with eyes that made him think of chicken hawks. A fast bright flash of teeth. Patty prodded him in the back. He nodded at Anita.

Windy pushed back her hair and lifted her chin at him. Patty's voice was a breath behind his ear. 'Girl-cousin never stop askin after you.'

They'd arrived at a time when the valley was foaming white, as if all the clouds that ought to be above them had left the sky and settled on the canes. The canes were pluming weeks too early. The weather had confused them. They feathered the air in waves, raised no odours on the wind and barely made a sound. But all that beauty was hiding a disaster. For it meant that the sugar had left the stems and made of the flesh a useless watery sponge.

That evening, Pynter sat slightly apart from them. His mother and Patty had their heads together. Tan Cee leaned against Coxy. Patty was pleased that her place was the one he'd opened his eyes in, and that she was the first to hear him speak with the voice of a man. Daytime was all right, she told him. Nights were dangerous. Oslo and the rest of his scooter-mad friends headed for the hills above the canes where they made leaf caves out of the bamboo. Peter did not go with them. He'd made a place for himself up Top Hill way, which he was telling no one about.

Anita would not tell them where she came from, or why she arrived so suddenly with her daughter, whom no one knew she had.

Been a long-long time, Tan Cee said. Too long p'raps. A pusson no longer knew Anita. They couldn't pull Anita close if she kept from them the one thing they could close their hands around: a lil bit of her past.

Anita leaned against the house and looked about her. She talked but made no conversation with them. She tapped her fingers against her legs, nodded at the things they said to her without really hearing them, smiled when they least expected it and reminded them of things she said they told her, months before she came. She wanted her own house, she said. She'd brought enough money for that. Deeka pointed at the plot of land where Columbus used to collect butterflies, a little way from Tan Cee's. And Coxy, who'd been staring at Anita above the flaming tip of his cigarette, told her he would build her house and that he wouldn't charge a thing.

It was then that Peter broke off his jostling with Windy and went into the house. He came out with Birdie's canvas bag and grumbled goodnight to them. At the edge of the yard, he looked back at Pynter, adjusted the bag on his shoulder and stepped into the dark. For he, Pynter, had started the trouble, not so? With a few words in Coxy's ear, he'd twisted the arms of the men. And instead of sticking around to see the problems that he left them with, he'd thrown himself on his back and played dead for all of three days.

When, the next day, Peter returned, he dropped his bag in the yard, waved at Windy, said good morning to the women and walked to the drum of water beside the house. He stripped to the waist and poured water over himself. His mother lifted her head at him, a trace of a smile around her mouth as she watched him scrub his face and arms. He was becoming a man. Brown as an over-baked loaf, the muscles already strained against his skin. There was the darkening smudge of a moustache which every now and then his fingers crept up to and paused over. When Peter raised his head, it struck Pynter for the first time that his brother had their father's eyes.

Anita passed all her joy to her bright-eyed daughter. Windy doubled the women over with her jokes, put her fingers in Peter's plate, fed herself and laughed with him. Peter crushed leaves between his fingers and held them under Windy's nose. The ant-blighted grapefruit tree was blossoming. Peter pulled the petals off the flowers and threw them in her face. She chased him round the yard. He found a caterpillar somewhere and placed it in Windy's palm. Something about the wriggling creature seemed to hold her. She grew still, passing her fingers over the white hairs that stood out from the body of the insect, like the prickles of a golden-apple seed. It was as yellow as the ripened fruit, with streaks of black and white along its side.

Deeka and his mother stopped their conversation, as interested in the girl now as she was in the insect she was holding.

Pynter heard her slippers on the stones. He lifted his head from his book and looked up at her.

'S'a butterfly,' he said, taking it from her. 'A lil bit of sun. A lil bit of waiting. Then de colours break out, get dry, turn wings. If …'

Peter's laughter cut across his words. 'He's a liar; don' lissen to 'im, Winny.'

Pynter handed the insect back to her.

'If what?' she said.

'If y'all let it live.'

Windy walked over to Deeka's rosebush and rested it on a leaf. Peter went to stand beside her. He held the tree and shook it, and the caterpillar tumbled to the ground. Pynter watched her face as Peter trod on it.

The next morning Pynter left for Glory Cedar Rise. Halfway up, he realised the girl was somewhere behind him, and that she wasn't alone. She rounded a twisty corner and did not seem surprised to find him standing there.

'What you followin me for?' He did not hide his irritation.

'I not followin you,' she said. 'We walkin same direction, thaaz all.'

He'd never been this close to her. She was older than Peter and him by one year, Tan Cee said. She didn't look it. She wore a single earring in her left ear. When she tossed back her hair, it sparkled like a struck match.

'Got a lot more hills round here to walk,' he said.

'I like this one,' she said, and pushed past him.

He watched the slippers slapping against her heels, pale as the skin of the palm of her hands. She climbed carefully, reaching out to balance herself by touching the trunks of trees, stopping only to brush her palms from time to time.

She came to the high mud bank that stood between them and the top of the hill, and he climbed past her. Glancing over his shoulder, he saw that she was holding up an arm towards him with an expression that was a mixture of expectation and reproach.

Without a word, he reached down and pulled her up. He could detect the pomade in her hair – the smell of lemons, and something else which came off her skin, almost like the smell of grapefruit blossoms.

She did not release his hand until they cleared the hill.

There was always wind up here. It came straight off the ocean, reared itself up, grabbed at their clothing and slapped them in their faces.

She was looking east, beyond the ridge of hills past which San Andrews lay. Columns of clouds, serrated like old sails, pushed themselves up from the ocean.

'Morning start 'cross dere,' he told her.

Windy lifted her face at him. He was distracted for a moment by the fine hairs along the nape of her neck. 'You laugh a lot,' he said. 'You hardly talk and your modder not sayin where y'all come from.'

She smiled and pointed past his ear. 'Wozzat?'

'Westerpoint. Rich people and their dogs live there.'

He named the hills and places just above their valley. Pointed at the spread of trees at the far end, just above the river, which he called Grass Water Bowl. And over there, on the hill that looked down on the ocean, the huddle of trees from which the people who came before them used to launch themselves and fly.

He took her hand, aimed it past the old stone mill, over the grey cane road and up towards the green rock rise that hoisted the trees above Old Hope.

'It got somefing up there,' he said. 'One day I might show you.'

She sat beside him. 'You talk pretty,' she said. She pressed her head against his shoulder.

He looked at her fingers and thought of cane. 'We cousins,' he said.

She eased her weight off him and nodded. She passed a hand across his chest and stroked his throat, and her pupils were like open doors which he wanted to walk into.

He returned to Windy during the days, up there on Glory Cedar Rise where the valley slipped away beneath them in a dazzling, giddying heave. But in the nights he took his bag and joined the young men in Grass Water Bowl. His arrival changed their tones and brought out the resentment in Oslo. He walked too quietly, they said, turned up at their gatherings too softly. He never forgot a thing and slept sitting, with his shoes on. And the nights that one of them dared to strike a match, all they saw between him and the darkness beyond his shoulders were his eyes.

They stretched themselves out in the leaf caves and talked in whispers, dropping off to sleep one by one, until their snoring joined the murmurings of the river and the canes.

A low mist had settled over the canes one early morning when Pynter stirred and woke them. He told them they had to move higher up the foothills, straight away. They watched as the jeeps rolled up the old cane road, the dim shapes of the soldiers spilling out of them, awkward and stiff-limbed, moving blindly through the fields, their searchlights scrawling crazy arcs against the half-light.

When, later, the vehicles left, Arilon came and stooped beside him. 'Dey practising on us,' he said.

It was true that as the weeks went by the vehicles came in more quietly. The men killed their engines and pushed them in more cautiously. They arrived at different times and approached from unexpected directions. They made wider circles and crept further up the hillsides. Pynter was worried then, especially when the Land Rovers drove off and his mind turned to the dogs that the soldiers hadn't brought yet.

During the days he would prepare Windy for the rumours that would envelope them. He told her how to look behind the soft words and the smiles of the women in the yard and follow the turnings of their minds. Right now, they were putting their heads together over them. They were searching for a way to kill their friendship. They got closer to it every time she left the yard to meet him on top of Glory Cedar Rise. When they struck, he said, it would be all of them together, even though the words would come only from the mouth of the one they'd passed the duty to.

And if anything, Patty's condition would be adding to their urgency.

His young aunt Patty was round as a full moon and the child in her was calling for odd things: the hard white flesh of green mangoes, the salty leaves of cheese plants, young June-plums so sour just the smell of them set the teeth on edge, strips of cinnamon and bitter mauby bark, finger-daubs of salt, Guinea peppers that were amber as the flame they carried in their hearts. Chalk and ash and charcoal. Patty strolled about the yard smiling foolishly to herself, her hands guided to the leaves of plants and the juicy stalks of grass. Deeka, his mother and Tan Cee spent their idle hours staring at her with still-eyed, dreamy fascination. They'd already started arguing over names: 'Dalene,' Tan Cee said, 'Dalene or Anisa or Melissa, or p'raps another Deeka. In fact, why not a second me?'

'Nuh, boys,' Deeka said. 'Another coupla fellas.' She would wave an arm at Peter and Pynter. 'Twins! In fact, two sets o' dem goin be perfect. That make four in one go, not so? That was, of course … ' She rested bright, assessing eyes on Patty. 'That was, if a pusson strong enough to manage it. Cuz this yard want more man. Any kinda man. A yard could never have too much man. Man good, even if dem turn good-for-nothing in the end. Man still good!'

They'd laughed with Patty throughout the evening meal, and somewhere near the end of it, they went quiet for a while. Leroy had to know, they said, cuz the last thing a pusson wanted was to have him meet her on the road like that and get surprised. Men go crazy over things like that, seeing a woman he convince 'imself belong to 'im, carrying another man child, so soon afterwards. Especially after all those years of nothing happening for him. It kill something in a fella. In these parts here – a fella who learn he got no life inside of him don't care no more for life. Not even his own. So, they should call him to the yard and Patty could let him know the nice way.

It was somebody else's invitation that brought Leroy to Old Hope. He was dressed as if he were about to start a new job. He stood in the road and called out Patty's name, his voice high and tight with anguish.

Patty leaned over on the steps, staring at her hands. She was shaking her head as if she were saying no to everything she saw there.

Leroy was calling her the way he'd been accustomed to, like they were together in a place all on their own. Patty only shook her head faster. When the calling became too much for her, she brought the heels of her hands up to her ears and kept them there.

He was a good fella, he shouted. Except for that last time. Was a mistake. He was upset. He would make the baby his. He would treat it like his own.

Elena decided to stop him from making a bigger fool of himself in front of all of Old Hope. She went down the path, stood on the bank above the road and called his name, the palms of her hand opened out towards him.

He did not come, but at least it stopped him calling, and apart from Patty's sobbing, and the crackling of the woodfire, the yard was very quiet.

They did not know exactly when Leroy left. They'd looked up and he was no longer there.

Deeka cleared her throat and Pynter was surprised at the sadness in her voice. Life happm, she said. People change wiv it. Besides, Patty was her daughter. And if she, Deeka, had to choose between a good man and no granchilren, or no-man-at-all and granchildren, she would always choose granchilren. Which didn mean her daughters s'posed to go off and bring baby home that way all the time.

It had Pynter wondering how his auntie's love for a man she'd been sleeping beside from as far back as he could remember could slip so easily into revulsion. Tan Cee had her eyes on him. There was a small smile on her face. 'Man do it all de time,' she said.

'You talkin to me?' he said.

'Who else?' she said.

'You tellin me what I thinkin?' He closed his book.

Something in Tan Cee's face retreated.

'You don' know what I thinking,' he said. He rose to his feet, stuffed his slingshot down his pocket. 'I takin a walk,' he said, and headed for Glory Cedar Rise.

Pynter stood with his back against a tree, watching Windy climb the hill towards him. The slingshot swung lightly between his fingers. He folded the weapon, shoved it into his back pocket and leaned over the brink of the hill to pull her up.

'Trouble comin,' she said.

'Trouble here,' he said.

'I mean Peter,' she said.

'I mean your mother,' he said.

'He your brother an' he hate you so much? Cuz of … '

'S'not that,' he said. 'He still play wiv you, not so? He don' blame you for nothing. Yuh see, I deprive him of somefing. He – he never been inside our father house.'

Windy went still against him. He felt himself struggling with his own hesitation. He'd never spoken of this before.

'I – I make somefing happm. I ask Paso to burn our father house. I went up dere one time, a lil time after he pass 'way, to make sure that Paso done it. And then I come home and tell Peter. I say to 'im the house was sufferin, 'twas fallin down on itself, yunno. He look at me, quiet like I talking to you right now, an' he say, "I never been inside my father house, Jumbie Boy. I never see inside it." Mos' times Peter don' remember in his head. But de rest of 'im remember all de time. And now, you come … and … '

Windy pointed past the trees to where their home was. They could see the roof of Patty and Tan Cee's house, and the upper skeleton of the new house Coxy was building for Anita. 'Down dere,' she said, 'who love you more, Pyntuh? Is Tan Cee, not so?'

She'd asked him that question before. He hadn't answered her. Now he felt he could.

'When I got sick, yunno, I wake up wiv my mouth hurtin. Down here too.' He touched his side. 'Deeka beat me up, she even force-feed me.'

Windy nodded.

'Who love you more, Windy? Somebody prepare to kill fo' you? Somebody prepare to die fo' you? Or a pusson who will hurt you, just to save you from yuhself?'

She didn't answer him. She took his hand and laid it on her own, seemed to lose herself in the contrast that they made, his dark as the shell of nutmegs, hers the pale brown of mahogany.

'Patty believe is Deeka,' he said. 'Is what she been tryin to tell me when I wake up in her house.'

He thought she sensed it too, the urgency he'd been feeling when he left the yard. The knowledge that if they were ever to come up this hill again and be together, they would never see what lay below them in the same way. That last look of Tan Cee told him so; they'd already decided amongst themselves.

Pynter reached for a stick and drew four figures at Windy's feet. He scratched each woman's name beside them. He erased the names and connected them with lines.

'You gotta think o' dem as one person, not four,' he said. 'This is Deeka.' He pointed at one of the shapes. 'She the eyes: she look at things, she read them. Tan is the feeling part. Patty'z all the niceness and the softness. My mother…' He paused, lifted the stick and pushed it in the soil. 'My mother is de hammer. When nothing else don' work, she hit.'

Windy was shivering. She'd folded her arms around herself and was leaning into him.

Did she think that when Anita arrived with her, said nothing about themselves – where they'd lived and why they came – that all they'd brought with them were their names? The women weren't interested in Anita. She, Windy, was the one who told them everything. They knew she was a town girl and that she wasn't from San Andrews. It had to be some place like Trinidad. Her feet told them that, her heels were soft as her hands and she always reached for slippers. Those hands had never lifted a bucket of water. She had no marks on them, no scars from lifting or peeling things. Her arms were like she'd just sandpapered them. Too many things surprised her and she ate too carefully. And they knew, he said, they knew even before it happened that he was going to like her, like he'd never liked no girl before.

'And what you know?' she said.

He took her hand and folded his around it.

'That your mother didn come to stay. She come to leave you here. She don' know what to do with a full-grown girl who she been standin between and any man who try to come near her. She lock you in so tight you hardly have a scratch on you from life. She follow you everywhere. She – she killin you wiv love.'

He lifted his head at the wall of borbook plants and cactus some way beyond the trees. He didn't tell her that the women also knew this, and that even if Anita wanted to take her somewhere else, they would not allow it.

The yard was quiet when they returned. His mother sat on the top rung of the steps with a grater and a bowl. Tan Cee sat in the shade of the large iron platter that John Seegal had placed there. Deeka was busy with the fire.

Patty would be in her house paging through one of his books for baby names. *Somefing different; somefing pretty. A name a lover goin like to call.*

He glanced at Windy briefly and went into the house. From the window directly above them he looked down at the jigsaw of his mother's plaits, and the neat crossroads that the partings in Windy's hair made. Tan Cee saw him there watching them and turned her head away.

Elena patted the wood and offered Windy a smile. Windy perched herself beside her, one leg pushed forward as if she were about to start a race.

'S'nice up dere, not so?' Elena said.

Windy nodded and said nothing.

'Nice an' quiet, and if you close them two pretty eyes o' yours is like de whole world turn a big wide cradle, rockin you to kingdom come. Ain't got no right or wrong up dere, especially when you with Pynter. Becuz dat son-o'-mine kin make a pusson believe anything. Problem is,' Elena popped a piece of coconut in her mouth, kept it there at the back of her jaw while she adjusted herself on the step, 'problem is, Miss Winny, it *got* right an' wrong. You an' my boy is first cousin, blood o' de same Bender blood, y'unnerstan? Dat's de first ting. De second is Pynter ain't got no knowledge of no girls yet. De time don't reach for dat, an' like I say, is jus' not right.' Elena began chewing. The coconut made a terrible crunching sound. 'And third – God give me eyes dat see everything. I see when nobody think I see, so if you and, er – ahem!'

Pynter had shifted his weight against the sill and they all looked up at him. 'Tell 'er, Windy, that she can't kill a dead thing twice,' he said. He hopped out onto the steps, rested a hand on Elena's shoulder and squeezed his way past them. 'See what I tell you, Windy? My modder is the hammer; she the one that hit.'

Elena flung the bowl at him, but he shot out an arm and caught it, glaring at her rage and laughing.

27

THEY'D BEEN FOUR months away from their yards when Paso came. Paso was the nephew who had taught him about poems and had shown him a way to see. From their perch on the hill above Old Hope, they'd watched the slow emergence of the human shape on the road below. As he came closer they could make out his red canvas shoes, then the thread of silver at the wrist, and his bright belt like a rainbow around his waist.

Pynter couldn't contain himself and began running to meet him. His nephew saw him coming and started laughing too. They met by the old iron bridge over which stood the dead stone mill. Paso made a doorway of his arms and Pynter stepped into it. The old dance was there, the same flash of a smile. 'Maan, you gone aall taaall and bee-yoo-tiful,' he said. 'In fact, you look like sumbady Ah know.'

The accent was American, a tease. Paso mimed a mirror with his hand and laid an arm against Pynter's. They laughed and back-slapped some more and then Paso's smile dissolved.

'Your people tell me y'all down here.' He looked about him and waved an arm at the trees. 'Which one is your mother?'

Pynter shrugged. 'I ask meself dat question all the time, cuz all of them believe that they my mother.'

Paso laughed again. 'Where the others?'

Pynter pointed at the hill above them.

'Gwone. I follow you.'

'What you want wiv them?'

The question stopped his nephew. 'Call me a reaper, Uncle. Make me a gatherer of rage.'

Pynter shook his head at Paso.

'I travel the island. I follow the troubles. I find people like y'all. I organise them.'

Pynter had heard about people like that in school, from bits of whispered conversations amongst the students from the north. He remembered the furtive lunchtime gatherings at the back end of the building. He pointed a finger at Paso. 'You one of them?'

'S'where de action is,' Paso said.

Pynter brought a finger to his lip. 'Marlis Tillock,' he said. 'Y'ever hear the name?'

He thought Paso would never answer. He remembered that expression: the tiny frowning hesitation, the steady eyes, the smile. The last time he saw it, his nephew had answered his question with a poem.

'Tillock,' Pynter repeated.

'He was one of mine.'

Pynter was suddenly aware of the babble of the river beneath them, the shivering of the old iron bridge under their feet. 'Yuh mean, you the one that, erm, gather 'im?'

'Organise, young-fella. Organise. Somebody have to do it. You goin take me to the others?'

Paso greeted them with jokes and they accepted him warmly.

'You look like him,' Frigo whispered.

'Nuh, he look like me,' Pynter replied. 'I'z his uncle.'

They took Paso past the belt of flowering white cedars, where the trees plaited their branches together and made an endless suite of rooms. It seemed perfectly natural that they should take him to that high place where they could light a masantorch at night and be certain that the light would not leak out. He shook their hands, asked their names again and wanted to know how their families were doing.

He told them why he was there. He asked them to lift themselves above the high green spine of the island and see themselves as part of a swelling tide of young people who ran from their homes at night. He made them see two streams, one flowing southwards from the north, another in the opposite direction. And they, he said, whether they were aware of it or not, had always been a part of these streams. They were part of others everywhere on the island, from the small, grey houses of galvanise and wattle that stood facing the sea, to those high on hillsides or locked in valleys full of ferns and boulders. Even the ones hidden amongst the lianas and the foliage further inland, they were all part of it, tributaries if they liked, that made that river what it was. And when those rivers met …

Paso brought his hands together, and in the silence that surrounded them, its effect was like a clap of thunder.

Pynter looked at the faces around him, the twitch of lips as Paso shaped his words, the catches of breath in the pauses between sentences.

Pynter slipped away and went outside. Darkness had grouped the hills together so that from where he stood they looked like the hunched shoulders of giants brooding over the cane fields. He whispered Windy's name, remembering something he'd told her. The sound of footsteps broke through his thoughts. Paso came and stood beside him. Pynter glanced at his nephew's face. He was looking out ahead of him, perhaps at the bright fleck of moon that hung over the hill.

'You do this all the time?' Pynter said.

Paso stirred. 'S'bigger than you think, not so?'

Pynter closed the front of his shirt. 'You say the same thing all the time?'

Paso cocked his head at him and smiled. 'All the time,' he said.

In all the years of not seeing Paso, it was the thing he remembered most about his nephew: the open smile, the beautiful teeth, the flash of eyes that went with it. He'd never stopped missing him.

'You didn finish it,' Pynter said.

'I don't follow you.'

'The metaphor, the river; you didn finish it. You didn tell them de colour of the water, when the two rivers meet.'

'You think I don' know that? Word reach me that you don't only have my face, you smart too. I been lookin forward to seein you. Don't spoil it for me now.'

Pynter shook his head, 'All I sayin is … yunno … '

'What you learn 'bout history in your school?' His nephew's voice was calmer. 'That all of it is in the past, not so?' Paso's arm made a quick contemptuous arc at the darkness before them. 'So how come it still right there in front of us? How come your people still killing demselves in it? For us, young-fella, history not something we look back at. History is now. To put it behind you where it belong, somebody have to break it. Get rid of it. An' yes, for that to happen, we goin have a few more Marlis Tillocks.'

Paso stuffed his hands in his pocket. In the distance beyond the hills, the soft white arc of headlamps brightened the sky from time to time. Dogs too, a long way off, were arguing with the dark.

'Tell them that then,' Pynter said. 'Not no story 'bout no river.' Pynter turned to face him. 'And you?'

'What about me?'

'Feel with your eyes, see with your heart. You 'member that? Well, they tellin me right now dat Victor want you more than all of us put together. Not so?'

Paso flashed a smile at him, turned and went to join the others.

28

OLD HOPE BEGAN dreaming and it was Patty who started it. She came down the hill each morning, her eyes dark and heavy with the disturbance of the night, and spoke to them in whispers.

She told them of women whose hair was a nest of snakes, dark rivers that ran backwards, gatherings of clouds that rained down scorpions on Old Hope, men as tall as palmiste trees covered in robes of flaming red, pregnant boys, rocks that bled, bloated babies with messages in their cries and fierce hot winds. The older folks tried to unravel these dreams. A brown and muscular river meant confusion, spiders promised money or deliverance, scorpions were spite, and a red-dressed man who danced the dance of palm trees meant that Shango, Orisha of all Orishas, had been awakened by the troubles in Old Hope and would not go away.

'Y'all talk like if trouble went somewhere,' Tan Cee said. 'But in dem dreams, you fly, Patty. You always fly. Dat mean … dat mean you not beat-an'-defeat, y'unnerstan? You not.'

These days Tan Cee hardly talked. She sat alone with her back against the iron platter watching the world through half-closed eyes. She lifted her head from time to time to look up at the house that her husband was close to finishing for Anita. They chuckled a lot, Anita and Coxy, and the sound of them together would turn Tan Cee's head, as if however often she heard them, their laughter never ceased to startle her.

Anita brought Coxy's meals to him. She sat beside him on her new step, dipped bread into her plate sometimes and held it up to his mouth. It was the only time that Tan Cee would not look.

Pynter felt the sinking of his auntie's spirit, watched the detachment with which she looked on the rest of them now, the flat-eyed daze of someone who had collided with something they could neither walk around nor climb over.

It was worse when Wednesday nights arrived and Coxy did not leave the yard. The first evening it happened, Coxy came down in his usual Wednesday get-up: the pleated trousers, the two-tone leather shoes, the soft white cotton shirt smelling of Cussons Imperial Leather soap and Alcolado Glacial. He stood at the edge of the yard with his chin pulled slightly inwards. He took out a cigarette and brought a fizzing match to it. His eyes met Tan Cee's and she stared back at him. There was a slight lifting of the corner of her lips, the tiniest thread of a smile and Pynter saw a shadow briefly cross his auntie's face.

Elena was leaning against the doorway.

'Somefing have to happm,' Pynter said, wrestling for words. 'Somefing…'

'Time,' she breathed softly, barely moving her lips, 'give my sister time. He not Leroy,' she said, lifting an eyebrow at Coxy's retreating back. 'He worse. You tol' Winny I wicked, not so? Well, I tellin you now, Tan Cee worse. Jus' give 'er time.'

She lifted Lindy off her shoulder and handed the child to him, just as she did every time he came home. While Windy moved around the yard, laughing with Peter, and glancing at him from under heavy, lidded eyes, he could not move. There was no one he could pass Little Lindy over to, since the child would not be held by anyone but his mother and himself.

He ruffled her lettuce-curls and grinned at her. This baby girl, so partial to the hands that held her, who laughed a lot in her sleep and would not eat meat, was, he believed, the picture of the stranger they had never seen: eyes dark and wide as river pools, limbs so slim and long they made him think of bamboo, and toes as supple as her fingers.

Elena kept her greased and prettily clothed all the time. He would watch his mother pause over the child sometimes with her head lifted as if she'd suddenly heard her name. She would finger the baby's hair, and then catch herself with a little start before turning back to whatever she was doing.

He loved to lay Lindy on his chest and talk, while she busied herself with parts of his face, or with pulling at his hair. Talking became easier because, these days, Lindy agreed with everything.

'You'z a wicked lil baby-girrrl!' he said. The child nodded. 'A nice one, though. The best. You'z a star apple, dumplin'-an'-fry-bakes and sapodilla chile.' Lindy poked at his ear and nodded. 'Yunno what a metaphor is? Is a lil bit like a parable – sometimes. Yunno what a parable is? Well, is a kinda metaphor. You goin stop squeezin me nose and lissen? Well, I been thinkin. Me an' Paso had a big argument about history. Yunno what history is? S'awright, I tell you next time. I tell 'im that de story about Sodom an' Gomorrah is about us right here in Old Hope. Y'ever hear 'bout Lot's wife? Dat's all dey call her. Lot's wife. She didn have no name, but she's de one everybody remember. God chase them out of Sodom and Gomorrah before he turn the whole place into smoke-an'-ashes. In them days, that fella,' Pynter wagged a finger at the ceiling, 'he used to lay down a whole heap of unrealistic conditions for ord'nary people. Y'hear me? He tell them don't look back, else they become a pillar of salt. De whole heap o' them keep their head straight. You kin imagine Missa Lot and all hi people runnin up dat mountain ketchin arse to hold their head straight, except the wife. She didn just look back, she turn round. She face it. And she was the only one who know what she see before she freeze up and stay right there and become seasoning for food, y'unnerstan? My father used to call that foolishness. I say the woman brave. I say that p'raps what she see worth all the salt she turn to, an' p'raps a damn lot more. She not like we. We don't look back. We 'fraid dat it … it … petrify us. Uh-huh. Yuh hear de word, Star Apple? Petrify! You wan' hear me say it again? Petrify! Well, none of Old Hope, in fact none of dis whole flippin island – they don't wan' to look back. But me! I'z Lot's wife. Uh-huh – dat's me. I'z she. I have to look back, y'unnerstan?'

Outside, they were choking on the laughter. As if he cared! Straight-head-people, all of them! He adjusted the sleeping child and closed his eyes.

Coxy's hammering woke him. The week before, Coxy had brought his Fire-Flyers to the yard, built Anita's roof and lifted it in place. There were windows now, a little veranda that over-looked a small garden. The floorboards had been laid in a single afternoon and the whole yard was steeped in the smell of paint and pinewood. Coxy promised Anita that he would finish the house before the hurricane season hit them. And he'd done as he promised. Already the river had become brown and muscular. And the mists that clothed the Mardi Gras were rolling down its sides in thick, grey swirls. They could hear the swelling ocean making a church organ of the rock caves beyond the Kalivini swamps.

Now that the house was almost done, Anita had no time for them, not even for Deeka. Apart from her daughter, Windy, the only person she laughed with was Coxy. She barely left her steps, although her laughing seemed to make her presence larger in the yard.

Lindy would lift her head and cry sometimes, and it brought on a kind of lethargy in Deeka, who moved in an aimless orbit around Tan Cee. His mother talked less, stood in the doorway more often, turned her head at every sound, exactly like Deeka used to.

Wednesday nights, Coxy stayed on Anita's steps with her and smoked. Sometimes they shared a cigarette. One evening, she eased herself up on the rung above him, made an arch of her body and covered his head with her hair. And while Coxy and Anita sat and laughed above them, all Deeka talked about was water – river pools and oceans – the kind of water a pusson got drowned in. Did they know there was a lil bit of sea east of where she came from that people called Nowhere? Waves did not rise and hit the rocks there. The ocean pushed against the land like a man heaving with his shoulders. The water was an indigo so deep you dipped an oar in it half expecting the sea to stain it blue.

There was a river that ran beneath the sea there too, that came all the way down from the north. The fishermen had a name for it, they called it the Cradle, although ignorant Old Hope men, who returned from building the Panama Canal, brought back a different name for it, Neenyo-something-or-the-other. A lot of careless man up north fall asleep in their boat sometimes and when dem wake up an' look round, de Cradle done gone and rock dem all the way to Venezuela. It happen to Deeka's uncle. It happen to him twice. And it would ha' happen to that foolish fella all the time if he didn decide to remain in Venezuela second time.

And past that far place where the Cradle ended … Deeka turned to Pynter, her eyes all hollowed out and pleading. Did a pusson know what was past that far place?

Nothing, Pynter said. Ain't got nothing past that place, just the underbelly of the world.

29

THE TROUBLE OUTSIDE had finally spilled over into Old Hope. Not the shootings and the small bonfires of protest that sprang up like a rash elsewhere on the island, but the procession of jeeps that took over the roads. A soft voice on the radio would announce the places where the roads were to be cleared by six o'clock.

Pynter watched their homes from his perch on the hill opposite. Paso walked the foothills, talking with the villagers, and when they returned, his nephew's language seemed to have changed his companions a little more. Oslo in particular became agitated about the news of the troubles elsewhere. Paso called them 'happenings'. He would name the soldier responsible for every atrocity, because each one, he said, carried the signature of the man who perpetrated it. Janus shot first and issued warnings afterwards. Manos pointed out the ones he wanted from the gatherings by the roadside, gave them time to get away, then went after them. Sylus stayed in his office in San Andrews, chose the places to send his men and told them the kind of youth to bring to him. He needed to tell them a lil bit about Sylus, Paso said, and he was going to take his time.

'Everyting I say now, people, I want y'all to remember. I want y'all to burn it in y'all brain, an' keep it there.' It didn't matter how a pusson come to know these things, he said. What mattered was he knew.

Sylus's office was a low building above San Andrews. Two gates led up to it, one for walking through, the other for vehicles. There was no night up there; it was always bright with flood-lights.

A shed of corrugated iron leaned against a tree at the back of the building, with a bolt which was always drawn across the door. There was a little swamp around it from the overflow of the bathhouse, and the whole place was overgrown with tannia plants and callaloo. Tillock and that young-fella Jordan would have been taken there, Paso said, glancing at Pynter. They would have been left sitting in that shed for three days before Sylus came to them.

Sylus had a face that women liked. He laughed easily. He had pretty hands and the smoothest face they would ever see on any man. He dressed neatly. He never hurried. But all that was nothing, said Paso. All that was a distraction. Sylus would pull a wooden stool between his legs and sit. At his feet he would lay out a dozen candles, a large king-size box of Anchor matches, three cartons of Phoenix cigarettes, five pieces of wire stripped from a truck tyre and cut to varying lengths, a cotton bag the size of a small football filled with freshly mixed concrete. And if he felt he needed it, he would reach into his shirt pocket for a thin length of leather that uncoiled in his palm like a snake. That strip of leather was what Sylus always left for last.

Paso got up. They followed him with their eyes.

'He not stupid,' Paso said. 'He smarter than the man who owns him. He knows what's at stake. He knows we going to take the island.'

Sylus also knew that Paso was down there with them. It explained the tension in his nephew, the way he looked down on the canes, the suddenness with which he stopped sometimes and listened to the wind.

It was the canes that saved them every time, their simmering protestations at anything that leaned or breathed on them, the readiness with which they slipped their saw-edged leaves into exposed skin and drew deep-throated curses from the soldiers. It was the deceitfulness of cane, the brittle bed of straw they laid down like a mattress over meshes of fallen stems, which could snap the ankle of a careless man like a biscuit. It was the maliciousness with which their prickles, white as filaments of glass, would bury themselves in the soldiers' eyes and nostrils.

The wickedness of cane saved them every time.

One afternoon they were puzzling over the weather, the fretful winds and sudden bouts of stillness. There was rain somewhere in the hills beyond the Mardi Gras, because the river was raging. But not a drizzle had reached Old Hope.

Arilon cut through Oslo's words about cadres and committees and reminded them that this was the perfect time for catching crayfish. Not the tiny kakados and red-tails, but the tiger-striped lings with claws that could crack a grugru nut. Pynter said he didn't eat them. Wouldn't put no creature near his mouth which had its stomach in its head.

They were still laughing at his words when they got down to the river. He left them struggling with the water and climbed to the precipice under which the top of the trees made an umbrella over the pool they called Young Sea.

Pynter pulled out a book from under his shirt and undid the plastic bag he kept it in. He listened to the river below and thought for a while about Sislyn. He hung his legs over the rockfall.

He didn't hear them at first. He was turning the pages of *The Master and Margarita* when they came. He was thinking of cats that talked, a fanged hitman with a bowler hat and red hair and a nicer name for Christ. Yeshua Ha-Notsri. He was going to take that name to Patty. He heard the rustle of the elephant grass behind him, and then a chuckle he did not recognise. He did not turn, not even when some cold hard thing rested on the nape of his neck and a voice told him to stand. Other voices were emerging from the bush behind him.

The soldier couldn't have been much older than him. The green khaki shirt hung off his narrow shoulders like a sail. His boots were thick with mud. The muzzle of the gun was hard against his left nipple where Windy touched him once. The rising coolness of the river crept up Pynter's legs and stroked his shoulders. He wondered if the young man felt it too.

There were five of them. Pynter could hear shouts in the distance. Frigo's voice, then Arilon's, a whistle high in the hills above them which could only be Oslo's.

He had no time. Just a fanciful notion which had just come to him from reading a book that Sislyn gave him. He moved before the thought completed itself in his head. His hand shot out and closed around the man's wrist and by the time his other hand had grabbed the soldier's collar they were already falling backwards. Everything became a whirl of green as their bodies broke through the branches. They hit the water hard. Pynter surfaced first, saw the young man rise in front of him, the shape of a scream his mouth was making before the river snuffed it out. There was pleading in his eyes. *You kill anover yooman been, you add their weight to yours. For de rest of your life, you carry them wiv you.* Patty's words.

Pynter reached out, grabbed the young man's shirt and dragged him onto the bank.

The babble of approaching voices, the sound of breaking undergrowth, did not worry him. He slipped into the water and let the river take him down its dark leaf tunnels.

His mother came running over the stones towards him. She closed a hand around his shoulder.

They brought him behind the house and pulled the clothing off him. He felt the quick querying fingers of Deeka down his shoulders and his legs. His mother slid a hand across his stomach while Tan Cee held him steady. Patty passed her fingers through his hair. Then Deeka stepped away and told them he was all right.

'The others all right?' his mother said.

Pynter said nothing.

Elena straightened up. 'Ole Hope man got boy-chilren down there too. Dey quiet. Dey too quiet. I don' know what dey thinkin, but dey too quiet fo' too long.' She drew him into the shadows of the banana tree behind the house and stood him there. 'All dis goin pass,' she said. 'Y'unnerstan? All this.' Her voice was the clearest he'd ever heard it. 'Pynto,' she said softly, urgently. 'Times like dese, you never come straight home, y'unnerstan?' She shook her head. 'Cuz is de firs' thing a pusson do when trouble reach dem, dey run home. You fink dey don' know dat?'

Elena slipped her arms around his waist and pulled him towards her. He felt her breath against his neck. He realised she was crying.

He smelled the tree before he came to it. It had taken him a while to get to this small plateau beneath the Mardi Gras. And there it was – a silk-cotton tree – its buttress roots splayed along the earth like the fingers of a monstrous hand. He knew what lay beyond the opening of its converging root-walls. Even now, the fruit bats shot in and out of it like showers of dark rain.

The only sign he'd found of another human presence here was an overturned bowl of rice, and markings in the soil beside it that looked like several crossroads. It was Santay's way of telling him that she too had been here.

Everything here was just as it always had been: the chipping away of beetles beneath the skin of bark, the chittering of bats so sharp at times it felt as if Pynter's eardrums had been struck by something solid. Further up the trunk he could sense the soft disturbances of birds. Where the mist-wet sunlight touched the leaves, he could hear the throaty conversations of mountain doves.

A young man named Zed Bender died here once. He, Pynter, was supposed to be this man born again. Zed Bender had died at the hands of a man who believed he owned him, cursing him to the end. Blood, Deeka had told them, had a memory of its own.

Santay was sitting with her back against her door-mouth. Her hands were white with the manioc she was grating in a basin in her lap.

'You goin stay behin' dat bush whole day?' she said.

She hadn't looked up. She covered the basin with a square of cloth and went to the oil drum behind her house to wash her hands.

'Wash yuh foot,' she said, and went inside.

It was still early. The canes below were hazy and untroubled. Gauldins swirled above them in dizzy, aimless circles. When Pynter washed at the oil drum, he was surprised to see the swelling belt of a bruise across his shoulders.

Santay came and sat beside him on the steps. She dropped a plate of fish and vegetables in his lap and while he ate she poured the contents of a small bottle into her palms and smeared it along his shoulders.

'I see you fly, Legba. I stay right here an' see you fly.' It was the new name she had given him. A warm and throaty chuckle bubbled out of her.

'Fall,' he said. 'Not fly.'

'De way dey come dis time,' she said. 'So ... so ... *heavy*.'

He told her about Paso.

'Is he dey come for?'

Pynter inspected a bit of fish, popped it in his mouth and nodded. 'They didn get 'im,' he said. 'Not dis time.'

The bracelets jangled. 'Somebody tell dem he down dere?'

He nodded again. 'Dey got Arilon instead.'

She got up and went inside, and when she returned she placed a handful of phials at his feet.

306

'Tomorrow and de next day, s'all de time I got,' he said.

'Who'z Marilon?' she said.

'My friend.'

Santay cleared her throat. She was busy with her headwrap for a while. 'Dat's why you come here?'

'Don' know why I come,' he said.

She reached for the basin of manioc. She lifted the cloth and held it in front of him. He swung his head away.

'S'de poison you smell,' she said. 'Most people don'. Dey take it, dey grate it, dey boil de badness out of it. Dey make farine, bread an' starch wiv it.' Santay dipped her finger in the milky paste. 'I been doin dat all my life. I never had no reason to do otherwise. Now,' she convulsed her shoulders and sloshed the white paste in her hand, 'now I want to strain it. I want to mix it wiv milk from de bark of a mangue tree, put it in dem bottle dere and give y'all to throw in other people face. An' dat can't be right.'

She convulsed her shoulders again. The paste dropped from the bowl in heavy clots.

They watched it trickle between the stones and settle there.

'Dat's how I know my time done pass. Ain' got no place in de world for people like me no more.'

She scooped up the bottles and held one out to him. He shook his head.

Pynter looked her in the eyes. 'I comin back, not so?'

'You intend to?' She flicked an irritated wrist at him. 'I don' know why you askin me! You don' have to go for nobody call Marilon. Nobody sendin you.'

'I have to go,' he said.

30

He expected Miss Maddie to topple over the edge of the veranda any minute soon. Most of her was already over the wall. She was shielding her eyes with both hands. Sounds were coming out of her, rapid and indecipherable. She was pushing her body further and further out.

'Coño,' she said. 'No créo … que.'

'I'm Pynter,' he said.

Her face was even more swollen than he remembered it, her eyes more puffed, and what before had been a hint of grey at her temples was cotton white now.

'Lord ha' mercy, I see you comin, an' I thought … I thought … '

Pynter offered her a smile.

'Cucaracha!' she muttered.

'I come to see Paso,' he said.

'Coo-nyo! De other one, he same like you?'

'He name Peter.'

She nodded. 'He same like you?'

'He name Peter.'

Miss Maddie swung her head as if he'd slapped her. 'Peter – he … ?'

'He more like yuh brodder, Gideon, but Peter much-much better lookin.'

'He not here,' she said. She lifted a hand to touch him, checked herself and dropped it quickly.

'Blood never lie,' she said. 'I mistake you fo' my boy.'

Her house looked smaller than he remembered it. The glistening white of the concrete walls had been replaced by the creeping brown of water stains. A fissure ran along the concrete walkway. The yellow walls inside the veranda had been clumsily repainted in places.

There was no trace of his father's house. No sign of the fire that had destroyed it. Weeds grew there now, and tall stems of honeysuckle held together by a riot of nettle vines. She'd planted peppers and sweet potatoes, red cabbages and pum-pum yams.

If he and Peter had children, they would say their father's name to them and tell them who he was. But it would mean little to them, even less to those who came after them. Rememberin was like watchin a pusson walkin a long road, losin them in the distance, disappearin with time. He looked back at Miss Maddie.

'You,' she said, turning her head to where the house had been, 'you had de best part of 'im.'

'Miss Maddie?'

The woman lifted her chin.

'Gideon, he got anything in common with my – with our father?'

He thought she wasn't going to answer him. She'd turned her head away. 'Love all yuh chilren same way,' she said. 'If you can't do dat, is better to pretend.'

She turned and left him there.

Later, he stretched out on the wall of the veranda and watched the night pass. Miss Maddie had stood behind the curtains of her window for a long time looking out at him. She'd brought him a bowl of soup and laid it on the little wooden table in the corner of the veranda. 'Paso not comin,' she said. 'Sleep with de window open.' He did not ask her why.

In the night Pynter thought about what she had said to him, that he had got the best part of their father. Those words reminded him of a walk he had taken with Tan Cee once. They'd come to a cool green place over the ocean, a place that seemed far removed from anywhere he'd ever been, as if they'd stepped into a dream together.

Tan Cee had nudged his arm. But he'd already seen what she was pointing at. There, amidst a small crowd of guineps, stood another tree. It was paler, wider and straighter than the rest, with leaves that shivered at the slightest breath of air. It stood back from the precipice that fell in a wide white plunge all the way down to the bottom of a cliff. The guinep trees were like a huddle of dark-limbed people round it.

'See?' she had said.

Tan Cee had nudged him closer, and he realised that it was not the tree that she was pointing at but small mounds of stone that stood up from the earth around the trunks like the piled-up heads of children. Here, she said, beneath this tree, on the lip of this precipice, was the place from which their people, the people of the canes, used to launch themselves.

'An' die?' he had asked.

'An' fly.'

'To where?'

''Cross dere.' She'd lifted her chin as if the ocean itself was a destination. To that place they had been brought from.

'A stone for each one that make it – an' I not askin you to believe it.'

If people didn believe that any more, she'd said, 'twas because they forget how to believe in things that used to come so easy once. 'Twas what happened to chickens, she s'posed: still had their wings, but 'twas long time since they forget how to use them.

She'd shrugged. It didn matter, though. 'What matter is, we the ones got left behind. Mebbe we the ones who 'fraid to fly. P'raps we didn wan' to go back to face de ones who hand us over.'

She'd turned towards the tree. What was certain was that hands had planted that tree there, shimmering and silver even in this leaf gloom. They had no name for it and it was the only one like it they knew. Old, she said, older than memory. Old as the people who brought the root with them. P'raps it was a tiny bit of root that got tangled in a woman's hair. Or it might have been the seed of some fruit that had slept in the bowels of a child. Maybe it was a special parting gift from someone, since it was the kind of tree you noticed even in the night. It guided you to itself, even when there was no wind. And it was true that in this quiet, windless day, he could hear it, in an endless conversation with itself.

He'd stepped back into the day with her, bleary-eyed and dazed. They'd looked past the cane belt up towards the foothills. Old Hope was no more than a gap between the rising hills, blue with distance. And he'd realised for the first time that a stranger to this island might lift their eyes up to those hills and never know that anybody lived there.

'Your modder, the others – dey give you tings you goin forget,' she'd said. 'I give you someting dat can't leave you.' She said it quietly, fiercely. Was distracted, for a moment, by the flight of a pair of birds making slow circles over the tiny island just offshore.

'Storm bird,' she said.

'Albatross,' he said.

'That the right name?' She'd shaped the word with her lips.

'Uh-huh.'

Tan Cee had looked at him. 'What make de difference, Pynto? Wiv you an' Peto? What make you get to go to dat high-falutin school an' Peter never get to come wiv you?'

'Was a mistake,' he said. 'A mistake dat y'all make. My father, when he left working in hi garden, he went home for good. The man I meet was not de man his chilren know. De man I meet was tired. He had enough of livin. An' all of de time I spend with 'im, my fadder was jus' waitin to die. S'like you standin here waitin to cross dat lil stretch of water to dat lil island over there.

I was de one y'all send to help 'im make de crossing. Cuz thaa'z the place I come from, not so? 'Cross dere? Little as I was, I was s'pose to know dat place. To ease hi passage towards it. And yunno, Tan, I help 'im. An' he pay me back. He used to tell me, he wan' to teach me every useful thing he know. He try. Even after Bostin come and force 'im to send me to school, he try. Dat's why…'

'You carry dat inside you all dis time?' she'd said.

'All the time,' he'd said.

The nasal tones of Miss Maddie and Paso's fretful mumblings woke Pynter early the next morning. The door to the veranda flung open.

'You didn bring 'im inside?' he shouted.

'He didn wan' to come inside,' Miss Maddie said.

Paso held him in a quick, tight embrace. 'You had me soo worried, Uncle. Thought I was goin crazy. I see you got de word.'

'Windy tell me,' Pynter said. 'S'how I know you awright.'

'I couldn give 'er a time. Jus' had to pass the word for you to meet me here.' Paso leaned suddenly into him. 'I hear about de flippin foolishness you wan' to do, and you can't.'

'Jus' tell me how to get dere. Walk me through the place.'

'You not goin nowhere.'

'Who goin stop me? You?'

'You might be me uncle, but I much older'n you – y'unnerstan?'

'I still yuh uncle, though. Tell me how to get there.'

Their argument brought Miss Maddie hurrying out to them. They were pointing their fingers in each other's face and talking in hot, rapid spurts. Her head moved with the wagging of their fingers.

'Crica!' she said, and went back inside.

Pynter finally got what he wanted out of Paso. There was a house above the Carenage in San Andrews, Paso said. He had

312

people there, almost as close as family. Better than family in some cases. There was another house much further south in the Drylands, a relative of theirs that Pynter didn't know. Paso listed the things that Pynter should look for in order to get to those places easily. Whatever happened, he said, and depending on where he was, Pynter should head for one of those houses.

'You still write pretty words?' Pynter said.

'No time,' Paso said.

'How come?'

'This, all this…' Paso waved at the air outside. 'Word reach me that you save a fella from burnin last Guy Fawkes Night. You into savin fellas?'

'You would ha' let 'im burn?'

His nephew straightened up. Even in the early-morning gloom, Pynter felt Paso's irritation.

'Tillock was your friend, not so? And that other lil one…'

'Jordan, he wasn' no other lil one. He was a fella big as me.'

'You didn't have Tillock and him in mind when you save dat fella, not so? Well…' Paso pushed his back against the wall, shooting his legs out at the same time. 'Next time keep both of dem in mind, okay?'

Pynter turned to Paso. 'I tell you what I work out,' he said. 'To kill a pusson, you have to make dem different. You have to change dem in yuh mind; yuh need to make dem less dan you. You have to feel you have de right. You feel you have de right?'

'If de reason big enough.'

'An' who decide de reason big enough? Not anodder pusson?'

Pynter slipped his hand along the waist of his trousers. He pulled out a small book and tossed it in Paso's lap. 'Page seventy-four. Wilfred Owen. English fella. Dey say h'was de greatest war poet ever live. In 1917, he join a war. Read what happm *inside* of 'im befo' dat same war kill 'im.' Pynter stood up. 'S'matter o' fact, I contend dat dat same war kill Missa Wilfred Owen twice. Keep de book, Paso. An' tell yuh modder thanks fo' me.'

Miss Maddie's house stood on the northern end of the ridge that ended at Glory Cedar Rise.

It was a steady climb up through the gardens of pigeon peas and sweet potatoes. Further on, through the brushland of sage and borbook, the soil coarsened under Pynter's feet, then became a trail of slipping gravel until he reached the small settlement above Old Hope they called Top Hill. He was less than half a mile from home, and yet the world was different here. The little wooden houses were as frail and brightly painted as kites. They seemed, in fact, to be held up by the winds that forever pushed against them, leaning into the blasts that came straight off the ocean.

The people up here were different too. They rarely came down to the valley. He felt comfortable under the children's dark-eyed scrutiny which took in everything and gave nothing away. As he walked along the track, they did not give him way, not even the youngest. To get past, he had to step around them and yet they took no offence when his shoulders pushed against theirs. In fact, standing as they were in this high mid-morning wind, their heads tilted at the ocean and their clothing flapping like boneless wings around their bodies, they seemed to be contemplating flight.

These were the true hill people of Old Hope, born and brought up in the middle of this skimming ocean wind. It had flattened their stomachs and lengthened their limbs and left them with that dreamy, far-eyed gaze. At least that was Deeka's way of explaining it.

Just when he was about to leave them, he heard the thud of naked heels behind him.

Pynter looked over his shoulder and saw a child – slim and long-limbed like the others, her hair piled up on her head like tufts of cus-cus grass – hurrying after him.

'Where you from?' she said.

'Down there,' he said, pointing past the trees to where he thought his home was.

She shook her head. She did not believe him.

'You been away?'

'Not been, I goin.'

'You don' look like Down-Dere people.'

'What Down-Dere people look like?'

'Not like you,' she said.

'How I look, den?'

She shrugged. 'Not like dem.'

Someone behind her called a name, a woman's voice, soft to his ears and musical. The child lifted a shoulder in acknowledgement.

She looked up at him. She'd tensed her forehead into a faint pleat. 'I ask too much question, not so?'

'That's what they tell you?' he said.

She shook her head. 'Nuh, dat's what I know. Don' know how else a pusson s'pose to unnerstan tings.' She'd become fretful and slightly restless. 'When you go away, you comin back?'

'Don' know,' he said. 'Don' know if I wan' to.'

Lil Miss Iona was smiling when she turned back to him. 'My brodder Glendo goin make a kite fo' me dis evenin,' she said. She turned and left him abruptly for the others. Halfway there, she lifted an arm and waved. 'When you come next time, I show you how to fly it.'

As soon as Patty saw him coming she came down her steps and pushed a finger in his face. Who the hell did he think he was to put so much worry in people head. And playing smart man wiv it too-besides, by coming to her place, knowing she was the one who could not stop him. But he shouldn fool himself, if she wasn' as big-an'-clumsy as she was right now, she would do to him the self-same things that were playing on Elena's mind.

She would stop him: she would break a leg of his, or hit him so hard he would go right back to sleep and she wouldn give a damn if he don' wake up this time, or if it mean they had to carry him on their backs for the rest of their lives.

Becuz a man walked out of this yard once. He left his woman and three girl-children dying for him. He left a yard full of stones and questions, and, however much they tried to wipe them off their minds, in all their years of living they could not make those questions leave them: was it becuz of them that he left? What was the one little thing they might have done to make him stay with them? These thoughts found a way to stitch themselves into everything they did.

And did he, Pynter, know what it feel like watchin a pusson who fill you up so much with demself walk off to some kind of death that they choose for demself? Like if they had a right to. Like if a yard full of stones and a house on a hill over the road was enough to stop the hurting. Like if it didn have a pusson in de world who had a claim on them?

His mother took it hardest. Did he know that? Eh? Elena give up on speech for years and 'twas desire that bring words out of her again, not for Manuel Forsyth, but for the one thing she wanted out of him: chilren.

You'n Peto. Y'all two. Two of you. Y'unnerstan?

And in all dem years, what did he think been happening inside of people, eh? What he think been takin place inside his modder head?

Well, a pusson goin tell him right now what Elena feelin – that nothing she allow herself to love that much will leave like this again. She rather get rid of it herself.

Which was why he could not go down to the yard today to face his mother, cuz one thing a pusson was certain of. He would never leave it.

And one last thing. Patty pointed a shaky finger at her stomach. She did not want to have to give this child his name. A pusson didn want to have to remember him like that.

His aunt's words seemed to have exhausted her. She sat back on her steps and fixed wet, accusing eyes on him.

He left Patty when the gauldins were heading towards their roosts up in the foothills. He'd closed his mind down to her pleas. He did not look back.

The air was thick with bird cries when Pynter reached Glory Cedar Rise, the hills directly ahead were already blurring in the dusk. He had not prepared himself for this journey. Paso had told him where to go and how to get there, and the names of a few people that he could go to if he managed to get Arilon out and needed to find some place to 'rest up'. There was a man named Hugo who lived in the only green-roofed building that looked directly over the Carenage in San Andrews. He could not miss it. That was the house he should head for first, he said. And if Hugo wasn't there, he should take Arilon south with him through the alleyways of the town and keep heading for the Drylands.

Night came fast. The sky was still full of birds hurrying to escape it. A new moon squinted over the hills of Déli Morne. The sighing of the canes had softened. His mind must have been adrift, for he heard her only when her footsteps stirred the leaves.

He was still staring ahead when a hand curved around his stomach and tightened. All he had to do was turn and she was in his arms.

They said nothing at first. Patty must have guessed that he was still up here and sent her or perhaps she came here on her own sometimes at night.

He lowered his face into her hair. Her lemon smell entered his head and made him shiver. She said his name. It crossed his mind that no one had ever called him like that before. He murmured her name. She offered him her mouth. He cradled her face and dipped his head. She held him tight and rocked him in the wind and he drifted with her, past caring.

31

TAN CEE SAW Windy emerge from the night. She did not come straight over to them. She stood at the edge of the yard, the fire-light lapping at the hem of her skirt like yellow water. She looked beautiful and lost there, standing in her red rubber sandals, her hair undone.

'Y'awright?' Tan Cee said. She cocked a thumb and smoothed the eyebrows of the girl. 'You seen 'im?'

Elena hadn't taken her eyes off Windy and she returned her stare. Deeka saw that look and it froze her fingers over the bowl of sorrel she was cleaning. Some mothers slapped their daughters down the very first time they saw that look. There were those who took it as the declaration of a war they'd hoped would never come, that look which said that their girl-chile was a woman, and the body she lived in was her own.

Tan Cee got up. She had things to do. She went up the hill to the garden of corn and sweet potatoes above Anita's house, her mind full of Pynter. They'd been crying for him in terrible, silent ways, Deeka especially. The Old Woman had become irritable and silent, was prey to hot flushes and could barely abide the sight of Peter. She was wanting this bright-eye, smooth-face, long-face dog of a gran-chile who looked at her as if he could see inside her head, whose funny edicated talk had her stuffing back a mouthful of chuckles. In all these hatin-an'-lovin years, it was this same lil Pynto who, after John Seegal left her, made Deeka begin to feel again.

Since he was a child, he'd told them what he needed but they would not listen. He told them when he returned with Santay that time, his blindness cured. They were all aware that he was seeing them for the first time. He was looking at them and matching their voices to their faces. He did not want to leave the woman's side. Santay had to put her hand behind his head and push him towards them. He came straight over to her, Tan Cee, folded his arms around her waist and looked up in her face. Even then, she saw the desperation in his eyes.

'Santay say I'll live if y'all believe it,' he said. He'd glanced over his shoulder at Deeka and tightened his grip around her waist. Had held on to her as if she were the only thing that could anchor him to this world. And with that one look into her eyes he'd claimed her in a way his brother, Peter, could never do.

It explained everything: those months of scooter madness when word reached them that he was riding his machine between the wheel-span of the tractors; the illness he'd brought upon himself which almost killed him. And that night he returned from the river, soaked to the bone, caked in mud, his clothing hanging off him, and later told them what he did to save himself.

For what was there left for a boy-chile to do when all his life a pusson tellin him he not born to live for long? That he didn have nothing to look ahead for?

He ain't got no choice but two, not so? He either run from the death a pusson keep holdin up in front of him, or he turn around and face it. He try to put his hands on it and bring it closer to his face. He try to understand it. That's what a pusson do.

Which was why Tan Cee didn give a damn if they all believed she was going crazy when she told them that it wasn't Arilon that Pynto was going after, it was the burden that each of them had left him with.

Tan Cee made her way through the garden on the slope above her house. From time to time, she stopped to run her fingers down the ears of corn, and if she was satisfied with what she felt, she pulled the corn loose and dropped it in the hammock of her dress.

It would be their first corn for the year.

Corn was in season the first time Chilway took Birdie off to jail. Corn was what Deeka fed them the night John Seegal walked.

Unsteady with the weight, she made her way down to the yard. There, she cleaned the fireplace, pulled some wood together and left the fire to rage for a while. When the wood had burnt itself down, she stripped the ears of young corn and laid them on the embers.

It was late. The half-quarter moon had started its downward arc towards the Kalivini hills. Old Hope would not sleep tonight. The air quivered with their fretful spurts of temper directed at the children. They were remembering Jordan and thinking about Arilon.

The children came first, drawn by the smell of the corn, and after them their mothers. When they were all there, Tan Cee looked up, red-eyed and blinking from the smoke. 'I can't figure no better way to pass de night,' she said, 'so we might as well eat corn. And somebody better find a story fast.'

Meena cleared her throat.

'Not you,' she said. 'We don' want to fall asleep. Patty, you goin start a song?'

Patty pretended not to hear her.

Tan Cee drew a large corn from the fire and held it up against the glow. 'A song for a corn,' she said, turning to the children. 'Else y'all starve tonight.'

Her hand disappeared for a moment and emerged with a small knife. She began cutting through the husk.

'Not with dat knife!' Elena said.

'What wrong wiv it?'

'You not givin me no corn you cut with dat knife.'

'A knife is a knife; I sure it cleaner dan yuh hand. Start singing, else no corn for y'all tonight.' She was rubbing her eyes and smiling. 'A song for a corn, y'all hear me? Sing Arilon song. It ain' got nobody in Ole Hope don' know Arilon song. Right now I askin' y'all to sing it.'

It triggered off the bickering and then the arguments, and finally the rush of jokes that helped to keep their thoughts off the one thing that pressed down on their minds.

Patty sang at last. Miss Maisie's voice, gruff and ugly on its own, eased in and seemed tempered with hers; then Peter's added itself to theirs, striving for a bass he did not have yet. The rest tumbled in quickly, each voice jostling for a comfortable space within the tune, and on finding it, making room for the ones that came in after: Lizzie's baby cry as unblemished as the day she was born; Elena's and Deeka's so similar a pusson could barely untangle them; Glenray and Nisa and Rachel frilling it with sighs and warbles and bird cries.

But the discovery was Windy. Her song voice came from the back of her throat, high yet hoarse and heavy-laden. She sang as if they were not there, with her head pulled back, her neck exposed and pulsing. They'd heard her hum prettily before, but never this open-mouthed, skin-tingling trilling. From the houses down below and on either side of them, and across the face of the hill above the canes, there came a surge of shouts and choruses.

> *Be a bird on a wind an' fly*
> *Be de heart of a child dat smile*
> *Be a bee, be a bird, be a butterfly*
> *Be all of a mornin sky …*

They listened with their mouths full of corn. Tan Cee raised her head. She dropped the husk of the corn she was holding into the fire and looked straight at the women. She was glad they came, she said. If they didn turn up she would've come out tonight and meet them. It didn have a pusson 'mongst them who didn know about Arilon and Pynto. But she didn't want them there to talk about those boys, or the soldier-hell everybody been livin these past five months. She wanted to take them back to the year after she brought her husband, Coxy Levid, to Old Hope. She was going to remind them of the night a young-fella name Solomon, from Déli Morne, danced and laughed and burned. They remember the months that followed – not so? They remembered those times when the men of Déli Morne and Old Hope were swinging machetes at each other the way a pusson did at cane? And if they remembered it the way she did, what was happening these days with Victor was nothing compared to those times. Cuz wimmen couldn't rest easy, since no right-thinkin pusson would have their man or boy-chile go out after dark. It got so desperate a woman would've offered a daughter or herself as some kinduva peace offering if that was going to stop it.

The women were shifting under her words. They were fidgeting their headties and heaving their shoulders in the firelight. It was clear to Tan Cee that they wanted to know where the hell she was taking them, why she was dragging them back to a terrible place of rawness.

But she would not be hurried or worried by their stiff-necked glowering. She would not. They could cut their eyes, suck their teeth and stewps their mouths as much as they wanted, she was going to hand them, one by one, the names of the cousins, the uncles and the cousins of the uncles whose blood, one unsuspecting night, had soaked somebody's soil somewhere becuz of a youth named Solomon.

And, like Solomon, these cousins and uncles were always beautiful, not so? Not because they been that way in life. But because their youth and the suddenness of their passing made them so.

Like they know, it got some illnesses in life that only time could cure. Time cool the anger, it clear up the bloodlust. It soften the edge of hard things. So, if once a year on Guy Fawkes Night, Déli Morne people come to Cross Gap Junction and hold up Solomon name in front of Old Hope, if they still want her husband, Coxy, or one of their men to feel what it like to dance and burn, at least, in these times, they give them a chance to save themselves.

Tan Cee paused and looked them over.

She didn't have to tell them that their men were up to something, she said. She was sure they knew. And Cynty wasn't there tonight to tell them, which was a shame, cuz Cynty know better'n anybody else in Old Hope what their men were up to. Cuz last night nine of them went to Cynty house.

Everybody in Old Hope knew that that lil man-friend who Birdie's woman was comforting came from Déli Morne. Old Hope knew that Tobias was the only person that Victor's soldiers got food and talk and water from. That lil fella laughed too loud and long with them. They took him in their jeeps on mornings, and dropped him off at night. Old Hope knew that too.

These nine men had all that in their minds when they went to Cynty's house, knocked on her door and called Tobias out. They'd walked with their machetes. They wanted to know where Arilon was. The sight of the machetes started Tobias talking. He would've talked till kingdom come if they didn't stop him.

There was a place above San Andrews that people called the Barracks, he said. There was a place outside that used to be a kitchen. A pusson knew when Sylus got somebody in that kitchen if there was a bar across the door frame, the way shopkeepers locked their shops. He told them that Sylus had been chasing after trouble in the north. News about Arilon would have already reached him. He would have left his men to travel back to San Andrews.

Tan Cee straightened up and swept the circle of faces with her eyes. 'Cynty tell me they make Tobias say the same things thirty-seven times, till the lil fella almos' fall down wiv tired. And they still not satisfy.'

Not satisfied because they'd already worked out how they were going to end it. It was what Gordon Kramer did that made her know this. He'd placed the point of his machete against the earth, leaned on it and let it slip between the stones of Cynty's flower garden, until just the handle was above the ground.

'Don't make me come back here for this,' he'd said.

Tan Cee let those words rest with the women for a while.

'Yes,' she said. 'They goin return. An' if dey can't find a reason, they goin make up one. Sure as hell they goin go back.'

For the trouble wasn't Arilon. It wasn't even Tobias's grinning ways with Victor's soldiers. The trouble these men had was with themselves. And there wasn't a face in front of her, right now, that did not know it.

The men had gone to Cynty's place itching with the humiliation of seeing themselves grow smaller in their children's eyes, becuz in all these passing months, they couldn lift a finger at the soldiers. They saw their manhood shrivel up an' die before their women's eyes. They looked on helpless when the soldiers stopped their jeeps and curled a finger at their daughters, when they traced the shape of their women with their eyes as if they weren't there. And shame bring blame, it make a pusson look for something to hit out at, and the only thing that they could turn on was Cynty's lil man from Déli Morne.

Tan Cee stood up. She dusted herself down and stared hard and long into the women's faces.

'Hold yuh men,' she said. 'Do what wimmen know to do to keep dem quiet. As for me, for what I know I have to do, I tellin y'all sorry in advance.'

Tan Cee rested a hand on Patty's stomach. She raised an eyebrow at Elena. 'Pynto goin be awright,' she said.

Anita's laughter drifted down on them. Tan Cee nodded as if she heard something in her sister's laughter and agreed with it.

She pointed at the moon, slipping like a broken teardrop down the Kalivini hills. 'Pynter goin be awright. Y'all know how I know dat?'

They did not answer her.

She told them anyway. 'I jus' done make myself believe it.'

BOOK THREE

Heart

32

PYNTER SAT ON the high ridge-road above San Andrews. By night the town was a random spread of lights hemmed in on one side by the depthless void that was the ocean. The lights from streets and houses gave the air a yellow glaze. He could make out the three church towers on Cathedral Street; the dead lighthouse, standing like an up-stuck thumb on the protrusion of granite and limestone where the harbour ended and the ocean began; and above all that, stencilled against the night sky, the high dark place that was Fort Grey, from the top of which a spotlight cut a wide, raw path down towards the harbour.

He knew it simply as the Fort. It was so old that the hunks of granite that had been cut and placed there by the people of Zed Bender's time had re-fused under their own great weight and become once more smooth and seamless rock. Not just a part of the hill but the hill itself. He could never look up at Fort Grey without a flaring sense of danger. He'd dreamt once of children, all dressed in crisp school uniform, leaping from the mouths of its cannons.

The faint hum of engines pulled him out of his thoughts. He allowed the slope of the road to take him down, covering the distance in that lazy, loose-limbed, hop-an'-drop lope that was neither run nor walk. He counted crossroads as he travelled: Morne Bijoux, Prison Cross, Richmond Turn, Croix-Fusil. At the bottom of the hill there was the rising thunder of traffic converging on San Andrews from the north. He stopped at the junction that went six ways and took the road Paso had described for him – a narrow, teetering path over which the walls of mansions rose. The path ended near the sea.

He wasn't sure what he expected but it was certainly not the large, flat-roofed house over the harbour. The rusted hinges of what used to be a gate were still buried in a low concrete wall which ran right around the house. A little way from the entrance on his right was the top of a giant flight of stone stairs carved into the hillside. It was hemmed in on either side by rows of little houses so tightly packed he wondered how people managed to move amongst them.

He marvelled at how close everything was. If he spat far out and hard enough he could hit the roof of the cinema below. A wide curving beach of asphalt was all there was between the shopfronts and the sea. From here he reckoned he could dive over the rooftops straight into the ocean.

He climbed the short steps at the back of the house and tapped on the slit door, kept tapping till a small brown face appeared in the single square pane of glass cut into the wall above his head. Massive eyes looked out at him.

'I'z Pynter,' he said. 'I here to … '

The door eased open and strong hands pulled him in. He was halfway across the room when the young woman stopped abruptly. 'The other fella?'

'Tonight,' he said. He gestured at the brightening day behind him. 'Where's Missa Hugo?'

'I'm Tinelle.'

'I'z Pynter. He there?'

She stopped again, sniffed and turned around to face him, 'You stepped on something?'

'Well … sort of.'

'Leave your shoes here. I'll boil a pot of water. I'll get you some clothes too.' She pointed at one of two blue doors to the right of her. 'Hugo's behind that door.' She flashed a quick backward glance that took in all of him. 'My parents won't like you here,' she said. And with that she disappeared.

He'd only seen women like her from a distance. They looked past him from the windows of their father's cars; or from perches on wide encircling verandas. He'd glimpsed them stretched out half-naked on bright-coloured towels on the lawns of Morne Bijoux, lawns trimmed so neatly they didn't look real. Women with up-tilted chins and rigid backbones who handed out their smiles like favours.

He expected the parents to emerge at any minute and order him out of their house. The young woman returned and seemed to read his worry.

'Canada,' she said. 'Somebody'll have to write and tell them that you here. Jeezus! You definitely need a douche! I'll get the water ready. I'll do some breakfast after.'

She disappeared again.

His awkwardness would not leave him. He leaned against the door frame, feeling useless in this large room with its heavy brown curtains, low, cushioned chairs and darkly varnished woodwork. The air was dry and sweet with the faintest suggestion of perfume. The odour seemed as much a part of the house as the colour of the walls. It was the young woman's smell. The house was full of her.

He thought of Patty's man-friend, Richard. Imagined his house to be like this, so far removed from the yard that his young aunt came from, like a different country.

Heaps of records lay scattered across the far corner of the room. Their covers were similar – a man suited in black, a stick in hand poised a little way above his nose, like a cock in mid-crow. There were three fat cushions clumped together in the midst of the records, scooped out in the middle by the weight of the body they were accustomed to. He imagined the woman sitting there, her legs pulled in under her, the thick plait of hair running down her back and brushing the fabric of the cushions like the tail end of a broom.

A row of bottles ran along a shelf above the cushions, their shapes and sizes as varied as the colours of the fluids they contained, from clear-water to a deep, mysterious purple-amber.

When he turned, she was standing by the blue door.

'How's Paso?' she said. She'd asked for his nephew the way a person would enquire about a brother or a lover.

'Awright,' he said.

'He phoned earlier from somewhere. He says that y'all are family?'

'I'z his uncle.'

She smiled. 'You say it as if you own him. You come for this fella by yourself?'

'Uh-huh.'

He pushed himself off the wall and turned to the line of pictures hung in a straight line around the room. The only house he'd ever been to with photographs on the wall was his father's. Old Hope kept their images of family in their heads, passed them on with words. There was a pattern in the way the photographs were lined up, they told a story. The first was of a woman standing with a man beside her. They were Europeans – hatted, gloved and dressed in white – so faded he could barely make out their features. As he moved along the wall, faces became fuller, the tips of noses shorter and more curved. The women's hair darker and more curled.

He paused at the farthest corner and looked back at the young woman.

She'd pulled her lower lip in between her teeth and was chewing on it slowly.

He strode across the room and unhooked the picture of the woman at the farthest corner of the room so that he could study it more closely.

'A picture missing – not so?' He said.

'You do this often?' she said.

'Do what?' he said.

'Walk into people's homes and meddle with their property?' She came towards him with a hand stretched out before her. She pulled the picture from him, replaced it on the wall, turned and twitched her nose. 'Go have a wash – you stink.'

'That is the way you talk to a pusson who arrives at your house as a guest? You think I have to be here. That what you think? I wouldln like yuh people either,' he said. 'Too stiff, too proper. Too glum. You look a lot like yuh granny, though.' He pointed at the photo of a couple sitting together on easy chairs with clasped hands, their hair brushed back in waves. 'They your mother-an'-father-in-Canada; not so? An' Missa Hugo?'

The young woman had gone very still. Pynter lifted his chin at the last picture of two small children on the wall. 'Yuh brother tall like me. Lighter-skin dan you. Different eyes he got. Grey o' green o' something, a lil bit like mine.'

'What make you say that?'

'It there,' he said, and turned away from her.

'You know this by, er, by just … '

She made a small step towards him, then checked herself.

'It there.' He nodded at the wall.

She strolled over to the picture of her brother and herself. She passed a hand across it as if she'd just discovered it. 'You could tell the colour of Hugo's eyes even if it's – this is in black'n white?'

'Yeh. Sorry.'

'Sorry for what?'

'You sound upset; I say sorry!'

'I'm not upset. And don't keep saying sorry, sorry, sorry like … '

Some time later he stood in a pair of her father's trousers which were too large at the waist and a blue shirt which, apart from the tiny spot of ink on the left pocket, was new. It was because of the ink, Tinelle told him, while gathering his discarded clothing with the end of a broomstick, that Hugo no longer wore it.

'What time, miss?'

'Don't call me "miss".'

'What time?'

'Past nine, just past.'

'Missa Hugo?'

'Give him another hour. Egg's ready!'

She got up and walked to the kitchen. She brought the food back on a little tray and placed it on the table next to him. He was lying on his side on the floor, looking at her through half-shut lids. Her face made him think of Ceylon mangoes – a smooth, thin-skinned amber-yellow. Her hips flared like a larger woman's. She was about to turn towards Hugo's door when she froze, realising perhaps that he'd been watching her all along.

He rolled over on his back. 'You don' think I'll make it,' he said.

'I didn't say that,' she said.

He shrugged and turned his gaze up at the rafters. 'I not so sure, either.'

She didn't seem to hear him. She was measuring all of him with her eyes. 'You, you really look like Paso. Difference is, I don' think I like you.'

He lifted his back off the floor and reached for the plate. He pushed the fork aside, lifted the tongue of fried plantain above his mouth and dropped it in. 'I not sure I like you either,' he said. 'I hate people who don' like a pusson for no reason and don't have the decency to hide it. But when you got upset I say to meself, "She upset, she awright. People who get upset is awright people."'

'The food's not running away,' she said.

Pynter licked his fingers. 'S'matter o' fact, me, I find you kinda awright, in a pretty sort of way.'

'Who's your family?' She'd turned her head down, trying to hide the smile.

'The Benders,' he said.

'Never heard of them.'

Pynter placed the empty plate on the table and stretched himself out on the cushions that smelled of her. 'I didn either,' he said. 'Not until my mother make me. Thanks for de food, Miss Tinelle.'

Hugo was as he'd told Tinelle – a thinner, paler version of his father. He had the largest, most carefully groomed Afro hairstyle Pynter had ever seen.

'Tin-Tin said you're Paso's … ?'

'Uh-huh.'

'Sorry, didn't introduce myself. Kwame.' Hugo fluttered a wrist at him.

'Kwa … ?'

'…me. Kwame – that's me. Means Saturday. African for Saturday. My slave name is Hugo.'

Pynter took the extended hand. 'I'z Pynter. And I'z a Bender since I born.'

Tinelle's eyes were darting between her brother's face and his.

He would be off next year, Hugo said, to study law. He was more or less working towards it. 'Tell Paso I'm disappointed he didn't turn up with you.'

Pynter soon got tired of the banter and grunted to everything that Hugo-Kwame-or-whatever-his-name-was said. These two were far removed from his world, especially this Hugo of the supple hands and fluttering eyelashes who talked too fast and too much.

'Paso come here often?' he said.

'Used to, but these two started quarrelling.' Pynter caught the quick sideways flash of eyes between them.

'Look, you're here to get your friend. You need to talk it through with Hugo, at least rehearse it in your mind.'

'I done rehearse already.'

'You don't need me then.' Hugo turned towards his door. 'Got some reading to do. Fanon. I just love Fanon. If you'll excuse me.'

'Get to know him and you'll like him,' Tinelle said.

'Don' matter. You know the Barracks?'

'Like this house,' she said. 'Used to play up there when I was a child.'

'You could tell me the best way in?'

'Don't have a best way in.'

'Tell me what you know.'

'I'll do better. I'll walk you past there later.' She glanced at her watch. 'Around five. That's,' she stared at her watch again, 'two hours before the curfew starts. You kin see most of it from the road.'

'You say it don't have no way in?'

'I didn't say that. I said there is no best way in.'

She pulled the curtains open. The light gushed in and made rainbows of the row of bottles. Pynter wondered what Paso might have told her about him.

'I'm not like that, you know,' she said.

'I know,' he said.

'I'll be honest, when they told me you were coming, I said you wouldn't make it, and definitely not on your own. Made more sense for you to come here first during the day and avoid the inconvenience of the curfew altogether. Would've saved you all that trouble and made a better impression, certainly on me.' She wrinkled her nose. 'I'll show you a couple of ways to get up there.' She turned to face him. Their eyes met and held. Hers were very wide. He thought of the older women in the photographs above their heads. 'It is possible for you not to come back.'

'I know,' he said. 'Who's the "they" who told you I was coming?'

'Whoever they are,' she said. 'You really don' know what this is about, do you? Paso asked me to find some way to stop you. I never heard him so distressed. He was sure that you would come here first. I told him it was too late. He shouldn't've passed the word on to the others, who have a lot more weight than him.

They want us to make sure you do it.' Now she seemed distracted. 'In this ... this night of terror, people need some light. Good news. Real news – everybody's dying for that right now. You go up there, you bring that fella back. S'like walking up to Victor and spitting in his face. It's like telling him we can go inside his bedroom anytime we want and watch him while he sleeps. That's why ... '

'And if I don't come back?' he said.

She lifted her head at him. He thought she looked afraid. 'We'll lose Paso,' she said. 'We'll lose him for good.'

She told him about Paso, how quickly he could make an impression on a group of strangers. It only took him a few days to pull a group of youths together, organise them, leave them with a leader and direction. Then he would move on. No one could motivate people as quickly as Paso. They called him Breeze. Did he know that? Paso travelled everywhere. And for all the years he'd been doing this, Victor and his people did not know what Paso looked like. But when they passed through a village they knew he had been there. They saw it in the gazes of the children. In the storm of stones that met them. Often enough, Paso was what stood between Sylus and many a quick confession. Which was why they wanted him so badly.

'That's all he worth to y'all?'

'No,' she said, nudging a thumb at Hugo's door.

Pynter thought how Paso's words had changed over time. 'Problems' became 'protests', then finally 'The Struggle'. 'Hope-for-Change' turned to 'Fight-for-Change'. Now it was 'The Cause'. 'Get-togethers' were 'cells' now. We goin to take the island, he had said, as naturally as if he had been announcing the coming of the rains.

Pynter listened to the soft rumble of the sea against the metal hulls of cargo ships in the harbour below. A hot wind shifted the curtains and deposited the smell of diesel in the room. 'S'big,' he said, staring at the young woman. 'All of it.'

Tinelle walked across the room and took up one of the coloured bottles. She held it up to the light, shook her head and put it back. She dropped a record on the spindle of the player and music filled the room. She returned to the bottle and poured herself a drink. The glass glinted in her hand like jewellery. Tinelle seemed transfixed by something she saw in the dancing amber of the liquid. Her stillness was like nothing he'd seen before. The window light was foaming down the nylon curtains and dripping along the front of her dress.

She remembered he was there and threw a glance at him. 'Brahms,' she said. 'To hell with Moz and Beet. Brahm's my fella anytime.'

She sipped at her drink and parted the curtains to lean out of the window. 'Paso suggested something else,' she said. 'I told him it depends.' She talked with her back to him. 'It starts small, a little hurt, an insult, the place and the way you're born. Some need you didn't know you had. Add that to all the other hurts and needs of everybody else, read the books that say the things you want to hear. Make your circumstances fit. It becomes ideology.'

She tossed her head and chuckled at the drink.

'Makes me wonder what the little hurt was that started Karl Marx off. For me it was Selima. We went to the same school together. We laughed about the same things, fought over the same fellas, got drunk at the same parties. She was the first to get arrested for a Black Power salute in front of the police station. Her father refused to pay the fine to get her out. It wasn't a simple thing for him. She brought disgrace on her respectable family. They kept her there for two weeks until I raised the money. Something happened in her head in there. She never told me. I think I know what it was.'

She went to sit on the cushions and lifted a finger at the pictures.

'Yes, there should be a picture there. I put it up but it disap-peared. We never talked about it. They never forgave me for not having eyes and skin like Hugo. Like it was my fault. Dad even asked my mother if I was his child. After me they stopped. They weren't taking any more chances. The burden of progeny – that's what I call it.'

The music died. She looked up as if the silence had alerted her to something.

'Why am I saying all these things! I … '

'You awright,' he said. 'I – I like your inside, what my auntie call yuh candle. By dat, I s'pose, she mean your soul.'

She looked up at him suspiciously. 'I wasn't asking for no compliment.'

'I wasn' giving you none.'

People were already making a dash for home before the curfew fell. The waves of thunder that rose up from cars and minibuses added an extra urgency to the decaying day.

As soon as they reached the road, Tinelle hooked an arm around his. 'You're my fella,' she instructed. 'We taking a stroll.'

She named the roads as they passed them, explaining where each one would take him. Her directions always led him back to her house. She told him she would show him seven ways to get back there. By the time she finished, he'd counted twelve, including a narrow culvert that would take him straight down to the harbour. This, she told him, was the real San Andrews: the webwork of drains, hidden steps and alleyways that could take a person anywhere without being noticed by the thundering world above.

Now that they had reached the road beneath the Barracks, she tossed her head and waved back at the soldiers in the passing jeeps. She was smiling at the men and instructing him at the same time about the buildings he should look out for: a yellow church, a reservoir with its tall graveyard of rusting pipes, the culvert that ran along it and a filthy drain that snaked between two rows of houses.

She tightened her arm around his slightly when they reached a white concrete road at the entrance of which a couple of men sat with rifles across their laps. Their eyes skimmed his face, paused on hers, travelled down her legs. The men said something to each other, looked up and grinned at her.

They turned a corner. Tinelle lifted her chin at a small overhang of rocks above the road. 'Up there,' she said. 'Turn right at the top and go along the line of trees. S'right in front of you.'

Then she turned to face him suddenly. He noticed a trickle of sweat running down her jawline. 'This is not a storybook, Pynter. This is real, y'understand? Things can happm t'you up there. Bad things.' She tossed her head. 'Come, I wan' to go home.'

On the way back, Tinelle held his hands much as a parent would a child, and when they were home she dropped herself onto the cushions.

'You been lyin to me,' he said. He walked over to the cushions and lowered himself in front of her. 'S'not your brother, Hugo, who run things round here. Is you.'

She shook her head. 'S'not so.'

'Why you lying fo' me?'.

'It's not like that,' she said.

'What not like that?'

She told him there was Hugo, but also many others he would never get to meet. They had ignored her sometimes and made mistakes. Serious ones. Now they did nothing without asking her what she thought. 'Some things become a problem, Pynter, if you put a name to them. Y'understand?'

He told her that he did.

'Paso said some things about you. I didn't believe him. Now … ' She shook her head as if to clear it. 'Your eyes.' She sighed. 'I can't decide … '

He took her hand. The lines in her palm came together in a wild, fluid convergence – almost as if someone had scrawled a big brown M there and forgotten to wipe it off. Patty told him once that all a person was and will ever be was written in the turnings of those lines.

'Pynter Bender,' she said, 'I never meet nobody like you.'

'Me neither,' he said. 'I – I want to be wiv you.'

She pushed herself up from the cushions. 'You hungry? Hugo's a good cook.' She stood above him for a while, staring down at his face. 'I look at you and the word that comes to mind is clenched. What's pushing you, Pynter? Because one thing I know for sure now, this is not only about your friend.'

'Don' know how to answer dat,' he said, and closed his eyes.

They woke him close to midnight. A candle was burning in a saucer on the glass table.

'My clothes,' he said.

Tinelle got up, but Hugo had already rushed into the kitchen and retrieved them.

Pynter stripped himself before them, and in that moment of tense uncaring he barely noticed Hugo's awkwardness and Tinelle's open appraisal of his nakedness.

'You miss a button,' Tinelle said. She unbuttoned his shirt and started all over again.

'Anything I can do, Pynter?' Hugo was holding out a small flashlight. Pynter shook his head. Hugo closed his hand around it. 'Nice, er, nice knowing you, man.'

'Same fuh me,' Pynter said.

Tinelle stepped out into the yard with him. He noticed for the first time that she'd changed her clothes.

'I'm coming with you,' she said.

'No,' he said.

'I – I can help you.'

'No.' His vehemence surprised him. He saw her wince and felt a sudden prick of contrition.

'Pynter, I know I shouldn't be saying this, but I – I don't want you to go. That – that's how I feel.'

'You just say you wan' to come wiv me.'

'That's different.'

'I don' unnerstan.'

'Didn expect you to.'

He turned to go. She called his name. Something warm and easy settled in the space between them.

'Go on,' she said.

He took the stone steps that led down to the sea and then found the drain that would take him to the reservoir and followed that. His shirt was sticking to his skin by the time he crossed the road they'd walked on earlier. Paso was right, it was like daylight up there, with floodlights blasting down from iron poles high above the buildings.

There was a swamp that stood between him and the fence – a high wooden wall with nails sticking up from the top, and packed so closely they were like the teeth of a ragged comb. Pynter followed the fence around, chose a tree and climbed it.

The buildings below him were long and low. They were laid out alongside each other the way those of his school above the ocean were. He saw the shed a little way off to the left. It was quieter than he expected. The sound of an engine came up from the town below, throbbed the air, then faded. A moon, yellow like a slice of pawpaw, hung above the darkness beyond, which was the ocean.

He did not know how long he sat there, his eyes half-closed and listening, wanting to find a pattern to this silence and finding none. The tree he sat in threw a thick shadow just beyond the fence. He thought he would need to climb much higher. He could not be sure of the distance he was from the ground. He scrambled up, pulled in his breath, held it for a while, and jumped.

He hit the ground hard. Something gave way in his left shoulder. The pain curled him up on the earth. He lay there for a while on the damp grass, and then, his mind a throbbing, hurting drift, he pulled himself to his feet and began to move in fast lurches across the grass towards the shed. The terrible numbness in his shoulders grew heavier. He lifted the bar with his one good hand and eased himself inside.

Arilon lay face down on the concrete floor, his right hand under his stomach, the other stretched out like a dead snake along his side. Pynter could smell his fear. He grabbed his friend and shook him.

'S'Pynter, Ari. Let's go.'

He shoved his free hand under Arilon's armpit. It was then that the first crushing wave of pain shot down Pynter's side and froze him. He rocked back, closed his hand on Arilon's arm and tugged.

'C'mon, fella,' he said.

They were out and running. The floodlights were bright enough to give some colour to the grass. They hugged the shadow of the fence.

Arilon was ahead of him, his upper body almost parallel to the ground. For some reason, he was following the curve of the fence while making urgent gestures at Pynter. It suddenly made sense when Arilon swung into the swamp.

Arilon lowered himself beside the fence. 'Dig,' he croaked.

Pynter barely heard him.

They worked against the stinking water that seeped into the opening they created with their hands. The pain and the smell of the rotting mud made Pynter choke on his breath. 'Can't go no faster,' he said.

Arilon did not answer him. He threw himself flat on his stomach and with his elbows tucked against his side, began slithering head first under the wire. Pynter followed him.

Then they were out and running again. Arilon, in whichever direction his terror took him. 'You goin nowhere full-speed,' Pynter growled. 'I come fo' you, so you follow me, y'unnerstan?'

On their backs amongst the pile of reservoir pipes, they filled their lungs with night air. Arilon cradled his hand against his stomach. The throbbing in Pynter's left shoulder rocked his body back and forth. From time to time, a whimper came from Arilon like the soft mewling of a pup. Pynter looked up at the moon, then down at the quiet spread of buildings below them. A sudden wind slipped into the rusting pipes and made them hum.

'Sylus,' Arilon said, 'I goin to kill 'im, Pyntuh. Fuh sure. One day...'

Pynter turned towards him. 'What Sylus make you say?'

He had seen the terror on Arilon's face when he rolled him over in that shed. He saw how far his friend was already gone, and the desperation with which he'd dug his way out through the swamp mud and set off in a blind and drunken plunge through the trees. Arilon reached up to his shoulder and tore the sleeve of his shirt away; he tried to grip the cloth between his teeth but he could not do it. Pynter took the strip and wrapped it around the damaged hand.

'Sylush wanf Pfasho, Fynter. Wanshim vaad,' Arilon said. He was touching his lips with such tentative strokes it looked like he was patting air. 'Y'hear me, man?

'Sylus want Paso bad. Dat's what you say?'

'Like de Devil want your soul.'

The growl of jeeps from the road above pulled them to their feet. Headlights swept the trees. Arilon pressed himself back down between the piles of rusting metal.

'We awright,' Pynter said. 'We awright, man. Let's go.'

Pynter did not see Tinelle on the steps until he collided with her knee.

'That's him?' she said.

When they entered the room there were three bodies stretched out on the floor washed in yellow candlelight. One was under the window at the far end of the room; another was against the wall under the picture of the grandparents. The third lay face down in the middle, using his folded arms as a headrest. Hugo was sitting upright on the sofa, his eyes shut and head thrown back, breathing heavily through his mouth.

'Robert?' Tinelle said.

The young man in the middle of the room lifted his head. He woke the others with a tap of his shoe against their ribs. Pynter watched him closely. Tinelle leaned over her brother and tugged the lobe of his left ear. Hugo came to life, staring wild-eyed about the room until he focused on Pynter.

'How – how did it go?' he croaked.

They turned to Arilon. His face was crushed, his lips and eyes swollen, and there was the stink of swamp mud. The three strangers rushed out of the room with Hugo after them.

'I'll prepare some water,' Tinelle said and hurried off.

Arilon was leaning against the doorway, swaying slightly. And to think that Sylus had only just begun to work on him. At least that was the sense Pynter had made of Arilon's chewed-up words up there amongst the pipes.

He was glad the others left them to themselves. There was something he'd begun to say to Arilon out there in the dark and now he wanted to finish it. Pynter traced the trail of mucus trickling down Arilon's nose, settling in the crevices of his swollen lips. He placed himself in front of him, but Arilon would not return his stare.

'You tell Sylus everything about us,' Pynter said. 'You tell 'im where we live and what we look like. You tell 'im all you know about Paso. And dat is worse, becuz till now, they didn know what Paso look like. Now they know.' He stuck a finger in the hollow of Arilon's throat. 'You owe me a life, fella. In fact you owe me two. Yours, fo' sure, an' Paso. Cuz s'far as I can tell, Paso good as dead.'

Tinelle came back into the room with a handful of clothes and dropped them on the sofa. 'For you,' she said to Pynter. To Arilon she said, 'I left yours by the bath.'

Later, washed and dressed in Hugo's clothes, Pynter lowered himself onto a chair. He was aching everywhere. At his yard, they would have laid their hands on him. They would have scrubbed him down with bush or bark, in water laced with powders and herbs, to soothe him and help him sleep.

They gathered around Arilon. After a tense, uncertain glance at Pynter, the youth tried to tell his story, but he couldn't do it.

Tinelle rested her hand on Arilon's, briefly. 'We got to get you out of here,' she said. 'First thing.'

'Later, I'll run them home,' Robert said.

Arilon wanted to go right now. He blinked at them through his swollen eyes. 'Trouble out there,' Tinelle said. 'And I should say this now.' She brushed her nose and turned away. 'Pynter's not travelling with you.'

'I take them together,' Robert said. The youth began striding across the floor towards her. Tinelle stopped him with her gaze.

'It doubles the risk,' she snapped. 'And besides, Pynter got that shoulder to look after.'

Robert lifted an irritated finger at Arilon. 'You really want to go first, fella?'

'I s'pose,' he said. 'In fact, I definitely s'pose I want to go first, specially if Pynter prefer to stay with Miss, erm, Miss Finelle.'

Hugo stood up. 'That's settled, then. Night all.' Tinelle muttered something and Hugo remained where he was.

Robert jerked a thumb at Pynter. 'That one make his own way, then. After you two finish with him, of course.'

Tinelle pretended not to hear him. She reached for the phone and dialled. She asked for a man named Simon. There was a shoulder she wanted him to check, she said. Could he remind her what to do? And, oh!, there was a hand too. A thumb. Was there …

Tinelle listened with her eyes closed. She put down the phone and came over to Pynter, asked him to curl his fingers in then straighten them. She closed her eyes and slipped her hand along his arm right up to his shoulders. Nothing broken or dislocated, she said. Most likely a torn ligament. She would bandage it the way Simon said and wait till he came to fix it.

Tinelle did the same with Arilon. She said nothing to him, just gestured to Hugo, who went into his room and returned with a small box which he handed to her. She spent a long time over Arilon's hand.

That night Pynter slept fitfully. In his dreams he was balanced on a high branch above the town and Arilon was calling him with soft gestures from below. When he woke in the middle of the night he saw that they had forgotten to blow out the candles. The room was washed in a reddish glow from two remaining stubs placed beneath the table. Tinelle was curled up amongst the cushions near the record player. Robert was on all fours above her, his head bent low, his whispers deep and pleading.

At first Pynter thought she was asleep, but above the breathing of the boys he could hear her saying, 'No.' Robert's was a grumbling insistence. And then they both saw him. Robert retreated to the middle of the room.

Pynter lay back and imagined Sylus searching the streets and alleyways for them. He wondered what, if they'd caught him tonight, they would have done to him. What might his last moments have been like? Certainly not like his father's – to whom death had seemed like nothing more than a willingness to shut his eyes on a world of which he said he'd seen too much. Perhaps he, Pynter, would have gone screaming in astonishment at his own blood, like Marlis Tillock, like Jordan. Like Zed Bender under that tree.

He pushed himself up on his elbows and looked over at Tinelle. Despite the presence of the others in the room, he felt alone with her. He mouthed her name and then gave it sound. Tin-nel-le. And when she stared back at him he knew then that he would never need to go down on all fours before her, and even if he chose to she would welcome him with those wide and quiet eyes.

33

I WANT TO BE with you, he'd said. And all she could think of when he left were his hands.

That's what Tinelle told him afterwards.

And because she could find no way of responding to those words, she busied herself with caring for his dislocated shoulder. She asked herself who the hell was she to fight it, to resist him. He puzzled her. He was a shy fella, yet so full of himself. *I want to be with you* – he'd said those words to her again. He was the type who talked and touched, which was why she always asked the kind of questions that made him talk a lot.

It was a good time for loving. Sylus's men were speeding through the streets, from late evening till the early hours of the morning, their jeeps making thunder along the Carenage below.

The grapevine hummed with talk of fresh arrests, more disappearances and Victor's new and killing ways.

It was a good time for the soldiers too, because the rains that fell in heavy curtains erased the blood left on grass and asphalt and concrete, hiding their crimes. But in the enormous silence of the cushions in the house above the harbour, they felt secure.

She had to teach him everything. Everything astonished him: her nakedness, the contrast their bodies made, the impossible warmth between her thighs, the way they fitted, how close to pain the sound of so much pleasure was. Everything was new to him and that made her feel untouched and new too. They loved with an abandon that mocked the stiffness of the portraits on the walls. Anything could trigger them, for her especially, she said, the sweat beads gathered on his upper lip.

'You know nothing about wimmen,' she said. 'What you been doing all this time?'

He paused from tracing circles around her navel. 'Livin to stay alive.'

'You nice,' she breathed finally. 'Nice enough to kill for.'

'You the kind who kill for love?'

'What make you think it is for love?' A smile crept across her face. 'You worry too much,' she said, throwing a leg across his stomach.

'I never worry,' he said.

But he did worry. He had to have words with Paso. He needed to let all of Old Hope know what Arilon did not say to him up there amongst those rusting reservoir pipes.

Every morning he opened his eyes to Tinelle's rafters, he told himself he was going to do it today, he was going to leave. But he did not count on the girl readjusting him in the way she did; making him want to close his eyes to everything but her. Because it was a good time; despite the curfews, it was an easy time. Love slowed him down, it was a kind of forgetfulness.

34

ARILON'S RETURN lifted the heaviness that had descended on Old Hope.

They greeted him with a new pair of trousers hung on the back of his chair, and a beautiful blue shirt laid out on its seat.

They wanted to know what happened. All of it. They begged him for the story behind every bruise and swelling on his body, especially how that bright-eye fella got him out. He must tell them what it felt like to get snatched back from the hell of Sylus's hands and be driven home in a fancy silver car.

Pynter Bender – Deeka Bender gran'son – what a fella! 'Twas that young-fella eddication that saved Arilon. Did he know that? A pusson was sure of it. In fact a pusson know it. It didn have no other argument for it. He study a whole heap o' science in dat fancy school of his, not so? He don' have dem whiteman eyes fo' nothing. Becuz everybody know that science is whitepeople obeah. They walk on water wiv it; they run the world wiv it. It make dem fly; it give dem underwater-boat-and-plane; and bullets as big as a house that mash up other people country. So, wicked as Sylus an' Victor is, they don' stand a chance against high science.

Besides, eddication is better than a ticket. It better than a passport too, cuz it take a pusson anywhere they like, includin the big-an'-soft-an'-wide bedroom of a nice-lookin girl in San Andrews.

It didn't matter at all that Arilon barely answered them. They put it down to the terrible thing that must have happened to him. For they'd seen his face and the broken thumb and something in his eyes that was not so different from what they'd witnessed in Jordan's the day Sylus's men returned him to Old Hope.

At least Jumbie Boy was all right. S'matter o' fact, he wasn' no Jumbie Boy no more. He was Missa High Science. And Ole Hope better prepare demself for Sylus and his men, cuz when you snatch a bone from a dog, you expect dat dog to turn around and bite you. So the men's attention turned to 'preparations' for the soldiers' possible return. They talked about the storm of stones their jeeps were sure to meet as soon as they entered Old Hope.

During the weeks it took Arilon to recover, he filled their nights with song, until one morning, his finger cured, he left his yard and went up to the foothills. They heard the sound of his chopping for the best part of the day. He returned with portions of wood – twisted branches and the convulsed roots of trees – and piled them in his yard.

They counted the days and waited, for, as Deeka Bender told Old Hope, there was a pattern in every madness and if there was a story in there, time was going to unfold it.

And, sure enough, one morning a few weeks later, Old Hope woke, cocked an ear up at the hills and what they heard was just the argument of birds, the sigh of cane and the snore of the wind in high places. Arilon's chopping had stopped.

He worked only nights with a masantorch, in the company of his own songs and the chipping of chisel into wood.

The morning came when word brought them down to the roadside. The twisted roots and branches had taken on the shapes of humans – people shapes whose bodies followed the contours of the roots and branches: limbs wrapped around or turned in on themselves; heads staring down at backbones; heels fused with neck and collarbones; skin shivering with the teeth marks of the chisel that chewed into them.

They had no name for this. They had no words for all the things those faces said. They had no measure for the feelings that it left them with. Although Muriel started weeping. 'Twas as if, she said, Arilon was telling her that he got a glimpse of the place Sylus had taken her lil boy, Jordan, and this was what it looked like.

Perhaps Anita had been taken to a place like that too. Perhaps she hadn't completely left it. A pusson couldn say for sure. What was certain was that she left her steps one evening, drawn perhaps by the gatherings in front of Arilon's house, and went to see for herself. The few times Anita strolled up Old Hope Road, women never stopped to talk to her. For she moved and looked like no other woman in these villages above the canes: the rust-brown hair that rolled down her head in coils and settled on her shoulders; big, cattish eyes; all that flesh that hadn't been firmed up by walking or hard work; and a smile that was too steady to be real. Still, they did not expect the screaming alarm with which she jumped back from Arilon's creations and the haste with which she retreated to her house above Deeka Bender's yard. And they certainly didn't expect her to come back for them with a machete.

Anita was calling them by names they'd never heard before. And as Arilon watched those shapes of frozen hurt become chipping under Anita's flailing machete, there was perhaps a glint in his eyes that looked like gratefulness. When there was nothing left but useless bits of kindling, he gathered the pieces and set fire to them. From now on, he would return to making beautiful furniture.

But those shapes that Anita destroyed did not seem to want to leave her. Evenings, she fought them in her yard. They were crowding her, she said. They were trying to get their hands on her skin. They wanted to steal her hair. She mistook mosquitoes for helicopters. She forgot her clothes sometimes, talked to people in the air, stood in the rain and danced and became a golden gloria lily with a singing voice more beautiful than Patty's.

And all the while, Tan Cee kept Windy at her shoulder. Nights, she brought the girl over to her house and made her sleep there. For they'd seen enough of this to know that those people in Anita's head were going to multiply. That some time soon, they were going to step out of Anita and merge with the people and the children around her, and that swinging machete would not know the difference. They explained everything to Windy.

One day Elena dressed herself in a way they'd never seen her do before and left for San Andrews. She returned in a white van, with five strapping young men beside her. Anita smiled at them as if she had been expecting their arrival. They threw a long white canvas shirt around her shoulders and laced it up, talking all the while to her, their voices soft and soothing like a chorus of urgent lovers. Anita was laughing as she went with them.

Elena sat on the stones and wept.

Tan Cee returned to her house and threw out what remained of Coxy's belongings: a bunch of photographs wrapped in a grey plastic bag, mainly of himself and his brother in Barbados; a wooden case packed with tools; a green transistor radio; a limp scattering of work shirts and trousers; and five boxes of Anchor matches. Deeka poured a cupful of kerosene on the pile, struck a match and dropped it on them.

Coxy wasn't there when the wardens came. He'd been working on somebody's house somewhere on the island. When he returned, he walked into Anita's house, pushed open the windows and returned to stand on the steps. He lit a cigarette and when the smoke cleared they saw that he was looking down on them. Coxy hung there a while, scratching his head. Then he went into the house.

That night Deeka had her eyes on Tan Cee; she was laughing too easily and teasing the hem of her dress.

'Leave Coxy to me,' Tan Cee said. 'Is all I askin. Please.'

She dropped the bit of yam she'd been eating on the stones and stepped out into the night.

Deeka turned to Elena and Patty. 'Y'all sister jus' wake up,' she said. 'An' … ' Her voice retreated in her throat. 'Like y'all dam' well know, is hell to pay.'

There was nothing they could do about Tan Cee. There was a saying in these foothills that a heart that loses its moorings drifts into a place much worse than madness. It gets bitter as a galba seed, and the quietness it sinks into is as unforgiving as a grave. Which was why when Tan Cee told them a couple of days later, 'I sendin Windy over to her mother house to sleep,' they barely blinked at her. They did not bother to point out that Coxy was still there and didn't want to leave. That he'd bought new blinds and hung them up himself. He sat on the steps the way he used to with Anita, smoked and hummed the songs she taught him.

'S'your modder house,' Tan Cee said. 'It belong to you now. 'Twill always belong t'you. De same way.' She closed a fist around Windy's hair. 'De same way this belong to you.'

Tan Cee scarcely ate. She walked the path between her door-way and Anita's when Coxy wasn't there, slept during the day and would spend the nights sitting on her step.

She remembered how the trouble had begun with Coxy. Pynter was ten at the time. He'd just returned to the yard from one of those night-time disappearances he used to worry them with. He was rubbing his throat with his hand. She remembered the trembling fingers, the rage in his eyes.

'If a woman married a fella, Tan,' Pynter said, 'dat fella s'pose to go kiss-up an' hug-up in anodder woman house?'

They played it like a game, the child telling her in bits and her fitting in the rest.

Soon she had a picture of the woman in her head – not only what she looked like, but the kind of person she was, the sort of clothes she would ask a man to buy her, the colours she preferred. What unmentionable things she would whisper in Coxy's ear to get the kind of answer that would make her laugh out loud and then roll over. How much of a man she made him feel; and why, over the years, even if Coxy always came back to her bed smelling of sex and frangipani, he would never want to leave the young woman he'd built that little house for. For such a girl could cost a man his soul. And she'd done so to Coxy even before he could lay a hand on her. So much so that Old Hope and the people of Déli Morne could never forget the price that Coxy had to pay for Wednesday nights with that Laughin Girl from Kara Isle.

Solomon had been Coxy Levid's best friend – the kind of friend a man told almost everything to: the amount of years that he, Solomon, had tried for children, and the shame he felt when he realised his life was cursed to dry up and die with him. It made a fella restless. It pushed him out there, searching for some woman to rescue him from oblivion.

That was the feeling that sent his best friend Solomon travelling north by boat to Kara Isle – the silent, arid place of docile men and beautiful women whose complexions ranged from sapodilla brown to the blue-black of star apples. The women, they said, were as silent as the island. That was why Miss Florelle – this Laughin Girl – stood out from all the rest. She did not fit in. Laughin Girls had no business being born on Kara Isle. She was not no ordinary Laughin Girl either, but a special one whose age didn show nowhere on her skin or in them big brown eyes of hers.

Coxy claimed her, in his mind, the very day Solomon brought her back and made her say hello to him. Solomon should have known straight away that there was trouble ahead when Coxy lit a cigarette and did not place it in his mouth until the fire reached his fingers.

A coupla months later, Coxy was still thinking of that girl when he began to build the house on the lil piece of land he won in a gambling game of rummy. He started building it before he made his intentions clear even to himself. He always make 'imself believe that piece of land was a secret. As if he think a pusson stupid. As if people never talk. So the little wooden house took shape in privacy, except of course for what he hinted to Miss Florelle. And even then it was always the kind of house that fit a girl like her: small-bone, y'know, put together perfect like a post-card. A pine house settlin back on twelve pretty legs, with flowers all the way around. She could just smell the flowers, not so? And the pine, didn she smell the pine oil on his fingers?

Florelle was his to have on the seventh of November – two days after Guy Fawkes Night, just a coupla days after Solomon danced and burned. It was the very first thing Coxy did after Solomon burned. He went to his friend's shack and told the girl that the house he'd built was hers. He said he planted canna lilies, spider plants, white anthuriums and frangipani flowers in the yard because he took the time to learn the things she liked. She would like the wooden veranda, which was not yet painted because the colours were for her to choose. Hers, as long as she allowed him in once a week to smell the pine of the bed he'd built with his own two hands, and sleep on the sheets she washed and ironed every week. Just once a week. The rest of the time was hers to do with as she pleased. Just give him Wednesday nights.

It was the thing he had had to do to get those Wednesday nights that Déli Morne did not allow Old Hope to forget. They threw it in their faces every Guy Fawkes Night. They would keep reminding Old Hope for ever of that fireball that fell on Solomon.

Solomon was laughing when it came straight out of the sky and fell on him, clothing him in blue. Blue flames – not yellow like it ought to be, but a hungry, licking blue that fed on him as if his skin were fuel. Solomon never stopped laughing. The terrible blue did that to him. It made him dance and laugh because screaming wasn't enough. They watched him till he fell at the feet of men too dumbstruck to do anything to help. Except Coxy, of course, who'd been battling with the flames that were feeding on his best friend. Coxy rushed over to the drum of water and started howling like a dog. How could a pusson account for that – cry out so hard-an'-loud and not mean it at all?

But Solomon brother told it another way. He swore Coxy went to the drum not just to cry but to wash the smell of high-octane petrol from his gloves – fuel that had no business in a Guy Fawkes Night. And besides, he saw Coxy Levid's lil smile as his brother lay there sizzling, and a whole heap of satisfaction was in that grin.

Solomon's Laughin Girl took her little brown case packed with personal things: a blue cotton dress, the nightdress that felt and looked like water, a very large bottle of Pond's Face and Hand Care Lotion, three shades of Island Palm lipstick, a bottle of Jeyes antiseptic lotion and a small plastic bag crammed with seeds, dried flowers and rooting things. She left with Coxy, he carrying her case, she the flowers and the seeds. The little mauve church hat with the perfectly rounded top that he'd admired so much on her the first time that they met was tilted over her left eye, the way the women in American magazines wore them.

Hard as it was, a pusson force demself to live with it. They fool demself into believin it not there – like a soreness you been carryin so long yuh mind make you ignore it. Becuz a pusson can't let a man inside demself the way she, Tan Cee, gone-an'-done, and then let him out so easy. Deeka was proof of it. A man was only gone when you let him die in you. But what if a pusson keep him there? What if even all the hurtin an' the hatin keep the love alive? How a woman s'pose to start to purge sheself of twenty years of that? Eh?

But over the years, something else had lodged itself at the back of Tan Cee's mind. It had made its own little nest in there, from the night Coxy started to sleep out. And it would not be shifted. It stayed in her head like this lil knife she carried.

This knife – she could not remember how she came by it; could not remember a time when she did not have it. Years of honing on the sandstone in the yard had reduced it to a bit of curved silver, bright as a first quarter moon, that felt natural in her hand.

She'd always felt comfortable with a knife. At nineteen she moved from grafting trees and harvesting the bark of cinnamon to things that bled. Had become so good at it no one within fifteen miles of Old Hope would have a tree or animal seen to by anyone else but her. She and the knife. They had made a name for themselves in Old Hope.

She began placing it under her pillow the week Coxy began to disappear on Wednesday nights. It just being there made her feel safer. S'matter o' fact, she hardly recalled she had it except on Thursdays. And if it wasn't for the occasional gelding, the grafting of somebody's fruit tree or the changing of her bed sheets on Thursday afternoons, she would have forgotten about it completely.

But there were a few times when she did remember it. Like the first night Coxy did not return from Anita's house. But that was only because she plumped the pillow a little too violently and it fell onto the floor.

She remembered it after the five men came and took Anita away, realising that, with her sister gone, Coxy had no intention of leaving Anita's house. That night she slept with the knife sitting on her mind. Shame did not allow her to tell the other women in the yard that exactly three days after Anita left, on that next Wednesday, he'd slipped the latch of her door and crept into her bed as if that space still belonged to him.

And she'd smiled in the dark and told herself that she was right in thinking that she knew him. That a time would come when the Laughin Girl would turn to someone younger, stronger and more interesting. That Anita would not always be there and he would return to her with what remained of the nothing that was left inside of him, which in their early days of loving was worth something, because taking care of it made her feel he valued her.

Now here he was offering his emptiness again.

But the years of not being claimed as she had been by him in the beginning had done something to her. They'd dried her up and made her unreachable with men. But in other ways she had grown strong and wet and fertile. She had a turned-in-on-yourself, don't-take-no-chances kind of loving for the children in the yard, for family. For anything that belonged by blood.

That one last time, she'd allowed Coxy back to her house so that she could say what she needed to say to him. And that time was done.

In a way, her husband made her laugh. He was one of those men who wooed with gifts and smiles. And a pusson couldn't tell which was more important, because the smile was what they saw first and remembered long after the gift got used or worn, or eaten, or simply thrown away. A pusson remembered the way his hands held it out as if it were the Eucharist itself, and the look in his eyes that went with it. And if he really wanted you, if you began to settle on his mind, Coxy started building things.

Perhaps Coxy thought he would surprise them all when he built Windy a pretty blue cage for birds. He brought home eight little yellow parakeets the next day, let them loose inside it and hung the little house up on the veranda. They began whistling and chiming straight away as if he'd let loose all the bells of Christmas inside that cage.

The little gifts of gold for Windy were not so obvious: the ring topped with a tiny blue stone that glinted on the girl's finger; a matching pair of earrings seven days later. Then, just yesterday, the finest of all gold chains with its own little heart dangling at the end of it.

It might have been the memory of foreman McKinley and the young girls in the cane that stirred a bunch of women to come to Deeka's yard. They was just passin, they said, and it cross their mind dat since they passin so close, they might as well drop by. And seein they already in her yard, it make sense to tell her what they been hearing about Coxy-in-dat-house-wit'-de-young-lady. Furthermore, nobody couldn say 'twasn't their business, becuz bad bizness is everybody bizness. And 'twas one thing to have dat foreman behavin like dog with poor-people girl-chilren. But this different. This inside a pusson yard.

Is help Deeka want? She want somebody to help her make dat dog-of-a-man see sense? Their men wouldn do it, cuz they follow Coxy like he's some kinda Christ. But they could. They could kick 'iz arse out right now. They could give dat sonuvabitch so much hell he wish he never see Ole Hope, far less come to play fowl-cock round here. They want some help right now? Cuz is help a pusson come to help.

There was not a person in the family who did not think that Tan Cee was going crazy. That in some funny way, Anita had passed her affliction on to her sister; for in that time too, the canes threw up their sweaty, rancid odour and filled her head with a dizziness that brought the chuckles bubbling out of her.

Tan Cee couldn imagine what Coxy was thinking. He really believe she was so sick-head-an'-weak she wouldn notice when he left for the rum shop? Or that when he returned some hour long past midnight she would be asleep? Or that she would not hear his hand brushing against the latch of the door? Or maybe he thought that she, Tan Cee, would hear him and not give a damn.

The girl was already struggling with him by the time she got there. And Tan Cee knew by the smell of him that Coxy did not have the guts to look his own nastiness in the face. Had to fill 'imself with rum to do it. Had to look for blamelessness in a bottle, so that he could explain his wickedness that way.

Men, they done worse than this wiv rum in them; they mistake nieces, daughters-in-law, even daughters for wives and got away wiv it.

She could just hear Coxy explaining it to all the fellas he sat with in the rum shop, with that smile that lied about his nature. She could see the look they would give him, the way they would shift their hips on the wooden benches, throw back their heads and knock back a glass of the hot white fuel to help them make a joke of the unheard of. A man joke. One they shared and laughed at 'mongst themselves, becuz Coxy Levid did for them what they didn dare to do themselves: leave de bed of yuh woman, take over her sister's, and when that sister gone, turn round an' take over de daughter. And they would reward him with a drink, because getting it second-hand was better than not getting it at all.

And he would not be blamed. They would ask him for all the details. Everything! They would part company in the dark after clasping hands and slapping shoulders. Laughing.

She found him in the dark, all right. Heard herself thinking even as she shifted the bit of silver in her palm that animals were more difficult. Pigs especially – funny creatures, dem! They always seemed to know when it was their manhood that her hands were reaching for.

35

SAN ANDREWS WAS like no town in the world. It could not die. Its face was turned towards the sea. It took everything that the hurricanes that came in from the ocean threw at it, fell flat on its foundations, then rebuilt itself straight after.

The people of Zed Bender's time had burnt it to the ground so many times they got fed up and turned instead to things that would stay destroyed. San Andrews simply took the punishment, shook the water and the ashes off itself and rose again like new.

Despite all his years of passing through it, to and from his school above the ocean, Pynter had never got accustomed to San Andrews. He'd been here three months with Tinelle and still he found the brightness of the place unbearable: the metallic heave of sea, the shimmering burn of rooftops, the dizzying strobe of steel and glass and paintwork.

Here, the houses clung to the hills above the harbour like barnacles – caught up, it seemed, in an endless tug-of-war with gravity – and when it was impossible for them to climb further up without falling back on themselves or taking flight, they flowed sideways around the hills.

Pynter would lie beside Tinelle listening to her breathing. Sometimes, to pass the time, he lit a candle and eased himself up on his elbow to watch her sleep. She was different from her daytime self: she dreamt aloud – laughed a lot and said his name sometimes – and when she woke she wanted him to talk to her, especially about the women in his yard who seemed to fill up his head so completely.

With the lifting of the curfew, nights in San Andrews were once more filled with the smell of roasted corn, barbecued chicken and the arguments of stevedores from the harbour below them. Hugo, her brother, was hardly ever there. Their father owned a small beach house on one of the peninsulas in the south, which he went to whenever the fancy took him. Now that Pynter had arrived, he was there most of the time.

Tinelle walked him down to the waterfront to the huddle of bars and wooden buildings, where they sat on stools, held hands like children and laughed at the antics of San Andrews women manoeuvring drunken sailors into corners.

There was a barman down there who knew her. Tinelle called him Capes. He was tall in his white cotton suit and swayed like a palmiste tree. His mouth was so packed with gold teeth he sounded as if he were always choking on something.

As soon as they arrived, Capes turned his back on his customers, retrieved an empty glass, polished it and mixed Tinelle a drink. 'Somefang new, Miss Lady,' he would say, 'A lil somefang that take mah fancy.' He would rest the drink on the table before her and step back, his eyes on her hands, nodding at them as if they were sharing a language that only he and Tinelle's fingers were party to. She would bring the rim of the glass to her nose, close her eyes and inhale; then look up at Capes, her eyes bright with discovery:

This rum born straight from cane juice. Rum agricole, not so? Guadeloupe or Martinique!

or

Cane sugar rum, this one. Brazilian. I sure of that. Add as much Coke and lime as you want, Capes. I still know it's Cachaça.

or

*Not Bajan, not Trini, not anything from this side. Too frivolous,
man. Too light. Virgin Islands more like – Cruzan?*

She never got it wrong. They spoke of flavours and proofs and
blends, of colours and styles and weight for a while. Capes would
look down his nose at Pynter, his teeth glittering like street
lamps. 'Orange juice fuh de baby-fella, not so?'

And while Capes took his time fetching the juice, Tinelle balanced the glass in the palm of her hand and told Pynter about
rum. It raised the hairs on his arms to hear her, for in the twelve
weeks that he'd been with her, he'd never heard Tinelle speak
more beautifully about anything.

'Rum is cane in a state of transcendence, Pynter. It is the cap-
turing of ghosts. That's why people right to call it spirits.
Because, you see, rum is the result of a kind of resurrection, y'understand? Is bringing alive a poisonous soup of fermented sugar
that people call a dead wash. Dead because that's what it do to
you if you foolish enough to drink it in that state. It's got sulphur
in there, it's got methanol and a whole heap of funny things
called ketones. But,' she would flick a finger at the glass, bring it
to her nose and inhale, 'somewhere deep in the heart of all of
that the spirit lives.'

And what did it take to exorcise it? A sorcerer. In the old days it
was a fella somewhere in the mountains, with a couple of steel
drums and some piping. He had something special. He had – she
would sip at the glass and wink at him – a relationship with steam.
That fella had an understanding of the exact point at which to
capture steam, bring it back to liquid and trap it in a bottle. Because
anything below a certain temperature was no good. Did he know
that? That there was a temperature you started to catch the spirit
from, and another that you must stop at? And the further up you
go, the hotter the rum, the more flavourful and deadly?

Cane – cane was amazing. Did he know anything about cane?

Pynter would sip his juice, shake his head at Tinelle and laugh.

Rum did not change her moods or dull the quickness of her movements. Nor did it soften the bite she brought to the arguments he had with her.

During the day, she answered calls and made them – her voice dipping so low sometimes all he heard were murmurs: bits of conversation, fragments of words, small silences; nods and winks and sideways glances in his direction; toes curling around conversations that sometimes lasted hours with voices she would never put a name to.

They all added up to something big. A plan. A great gathering of youths the likes of which the island had never seen before. He thought of the picture of converging rivers that Paso spoke to them about in the forest above Old Hope. Only this time he imagined Tinelle and the people whose names she would not even say in her sleep, standing on some hill above it all, directing the flow of the flood.

It began as the root of an idea, which, over the weeks, grew so complicated he'd given up on following it. There were security and logistics to consider. There were warm-up speeches and keynote addresses and possible contributions. There were worst-case scenarios and exit strategies. There was also Paso. They were going to leave him for last. Paso would use those pretty words of his to erase the fears and stir the love. His words would draw them closer to the thing that everyone was heading towards. They were counting on Paso to send everyone home on a high.

She'd come to the end of one of those conversations which hadn't lasted long. She'd got up earlier than usual to make the call and at the end of it Tinelle put the phone down chuckling. She saw him staring at her.

'What?' she said.

'Take Paso out of it,' he said. He'd raised himself up on his elbows from the cushions. He spoke quickly, breathlessly about the night he went for Arilon and what he knew for certain. 'Sylus,' Pynter said. 'Arilon tell 'im everything, especially 'bout Paso.'

'You don't think we figured that out?'

'Who figured?'

'We did. Look, Pynter.' She dropped herself beside him. 'It had to happen. Paso knows that too. That's why he's never on his own these days. Paso's all right, believe me.'

'He not! Tell 'im I say he not!'

'I spoke to Paso yesterday. You were sleeping when he called. He even asked me how you were. Listen, Pynter, you not made for this. It was the first thing Paso told me. You think … '

'Lissen to me, Tinelle!'

'Go easy, fella, you squeezing my hand.'

Pynter walked out onto the veranda and raised his head up at the Fort. Even in this sizzling brightness, it still looked grey and separate. It was the only thing in this town that did not throw back the light. He turned his gaze towards the corridor of islands that began where the harbour ended – a blue-black procession of rocks that pulled his vision northwards until their shapes were smudges in the distance. The first sun cut a bright yellow path straight through them, ending, it seemed, at the very foundations of the house in which he stood.

He was looking at the bright knife-edge of the horizon and thinking that Tinelle might be right. He'd imagined his way towards something that served only to frighten him. He was different in San Andrews. There were just San Andrews and Tinelle, and the way she wanted him to be. She wanted him to be like water, she said, and fit whatever shape she needed. That meant absorbing her instructions while pretending not to hear them.

'You worry too much,' she said. 'I want you to trust me.' She slipped an arm around his waist and pointed at the procession of islands. 'El Dorado Road,' she said. 'That is what I call it. That's the road that takes everybody off this island, even the planes follow it.'

Those rocks ended in a kind of hell a few miles further out. It was where the spine of the island dipped into the sea. There was a live volcano beneath the waters, the remains of the fire that had risen from the ocean and built the island. It made a cauldron of the currents that met there. Just beyond though, a little way past that, the ocean quietened and deepened. Its surface was so flat and sleepy a foreigner who saw it once had named it Dreamwater.

Tinelle tightened her arm around him. 'Pure calm,' she said. 'In the midst of all that violence. Like us.'

'T,' he said. Her shoulders stiffened under his hand. 'I have to walk. I have to go out.'

Apart from their night-time trips to the harbour, he'd barely left the house. He'd lain with her and talked. He'd fallen asleep to her music and her voice. He'd followed her with his eyes until he could tell what she meant or wanted just by touch or gesture. He'd uncovered ways to love her that exhausted and amazed her. But over time the yard had become a pulse inside his head, the absence of the women's voices a dull ache in his stomach.

'Tired of this place?' She said it like a joke. He saw the worry in the way she looked at him.

'I have to see my Aunt Patty,' he said.

Tinelle raised her eyes at the church towers on Cathedral Street. 'You'll come back?'

'That what you want?'

'F'course,' she said.

He'd been sending notes to Patty at the store through the woman who came once a week to clean the house.

He always wrote the same three lines.

I'm alright.
Coming home soon.
Pynter

Patty would reply in the same style, almost as if she were mocking him.

We alright too.
Take your time.
Patty.

His aunt spotted him across the street and came out of the shop. She leaned against the glass front and began fanning her face with one hand. She'd straightened her hair and pulled it up in a high bun, with a large silver comb on either side. Her face looked fuller, her gaze more distant. He hadn't seen his aunt for almost four months. Now he saw how much the baby she was carrying had changed her.

'What wrong?' he said.

'I tell you somefing wrong?'

'How'z everybody?'

'Who'z everybody, Pynto?'

Pynter stepped closer to her, peering into her face. 'What wrong, Tan Pat?'

She angled her head away from him. 'Is lunchtime,' she said. 'Come wiv me.'

He walked with her through the market. She moved slowly – a careful sideways walk in which her shoulders took the impact of the people who pushed past them. He realised she was fearful for the baby and stepped ahead of her. Patty hooked a finger into his belt and steered him forward.

She did not speak to him until they were sitting in the little restaurant that looked down on the sea. She made him order her food and place it in front of her.

'Is Celia,' she said. 'She not awright.'

He almost asked her who Celia was. Apart from Deeka, he'd never heard anyone else use Tan Cee's proper name.

Patty said she was going to tell him everything. She dropped her voice. She forgot her food and fingered the buttons of his shirt while she spoke.

It happened a few weeks ago. How come nobody let him know? Well, 'twas becuz that was what Tan Cee said she wanted.

'She don' want you to come home an' see her like she is now. She don' want you to meet 'er this way,' Patty said.

'What way?' Pynter made to get up. Patty closed her fist around his shirt.

'I goin home,' he told her. He moved to get up again.

'Lissen to me! You don' lissen! That's yuh problem. You never lissen! An' you make trouble fo' people when you don't.'

He tried to get up a third time. She pulled him down. Patty glanced at the bulge of her stomach and stared straight into his eyes, as if to say, she would fight him if she had to despite her heaviness with child. He sat back.

His aunt picked up her spoon and wagged it in his face. 'You have to unnerstan this, Pynto, not everybody like de world to see dem naked. Specially de ones dey close to. Nobody kin love you like Celia gone and done. You unnerstan dat? Even I not sure I unnerstan it. But she tell me once dat you'z her child becuz you feel like dat inside of her. From the first time she lay dem two hands of hers on you and stain dem with your birt' blood, she make you hers. Not even Elena kin fight dat. Tan Cee don' want you to see her the way she is right now. She'll call you when she ready.'

She dropped the spoon and pulled a kerchief from her bag. She wiped the corners of his eyes.

'I hope – I hope everything make sense later. So help me God, I not always sure. I not … Love an' hate, Pynto. They live in de same place sometimes. You say dat to Chilway once – that time he come for Birdie. Lil boy as you was, you teach Chilway somefing. I never forget dat.'

Coxy was going to be all right, she said. That was if he could find something else to hold on to that make him feel like man. One thing was for sure though. He would have to learn to walk again.

'The police came. A lot of them. And it was all Deeka could do to make Ole Hope wimmen keep their mouths shut. Didn have a woman in Old Hope who wasn' there to help Tan Cee with a story of some kind. They left the police believing that Coxy used to throw 'imself at every woman in Ole Hope, includin a whole heap of ole-wimmen. S'matter o' fact, Tan Cee didn need to say nuffing fo' herself.

'Dey got so much statement from so many of dem wimmen, police people run out of paper. They would ha' been writing still if they didn decide 'twas too much information.' Patty shook her head. A soft laugh came from her. 'Dem police put it down to self-defence – self-defence of Windy.'

Pynter frowned at her. Patty flashed him a dark, condemning gaze. 'The problem wiv you is dat you think too straight – dat's what. How'z de lady?'

'Tinelle?'

'That her name?'

'Uh-huh, she awright.'

Patty waved her spoon. 'God not fair sometimes – an' I don' care if I burn in hell fo' sayin dis. He wrong to make you an' Windy family. One thing he do right, though – he make sure you wasn' home when Coxy try to trouble her.'

Everybody else was all right, she said. Even Deeka. And she, Patty, wouldn't be coming back to work until she had the baby.

'And then?'

His aunt lifted her shoulders and dropped them. 'Richard got to make up hi mind: I go to his house o' he come to mine.'

'He'll never come to yours.'

Patty soured her face. 'One thing I know fo' sure. I not goin be nobody woman-on-de-side.'

'He got a woman on de side?'

'You know a man who don't?' She seemed lost for a while in the thrashing of the water below. 'S'not de govment that got to change first, Pynto. Is y'all, you fellas. If govment change and y'all don't change is de same trouble we headin for.'

'Richard done you something?'

'Course!' Patty giggled like a girl and gestured at her stomach. He laughed with her. She raised an eyebrow at him. 'Lordy! Girlfrien' teachin you to laugh dem pretty laugh too?' She was laughing so much now, she had to hold on to the chair.

Patty quietened. She was assessing him with that deep-eyed, yard-woman look of hers. 'She'll try to change you, Pynto. You mustn't let 'er change you, becuz…' She touched her chest then brought the same hand to his heart and pressed it. 'We stronger here. Unnerstan? Becuz of de life we live.'

The gesture seemed to remind her of something. She pulled an envelope from her purse and handed it to him. 'Somebody lef' it in de store fo' me to give you. Nincy say it was a man. I been carrying it around fo' weeks.'

'What's the real reason, Tan Pat?'

'Fo' what?'

'Why y'all don't wan' me home?'

'I jus' done tell you, Pynto Bender.'

Patty chose a different route back to her work. The street they walked on was quieter and cooler. Even here people passed and waved at Patty, or called her name and smiled. She pointed across the street. 'Look in front of you, Pynto. What you see?'

'Some people and some buildings, Tan Pat. This a new game you play after lunch?'

'No, dere, look! I see "Patty's",' she said. 'Right dere. I see my name on dat place I goin fix up.' She pointed at a small building at the side of the road. The wooden windows were the old kind, the ones that were kept open with a rod. 'I see my own lil store, Pynto, wiv me an' Windy at de counter. I work out de rent. I work

out how much money I need to start wiv, an' how much I got to
buy an' sell. I know who I goin to buy from an' I know who goin
buy from me.' Patty lifted her chin at a group of passing people.
'I follow a coupla dem sometimes, to watch what dey leave home
to buy. A thousan' o' dem pass every day. I want only fifty in my
shop. An' if I can't double dat number every day, my name not
Patty Bender.'

Her eyes were fixed on him.

'In five years' time, dat lil store right dere goin take all my
famly out of cane, y'unnerstan? I work out every minute.' She
pointed at her head. 'I got everyting in here. You – you believe
me, Pynto?'

'Course,' he said. 'Don' jus' believe, I know.'

She'd turned slightly away as if she did not trust his answer.
'How come you know?'

'Becuz I hear you say it, Tan Pat.'

Patty turned him round and wrapped her fingers around his
belt. 'That's why I say it to you first, Sugarface. Gwone, driver!
Drive me.'

Dear Pynter
This is a quick farewell and also a reminder.

*I'm leaving tomorrow for reasons which I can't go into
now.*

*I'm handing this note to a friend of mine who will pass it
on until, hopefully, it reaches you. I'm counting on the fact
that it's a small place and somebody always knows somebody
who should know. I hope it reaches you in time.*

*On the 5th of May, drop whatever you are doing, go to
your school and register. Registration begins at nine. Be there
early. Too early is preferable. You will receive your number
and the dates of your exams. There are six papers. The dates
are staggered. I've written them on the back of this note. Get
there on time for each of them. Sit them.*

I'm not interested in good results from you. I want something better.

You live, you think, you see, you feel. Bring them all together in those sittings. Remember everything. Read every question three times. Double check exactly what they're asking you. Use every minute of the time you have to answer only what you're asked. Don't opinionate, substantiate. Don't defer, refer. Make the facts work for you. Offer the examiner your mind. A foolish one might mark you down. A thinking one will reward you for your insights. You think you're special. Prove it.

I'm not wishing you good luck, Pynter. It's never been about luck.

I take it that you've been doing the work. Go finish it in June.

Always, Pynter, always – I carry you inside me.
Sislyn Chappel

36

TINELLE BEGAN preparing him for a visit to her aunt. It was the week after he'd astonished her by asking for a pen and telling her he was going to sit his exams.

She was going to introduce him to her entire family, she said. That, he learned, was a single aunt who lived on a hill called Morne Parnasse, over Temple Valley. Aunt Linora lived at the 'ancestral home' built by her 'great great and greater still' grandfather ten years after he arrived from Scotland. Morne Parnasse was where the McMurdos first planted themselves on the island and took root. The Old Man – Tinelle talked as if she had known him personally – had decided to name the building Troy. And whatever Pynter did, he must remember this: Aunt Linora's son, Laban, was studying Philosophy in London.

Troy was a ponderous wooden structure on stone pillars, painted cream with a veranda that encircled the house completely. There were large windows on every side. It had its own wide stone road that led up to it, paved with slabs of lichen-covered granite that had gone lopsided in some places. Tall walls of ancient hibiscus stood on either side of them. Their limbs were padded with green moss. It reminded Pynter of the old plantation houses further inland.

Tinelle had given him a hive of advice about how not to act in the presence of her aunt. Aunt Linora's first impression of him had to be a good one. Aunt Linora never changed her views after a first impression.

He hated the bright green shirt Tinelle bought him. She asked him to wear it nevertheless, for her. He was suspicious of knives and forks but ate with them during the week Tinelle was getting him ready. It brought to mind Patty's preparation for her new job in San Andrews. His young aunt had given up her spoon for the inconvenience of those two flimsy bits of metal, her grace before meals replaced with a muttered recitation which she said exactly as she would a prayer.

> *Knife on de right,*
> *Fork on de left,*
> *Keep de chat light,*
> *An' to hell with de rest.*

He used to laugh at her. Now he ran the rhyme over in his mind every time he took up the knife and fork. 'S'a wicked, sadistic so-an'-so who invent dese tings, Tinelle. People not s'pose to relax and enjoy de food dey eat?'

'They look beautiful in your hands,' Tinelle said.

'Gimme a spoon, girl.'

'Having a meal and eating food not the same things, Pynter Bender. Remember?'

She'd cut his hair. 'You've got Indian in your blood?' she'd said.

'Nuh, I got only blood,' he'd said. He'd glanced down at the soft nightfall of hair Tinelle had just snipped off.

'What you thinking, Pynter Bender?'

'Goldin apples. Green ones. They hard, they sour but they sweet. I missin goldin apple.'

He'd refused to change the way he spoke and, sensing his rising irritation, Tinelle had backed down quickly.

Linora was a little lady, older by far than the smiling woman he'd seen in the photograph in Tinelle's house. She could not keep her hands off Tinelle. She hugged and kissed and tugged her, while chiding her for not phoning. Didn't she remember the number? It was still working. Never had it disconnected, because Laban called every Christmas. Did she know that Laban called home every Christmas? Been calling for the last five years without fail? And Hugo. How's Hugo? Always said he should be doing something legal. The boy was born judgemental. Remember him as a tiny child sitting in the yard with a stick in his hand passing sentence on the chickens. Did she know it was on her insistence that their father, Richard, began to prepare Hugo's mind for law? And her son, Laban – God, that boy was a born philosopher. His very great grandfather must have been one. Only a philosopher would travel all the way from Scotland and come to set up house and family here.

Tinelle pounced during the pause.

'Auntie Li, this is my boyfriend, Pynter.'

Auntie Li looked him up and down. 'Fine young man. A bit, er, tall. But then I always notice because, apart from Hugo, us McMurdos aren't.'

'Nice to meet yuh,' Pynter said.

'How are you?' Her tone now matched her eyes exactly. She was a paler version of Tinelle's mother. She'd bleached her hair a subtle silver and was tucking it in and patting it as if to assure herself it was all still there.

'I'm fine,' he said. 'And you?'

Linora shot a finger in the air. 'Oh! Tinelle, I found it! I found that picture you were pestering me about. Your great-aunt. You never knew what she looked like, did you? I'll show you where I found it. God, you'd never believe it! Come on, child!'

Pynter stepped out of the door. He propped himself up on the veranda, and followed the chirping of the woman in the house. There was a soft fluttering above him. He turned his gaze up at the old soursop tree which leaned against the house. He saw the bird, grey as ash, moving clumsily through the branches, a cuckoo myuck. He thought how odd it was that it should appear so early in the year, and then he remembered that it was already dry season and this, the world's saddest bird, was cursed to quench its thirst from the leaves of trees. He'd wondered when he was a child how they survived the long dry season.

The veranda was covered with patches of peeling paint, the crevices in the woodwork were caked with lichen. On the slope below him, lime trees had taken over the orchard of low-growing pawpaw, Julie and Rose mangoes. The pawpaw fruits were shredded by kongorees, birds and lizards. Further down the hill, the green gave way to a kind of darkness and a chill that he could feel even from where he sat. For there was no sensation like the chill that seeped from the roots of a dying cocoa plantation. And if anyone needed proof of it, it was right there in the bright, parasitic spread of love vines.

He wondered if Tinelle's cat-eyed aunt knew what was happening. The forest was moving in on her. In ten years' time, perhaps sooner, Linora and Troy would be swallowed up.

In the house the woman flitted about like a child, fussing about Laban. He would be back in two years. Then he would fix the veranda, pave the path with stones like his great-great-grandfather did when he first built Troy. She turned to Pynter. Did he see those stones out there, those flat white ones laid down along the side of the road? The grass was all over them now but her very great, great-grandfather laid them down himself. Scottish – Tinelle and all the McMurdos on the island were from Scottish stock. Did Tinelle tell him that? The name itself said so. Proud, hard-working people the Scotsmen were. Blue eyes too. Where her very great grandfather came from they all had sky-blue eyes. Did he know that? Blue eyes like Laban had been born with. He lost the blue as he grew up, though. Always said it was the climate. Had to be the climate. Too much sun and certain, erm, associations.

The grey eyes were now averted, the chin pushed high. Certain associations didn't do the family any good. Definitely not. She was a God-fearing Christian woman, but she had to say it, certain unfortunate associations caused the McMurdos to lose those marvellous blue eyes. It was up to the women to keep things clean. That was why McMurdo women should never go that way. Or that would be the end of it.

'End of what?' Pynter asked.

'You a strong-looking young fellow. It would be nice to have somebody cut those fruit trees down, especially those pawpaw. God! I can't stand the smell of those things. Did you know, Tinelle, when Laban left there wasn't half as many down there? Why on earth do they grow so fast?'

'Don' worry, he goin' cut dem when he come,' he said.

'It'll be all done by then, I hope.' The woman laughed.

'I hope so too,' Pynter said.

'If I didn't know better,' she smiled, 'I would have said you've got hazel in those eyes.'

'Is de hot sun in we backside,' he answered drily. 'It bleach out some people eye, yunno.'

A figure crossed his vision. A shadow at the back of Linora. He could not keep his eyes off the girl who moved about the house. Linora's servant was a long-limbed young woman of about eighteen. She reminded him of the people on Top Hill, those he'd described to Tinelle as 'the people of the wind'. The woman kept referring to her as 'D', mainly when she was telling Tinelle about some new recipe she'd read about in Harpers and asked the young woman to try out.

Linora was a strange woman, Pynter thought, and Miss D there, D for Delia or Doreen or Daphne or whatever, hugging the shadows of this flippin house jus' like a ghost. Why the hell didn she come forward?

'Darky's getting quite good at it. Last time I had the La Fortunes over. She did a gorgeous flan.'

Tinelle had finished rearranging the basket of dried flowers on the piano in the corner. She eased the lid of the instrument open to expose a row of black and yellow keys.

'That's what de "D" stand for?' he said.

Linora looked brightly up at him and mumbled that he must not mind the words of a tired old woman. Just a friendly joke between herself and Syl. In fact Miss Syl didn't mind at all.

Miss Syl was now beside the sink with a handful of radish under the tap. The girl was pretending not to hear them.

'As long as people call me by my real name. My whole name,' he told her quietly. 'Besides…'

'Laban sent any pictures lately, Auntie Li?' Tinelle asked.

Tinelle's mention of pictures did something magical to Linora McMurdo. She was more than glad to show him the pictures of Laban – a student of Literature and Philosophy in London, England. Pynter was genuinely intrigued by the pictures of Laban as a baby, Laban as a boy with his uncle in New York, Laban as a young man holding up a handful of snow in Canada, Laban graduating from college in Chicago, and finally Laban and his English girlfriend against a small red car 'in Knightsbridge'. Linora explained how it was his very own car which he'd bought last year with the money she had been saving up for him from the first month he was born. Five dollars a week for twenty-five years is quite a bit. Did he know that?

'Six thousand, five hundred dollars,' Pynter said, almost before she'd finished.

Not many students, not even English people, could afford to buy a car like Laban's. Did he know that? He sounded like a smart boy! Did she know his family?

'I'm Pynter, Pynter Bender.'

'Ben … Oh, Benoit! The Benoits. You a Benoit.' Linora's face lit up. 'That's where you get the height. Which one of the brothers is your father?'

'Not Benoit, Bender.'

She looked doubtfully at Tinelle. 'Ben-uh-der. Never heard that name before. From?'

'Old Hope.'

'Eh?'

'Old Hope. I come from a lil cane village name Old Hope.'

Tinelle was brushing her fingers across the keys of the piano.

'Yes, well…' Linora got to her feet and looked vaguely about the room. 'You'll excuse me, er … T? Those orchids I've been trying to grow, you remember? Come, I want to show you how I've been getting on. Laban sent me this wonderful book about growing orchids. All sorts, my dear! Excuse us, er, young man.'

Linora and Tinelle went into the dining room, leaving Pynter to drift about the house on his own. He went into the kitchen and there was Miss Syl again. She was leaning against the dresser. She'd folded her arms and her eyes were on him, probing him. A Deeka gaze. She was telling him she knew him.

'Don' let 'er call you no fuckin D-fo'-Darky,' Pynter said, washing his hands at the tap. 'Y'hear me?'

Miss Syl moved towards the door that led into the flower garden at the back. 'She don't like you,' she whispered. 'Dat's what she been tellin de girl in quiet. She fink you not good enough fo' her.'

Pynter dried his palms on his trousers. 'She can't stop six. The quenk! What's your real name?'

'Selina. Everybody call me Lina at home.' Lina was grinning, probably at the name he'd called the woman.

'I'z Pynter.'

'She like you?'

'I don' flippin care.'

'Not she – Miss Dolly-face, I mean.'

'Of course!'

'Only fuh your looks?'

Pynter shook his head. 'Not only. Don't let nobody fool you. You pretty like hell. Nicer-lookin than dat half-bake son she got. And if … '

Lina's face went dead. Tinelle was standing in the other room, her back against the partition, looking across at them. He had never seen her look so small and vulnerable.

'See yuh,' he mumbled.

Lina nodded, her eyes shifting to the floor.

'I gettin outta here, Tinelle.' His voice was loud enough to fill the house. 'You comin or you stayin?'

'We came together, not so?' Tinelle sounded plaintive.

Linora saw them to the door. 'Think about what I told you, Tinelle.'

'I can't remember everything you told me, Auntie Li. You told me so much, dearest.'

Outside, Tinelle plunged her left hand into Pynter's pocket and turned her face up to him. Temple Valley lay blue and beautiful below them, and above them were great walls of hibiscus, probably planted there by the blue-eyed grandfather from Scotland.

'Hibiscus and begonias,' he said. 'The names always nicer than the plant. Begonias remind me of my aunt, Tan Cee. Begonias especially.'

'She crazy about plants.'

'She know plants. Tan Cee is plant modder.'

'Not her, Aunt Li.'

'Oh she! She jus' crazy, full stop!'

'Not crazy. Just living her life for Laban.'

'And you don' call dat craziness? Like de world begin and end with dat chupid fella name Laban. What's so special about 'im anyway?'

'He's her son.'

'I'z also my modder son, but she not sitting down and waiting while the whole world tumble down around her. Dat's what Silly Lily doing.'

'Stop it!'

'Stop what! Stop my arse! I putting it to you dat Linora de loveless not crazy about no plants. Is appease she tryin to appease them. Becuz them coming fo' her. Dey closing in! You watch that forest down there and, mark my words, your Aunt Ugly Lily better watch she arse, becuz de forest creepin up to get she tail and it goin to finish her off long before she live to see you married to a D for Darky like me.'

'Pynter! You shouting.'

'Sooo! I kin flippin shout loud as I want. I not inside dat fallin-down house no more. I don' know what de hell you bring me here for. If you come to my yard, dey will treat you proper. Dey won' call you no Pale Face, or Red 'Ooman, or Brownie. Dey will treat you like you was a flesh-an'-blood pusson.'

'Pynter!'

'Don' call my name. In fact, I surprise you know it, seein as Lily de lyin, loveless, lonely little … '

'Pynterrr.'

They were at the end of the road, against the iron gate. He pulled her to him, still angry and drunk with it. She was crying. He glimpsed Lina at the side of the house looking across at them, her hands on her hips. The old woman had come out too.

When he raised his head again, Selina and Linora had vanished.

They were on the road above San Andrews. He was marvelling at the red trail of flowers discarded by the high flame trees that stood above the twisting strip of asphalt when Tinelle began talking. Didn't he want to know what Auntie Li was saying to her? Did he realise she loved him? She'd never said that to a man before.

She was speaking so quickly she had to stop to catch her breath. Laban, she said, was never going to give Linora the grand-children she wanted so desperately. He was not planning on returning. He had no interest in family. Would not have one for the sake of continuing his or anybody else's name, for the same reasons that Hugo did not give a damn about children either. What she could never bring herself to do was explain to her aunt that Laban loved living abroad. He saw himself as being in a state of waiting. When Linora died he was going to sell the house and the land it was rotting on.

Tinelle looked up at the hills, at the green waterfalls of leaves and trees and vines. She stopped and turned to face him. 'With Hugo and Laban out of it, there's just me to carry on the family name. Or us McMurdos will disappear off this island.'

'Never mind. There's lots o' you in Scotland!' Pynter said.

'I'm not joking. My children will have to carry my name.'

'Call all of them Tinelle then.'

They were still fretting at each other when they got to the house. Something restless and unsated sat between them.

Tinelle went into her room. Shortly after, she emerged wearing a purple dress. It swirled around her naked feet.

'Shower now and change, please, Pynter,' she said.

She'd put on some music when he returned. She was standing in the middle of the hallway. The windows were thrown open to the town. And the yellow night glow of San Andrews was all the light there was.

'I want this back, Pynter. I want us to rectify what went wrong today. In here.' She touched her chest. She pulled her breath in and looked away. 'I want to dance with you till we fall asleep. Or get so tired we can't think or feel any more. And when we wake up, I hope … ' Her voice faltered.

She reached for his hands and opened his arms. He folded them around her.

'Who's the voice?' he whispered.

'Millie Jackson,' she said.

Up there in the big white house above the harbour, they swayed together in each other's arms and he was alive to the brush of her lips and her whispered words. The sound of the sea became a soft snore in the distance.

37

PYNTER CAUGHT THE smell of the canes as soon as he reached Old Hope. He'd been away for seven months and he wondered how they would receive him.

His mother was the first to spot him at the bottom of the hill. She straightened up over the pot of oil-down on the fire and laughed out loud, which brought Deeka and Patty hurrying and they too started laughing when they saw him. Tinelle had cut his hair and parted it on the left. She'd greased and brushed it until it shone blue-black like a corbeau's wing, with little waves laid out along the top like neat potato banks. He'd bought himself a shirt with copper studs around the pockets and cream buttons at the front which glowed like polished ivory. He'd left the top two buttons loose and tucked the tails of the soft white shirt into a pair of flared denims. The shoes he'd left the yard with all those months ago were as clean as if he had just taken them from the box.

They laughed him all the way up the hill, pointing out how fast he'd grown, how tall de fella look now. So easy-walking too! With a pretty smile and a body that only a whole heap o' Town-Girl-lovin gave!

Elena licked a finger and brushed his brows, teased back the quick of his fingernails and studied them. She examined every inch of him. 'Now you know what only man s'pose to know 'bout woman, you still believe you'z a man?'

Pynter smiled and wrapped his arms around her. His mother nudged him off and stepped back.

'Lord ha' mercy. As if I never see this boy before. Look what six months gone and do to 'im.'

He brushed her cheek with the back of his hand. 'Ma,' he said.

'You hungry?' she said, and turned towards the fire.

Pynter didn't answer her. He walked over to Deeka, who was leaning against the door frame, bothered it seemed by a thorn or something in her finger. She felt frail in his arms, all nerves and angles. He was reminded of the bird he'd pulled out of the sky up there beneath Zed Bender's tree.

'Kabinda,' he said, calling her by the name he'd always used as a child, with the voice that belonged to that time.

'Gloria Lily Boy,' she whispered. She adjusted her headwrap and hurried into the house.

Patty had her baby in her arms. She told him that Tan Cee was not there, that this would be her third month at Santay's. A woman in blue visited just once, she said. A couple of months after Tan Cee's trouble with Coxy. She'd prised Tan Cee's eyelids open, asked her a few questions and after a whole morning of talking to Deeka and writing things down, said that Tan Cee was a problem only to husbands who went off with the sisters of their wives and were bad-minded enough to want the daughters of the wife's sister too. The village males, she added, should be exemplary for a couple of months, at least.

Patty passed the child over to him. The baby's fingers curled around his thumb.

'What you goin call 'im?' he said.

'Windy don' wan' to see you,' Patty said. 'What you done to her, Pynto, that night, that night you left?'

'Same thing she done to me, Tan Pat. Everyfing and nuffing. I try to ferget her like y'all want. I can't. An' Tinelle don' make no difference.'

'What goin happm to Miss San Andrews?' she asked.

'I stay wiv Tinelle. Don' look at me like dat, Tan Pat.'

'Like how?'

'Like you sorry fo' me o' something.'

'Not fo' you, Pynto, fo' them.'

'I done them somefing?'

He stood up, holding out the sleeping child to her.

Patty folded her arms and sucked her teeth. 'You walkin off already? As soon yuh seat get hot you want to walk. Dat's easy, Pynto. De hard part is sitting down and lissenin when I got serious tings to tell yuh. You should ha' lef' Windy alone. Some things you don't touch if it goin stick to your hand and stain it, no matter how nice it look o' feel. You leave it alone. You walk 'way from it. Windy is your fault.' She spoke without looking at him. 'You don' know the worry we had when we see the way that girl-chile fix she eyes on you. Cuz we know you. You not like Peter. Peter will do somefing foolish, check 'imself and run away in time. Not you, you want more. You want her head. So what you do? You find a way to walk inside it. You use all dem pretty words o' yours to make a seat fo' yuhself in dere. You siddown like a shadow inside that girl-chile mind. Now she won't do sheself a favour an' push you out of it.'

'Tan Pat…' he said. He was shaking his head at her. Patty stopped him with a quick impatient gesture.

'Got a fella who pass in a car every day. Nice fella. He see her first time. He come back. He want to talk to 'er. He come back every day. He keep tryin. She look at him but she eyes don' stop on 'im. All I see her doin is comparin. She lissen to 'im like she makin believe is you she hearin.' Patty levelled a finger at him. 'You know what dat feel like? To full up yuhself wiv somefing you can't have? To know it there, and it never goin be yours? If you want to unnerstan dat, go talk to Birdie woman. S'matter o' fact, go talk to Tan Cee about it. It sour a pusson life, y'unnerstan? It make dem want to quarrel wiv God. I askin you, Pynto, how it feel to have a woman any time you want her, no matter who she livin with or married to? Dat make a fella feel good, not so? But it blight a life, y'unnerstand?'

He raised his hand to try and stop her.

'It 'mind me o' dat Zed Bender fella you s'pose to be and dat Essa Bender girl who s'pose to come an' take you back. If dat was true, I ask meself what kind o' love could make a woman want to do dat, eh? To follow a fella even after death? I askin you, dat the kind of love you been after from Windy? An' if so, what about her? Eh? What about Windy?'

He stood up. This time Patty took the child from him. 'You cursin me,' he said.

'I tellin you de truth.'

'You my aunt, so I can't tell you what I thinkin now, the way I want to tell you.'

'Well, Pynto, if … '

'Lemme finish! You talk a lot and I lissen. Now lemme put my coupla words t'you. I don't know men. I hardly been around dem. I don't even know if I like dem fo' company or friendship. S'always been y'all – wimmen. If yuh want a different kinda man,' he pointed at the child, 'you got yuh chance with dat one. I tell you somefing else. What I feel 'bout Windy frighten me too. She not de only one dat 'fraid.'

He was on his way out when her voice came at him. 'I name de baby after you, Pynto.'

And then he could hear her making bird noises at the child and chuckling to herself.

He'd come home during the time of the boucans when, late evenings, Old Hope piled high the carcasses of old crops and set the hills alight so that the smell of wood smoke clung to everything in the valley. Even food and water tasted like the closing of dry season.

Later in the evening, when the flutter around his arrival had subsided, he sat in the yard and looked up at the blazing hills. By then he'd washed off the Eddison Farley's Supreme Cologne, and treated his armpits to a smack or two of stinging Alcolado Glacial. The smell of Topaz Hair Pomade, London Ltd had been replaced by the coconut from the coarse blue soap that Elena handed him with the order to, 'Go wash dat town girl off you, boy!'

He'd watched Peter busy himself with the fire. He had changed, Pynter thought, or perhaps it was he who was different.

'What you come back here for?'

'Don't talk to me like dat, Peter.'

'I talk as I please. I don't want you here. Is only trouble you bring and you don' stay round long enough to see what happm after. This time I won' 'low it.'

Pynter felt like a stranger in his yard. Peter was trying to protect them from him. If, in the past, Pynter had claimed their father as his own, Peter had made their mother his.

'I'm not leaving now,' he said. 'Not until I ready. Put that in your pipe an' smoke it.'

'I make you leave if I have to, and not even Tan Cee kin change that.'

For what remained of the week, his mother told him, in every way but outright, that the yard was no longer a place for him.

'You an' Miss San Andrews fall out?'

'Nuh.'

'I ain't got electric light.'

'I didn born with electric light.'

'You pass de age fo' sleepin on de floor. Peter don' sleep on de floor no more.'

'I'z not Peter.'

'Besides, I don' want you to go near Windy.'

'Is Windy not comin near me.'

'And don' start no argument with Peter.'

'I not makin no argument wiv Peter. Is Peter hate my guts.'

'Don' say that! Peter is your brother.'

'You sure?'

The canes were dying: the Otaheites, thin and hard as the people who had fed them with their lives, the dark-barked Creoles, the light-striped Caledonians, and the king of cane itself, the moving sea of Cheribons that had ruled their lives longer than anyone could remember, no longer made this valley shiver with their whisperings. They had been replaced with the new aggressive strains that had numbers – D625 and POJ2878 – instead of names. What Old Hope said to the man who came and made them change the way they planted cane was proving to be true.

In the first few years the Numbers thrived magnificently. But they were fooling no one. To grow so fat, so fast on ageing land meant their roots were doing something secretive and harmful underneath. And now it was there for all to see. The land had blanched and soured with the phosphates it had been force-fed. And wherever the rains had fallen and settled, the soil was iridescent with bacteria. There were bald patches everywhere, and the wind threw up the smell of chemicals and decay.

Men and women left their yards the usual fore-day morning and returned home in the afternoon to sit on their doorsteps and contemplate the fading green. For in the shifting of the hues, the yellowing of the green, the spreading, orange fire of the love vines and the purpling of the shade below the bamboo and the almonds, they saw not only the passing of the old things but the closing of their future too.

Pynter watched Frigo walking up the hill towards him so slowly it was as if his friend were wading through the odours of the rotting canes. He was wearing a collarless white shirt similar to Paso's. He walked with the same dreamy-eyed distraction. He even wore a coloured belt.

'How yuh, Pynto Bendup? S'a long time, fella.' Frigo brought both of Pynter's hands together and clasped them in his own, Paso's gesture.

'Seven months,' Pynter said. 'Where's the others?'

'Gone. Gone home. Drop de struggle, Pynto. Arilon, he come to see you yet?'

'No.'

Frigo's lips closed down like a curtain over his teeth.

'S'awright,' Pynter said. 'People change. You too, Frigo. You change.'

'What San Andrews like?'

'Quiet.'

'An' de people?'

'Quiet.'

Frigo turned his face up at the hills. 'Dat's de problem. It too quiet now. It gone quiet everywhere. We goin to change dat, Pynto Bendup. We planning a big one. Big! That burn we burn Victor last time ain' nothin to compare. Paso call it a Gatherin. In Si-Monde. You know dat big place by de sea where dey used to race dem horses? We gonna call a rally of every man, woman and child on this island right there and we gonna put Victor on trial. Like they do in court, y'know? Put de sonuvabitch on trial for all de crimes he commit against we. Against me. Us. De people. We goin to try 'im for all de world to see. Try 'im in … in, er, how Paso call it? Oh! In absentia. Dat mean in the absence thereov! Not so? And when we finish try him with judge, jury, due duress and process; when we finish process de sonuvabitch, we gonna sentence 'im.'

'What happen after y'all find Victor guilty?' Pynter said.

Frigo's smile was beautiful. 'He stay guilty.'

'Y'all been planning that a long time?'

'Long enough.' Frigo squinted at him. 'You keep sayin y'all, like if…'

'And how soon dat due to happen?'

'When de right time come. Why?'

Tinelle answered him like that too, these days especially. Responses that were not answers. Now Tinelle and he preferred not to talk about these things. For it soured their ease. It made her wary and tight-lipped with him. It was one of the things he'd learned about the way they loved now: much of their happiness depended on avoidances.

'Just want to know. Thanks fo' coming, Frigo. I 'preciate it.'

Frigo seemed to want to say something but couldn't bring himself around to it.

'Say what you want to say, Frigo.'

'De girl, she nice?'

'Which girl?'

'De red woman in town. De one who they say turn your head.'

'Who say?'

Frigo grinned. 'People. She nice?'

'Nice is not de word.'

'What is de word, den?'

Pynter got up, stretched and yawned. 'She's not de reason behind nothing.'

'She nice?'

'Like I told you, nice is not de word.'

Pynter realised that it wasn't Frigo's old friendship that had brought him here. A pusson just wanted to get a better look at the bravery or stupidity that made a hero of Pynter Bender in Old Hope. The villages above the canes had all heard of him. In front of the evening fires, they'd fleshed out the little they'd gathered from Arilon for the benefit of the children. They explained how Pynter Bender, Elena Bender's boy, was born funny, born blind. He was a spirit-chile that found its way into the world by sneaking behind a natural-born; how he became a bat and flew above the fences of barbed wire and liberated Arilon.

Pynter cleared his throat. 'You know where Paso is?'

Frigo shrugged. 'Who wan' to know?'

'You one o' the fellas that s'posed to protect my nephew?'

Frigo smiled. 'People change, Pynto. You lookin at me an' you thinkin I not up to it? You thinkin … '

'Tell 'im I want to see 'im.'

'I not so sure 'bout dat, fella.'

Pynter advanced towards him. 'I want to tell you somefing, Frigo. Paso will not live past this "gatherin" y'all planning. I know this. Nobody need no magic to unnerstan that. And if y'all just stop and think 'bout it, y'all will see exactly what I sayin.'

Frigo laughed. 'Everybody want Paso life, like … '

'Tell 'im what I tell you, Frigo.'

Frigo turned. 'I see what I kin do, Pynter.'

'Don' jus' see what you kin do, Frigo. Do!'

'You missing Tan Cee?' Peter's voice was a whisper in the dark.

'Ole Hope is a different place without Tan Cee, Peter.'

'Who's behind it, Pynter?'

'Behind what?'

'De trial o' Victor.'

'Paso.'

Peter seemed to sense the worry in him. 'What gonna happen?'

Pynter lowered his head. He touched his brother. 'You remember that night before them soldiers come for Birdie?'

Peter nodded.

'You left the yard. You was out there for a lil while in the dark. Then you come back. You went straight inside the house to tell Birdie he couldn go back to jail else he'll never leave it. What happm out there in the dark? What make you know?'

Peter stirred beside him. 'Don' know. Didn fink it. I jus' know.'

'I tell you how you know. You do two things that night: you didn fool yourself and you went all the way. You saw dem soldiers come fo' Birdie. You know Birdie mash up eight of 'em already before he break loose from jail. You know if they take 'im back to jail and hit Birdie, Birdie goin go crazy. Ain't got no fella in de world goin strike Birdie an' Birdie won' strike 'im back. You add all o' dat up in yuh head. So quick, Peter, you didn even know it happen. All you had befo' you was de answer. Patty an' Deeka see it too, but they didn want to believe it. They stop demself halfway. They fool demself wiv hoping dat it not goin happm. People do that. People do it all the time. Dey fall back on hope, specially when the obvious is jus', well … unthinkable. You, you didn let hope stop you. Dat's how I know Paso wouldn come out of dis gatherin alive … and I can't get nobody to lissen. Before I come here, I write it down for Tinelle. I left her a letter. I explain to her that in all them years that Paso been mobilisin, that gathering is the only place where Sylus sure to find him. They been lookin for him for years. He frighten the hell out of dem, y'unnerstand? They been tryin to put a face to Paso from time. Now they got a face for this one lil bright-eye fella who kin bring the whole island out in one place, point hi finger at Victor and convince everybody with a coupla words that he's a criminal. Now they got this one chance to get 'im. You don' think they goin do whatever the hell it take to do it? Put yourself in Victor place an' tell me who you'll go for first, the thousands dat make de trouble or the one pusson dat make de thousands make de trouble? An' besides, who got the guns, eh? Who got the guns, Peter?'

'Paso could leave dis place, not so?' Peter said.

'Paso will never leave this island.'

'Why?'

'Cuz he don' feel he belong.'

'Don' unnerstan.'

'Wouldn make sense if I tell you.'

'You tellin me I stupid?'

'Nuh. Paso wasn' born nowhere. He born in the middle of the sea, somewhere between Puerto Rico and this island. Pa told me that. Paso carry dat knowledge wiv 'im all de time. He talk 'bout it even when he don' know he talkin 'bout it. How a pusson make demself belong to a place, Peter?'

Peter shook his head.

'They give themself to it. They commit.'

'An' I not s'pose to unnerstan dat?'

'Didn mean it the way you take it.'

The fires on the foothills had been reduced to the fitful glow of embers that brightened with every passing wind, like the eyes of demons in the dark.

Peter stirred. 'You know what people saying about you?'

'No.'

'You brave.' Peter chuckled. 'You know why?'

'No.'

'Cuz you bring back Arilon.' Peter laughed louder.

'Something wrong wid dat?

'Dey say you could ha' never get away if you didn shorten dem arms o' yours and make them turn to bat wings.' Peter's laughter must have reached the foothills.

'You are my twin. If I am like that then you are the same.'

'You are my two-win. Ef I um loike thort! You turn speaky-spokey too? Seven months and you talkin as if you got a lump o' mud in you mouth. Spit it out!'

'It might fall on you.'

'Never. I don' wear nothing dat don' suit me. What she look like?'

'Who?'

'De girl.'

'Tinelle?'

'Dat's she name?'

'Yep!'

'Tell me 'bout her.'

'Tell you what?'

'What she look like, how she talk, de way she treat you.'

Peter went quiet.

'She nice,' Pynter said. Whatever changes they saw in him they'd put down to Tinelle.

'Like I say, she nice. Brown like one of Uncle Birdie bread. Warm like bread too. That is how I think of her especially. Just warm. She teach me somefing, Peter.'

'Wozzat?'

He did not know how to say it. The words felt awkward in his head. 'Tenderness. Y'unnerstand dat? Love an' violence – dey don't have to go together.'

When Peter spoke again his tone was gentle. 'She pretty?'

'I never hear nobody say she pretty, 'ceptin me. But I know one fella want her desperate like Sylus want Paso life.'

'S'posin 'twas me who meet her first?'

Pynter laughed.

'What de hell you laughin at?'

'I don' know how to answer dat cuz I don' know how you'll mix with her.'

'You tellin me she too nice to mix wiv me?'

'Jeezas Christ, man!'

'Lemme tell you something, fella. If I did meet dat girl before you or even same time as you, she would ha' been mine. In fact, if I meet her tomorrow and I want her, she'll be mine. You know why?'

'Nuh, tell me.'

'I more of a man than you. That's why. I no saga boy, no sugar-mouth sweet man. But I'z a man, a big man, y'unnerstan? Is a long time now dat I gone flyin past you. So don't think dat becuz you got a stupid lil piece o' red-skin girl in town dat anybody kin own, dat make you special. It don't, cuz I could take she from you any time.'

'You jealous, Peter. And you ain't got no frickin reason to be jealous. Jealousy eatin y'arse and you don' know what to do with it. You got no reason to be hatin me. Cuz you never had nobody tell you that you not natural, you not born to live, you not good for much 'ceptin for yourself. My life been like a line you draw in de dust with your toe that any wind or any absent-minded hand or foot could rub right off like dat, as if I never been there. They talk about me only in the present, or the past. What I am; what I was. I don't invite no future tense because what's the use if I not going to be there for long? So they build everything around you. It always there in their words, in their expectations, in their idea of the future for this family. Dat's why you ain't got no flippin reason to be jealous.'

The next day over dinner he told them he was leaving. Elena stopped chewing for a while. Patty smiled at her as if to say that, despite her silence, she could hear her perfectly. And Peter, who from the day Pynter arrived had decided to eat standing with his back against the night, sat down. Windy, who was still avoiding him, placed her bowl on the ground between her feet, got up, stepped out of the rim of light and disappeared.

Elena chuckled. 'She won' sleep tonight,' she said. 'She'll walk up and down in that house like her mother used to.'

His mother ate with her fingers, something he had not noticed before.

Patty leaned against him, jostling until he adjusted himself to accommodate her. The beautiful fingers went back to stripping the thigh of the chicken. 'Fix yuh face, Sugarboy. Cat eat you tongue?'

'S'pose I did come to stay?' he said.

'You didn,' she said. 'You fink a few lil ole words could change de truth? And you know what's good?' She dropped her voice. 'I see Elena happy fo' the first time in years. She believe the trouble finish.'

'S'not over yet.'

'Dat's what your modder feel an' we should leave her feeling good for as long as it last.' Patty looked up at him with troubled eyes. 'Eat in peace. Arilon bring your books up for you from where you left them by de river.'

'I don't need them no more.'

'They yours.'

'I done the exams. I'm sick of them.'

'They still yours. Don't leave them here when you going. Peter! Bring your brother bag o' book!'

Patty rested a hand on his knee. 'Another time, Pynto. Another time. I hope everything make sense later. But you got to go. Cross water. And San Andrews nearer overseas than here.'

38

THE NEW YEAR crept in so quietly Pynter hardly noticed when it arrived. San Andrews looked like a picture postcard. Mornings, the grass was wet with dew. The big trees lining Canteen Road were already discarding their leaves in preparation for the dry season.

This, he told Tinelle, would be his nineteenth dry season in the world. Pynter scrawled the year in yellow on a square of paper, underlined the number – 1974 – with a red marker and hung it beside the portraits on her wall.

The island was tossing with a new disquiet, one that had started at the tail end of the previous year. They'd called a great gathering in the hills by the sea, listed twenty-seven crimes against Victor and tried him 'in absentia'.

They had been generous, they said. They left out the hundred or so 'atrocities' for which they judged him indirectly responsible. They'd had witnesses who gave long testimonies. At the end of it, Paso spoke as planned, and told the thousands about another gathering to come, when there would be even more people, this time in San Andrews on the half-mile spread of asphalt that looked out on the harbour called the Carenage. Together they would cripple the island.

Tinelle and Hugo returned from their nightly planning meetings to the breakfast Pynter prepared for them. He'd stood at Hugo's shoulders a couple of times and learned the way he cooked. Now

Pynter watched them eat, hardly taking in the driblets of conversation that animated them.

By the time they finished, he knew what Tinelle's mood was. He got up then, strolled over to the row of bottles, selected a few and mixed a drink that matched her mood.

> *Devil's Tail fo' tiredness: one and a half ounce light rum. Just one ounce o' vodka. One tablespoon lime juice. Grenadine – one teaspoon. Measure the same fo' brandy. Ice: half a cup. Blend dem!*
>
> *Lounge Lizard cuz she feelin good: half ounce dark rum plus amaretto – same amount as de rum. Nuff Coke. Full up de glass wiv ice. Pour everything in. Nice it up wiv a slice o' lime. Give 'er with a smile.*
>
> *Dat need-for-lovin-look. Is Undertow she want: gold rum, gin, lime juice – one ounce of each o' dem. Half dat amount o' Creme de Noyaux, or something close. Guava syrup, lime peel. Gwone, Missa Bender, blend dem.*
>
> *Now add a slice o' lime.*
>
> *She upset; she want to sleep. Dat's Devil-Poison. One ounce Jack Daniels; one hundred proof o' mountain dew o' anything really hot. Ice. Shake. Strain everyting. In a coupla minutes, carry 'er to bed.*

He showered her. He washed her hair. He lay beside her and read while she slept. Once he pulled a slip of paper from his pocket and wrote some lines he suddenly remembered from the pages of his Uncle Michael's book.

> *Where shall this loving lead us …*

The rustling of the paper must have woken her. He felt the tips of her fingers on his thigh. She was staring at him with a wide-eyed, wondering gaze. 'What you doing to me, Pynter?'

He'd smiled at her and closed his eyes.

Paso had become an incubus on his mind. He lost his appetite and would toss awake at night with worry. He made himself recall whole passages from books. He composed poems in his head and kept them there. His agitation was an illness that was spoiling the way he was with Tinelle.

Not long after that first gathering, he heard Tinelle talking on the phone and he was sure it was Paso she was speaking to. He walked over to her and placed his head against Tinelle's. She convulsed her shoulders, told the voice she would call back, went into her room and locked the door.

When she came back to him she looked into his eyes. 'What's happening, Pynter? What's wrong? You making yourself sick. Look at you – you lost so much weight, I hardly recognise you. What's going on with you?'

He held up his hands at Tinelle. 'I awright, Tinelle. I awright now.'

His words did not convince her. 'There is something deeply selfish about this too,' she said. 'That's what's really getting to me. We'll have more people out there than you can count, and what you do? You killing yourself over Paso. Not Hugo, not me, just Paso.'

She'd gone to the record player and lifted a disc from the floor. She held it round the edges and blew on it. He watched her hands as she dropped it onto the spindle of the machine.

'We can't stop this, Pynter. This island already stirred up. Victor stirring one way, so we have to stir the other way or else everybody drowns, including you. We've been counting from the time this started. We were counting again last night: the disappearances, the accidental shootings; the people like us who leave their homes to visit a friend or family and never arrive. Not to mention the ones Victor sends back to us so frigged up you could hardly recognise them. Two hundred and seventeen, Pynter. Two hundred and seventeen. I want you to keep that number in your head. Why? Because we insist that this island is not Victor's back garden? That we want a future different from the one he decides for us? That we don't want no independence from no England if it means we still kissing England's arse? I'll tell you something else.'

Tinelle lifted the record off the player, flipped it over and dropped it back onto the spindle.

'I'm clear about one thing. You my man, you not my mind.'

He pushed himself up off the chair. 'Make sense,' he said. 'Everyting you say.'

'Then how come we can't agree on anything?'

'Cuz, like you say for yourself, my mind is mine and I will check out whatever try to enter it before I give it a place in there.'

The words came out more fiercely than he'd meant them to. Tinelle and he – they'd suddenly become strangers in this room and the detachment he felt surprised him.

'Come,' he said. 'I want to show you somefing.' He took her hand and urged her towards the door.

Tinelle's house stood like the prow of a ship above the Carenage. A few alleyways radiated off the space like spokes in a wheel. From the veranda he pointed at the spread of asphalt down below. The evening sun had bleached it almost white. People drifted about down there like shoals of fish, the reds and greens and yellows of their clothing burning bright like daytime torches.

'What you see down there?' he said. He sensed her irritation and ignored it. 'I see two end of a road that bring you in and out of there. I see five little alley-road that run off it. I see the sea in front of all of dat. I see a trap y'all makin for y'all self.'

Tinelle shook herself and glared at him. He rested a pleading hand on her shoulder.

'I ask meself: what happm if five thousand people have to get out o' dat lil place in one go. Eh? My problem is,' he dropped his voice, 'I not jus' thinkin 'bout what Victor an' Sylus done to people already. Dat's history. I keep thinkin o' what dey capable o' doing. I wish I could stop an' give meself a easy time.'

Tinelle leaned into him. She slipped a hand around his waist. 'You worry too much, that's all. Another week to go and then …' She elbowed him, winked at him and chuckled. 'This is all the standing I'm doing for the rest of the day, Pen-Ben. Y'hear me?'

'Undertow.' He shrugged and followed her inside.

39

T<small>INELLE WAS QUIET</small> with him the morning of the march, although she laughed easily with Robert and the three young men who came to meet her. They were wearing T-shirts and sandals, their hair so carefully groomed they could have been going off for a lime.

They spoke to each other in lowered voices, which dropped almost to a whisper when Pynter was near them.

'Look, Pynter, I find this embarrassing. You understand? You have to be with us. Do you understand? If you can't do that with me, then ... '

'Then?' he said.

'Do I have to say it?'

'Nuh,' he said. And then more quietly, 'I'll close the door behind me.'

Tinelle jerked her head as if he'd struck her. She looked back at him just once before the green and yellow headscarf disappeared down the steps to the Carenage.

From Tinelle's veranda he could see everything.

The schools had tipped their children into the streets. They were streaming down the roads towards the Carenage, the sound of their shoes like the lapping of storm water on the warm asphalt, their white tops foaming in the bright mid-morning sun, the coloured ribbons of the girls glittering like coral.

They raised a hum that shivered the air above the town.

There were thousands of them, singing an anthem that looked forward to a time of overcoming.

And Paso was there, a dot in the distance.

The collarless white shirt his nephew wore fluttered in the sea wind like a bit of tissue on a branch. Pynter saw no soldiers. There were no jeeps. At either end of the road were a small cluster of crawling trucks, packed high with crates of soft drinks, the bottles glittering in the sun. It wasn't what he expected.

There was the crackle of a loudhailer. Somebody announced Paso's name and when he rose on the crates the crowd erupted. Paso raised a hand and everything went still.

Pynter could not hear him but whatever he said raised a storm of laughter from the crowd. Their laughter brought the chuckles out of Pynter too and made him marvel at his nephew. There must have been six thousand there. It wasn't as he expected at all. The trucks of soft drinks began making their way towards each other, parting the crowd. The men on the trucks dangled their legs down the sides of the crates, lifted their caps and waved them at the crowd. They were nodding their heads and laughing. The men who'd been standing on the streets just away from them had now joined the crowd. They were also wearing caps.

Pynter followed them the way he'd followed Tinelle's green and yellow headtie all the way to the space beside the stage. It was easy to trace these men, for they created little eddies in their wake. A strange kind of turbulence it was, because it did not look like jostling. And yet it grew and spread itself throughout the gathering the way wind walked over water.

The megaphone crackled. A man's voice, bright as a blade, cut through the air and suddenly the stage was no longer there. Just the spreading turbulence.

And all this time, nothing in the sound of the crowd had changed.

But then the guns went off. Even then it was not as Pynter expected. There were no falling bodies, just a mass of milling colours, a rising whirlwind of voices from down below and the awful crack of sun-heated soda bottles exploding on the asphalt. Then the spillage of bodies into alleyways, and the overflow of people into the sea.

Pynter knew that he was shouting, even though he could not hear his own voice.

He was taking the steps in twos and calling Tinelle's name. He threw himself among the press of limbs and torsos.

And even then in the tearing struggle forward, with the bottles exploding like glass grenades around his feet, the splinters flying everywhere, the fizzing fluid burning in the gashes that they made, he worried for his eyes.

He pressed a hand over his face, his splayed fingers scissoring the world before him.

He found Tinelle pinned against the doorway of one of the stores. She'd lost her scarf. She had one hand over her mouth and with the other she was pushing against the shoulders that were crushing her. He could see the exhaustion on her face. He reached for her just as the tide of bodies began to suck him backwards, and as he stretched for her, a surge of fierceness welled up in his gut. Tinelle was his woman. Every time she'd offered herself to him up there in her house above the harbour, she'd been giving him permission to claim her. Tinelle was his woman. She was all he saw and wanted.

When he got to her he tore off his shirt and covered her head with it. He brought his lips down to her ear and told her what she'd said to him so often in their early days of loving: relax, don't fight the tide. And by the time they slipped into a side alley the thunder had subsided. They heard the sound of gunshots in the building just above them. Then everything went quiet.

He took Tinelle through the back ways on the narrow stone paths he'd discovered during his night walks. He stopped only when a fit of coughing took hold of Tinelle and doubled her over.

When they got home Hugo was already there. He was sitting on the floor with his head thrown back against the seat of a chair. The only sign of the trouble Hugo had just escaped from were the blood marks on his shoes.

Pynter eased Tinelle down on the cushions. He went to the kitchen, lit the stove and set a pot of water on it. He lifted a couple of towels from her room, returned to the kitchen and waited till the water warmed.

She was exhausted. There were small gashes at her temple where flying glass had struck. Pynter pulled off her shoes and began working on her the way he'd seen the women in his yard do: from her head down. He loosened her hair and picked out the bits of debris. He extracted the flecks of broken bottle embedded in her arms and legs. He wiped her down, Vaselined her bruises, wrung the still-warm towel and folded it around her feet. She barely winced. Her breathing quietened. She was still crying when she fell asleep.

He tended his burning feet the same way he'd tended Tinelle's. Felt as if some part of his self had decoupled from his body. All he remembered now were Tinelle's words about his fear for Paso's life: 'You're grieving for a death that you've invented.'

Until Paso he'd never understood loss. Not until he'd lived this helplessness and hurting during the few weeks of madness that sent him on his night-time walks through the ghost roads of San Andrews. It amounted to the same thing in the end: hurting for something that could not be rescued or held on to. How much worse it must be then for the women in his yard. For him it had been easier: all this grieving had taken him somewhere; it had led him to accepting something he could not change.

Night was darkening the church towers in the distance when Pynter got up and took his bag. He'd packed only the things he came with.

'Where you going?' Hugo said. He went to the doorway and blocked it with his body. 'Stay with her,' he said.

'She's awright now,' Pynter said. 'I got to get home.' He was thinking of the curfew that was sure to close the island down. In fact it had already fallen, for there was an absence of human sounds out there that came only with the curfews. 'And like Tinelle done tell me.'

'I don't care what she told you. Stay with her.' Hugo left the door and took a long stride towards him. 'Like you gone stupid or something, Pynter?' He was shaking his head and staring at the bag in Pynter's hand. 'You make it look so easy, man.'

Pynter shook the bag in his hand. 'Is what she want. She sleepin now.'

'She went to sleep knowing that you there. That's not the same as ... I have to spell it out for you? You and him. You're the same. Pride and ice. Both of you. Y'all even wearing the same face. Me and my sis – somebody's playing a joke on us, man.' He reached out suddenly and plucked the bag from Pynter's hand. 'Stay with her, Pynter. Please.'

Hugo tossed the bag onto a sofa and led Pynter out to the veranda. The Carenage below was no more than a grey space now, littered with the debris of the day. The sea threw back the glow of the dying sun. On Cathedral Street, the three clock towers struck seven.

'You take everything somebody tell you in vexation for the truth?' Hugo said.

Pynter shrugged. 'Depends.'

'Even out of love?'

'Didn see no love in dem words,' Pynter said.

'Try hearing with your heart next time.'

He almost told Hugo that those were Paso's words; that when he heard them first time, they felt like the beginnings of the real alphabet to life. Instead, Pynter said what he believed was the only thing that sat beneath their words now.

'I hope Paso awright.'

A burst of static pulled their gazes towards the settlements below. They could hear the chords of a guitar and it raised the hair on Pynter's arms. Bob Marley's voice – sad and angry and plaintive – rose up into the air:

No sun will shine in my day today

The music stopped abruptly.

They watched the night roll in. In the spreading dark a line of lights were moving out towards the row of islands.

'Fishing for the missing,' Hugo said. He sprang to his feet, made a strangled sound and rushed inside the house.

40

Paso died swimming.

When Pynter heard, he simply lifted his head at Tinelle and said, 'He was born on the sea, yunno dat?'

Tinelle would not look at him.

By the next day news of Paso's death had reached every corner of the island. Pynter paced the living room, pausing occasionally to part the blinds and look down on the town while Hugo and Tinelle slept or cried off their rage in bed. The radio droned on. Pynter barely heard the voice of the announcer, whose reading of the news had become so stilted she was made to do it with a man who interrupted more and more or took over sometimes. He wondered why Victor did not get rid of her altogether since her heart was not in it.

On the third day they broke the curfew in their hundreds to go to see what Victor's soldiers had done to Paso. There were no tears amongst them either, just the silence and the numbness. Pynter thought that there would be no end to the stream of people making their way up the hill to see his nephew for the last time.

Miss Maddie was sitting straight-backed in a chair when he arrived. Pynter stood before her, touched her briefly on the back of her hand and said, 'I sorry about Paso.' As the night deepened, people arrived with masantorches and left them burning in the yard. They went into the house, returned and pronounced Paso beautiful in sleep.

Miss Muriel, Jordan's mother, lit a fire and began preparing coffee. Missa Ram conjured a bottle of white rum, broke the seal and doused the steps of the house before pouring a mouthful down his throat.

Much later in the night another group of men arrived and made a small circle on the grass. Pynter was interested in these last arrivals, Old Hope's fishermen, men who'd long lost their fathers and their faith to the sea. They sat and told stories, the drumbeat of their voices drawing people towards them the way the masantorches sucked the gnats into their flames. Pynter stayed for the talk about the two children whose brother–sister love took them to the seashore, where they left everything they owned and swam out to meet the ocean, and whatever else was waiting out there for them. There was never a waste like dat pretty-face fella lyin down so peaceful inside dere, they concluded.

He'd lost a sense of the time when he got up and walked away from the circle.

Pynter wondered about Oslo, the young man whose back he'd almost broken. Oslo had made himself a disciple of Paso. No one had heard from him or seen him. Over the past couple of days, word reached them that Frigo was now in the hands of Victor's men.

He took Tinelle to the little gully behind his father's house he hid in as a boy. He told her about the man who used to sing like a rain-bird and the woman who came laughing through the patches of sunlight to lie with him there. He told her how he had called this place Eden and how it had given him the first idea of the promises that lay beyond childhood. Pynter wondered what had happened to Missa Geoffrey and Miss Tilina, whether they'd found another place. There were birds like that. A person tampered with their nest, they moved away and built a new one somewhere else.

It was there that Pynter spoke to Tinelle about the letter Sislyn had sent him. He fished it out of his pocket and showed it to her.

That letter, he said, was proof of what he'd been so desperate to have her and her people understand. Sislyn could have given that note to anyone, anywhere on the island, and it would have reached him. The island worked liked that. It was a web of threads. You held any end and shook it, it got felt everywhere else. It meant that there was not a person on the island that another could not get to if they really wanted. He believed that Paso also knew this. There was that look that Paso carried all the time, he said: the certainty of his passing.

41

ONE SUNDAY MORNING Pynter was woken by steel-pan music. It was like nothing he'd ever heard before. It stirred the quietness that had descended on the house in the months since Paso had drowned.

'Who's dat pan-man, Tinelle?'

Tinelle threw a quick, hot glance at him. 'He name Simone. Go on,' she urged. 'Ask me another country-boy question.'

'She your friend?' he said.

Tinelle would laugh at him if he told her that what he was hearing did not feel like music but a kind of conversation. It sounded like a woman speaking to herself of loss and hope and wanting. It took his mind off Tinelle.

He sat up and pulled on his clothes. Tinelle rose with him and dressed.

They did not take the road but rather the ancient alleyways, the meandering brick roads and stone steps carved into the rocks on which the town was rooted. He stopped beside a stone wall once and held out a hand to Tinelle. She pulled back from him, staring down at his hand as if it belonged to a stranger.

The music had stopped by the time they emerged amongst houses that sat at the edge of a wide gravelled yard high above the sea. Below them was Cathedral Street, with its rows of flower-draped verandas and the dark indifference of Georgian glass windows and grey stone paths.

Pynter saw the shape of the young woman first. She was standing against the cast-iron railings with her back towards the sea. He felt he knew the exact shape Simone's face would be, and the way the small birthmark that sat like a tadpole just under her cheekbones would creep up the side of her face as she parted her lips to say hello to them.

Simone uncrossed her legs and straightened up. She was as tall as cane, with eyes like Patty's.

Pynter extended his hand and brushed her fingers. 'How yuh, Simone?'

'I fine, and how you been?' Simone's fingers wrapped themselves around his.

'Awright,' he answered. 'I been hearing you.'

He released her hand. The tadpole tremored briefly. Simone leaned forward. Pynter brought his palms to his face and held her gaze. She seemed frozen by the gesture.

Tinelle's fingers crept up the back of his shirt. Her hand became a fist against his spine.

'Let's go, Pynter,' she said.

He sensed in Tinelle a warning that he'd better kill whatever it was that had made him hold this woman's gaze like that. He turned with Tinelle, swung his head around just once. Simone had turned around, her elbows on the railings, looking out to sea.

They'd barely arrived home when Tinelle broke her silence – a quiet, deadly rage that made her face go pale. 'I thought you said you didn't know her,' she said, her voice tight with accusation.

'I didn ... I ... '

'Then how come she asking how you've been? That long-neck bitch...'

'Don' call her no long-neck bitch, Tinelle!' His anger surprised him.

'She got Cecile Younger but she still cutting eyes at you.'

'You don' unnerstan. She not … '

'But she better watch her arse with me. Y'hear? You too! You mess with Cecile woman, Cecile don't have no problem messing with you, y'unnerstan?'

'To hell with Cecil whoever-de-hell-he-is. Gimme a chance to talk.'

'I say Cecile, not Cecil.' She'd paused for him to take that in. His face must have registered the surprise because she laughed in his face. 'That place you come from in the country only teach you life in black and white, not so? Grow up, lil boy!'

'Don't call me no lil boy,' he grated. 'And don't rush me neither. Y'hear me? Don't rush me! You rush me an' you askin for trouble. Town people got life? What life town people got? You call dat life? Life my arse.'

He stepped out into the yard and slammed the door behind him.

He wanted to walk. He took the road which swept down towards the bridge over the river at the edge of San Andrews. It was a deceitful road, for it did not deliver the easy downhill stroll it promised. He would turn the corner and there, before him, would be the mountains rearing up in great frozen waves. The road would narrow abruptly and begin to rise like a grey serrated scar towards the purple heights, burying itself in the mist up there. That steady, crooked climb delivered the vehicles which dared to climb it to the murderous downward drag of gravity on the eastern side of the island.

He heard the hum of tyres behind him and his heart flipped over, for there was not a person on the island who did not recognise the sound of those high-ridged tyres on hot asphalt. There wasn't a child in Old Hope who did not understand its meaning, for it had been said to them so often it hummed like tinnitus in their ears. That – that was the sound that Jordan did not hear, or hadn't been listening out for, when Victor's soldiers lifted him off Old Hope Road.

The first Land Rover went past him. He caught a glimpse of green caps and an arm hanging out of a window. He was not worried. It was early afternoon and even if the curfew had never been lifted after Paso's passing, the island had tested it and pushed against it until it finally gave way.

The other vehicle stopped behind him. It was then that he heard the grating of gears ahead and saw the jeep that had just gone past reversing towards him.

He'd always wondered how the soldiers did it. What was it that had made it so easy for Sylus's men to lift someone like Marlis Tillock off the road, or so many of the others that he'd heard of? Pynter looked about him, was surprised he was so calm. He scanned the high mud banks on either side of the road, the tall wire fences planted on each of them. Of all of the six roads he could have selected out of San Andrews, his feet had taken him down this one.

The door of the vehicle behind him slammed. A man stepped out of the jeep in front. He approached Pynter with a stiff-backed strutting gait, his eyes never leaving Pynter's face. Others followed him. Pynter learned their language quickly: the pressure on his wrist that urged him backwards, the sharp jerking of their heads which ordered him to enter the back door of the humming van behind, the abrupt finger directed at the metal rise above the rear wheel which meant he was to sit there.

In the busy silence he felt a bitter rising in his chest, a shivering dislike for Tinelle which the smiling man beside him must have mistaken for fear. For it was Tinelle's goading that had brought him here. Her daily chipping away at so many things inside him. Her puzzling pettishness with him, no different from the way his aunt, Tan Cee, used to be with her husband. These women – he did not understand them. They were strong as God in every way, fearsome when they had to be with every human in the world, except with the men they loved.

Pynter pressed his head against the metal of the van and closed his eyes, navigating the rest of the journey by the movements of the jeep and the sounds outside. He knew they had arrived when the men stopped talking and the vehicle made a sharp turn. There was the sound of tyres chewing into gravel, then they stopped abruptly.

The Barracks throbbed with the voices and laughter of men. The windows were wide open. Two men sat chuckling on chairs beside the doorway. Their laughter died and their faces closed down when they saw him. A young man – all bones and eyes – looked out of a window, rolled slow eyes over him and pulled his head hurriedly inside.

They led him into the building through corridors painted green, with doors that stood half-open, offering glimpses of naked feet and shoulders dark and gaunt as scorched wood. They stopped him at a white door and knocked on it. A voice rough as gravel came from the other side.

They pushed him in and closed the door.

A man was standing with his back against a large window that flooded the room with light. He wore a white shirt, as carefully ironed as the ones Patty went to work with, and pale khaki trousers that matched his sandals exactly.

If this was the man that had come for Birdie all those years ago, Pynter could not remember him. Not the slimness, or the angles that his body made against the light which made him think of Deeka.

Paso had been right about Sylus's hands. They were slim and long and tapering like river reeds. They were hanging at his sides, the tips of his fingers brushing against each other as if he were clearing them of dust. A tension came off him like electricity.

The man's eyes were on him. It lasted for ever, that gaze, in which time Pynter's senses were filled with a rising sense of danger from this slim-boned, dark-eyed stranger who'd murdered his nephew, robbed Jordan of his mind, done something so awful to Marlis Tillock that the sight of it had changed something in John Coker, their headmaster, too. He was remembering the last thing his uncle, Birdie, ever said to them before he escaped the island. That there was not a soldier or jail-keeper in the world who would not destroy a man if he could convince himself that he should do so. These men lived it as a privilege. There was pleasure to be had from that – a man's power over life.

Which was why, he said, you never provoke them. You never offer them the reasons they are hoping for. In fact, you work on them the other way. You try to remind them of something they felt, or could feel weak for: you widen your eyes, you soften your face, you pretend stupidity or innocence. You show them that you're hurting long before they try to hurt you. And if you could make a woman of yourself, you do your best to become one. Or better still, you become their mother, because on this little island there was just one thing that even the wickedest of men held sacred – their mothers.

He'd seen it every time – how a dying island man always fell back on two names: God for insurance, and their mothers for comfort.

'You the first,' Sylus said.

'First of?'

Sylus sat on the table, brought his hands together and leaned forward towards him. 'You not 'fraid. You make me want to make yuh 'fraid. Whooz yuh people?'

'Paso was my family.'

Sylus stretched an arm up towards a shelf above him and took down a small brown box. It jangled briefly. The man laid it on the table, slipped his fingers beneath the lid and pulled out a handful of keys. 'Suh, you come lookin fuh me?' he said.

Pynter looked Sylus in the eyes. 'I been wonderin about you, specially since Paso, erm, gone,' he said. 'I been wonderin how – how many times you die, jus' imaginin your own passin. I wonder if it ever bother you, knowin dat it hardly got a pusson on dis island who don' wish to destroy you. A coupla times, I tell meself I wan' to meet you, just to ask you dat.'

There was no reaction from Sylus. There was a knock on the door. A thin arm pushed it open. A shoulder appeared. A harassed-looking young man came in with a small red canvas bag. He raised his brows at Sylus, who gestured at the table. The youth left the bag there and avoiding Pynter's gaze, eased himself out and pulled the door behind him.

Pynter nodded at the bag and said, 'You kill a man, you add his weight to … '

Sylus moved so suddenly it caught him unawares. He expected the man to hit him. He'd already imagined that was what the keys were for. Was so sure of it he had to struggle with himself not to bring his hand up to protect himself. He willed himself to remain as he was, even when Sylus closed his fingers round his throat and pressed his head hard against the door. 'Lissen, fella, you fink you a bad-john? You fink you kin stan' up in my face an' gimme yuh shit-talk? You fink I don' know how to soften you? You play wiv me, I spoil yuh head right now, y'unnerstan?'

Sylus stepped back. He flicked his hand as if he were shaking water off his fingers. He walked towards the bag on the table.

'Somefing Paso say about you. He say you better dan de people dat you work for. Or you used to be.'

Those words straightened Sylus up against the window. 'Wozzat?' he said.

'You hear me first time,' Pynter said.

Sylus looked down at the bag, then at his hands. He sat back on the table, his legs stretched out, the pleated ridges of his trousers sharp like the edges of knives against the light. 'He send you?'

'He dead.'

Sylus levelled a finger at Pynter's face. 'You part of all dat madness too? You … '

'I born in it.'

'Dat communist fella say dat fo' true?'

'My nephew?'

'He yuh nephew?'

'Uh-huh!'

'Dat's why you wear hi face?'

'Dat's what Paso say,' Pynter nodded.

Sylus dropped the keys on the table and called in one of the men from outside. 'You de first,' he said, and his hand shot out and closed around Pynter's neck. He spun him round and shoved him roughly through the open door. 'Useless lil jackass,' he shouted down the corridor. 'Don't bring 'im here again.'

They dropped Pynter off exactly where they had picked him up. On the way back, the driver looked at him as if he'd been privy to some kind of sorcery with Sylus. He offered Pynter a cigarette, and as the van rolled off, the soldier honked his horn and waved.

That night Pynter slipped into bed behind Tinelle. He traced her spine with his eyes, placed his lips near the edge of her pillow. He knew Tinelle was not sleeping. He knew that by her breathing and the stiffness of her neck. The irritation he had left her house with had been replaced by a hollow craving in his gut. A desire for the only kind of warmth that could kill the chill Sylus's eyes had left in him.

He lifted a hand and brushed her neck. Suddenly the bed erupted and she was on him and it took a moment before he realised that Tinelle was not fighting him but loving him with a terrible rage. She'd closed her teeth on the skin of his shoulders. He brought his mouth up to her throat. They wrestled and cursed until they were exhausted, and then with a tenderness that reminded him of their early days of loving, they held hands and spoke in whispers.

'She touch you,' she told him quietly, 'and I'll kill the bitch. It will happen again – and you won't even have the decency to lie about it. I know you. You see something, you want it, you go for it no matter what. But I won't take it, y'hear me? I won't take it. I'll give you so much hell, you'll wish you never born.'

42

BECAUSE PYNTER did not go to Simone, she came to him.

He was on the veranda when he saw her walking across the Canteen playing field towards the lagoon some way beyond the pier. She was wearing a pale blue towel and was heading for the jetty. He thought of gauldins as he watched her walk – all length and glide and smoothness. She dropped the towel on the lip of the pier and, with that slow unbroken stride, stepped into the dark water, becoming a bobbing head there. He realised that he wanted her. He wanted her for something more than what Tinelle had shown him in all the months they'd been together. She had crept into his head, so that nights and days and mornings he could not shake her from his mind. So he went to her. He went to her and dived into the water after her. She pulled herself onto the platform and sat there glaring down at him. She'd cropped her hair very close, which seemed to accentuate her lips and cheekbones. Drops of water beaded her brows and she glistened in the sunlight.

Pynter took in a lungful of air and dived. The bottom was a great way down but he kept going until his head began to hurt. And when the pressure on his eardrums was unbearable, he hung there before rising very slowly.

When he surfaced he looked up at her. 'I jus' wan' to tell you, Simone, that I think you nice. Not no ordinary nice but special nice. And I come runnin down here like a fool becuz I couldn hold it in no more.'

They met in the cove beyond the Carenage, below the place where the colony of lepers used to live. There were hardly any words between them. Afterwards, he would look down at her face, dusted with coarse white sand, and wonder at it. She would stir and look back at him quietly, uncaring of her nakedness, and then draw him to her again, and hold him there until he drifted into a kind of sleep. Simone would blow into his ear then, and he would lift his face to see the first lights of San Andrews tossing yellow, oily patterns on the water of the mainland just beyond.

At some point during this numbing, hollow drift in which his mind wandered off to nameless, lightless spaces and faces as insubstantial as smoke, his body would be further stilled by a creeping sense of danger, but there was no urgency to it, no quickening of the blood.

She always hit the water first, pulling ahead with long, sleepy strokes, never once looking back to see how he was doing until her fingers touched the pier. And she would head for home without a backward glance while he went the other way.

Tinelle was waiting for him on the veranda one evening when he returned. Her legs were swinging over the edge into the void below. 'This is your punishment for Paso, not so? You blaming us for what happened to him?'

Pynter looked past her shoulders at the buildings beyond. 'I sorry, Tinelle.'

'I could ask you to leave right now, but that don't feel right. It's not what I want. She's done this before, not to me. She's done it to a couple of my friends. She sees a fella, she likes him, and she doesn't give a shit about anybody else. It hit me last night that it's always the same type of fella. The dark ones, the slim ones. Then she drops them and moves on. Like she's sampling men or something. Like she's looking for something that's not there. I hate women like that.'

Tinelle sucked in a lungful of air. 'I'm not taking this, Pynter. I'm not. Hugo asked me to be patient with you. He keeps saying … ' She came off the veranda and stood in front of him. 'I want a promise from you.'

He nodded.

'Don't go back down there. If it wasn't for Hugo, I – I would walk away from this. On principle, I … ' She covered her face with her hands and turned away.

'I'll stay,' he said.

She wouldn't let him speak to her about it. She did not want to hear his confusion. She put it down to men – the dog he was, like all the other men she knew.

Tinelle was on the veranda the next evening. She looked down grim-faced at Simone, who walked across the pier as usual and, not seeing him there, turned around as if she'd forgotten or lost something. Simone left the blue towel on the boards and dived into the water. From where they were above her, Pynter could see how beautifully she swam, her strokes hardly breaking the surface of the lagoon.

He became aware of Tinelle's eyes on him. 'Pynter,' she said, softly. 'She gives you anything that I can't give you?'

He shook his head.

'Then why?'

'S'not you, Tinelle. Is me.'

It was their fifth evening of standing at the window. Tinelle hardly ever looked down at the lagoon any more. Over the past few days, he'd felt the hardening in her. Her gestures had sharpened. She spoke to him with an abruptness meant to keep him away from her. She refused the drinks he mixed her.

He'd been following the figure in the water. Tinelle must have said something to him, but he didn't hear her. She'd prodded him hard. He turned around and she was suddenly ablaze.

'Go on! Go down to her, you sonuvabitch. And make sure you make up your mind when you come back. You tell me what you decide, y'understand? And if you can't decide, I'll decide for you.'

He heard her in her bedroom slamming drawers and dragging things around. Tinelle came out a short while later and stomped out of the house.

Simone was looking out to sea when he arrived. He was sure she heard him approaching but she did not turn. She was sitting on the lip of the pier, with her toes grazing the water. She did not seem surprised to see him.

She greeted him the same way she had when he first met her. 'How you been?'

'I been watchin you,' he said. 'You swim like a dream.'

A strong breeze was stirring up the lagoon. He followed the circling of gulls above their heads. He sniffed at the wind and thought that behind the smell of diesel he could pick out the odours of mimosa.

'Let's go.' Simone flicked a foot at the water.

'No,' he said.

'I not takin you from her,' she said.

'Is not you to decide dat,' he said, lowering himself beside her. 'I come to talk.'

'We'll talk 'cross dere.' She nudged his arm. 'Let's go, Pynter.'

'No,' he said. He imagined Tinelle looking down on them from up there. She would see two dark people-shapes against the darker waters of the lagoon, with their heads almost touching.

Pynter took Simone's hand and stroked her fingers. 'Ever hear the story about the fella an' the girl who left everyting behind and swim out?'

'Everybody know it.' Simone turned her head. Her eyes were like the waters of the lagoon. 'I like dat. De love stay clean dat way. You take it with you when it still perfect. It don' die or go away. Life don' dirty it or spoil it. That make sense.' She smiled at him. 'That's what you want to do?'

'I want to live,' he said. 'I want Tinelle.'

'I not takin you from her.'

'You sure?'

Simone traced the lines of his palm with a finger. She looked at her palm beside his. They were so similar it made his heart flip over.

She pointed at the little beach across the water. 'S'gettin late. Let's go.'

'I can't,' he said, and stood up.

Simone turned her head up at him. 'Another time?'

'You nice,' he said. 'Nice enough to die with, and that's de problem.'

He felt so tired when he got to Tinelle's house, all he could think of was sleep. He sat on the wall of the veranda and stared out at the islands for a while. The decaying evening left traces of red and amber sunlight on the waters of the harbour. And for no reason he could point to, something in him crumbled and he began to cry.

43

SATURDAY NIGHTS, Tinelle and her friends converged on one of the houses above the town and danced to a radiogram that was played so loud everyone said it must blast a hole in the roof of the world. Pynter began to live for those weekend raves. They started an hour before midnight and took them half-drunk, delirious and thrashing through to the very early hours of the morning. Their dancing would briefly take their minds off their war of attrition with Victor and the loss of Paso.

It was the stiffening of Tinelle's spine that would alert Pynter that Simone had arrived, and, however hard he tried, he could not prevent himself from lifting his head. Likewise, Tinelle said that she could tell from his movements when Robert was around. He called Robert the Floater, because that was all he seemed to do: float around the room, dance with whichever girl chose to dance with him, his eyes constantly drifting in Tinelle's direction. It was this tension that kept Pynter and Tinelle close.

'He's not like you,' Tinelle said. 'He's amoral. I can do no wrong. You understand that?'

Pynter wasn't sure that he did.

There were moments when he left the milling feet and flailing limbs and stepped out into the early morning that always smelled of yellow poui and mimosa. Up there, high above San Andrews, there were fireflies and the air was thick with the tik-tok-tinkling of forest insects. And the same questions returned to Pynter every time: what did men like Victor do on nights like these? Had he ever marvelled at a morning? Tasted air so sweet it made him dizzy and just glad to be alive? Had he ever loved a woman or a child so much it made him feel blessed and helpless at the same time? Did he feel like a fool sometimes? Who were these people, and what was he doing here amongst them?

He would drift back to the party, and Tinelle and he would bum a ride in the car of one of Tinelle's friends, run the short distance across the yard and throw themselves at each other on the cushions in the hall. He'd snugged himself down in San Andrews and it felt all right. But he knew it was too perfect to last.

Pynter was under the shower washing off the grime of one of the hottest days of the year when Tinelle came running in to tell him that Sylus had died with a harpoon in his gut and nobody knew who did it.

'Robert just phoned,' she said. 'Sounds like a terrible way to die.'

'You sound sorry fo' 'im,' he said.

'You didn't use to be like that – where you get that hardness from?'

'From livin a hard life, Tinelle, made terrible by people like Sylus. Who gone an' done this?'

She shook her head and walked over to the record player. 'I don't even want to think of the consequences. We gone past that stage,' she said.

'Gone past?'

'Confrontation, murder.'

'I was never there,' he said.

'Of course, you're like Jesus, who absolved himself of everything, Pynter Bender. Remember what happened to all that righteousness? S'gonna be bad, Pynter. Bad for all of us.'

He turned away from her, parted the blinds and stared down at the Carenage. It was beautiful down there with all that sun on water. It would always remain beautiful. The tourists would come, take their pictures and leave, and that was all that they would see – the brightness and the beauty. Not what lay behind them. Not the awful memories that hung above it like an invisible caul.

'I have to go home,' he said.

'You can't. Hugo's hardly here and … '

'My mind made up.'

'You go to your place, they'll take you like they took your friend, Frigo.'

'Fuh what, Tinelle?'

'I'm trying to tell you something, Pynterrr. It happened on your side. That place y'all call Saint Divine,' she said. 'It's y'all they'll be searching for. Why else you think everybody's calling me?'

He sat down and looked up at her. 'Everybody left for home, Tinelle. Y'unnerstan?'

'Talk for yourself. Not the others.'

'I'll speak for whoever the hell I want … '

'Who would want to write Paso's name on the harpoon of a fish gun and shoot a man with it?'

He rose to his feet and walked out to the veranda. He stood there rubbing his head and staring down at the town. Tinelle hurried out after him and closed both hands around his belt.

'I drag you with me if I have to!' he said.

'Go ahead,' she said. Her eyes told him she meant it. He cursed her, swung her round, lifted her off her feet, carried her inside and dropped himself on the cushions with her still holding on, until their struggle became something to laugh at. She finally released him.

He left the house running.

Oslo was leaning against a small Seville orange tree at the left of the little house he'd obviously built himself. Everything here was new. The wooden house was barely settled in the ground. The yard was still no more than a clearing cut out on soil which had not been walked on to give it the worn and rooted quality of a true yard. There were stones everywhere, covered with washed clothing. Pynter recognised those stones as the type he found in Gaul and on the strips of unused land close to the river. It would take a determined man a lifetime to dig those boulders out.

Oslo spoke as if he had been expecting him. 'Long time no see, Pynter Bender.'

'Couple of years, Oslo.'

A young woman appeared from the back of the house. She began picking up the clothes.

'You know why I come, Oslo; not so?'

'No. Why you come?'

'You cross my mind this morning and I thought I had to come.'

Oslo grinned at him. 'You cross my mind too, a coupla times. I hear you sell your soul to a woman in San Andrews.' There was a sliver of silver on one of his upper front teeth, exactly like Birdie's.

''Twas a mistake, Oslo, passing Sylus out like dat.'

Oslo's face tightened. 'Don' know what you talkin 'bout.'

'I feel sure enough about this to come all this way to see you,' Pynter said.

'You accusin' me?'

'Yes. I just want to unnerstan what make you do it.'

'And if I say I didn't?'

'I'll choose to remember that.'

'I don' have nothing to say, Pynter. You mad, you know that? Town Boy!' Oslo laughed. 'Y'all gone soft. Everybody gone off, or gone soft. Like nobody don' remember Paso and dem school-children on de Carenage, and Jordan and Frigo! Your friend! Like all those years was for nothing. A waste! I refuse to let dat pass just so. For nothing. If I have bad dreams and still find meself running like hell in my sleep to save my life from soldiers, is not because I want dat to happen. Y'hear! We become what dey make of us. I still remember that. You was the one who put dem words together. Was the smartest thing you ever say. Now look at you! De way you stand up, de way you talk! You don' know if you goin or coming! Pynter de petty bourgeois! Tell me, when last you see yuh modder?'

'Leave my family out of it,' Pynter said. 'My modder is my business.'

'Rumour have it dat you leave your yard fo' good, like you 'shame of where you come from.'

'And y'all believe that?'

'I tell you as I hear it. Y'know what I don't like about you? You behave as if Christ live in y'arse. Like you spend all your life in this shit looking for purity, and you still expect to stay clean! You got a problem, Pynter Bender.'

'I'll tell you what my problem is, Oslo. I looked hard inside a man's soul once. He kill a boy, see? Kill a boy out o' jealousy. Take nine years o' my life to work that out from the lil book he used to write in. And the kind o' torment it bring down on him, I not wishing that on nobody. And then there was Harris. You 'member Harris? Got pass away in his own house for a piece of bread. Harris was my friend, the first friend I ever had. Full of life, brimming all over with it, and then one night the man who share hi house with him take all that away. One day something happen. I had the chance to look in the eye of the man who done it. He carry the same intention to murder me. I tell you, man, I saw the Devil there in dat lil piece of bush behind my father house I used to call Eden; and I tell you this, Oslo: no anger, no hate, no cause in the world, could make me want to 'come like that. S'not even that I don't have it in me. I have. But I make that choice long time ago. Y'unnerstan?'

'Oslo? You want to eat now?' The woman was at the door with her hands on her hips.

Oslo began walking towards the house. He stopped at the steps and looked back at Pynter. 'You too nice to eat me an' Mary food?'

Pynter sat at the table and picked his way through the plate of soused herring, sweet potatoes and bananas. Oslo had told Mary that Pynter did not want her food, but she filled a plate and placed it in front of him anyway.

Oslo wanted to know as much as he could about 'de softies' in San Andrews. Pynter answered him with grunts while studying the titles of Oslo's books. They were mainly westerns by Louis L'Amour, and Perry Mason novelettes all stacked next to a massive Bible.

'You still read, Pynter?'

Pynter nodded.

Oslo raised a finger at him. 'I show you something, then. Mary?'

'What?'

'Gimme de box.'

'Which box?'

'How you mean which box? De box!'

Mary dragged in a box of books from the next room.

'These,' Oslo's voice dropped to a whisper, 'every single one o' dem banned by Victor. I got forty years' worth o' jail in dis lil box here. Mebbe more. Ever hear 'bout Lenin?'

Pynter nodded. 'My town girl have a whole heap o' dem.'

'Ever read any o' dem?'

'I prefer poetry.'

'You gone soo sooft!'

'I still prefer poetry. People worried about the trouble this gonna start.'

'Who is "people"? You?'

'All of us, including those who decide to go home and stay home and not have anything to do with this tug-o'-war no more.'

'It ain't got no going home until this thing is over proper, fella. S'far as I concern, it ain't got no home to go to. For nobody. You don't realise dat?'

'And who decide dat?'

The teeth flashed. 'Me! If nobody else goin decide, I will decide! Something happen to y'all dat I don' unnerstan. Is like … like if … '

Pynter watched Oslo grapple with the words. 'Put it this way, Oslo, this is more about me trying to unnerstan myself through people like you.'

'Jeezam! You even talk like dem.'

'Like who!'

'Them people you mix with.'

'I always talk like dat.'

'No way! I remember you, fella. Sharp like a knife and uptight! Like you was vex with de world. Vex to bust. I never used to like you but I 'member you for dat. Where all dat gone?' Oslo slowly worked his jaw over a piece of yam. 'Lissen, fella. You still got dat pen?'

Pynter reached into his shirt pocket and held up Sislyn's pen. Oslo took it carefully and held it against the window light. 'It got ink?' He slipped off the cover, spread his left palm flat and retraced the strong dark lines there. Oslo smelled the ink and chuckled. 'I still envy you this, you know dat? 'Twas like when you sit down with dis pen in your hand, you was protected. Nobody could reach you. I used to hate you for dat. Paso used to tell me that you write good. You gonna write about – about, erm … ?'

Oslo's own question seemed to have done something to him. For the first time he appeared uncertain.

'Don' know.' Pynter eased the pen from Oslo's fingers. 'I see tough times ahead, Oslo.'

'You talk as if tough times went somewhere.'

'Somewhere in the back o' my mind I come here well prepared to straighten you out.'

Oslo smiled. 'This is not like last time, fella. Times change. I won't let you get away this time. I mean it.'

'We still got time,' Pynter said. 'Like you say, this thing not over yet.'

Pynter was looking out at the islands and reliving his conversation with Oslo when he heard a soft knock at the door. He wondered why anyone would come to Tinelle's house in the middle of a curfew. He eased it open and there was Patty, dressed the way she used to when she and Leroy went for Sunday strolls down Old Hope Road. She wore the same shoes too, and the khaki trousers she worked the canes in. Lipstick glossed her lips like purple plums and her hair was pulled up like a mountain rearing back on itself.

She stood on the steps wavering like a palm tree in a soft wind. Pynter kissed her on the cheek and stepped back from her. He could see that something had frightened his young aunt and, whatever it was, it had brought her through the curfew to see him. He was certain she was sent. She took a seat on the wall of the veranda. She started fanning herself and looking around as if she'd just landed in a foreign country, swinging her head at the buildings and the sea below. 'Y'all not 'fraid this house toss y'all down dere one day?'

Pynter went inside and brought her a drink. He handed her the glass. 'How you come here?' he said.

'Where the girl?' she said.

'Sleeping.'

'Pynto, you love dat girl?'

'Like sand.'

'Like?'

'Sand – a whole heap.'

'Dat's why you burning yourself up over her?'

He smiled.

'You gotta eat more greens. You get sick if you continue like dat.'

'Like what.'

'I not stupid. You greedy fo' dat girl and you not eatin proper. You goin dry up if you go on like dat.' She cut angry eyes at him. 'Fellas always do dat! Y'all behave as if it ain't got no tomorrow. Look how pale an' dry you get!'

A hard wind scrubbed the eaves of the house. She looked up quickly. Now she was turning the glass in her hand. He watched her fingers.

'They come fo' you, Pynto. Soldier-fellas come to de yard askin fo' you an' Oslo.'

'I didn do nothing,' he said softly, weakly.

Patty shook her head, as if to say he'd missed the point.

The whispering of feet on the floor inside the house made Patty look up. Tinelle came to the door and seemed transfixed there. Patty lifted her eyes and smiled at her, and Tinelle's face relaxed.

'This is Tan Pat,' Pynter said.

Tinelle walked over to Patty and kissed her. It was as if they'd always known each other. Patty seemed to understand this. She took Tinelle's hand and rested it against her cheek.

'A little bit o' bizness between family,' Patty said. Tinelle returned Patty's smile and went back in.

His aunt dropped her voice. She'd counted twelve men, she said. They said that he, Pynter, had some questions to answer concerning Sergeant Sylus. They were not interested in Peter. They were sure that only Pynter could help them. He was the one that looked like the communist-fella-who-got-what-he-was-askin-for, not so? One of the men had taken out a piece of paper and read out some names. Oslo's was there, and a couple of others that no one in Old Hope knew. Pynter's was the last. Deeka swore on her life that Pynter knew nothing. They wanted to know how Deeka knew that. She told them she was certain because her grandson was no longer in the country. That worried them a little until Windy started crying.

They'd narrowed their eyes at the girl and told Deeka she was lying. And furthermore, she and the rest of the yard could look forward to a whole heap of sleepless nights until they found Pynter, or until Pynter came to them. Deeka followed the men down to the road, threatening them with murder. The men laughed at her, said good night and left.

Elena went to Cynty's house to speak to Tobias but the little man was no longer with Cynty. Cynty sent him away for reasons she would not tell Elena. Except to say that Tobias talked too much. He couldn't help it. And in these times a talking man was a man whose mouth was just as bad as a gun. What Cynty knew was that the wardens in Birdie's prison were preparing themselves for a fresh crop of young people. Somebody had to pay, somebody from anywhere would do. But Old Hope made more sense. It was where Paso came from. And it was a couple of hills away from Saint Divine where Sylus got passed away. And the little they got from Frigo when they caught him was enough to send them looking for Oslo and Pynter.

If Patty weren't already so upset, he would have told her what he was thinking while she talked. That there was no way through this. They would find him, sure as rain. Like they found Paso in the end. Instead he said, 'How's Tan Cee?'

'She good. Much better. I … '

'I want to see her, Tan Pat.'

Patty didn't answer him. She pushed her hand into her bag and pulled out a purse. 'Wish I had more. S'everything I got,' she said.

He shook his head but Patty stuffed the purse in his hand.

'How you getting home?' he said.

'Same way I come,' she said, pointing at her feet. It was all of eight miles to Old Hope. Night would meet her on the road.

She placed a hand on his shoulder. Now, she was looking at him with Deeka's eyes.

'Lisen to me,' she said. 'You not leaving like Birdie. Y'unnerstan? You not runnin from nobody like no criminal. When you leave dis place you leave here like a man. Full of all de dignity we teach you. Is what I want, is what Deeka want. Is what Elena an' Tan Cee want. Tomorrow I goin talk to dem soldier-fellas. Got a coupla dem who come to look for me an' say hello all the time at de store. I goin find Chilway an' talk to 'im. He got to have soldier friends he know. I'll walk through a million curfew if I have to. Let dem shoot me if dey want; but you not leavin dis islan' like Birdie.'

He wanted to walk with her out to the road but Patty waved him back. He watched her till a bend in the road hid her from view.

The island sank into a well of silence. Tinelle said that the problems would begin when they started reading out names on the radio. Pynter sat with her in the darkness of her father's house, feeling that the whole island was crowding in on them.

The thought of the soldiers separating him from her filled him with a fear he sometimes choked on.

If Tinelle hadn't been so sure that the trouble would blow over, he would have gone and handed himself in. Sometimes he caught her in the kitchen staring at her feet, her eyes red, as if she had been crying, even though he knew she wasn't.

He heard the footsteps long before the man entered the gate, a heavy, solid stride. He felt Tinelle's weight on him. Her mouth was hot against his neck, her legs wrapped around him as if she wanted to take him whole inside herself and hide him there.

A knocking at the door, hesitant at first, then firmer. He pulled himself to his feet, dragging Tinelle up with him, and walked to the door.

'Pynterrr,' she said.

'I fed up,' he said.

Outside, the man called his name. Pynter pulled open the door.

He did not recognise the shape, standing as it was with the lights of the town behind it. Not at first. His mind presented him with a quick picture of Birdie, then abandoned it as soon as Peter said his name.

His brother slipped inside quickly. Pynter guided his brother through the darkened hall.

Suddenly Pynter felt at ease. Peter seemed to have the same effect on Tinelle. She dropped all the precautions she'd taken so far and lit up the hall with candles.

Peter stood in the middle of the space looking quietly across at him. Tinelle's eyes could not stop from shifting from Peter's face to his. Pynter thought he knew what she was seeing – they barely looked like brothers. And standing there, solid and at ease inside his body, Peter looked exactly like their father.

'Deeka send me,' Peter said. 'S'matter o' fact, I tell dem I comin cuz somebody got to take care o' you, fella.'

'S'kinda late.'

'They come to take you, dey have to take me too.'

'Go back home,' Pynter said. 'People don' want you here. You waste your time coming an' I wasting my time talkin to you.'

'Don't talk like that, Pynter!' Tinelle's voice startled both of them.

Peter turned to Tinelle. 'He tryin to make me vex – so I could walk out of this house an' go back home. Tell de backside, I not goin nowhere until I finish tell 'im what I come to tell 'im. A fella come home to look for 'im yesterday. No, not dem.' He shook his head. 'A short, lil man. Important-looking fella with a pretty walkin stick and glasses.'

Pynter shrugged. 'He say who he is?'

'Deeka couldn't remember that part, 'ceptin that the name was long, like a govment man o' something, with a whole string of things hook on to it.'

'A string of?'

'Titles an' tings like dat. Deeka couldn remember everything and she was de only one that meet 'im.'

Pynter's mind shifted back to a time in his father's house when a man with a stick with the head of a lion arrived and frightened Manuel Forsyth into sending him to school. He hadn't seen Bostin since. 'This fella, he walk like he prefer to fly?'

'Deeka say he walk tiptoe.'

Pynter smiled. 'Bostin. He tell Deeka what he want?'

'He want to see you. Urgent. Ask where he could find you.'

'And?'

'Deeka cuss de man. She tell 'im to haul 'iz arse from her place befo' she knock 'im down. He put this in she hand and leave.'

Peter handed him a letter.

Mister Pynter Bender,
Hello and how are you?

I estimate that you would be around nineteen years old now (hence the salutation 'Mister'). I hope you do not deem that it is too late for me to congratulate you on your A-level results. Being responsible for overseeing such matters now, I was made aware of your outstanding performance the very day the results were expedited to my offices from Cambridge, England.

I expect that you will now appreciate the basis for my altercation, many, many years ago, with, if I may say so without undue offence, your very recalcitrant father.

A number of conjunctures precluded me from making certain openings possible for you (based entirely on your impressive academic performance, I may add).

I have been made aware of the circumstances surrounding yourself at present through very confidential sources. It is with concern and curiosity that I present this request to see you and discuss possibilities.

There may be something I could do.

You will, I presume, appreciate the extremely sensitive nature of this missive coming from a person of my placing and position. Therefore, subsequent to reading its contents, I urge you to destroy it.

Yours Faithfully

Bostin Uriah – PTECO, ANCEEDP – Ministry of Education & PP of the SRBE.

'Writes like a politician,' Tinelle chuckled.

'Better than that,' Pynter said. 'I remember telling you about him once,' he said to Peter.

Peter nodded. 'Long time back. Y'all was in touch all dis time?'

'No.'

'Then how come...' His brother seemed to change his mind about asking the question. Peter shrugged. 'I'll bring him to you if you want.'

'How?'

'Anyhow.'

'From where?'

'I'll find him.'

'In this curfew?'

'In any curfew.'

'Bring him, then.'

He had to hand it to Bostin. He was dressed as meticulously as Pynter remembered him, a grey polyester shirt and blue trousers whose seams were pressed to a knife's edge.

He was now Principal Teacher Education Concerns Officer, Advisor on National Curricular and Extra-curricular Education Development Policy ANCEEDP (pronounced, Add-Seed, he instructed), with an eye firmly fixed on the Statutory Regional Board of Examination. He had cultivated a little paunch, as was becoming a person of his position. The cane, imported from England, silver-capped at either end, rounded the image off perfectly.

Pynter liked listening to him as much as Bostin enjoyed being listened to. Tinelle stifled her laughter in the kitchen while she prepared him the orange juice and Jacob's Cream Crackers that he asked for.

No food, thank you. Jacob's Cream Crackers with a pat of Blue Band margarine, Blue Band Gold if there was any about, would do him fine. Thanks ever so much, Miss McMurdo. Did she know that McMurdo was a Scottish name? A nice match one would say, he nodded at them. Nice. Not all names had to have a history. In fact, a few names without any history at all were making history right now. Indeed, it was a common thing for commoners to marry into history – no disrespect meant, Mister Bender. Just look at the royalties of Europe! A handsome young man with a brain like that and a very pretty lady with a bit of history behind her name could do very dramatic things indeed. If he had his way, there would be a Ministry for the Family. Yes indeed! A Ministry for the Foundation of Society. He would name it personally, because that is what a family is, the foundation of society. And who will head that Ministry? A Minister, of course, he smiled, a Minister. And bright young people like Mister Bender there and pretty Miss McMurdo here will have a definite place in it. A well-paid place too.

'You said you wanted to discuss, er, possibilities?' Tinelle slipped in politely.

Bostin looked up. 'I said?'

'Not tonight. In your letter to Pynter.'

'Ah! You also read my letter?' The eyes popped wide with pleasure.

'A wonderful letter,' Tinelle purred. 'The, er, possibilities for Pynter?'

'Self-taught, you know. If I may say so of myself, a perfect example of self, uhm, enhancement. Yessir. I am very much that. I'll tell you something else.'

Bostin frowned at a crumb on his knee. With a single finger, he flicked it into his palm, scrutinised the offending particle and then brushed it off onto the saucer.

'I'll also tell you this. If I had the opportunity, I would have innovated something by now – some invention of importance, because I am an innovator. I was innovating since I born, researching and exploring. That's what my parents told me and I have no reason to be dubious about what they said. Innovating is my nature. I see you laughing, Miss McMurdo, but my father, if he was alive, that is, would make a point of letting you know that. Anyway, I'm here to discuss another matter of urgency. I solicit your pardon. Jacob's crackers and Blue Band margarine always get me talking.

'Now! Young man! Like I said in my note – I assume that you have destroyed the missive as requested? Yes? Good! As I indicated, I am aware of your present predicament and apart from my historical interest in you – I consider you one of my protégés – I have been prompted by certain interested parties to, er, to bail you out, to use their expression. And, granted my current position as Policymaker and Advisor, we've all agreed that a scholarship is just the thing.'

'Who's the interested parties?' Pynter studied the man's face closely.

'I am not at liberty to say, sir. But believe me they're well-meaning. One of them I understand you had some association with? Some people have a conscience – a rare thing in these times, if I may say so myself.'

'Which person I had association with that I don't know nothing about?'

Bostin responded with an expression of sympathy. But that was all, he wasn't giving anything away. There was no one Pynter could even vaguely think of apart from Sislyn. But Sislyn would know nothing about his present situation.

'Tell me about the scholarship.' Tinelle came around and wrapped her arms around Pynter's shoulders from behind.

'Ah! We get these offers sometimes during our overseas missions: meetings, summits and, er, colloquies, you know, offers that nobody don't really know what to do with.

'If, say, a North Korean offers your country a scholarship in tyre manufacturing, what you tell them? No? Nooo! You tell them, yes. Yes, thank you, a scholarship in tyre manufacture is the most important economic input your country will ever receive, even though you never saw a rubber tree in your life! They know and you know you will never take it up because your country don't make tyres and it never will. You catch me? That is what we call aid. Some kinds of aid, I'm reliably informed, is not offered to help you. What matters here is the offer itself. These North Koreans could be like that.' Bostin looked up at him. 'You would like to go North Korea?'

'North who?'

Bostin's eyes settled on his shoes. 'Well, young man, nobody will be looking for you there. Besides, they are very gracious people. That's what I hear.'

'I thought you talkin about a real scholarship.'

The man lifted his eyes at Tinelle as if imploring her to help him. She refilled the empty glass and placed herself beside Pynter. Bostin eased his handkerchief from the pocket of his shirt and began patting his forehead.

'They speak English?' Pynter said.

Bostin shrugged. 'Everybody do.'

'In Korea?'

'You'll pick it up – Koreanese – er, the way Koreans talk.'

'Nobody else in de world speak Korean except Koreans. Who I goin to speak Korean to when I come back? Or p'raps y'all don' intend for me to come back?'

'Y'all? Who, might I ask is "y'all"?'

'You work for Victor, not so?'

'Excuse me, sir, I don't work for no Victor! I does work for de Civil Service. Education, it is my belief, transcends politics.'

'My arse! Not here. Dat's exactly why you talking to me right now about some kind of flippin banishment in some country on top o' de North Pole.'

Bostin leaned forward. He'd dropped the handkerchief on the floor and seemed unaware of it. 'You smart, young Bender, I give you that. But you also very stupid. I am advising you to take it because is all I can offer now and it did mean a lot of hard work on my part to get it. Take it if only because is the quickest way out

441

of your troubles. The time might come when you could even make something special out of that.'

'No.'

'Don't tell me you prefer to stay here and … And … '

'Get kill? Don't worry, Mister Bostin, Education Ruler of the Universe. I not going alone.'

Bostin swiped his walking stick across the table and knocked the glass of orange juice onto the floor. He slammed the door behind him.

Tinelle sat back on the cushions, crying.

'Bostin will come again,' he told her. 'And unless he come back with something better than North Korea, I'll refuse again.'

'You damn fool. It will be too late.'

'So be it.'

'Stuupid!'

'Thanks.'

Bostin did come again. This time, he said, pulling several sheets of paper from his briefcase, he'd brought Finland, and of course Sweden was a possibility, although he would not advise that personally, since life was too much of a distraction there. Holland was also noted for distractions of that sort. He'd even got hold of Austria which, he was told, was quite wonderful and rare. Would he consider Portugal if it ever came up? He would put the word out that he was looking out for Portugal and that nobody should touch it because it was already booked by him. Pynter may even get a big one. Only last month Briarson, his Permanent Secretary friend, found Switzerland just lying there beneath a set of memoranda, for months. Nobody noticed it. Briarson's daughter was there right now studying languages in Berne. Had he ever heard of Berne?

'Germany,' Pynter said.

'Beg yuh pardon?'

'You got anything for Germany?'

Bostin straightened up. 'Germany? My God, boy. Like you forget Missa Hitler!'

'He dead long time now.'

'Ah!' Bostin laughed. 'Not from what I hear.'

'I will take a scholarship to Germany, Missa Bostin. You got one?'

'Why you want to go there?'

'Cuz it ain't got nowhere else to go.'

'But you'll have to learn that language. God! Is not de prettiest language in de world to learn, you know!'

'Is easier dan Koreanese.'

Bostin lowered his eyes.

Pynter felt a sudden flush of warmth for this stranger. He'd heard about people who did that sort of thing – social projects that Sislyn claimed followed a person throughout their lives. Bostin looked like the sort who would follow a person right through life, just to see if his ideas about them were right.

'Tell me, Missa Bostin, why you never leave to go nowhere?'

'If everybody go, who goin be here to send de last one off?' Bostin threw his head back and laughed. He stared up at him, all teeth. 'That one tickle you, eh!'

Was Pynter honestly interested in Germany?

Pynter told him yes.

He would begin working on it tomorrow. Did he have a passport? No? He would do the necessary correspondence to make that happen quickly – say, in a couple of days? Another thing, it would make things easier if he used his father's name. Did he know that he was christened Pynter Raphael Forsyth Bender? Yes? Well, Raphael Forsyth on his passport and on the paperwork will not raise a question anywhere since nobody nowhere knew him by that name. Money – did he have any money? No? No need to worry, a discretionary stipend would be in order and of course relatives and friends may want to make contributions.

Bostin got up and extended his hand. Pynter sidestepped it. He embraced the man. 'Thank you, sir.'

'Well,' he cleared his throat. 'One has these ideas, you see, these longer-term agendas, and occasionally one wants to get at least one item safely through.'

After Bostin left, Pynter dug into his bag and took out the money Patty had given him. Each note was folded as neatly as Bostin's handkerchief. He weighed the packet in his hand. It was all the money Patty would have saved from the time she started working. She had handed him her future. He was holding her store in his hands.

He dropped it on the cushion beside Tinelle. 'A time will come, Tinelle, when I'll ask you to give this to my aunt. Tell her I forgot it.'

44

By the time they were ready for him to return to the yard, another curfew had silenced the island. Still, it was a good time, Peter said, for it was the Season of the Souls and Tan Cee had emerged from the silence she'd sunk into. Santay had fed her herbs, boiled leaves and roots and grasses and made her drink them. She'd soaked her every day in a stew of herbs and resins. She'd sprinkled her with powders, drawn lines and circles in the dirt and had her stand on them for hours. Now his aunt was whole again.

Tan Cee traced the muscles of his arm, pulled his eyelids apart and blinked in horror at his eyeballs. She brought her nostrils to his armpits and pretended to faint. She walked him through her herb garden, crushed lemon grass, santa maria, bay leaves and black sage between her fingers and brought them to his nose. She yellowed his face with the pollen of okra flowers and showered his clothes with prickles. She sat him down and peeled golden apples for him, placed the salted slices in his mouth and watched him wince as the sourness spread across his tongue before melting into sweetness. She whistled tunes she used to sing to him as a child, warbled, clucked and cheeped them till he was a ball of laughter at her feet. And then she kicked him on his behind and said, 'You think you is a man, you think you is a man. You stray-'way dog!' And then, still bubbling like a pot on the boil, she helped him to his feet and told him. 'Go bathe an' sleep, cuz I keepin y'all up tonight.'

Pynter took in the dark heap of manioc, the large mound of firewood beside the giant metal platter beneath the June-plum tree. 'Farine,' he said. 'You makin farine tonight?'

'Mind yuh business,' she replied, and with a thump on his back she hurried him off to bathe.

Later, it was Pynter's little sister who woke him. 'Tan Cee say to wake yuh, an' you wouldn get up, so I bite you!' Pynter lifted Lindy onto his shoulders and went out to the yard. A low moon floated over Old Hope amongst a bright scattering of stars. The air was thick with the smell of manioc.

Deeka was stoking wood beneath the large platter. The masantorches were lit and everyone had spread themselves around the yard. Pynter placed Lindy on her feet and went over to Tan Cee.

'I was thinkin 'bout you all de time,' Tan Cee whispered.

They'd already peeled away the rough skin of the manioc. The bared flesh glistened white and ghostly in the night air. The milk from the leaves and stem could blind a person in minutes. And the juices in the roots were a slow and painful acid in the blood once they got in there. Yet it was food in the hands of Tan Cee and these deep-eyed Old Hope women. He'd seen them make bread as delicate as sacrament from the white flesh and the poison, and starch so pure it had the translucency of glass.

They'd brought the season forward for him: Cassava Time, when old grudges and wars were abandoned, and past insults and hurts discarded like old garments.

Deeka's fire was now a growling beast beneath the giant platter. Peter and Tan Cee had propped their graters on the sheet of galvanised iron near it, preparing themselves for the grating.

Peter raised his head and warbled. A slow, beautiful trill came back from somewhere in the dark and Windy stepped into the yard. Pynter laid his back against the stones and closed his eyes.

There was the giddy-sweet stench of cassava, the wet whisha-whasha of graters chewing into the soft roots, the deep-chested grunts of his mother, Peter's exhalations. Women's voices stirred him. He sat up and saw Santay leading seven women up the hill. Their greetings were muted and musical. Santay wrapped her arms around Tan Cee and rocked her. They were laughing now, all nine of them together.

The draining of the grated paste was over. Pynter envied the ease with which Peter lifted the heavy drum and carried it beneath the house. Windy had moved to stand beside his mother.

The women tossed the paste into the hot platter. Patty and his mother were lifting the long oarlike spatulas and turning the substance till it became white dust on the heated metal. And with a sweep of the hand that was both a benediction and a boast, Tan Cee scattered mint, bay leaves and powdered cinnamon into the mix. Windy tasted and pronounced the whole thing wundaful. Peter laid a basin of special paste before the women. They scooped it up into their palms, patted and pulled and rounded it to an impossible perfection. Baked, it became brittle like dried leaves. Tan Cee broke the first one, brought it back to flour with a vigorous twisting of the fingers, scattering the result to the four corners of the earth. And before she could say the words, Pynter heard them coming from himself.

'Ago, Legba. Ago!'

Pynter dipped the big white biscuit into his cup of hot cocoa. Patty came and sat with her back against his. Lifting his head with the first bite, he saw a thin, red thread of light running across the peaks of the Mardi Gras.

It would be the first day of the Season of the Souls.

'Make me a promise, Pynto.'

'Uh-huh?'

'You never stop makin words.'

45

THE SEASON OF the Souls began with the thunder of last year's corn dragged down from rafters, followed by the strewps-strewps-strewpsing of graters chewing the yellow seeds off the husk. Thin films of lard hissed in hot cast-iron pots and everywhere the air rattled with a rain of maize on metal.

Nights, the thoooka-thookuh of pestles crushing the parched corn in heavy wooden mortars shook the earth like heartbeats. And in the morning, miraculously, there was asham – the result of the roasted corn, pounded so fine it was textured talc – mixed with sugar, hints of clove, black pepper and flourishes of cinnamon and nutmeg.

Tan Cee made cornki – corn flour sweetened and mixed with coconut juice and spices, then steamed in a large butter tin covered with young plantain leaves. Corn, she reminded him, was food fit to feed the souls of all the Dear Departeds of Old Hope. For the Season of the Souls was the season of the dead – a time of penance in the midst of plenty. And unseen though they were, their spirits populated Old Hope. That was why during the week ahead the whole village would give witness to the presence of ancient uncles, past aunts, parents and grandparents gone, and little children who, though God had chosen to take them before their time, made themselves manifest in everything. They were there in that wind that stirred the dark outside and made the flames dance briefly.

There were special meanings in the way leaves unanchored themselves from trees and came sailing down to land in someone's pocket or even in their bosom. Did he know that? Did he?

Pynter knew that. He also knew that Deeka Bender would be first to light her candles and place them in two snaking lines along the path that led from Old Hope Road right up to her door. If John Seegal or any one of those long-gone folks who populated her memory decided to return to her in spirit, their journeys would be guided by the candlelight out there.

He had never been more attentive to the pulses of Old Hope. He wondered if this was because he had chosen to be with Tinelle.

The Season of the Souls was also a time of penitence for all the hurts inflicted on the innocent. Old Hope spoke in hushed tones, remembering Jordan, Frigo and Paso – the victims of a war that had consumed them all. Even Pynter spoke more slowly, leaving the necessary silence between sentences, just in case the ghosts of Old Hope were listening and wanted to put in a word or two. For hadn't his whole life been explained by these same ideas which made this funerary celebration possible? Hadn't he been one of those who had left the world for what Tan Cee called the Middle Air? It was the place from which they said he'd come and against whose tug he had been pulling all his life. Everyone believed it from the moment he was born. Jordan and Frigo and Paso were somewhere in the air and looking on.

Pynter wanted to take all this with him. He wanted to carry all those voices that had, undefeated by the canes, surrounded him from birth: the goading, insistent voices of the women of the yard.

On the second day, Pynter decided to follow the crowd to Déli Morne. It was the annual convergence of elders on the garden of crosses and flowers on the sloping ridge above their valley. Up there they would set about clearing last year's growth of weeds and grass. They would plant fresh flowers and leave burning candles at the gravesides. That was Old Hope's way of putting all those memories back to rest.

Paso's place was beside a flowering tree Pynter did not recognise. In the fading light, its big, red bulbous flowers were as still as sleep. Pynter wondered who could have been remembering his nephew so diligently.

And then in the half-light, a slow figure appeared. Miss Maddie came towards him, hesitantly but without fear. By then he had placed most of his candles around Paso's mound.

His sister had grown older over the months he hadn't seen her. She smelt of the peppers she grew around her house.

She patted the side of her head. 'Lordy! I almos' thought that … Good Lord!'

A wicker basket hung from the curve of her elbow. He saw a pack of candles there, a box of matches and a little huddle of dried leaves.

'You and *him*,' she said. 'Same everything … Same … '

Miss Maddie was pointing not at the mound but at the flowering tree. She dropped the basket at his feet, stretched the other hand out and stroked his face. He allowed her fingers to follow the line of his jaw, the curves of his forehead, neck and cheekbones.

Miss Maddie finally dropped her hand and glanced down at the mound. Paso's tiny headstone was veined and wondrously luminous in the evening light.

In loving memory

Paso

1947–1974

'Blood-love,' she said. 'Blood-love – that's what I see between you and Paso from the first time. Blood-love. Past all the hate you feel you ought to hate us, you can't run way from blood.' Miss Maddie turned her gaze up at the hills, squinting as if she were facing an early-morning sun. 'If the Old Man was alive, I know what he would've done. He would've put you two stand up in front of us. He would've point at the way y'all turn out and laugh at Gideon and me.'

The sun had left an orange scar at the western edge of the Kalivini sky. It would remain like that for another hour – half-drained of light, and so purple it coloured the whole world blue – and then the darkness would be absolute.

Pynter struck a match and allowed the flame to creep right down to his fingers. Miss Maddie watched it burn.

'So how you been? You and, erm … '

'Peter.'

The old eyes had gone soft and vulnerable, as if what he said from now on would make all the difference in the world.

'Like we always been,' he said. He knew he was not telling her much; but what was there to say, unless she wanted all nineteen years of his and Peter's life laid out before her? Still, he had no right to deny her this, because, for ageing women like Miss Maddie, remembering was all there was to look forward to.

He struck a match and held it to his candle. 'Peter got Pa body and Pa voice. My brother carry all of Pa inside him.'

'I want to see him,' she said. He saw the agitation in the shifting of her shoulders. 'You de smaller one, not so?'

'Smaller but taller.' He lit another candle. This time Miss Maddie averted her eyes.

'You had one uncle pretty like you – y'know that?'

'Michael – yes. He kill a boy an' then himself.'

She looked surprised. 'You heard 'bout him?'

She began pulling at the weeds around the grave beside Paso's. 'Dey'll like you – girls. Take my advice, sonny. Get one girl – you got a girlfriend?'

'Uh-huh.'

'She nice?'

'I like her.'

'She from good family?'

'She thinks so.'

'Stick to her, then. Like that you get to know your children.' She lifted a candle from her basket, lit it and brought the flame to his.

Pynter turned towards his sister. 'I goin away tomorrow – to Germany. Fo' good, perhaps. Got to pack my things tonight.'

Miss Maddie straightened up and wiped her brows. 'Germany,' she coughed. 'Dat a far place to go to, not so?'

'I need to cross a whole ocean to get there,' he said.

'The girl – she go with you?'

'No.'

'You send for her?'

'No.'

'She wait for you? You can't go closer? Trinidad? Go Trinidad and let the girl come meet you dere.'

'I'm goin to study.'

'Study what?'

'I don' know.'

She lifted the end of her frock and wiped her eyes as if to clear them and noticed that she'd made a mess of her clean blue dress. 'Gwone, son. Paso was glad to see yuh.'

Pynter turned to walk away, lifted his hand and waved. He did not look back.